"Who shall separate us f

"No on

Kathryn Wright

UNSUITABLE

Nicola,
Praying God blesses you as you read this book!

Kathy

UNSUITABLE

Kathryn Wright
Margaret Locklair

a novel

Tate Publishing & *Enterprises*

This novel is a work of fiction. Names, descriptions, entities, and incidents included in the story are products of the author's imagination. Any resemblance to actual persons, events, and entities is entirely coincidental.

The opinions expressed by the author are not necessarily those of Tate Publishing, LLC.

Published by Tate Publishing & Enterprises, LLC
127 E. Trade Center Terrace | Mustang, Oklahoma 73064 USA
1.888.361.9473 | www.tatepublishing.com

Tate Publishing is committed to excellence in the publishing industry. The company reflects the philosophy established by the founders, based on Psalm 68:11,
"The Lord gave the word and great was the company of those who published it."

Cover design by Blake Brasor
Interior design by Chelsea Womble

Published in the United States of America

ISBN: 978-1-61777-598-7
1. Fiction, Christian, Suspense
2. Fiction, Coming of Age
11.07.01

DEDICATION

To the glory of God.

ACKNOWLEDGMENTS

Heartfelt thanks to our husbands, Randy Wright and Ernie Locklair, to everyone who prayed for our writing sessions, to Brenda Ryan and Regina Meares for their constant encouragement, and to the reading brigade: Cindy Gragg, LaDonna Alexander, Mary West Daly, Terri Parker, Genie Mezick, Lois Fatkin, Mary Jane Evans, Debbie Smithson, Katy Heit, Andrea Wright, and Brittany Daly. Thanks as well to the Conway and the North Myrtle Beach, S.C. police departments for their technical assistance, and to Al Ginn for his insightful plot "interrogations."

CHAPTER 1

On the second day of spring, when the purple finches descended like feathered raspberries, the men in the long car came to take Rose's daddy.

She stood in the flower bed, watching, digging her toe between the tulips. The men slid her daddy's stretcher into the back of the car. But instead of clambering in beside him to start an IV, they simply climbed into the front seat, closed their doors, and backed quietly down the driveway.

Rose saw that she had completely uprooted a tulip and that her canvas shoe was covered with damp black dirt. She wiped it on the doormat as her grandmother had taught her and pushed hard on the back door. She needed to ask when the men would bring her daddy back. Rose didn't consider asking her mother. She would ask Papa instead, who knew everything. But Papa didn't answer, only picked her up and held her where she couldn't see his eyes.

Two days later, at the church, Rose listened with all her might, remembering something her daddy had said, something very big that had made him look at her as if he were mapping her freckles again.

"Rose," he'd said with a labored smile. "One day soon, you . . . and Mom . . . and Papa . . . and Grandmom are going to the big church. Mr. Tommy's going to ask everybody a question. I want you to know the answer. Okay?"

Rose had nodded, twisting her fingers up under the elastic of the fitted sheet, waiting.

"Okay," said her dad, struggling to prop himself on his elbow. "Here's the question. Mr. Tommy will say, 'Who…shall separate us…from the love of Christ?' And he'll wait a second, and then he'll read a good, long answer. But I want you to know the short answer! I want you to whisper it out loud—right there in church."

Daniel whispered in Rose's ear. She nodded and whispered it back. He studied her eyes, then slid back down on his pillow, his face twisting strangely.

"Okay," he said again after a few seconds. "Let's practice." Slowly and meaningfully, he asked, "Who…shall separate us…from the love of Christ?"

She practiced.

"That's good, my Rosie," her father said hoarsely. "Will you remember that for me?" He fixed his luminous blue eyes on hers as if he could see all the way to her memory. "Never forget it?"

She nodded gravely and gave him the "promise" sign, wondering at the throaty voice, wondering why his eyes were closing so soon.

"Okay." Her father smiled, and in a minute, he was breathing evenly again.

A nurse stepped in, held his wrist, wrote something in a notebook. She settled into the green chair near the bed, studied Rose thoughtfully, and patted the cushion. "Sit with me?"

Rose shook her head. She stepped out into the hall and sat down on the polished pine floor, where she could hear her daddy's breathing.

In a few minutes, her mom came down the hall, eyes swollen. With a hopeful look, Rose reached for the coloring book she kept on the bookcase. Marcy always got better when they colored, and Rose considered this an especially good book, with zebras and toucans. But her mom just bit her bottom lip and shook her head.

The nurse stepped into the hall, closed the door after Marcy, and looked down. "Tropical birds!" she stage whispered. "I haven't colored in a long time! May I?" Rose led her to the kitchen table and with one ear listened to the woman's chatter and with the other strained to hear something from the bedroom.

Every morning for the next four days, Rose and Daniel practiced. But on the fifth day, Daniel got as far as the word *separate* and went back to sleep. Rose hesitated, then finished the question for him and whispered the answer in his ear.

The nurse stepped up quickly, and Rose returned to her spot on the hall floor until her grandmom told her it was a good time to play outside.

Once the long-faced men with the long car took Daniel, they did not bring him back. Instead, the house filled up with people who looked at Rose longer than she liked.

"Where are we going?" she asked, when Grandmom led her to the back bedroom and pulled a sky-blue dress with pintucks over Rose's strawberry blond curls.

"To church," her usually talkative grandmother had said, and that was all. But it was not church as usual. The whole atmosphere was peculiar: midafternoon, not morning. Sunlight streaming through the wrong windows. Not a single other child.

Rose barely recognized her mom, who looked small in her black suit and dark glasses and didn't walk straight.

Though her four-year-old legs dangled a foot above the carpet, Rose kept still and listened with both ears when Mr. Tommy stood up behind a big wooden box topped with red blooms. He smiled straight at her and began to speak. Rose didn't understand much of what he said. But after a long time, she heard what she was waiting for.

"Who…shall separate us…from the love of Christ?" Mr. Tommy asked slowly, his voice sounding cracked.

She felt a small thrill that it had happened just as her father had said. Quickly, before Mr. Tommy could say another word, Rose followed instructions. Loudly enough for the front two rows to hear, she whispered Daniel's answer, practiced to emphatic certitude.

"No one!" breathed Rose. She held on tightly to the edge of the pew, aware that heads were turning.

Not until she got to the cemetery did Rose figure out the box. Flinging an agitated glance at her mother, Rose could see no change. Perhaps Marcy didn't know what was in the box. Rose would not tell her.

Fourteen Years Later

Late March had been unusually cold, the spring flowers late to bloom. Each time Rose remembered, revulsion crept like chill bumps from the top of her head—washed over her body in freezing waves. It was almost summer now, but no matter how sultry the night, she felt the cold, heard Jack's whispered, bourbon-scented command: "Not a sound!"

But Rose *had* cried out, involuntarily, and felt a hand descend over her mouth and nose. It was then that Jack proved himself an astute judge of character. His threat was perfectly chosen, the words measured and emphatic: "Miss Marcy couldn't cope with *this*, now, could she?"

Shaking her head, panicky in his grip, Rose had accepted his unstated terms. She would not tell.

CHAPTER 2

"Get a move on, girl!" An irritable voice from behind shook her out of her reverie. *Get,* she thought. *Verb in the imperative mood. Understood* you *as the subject.*

Mechanically, Rose moved forward to close the gap in the line inching toward the application desk. Two more people ahead of her, three behind. She glanced again through the résumé, found no typos, and picked up the thread of her musing.

She could still see the detectives' faces, hear the doubt in their voices as they asked the same questions over and over. Rose knew her sketchy answers hadn't satisfied them. Jack was gone. Other than the police, should *anyone* care? One note of comfort played behind her fractured thoughts: her mother was safe. Nothing else really mattered.

"Hey, statue," came an acid voice behind her, "whatcha doin,' putting down roots?"

Rose decided to pay attention to where she was. A minute later, she stepped up to the desk, introduced herself, and produced the classified ad from the *Sun News*. The no-nonsense woman studied Rose's face as she handed her an application and pointed to a booth where she could sit to fill it out. Shifting into test-taking mode, Rose read the directions twice and started writing. Coming to the blank marked *age*, she penned a number that looked ridiculously young for the way she felt.

Barely eighteen, she felt all used up.

Height: five feet four inches. Weight: 119. The five extra pounds she'd been trying to shed had melted away. Considering that a wave of nausea hit her almost every time she thought about her circumstances, the weight loss was understandable.

Rose turned in her application and returned to the big, empty booth by the front window of the Picket Fence Pancake House to wait for an interview, dimly aware that five sets of eyes were burning through her back. The other applicants had already formed a union. A mocking laugh sounded behind her but stopped short of the wall she had erected around conscious thought. Rose simply shrugged and returned to what was left of the Plan.

The Plan had its origins in the first thirty minutes after Jack's wordless retreat from her bedroom. Rose had rushed…alternately sick, sobbing, and holding her breath for fear of waking Marcy… to the small bathroom that adjoined her bedroom. A near-scalding shower. Another. Jeans, a heavy sweater, a thick overcoat, and tennis shoes. She tiptoed down the stairs, noting with helpless irony that her mother was crying out again in her sleep. Rose silently unlocked the back door and spent the frosty hours until dawn wrapped in a quilt in the front seat of her mother's car, the doors locked, locked, and relocked. At daybreak, Rose rushed to school, tearstained and furious, conscious that Jack was undoubtedly still sleeping off his night before.

The next four nights she spent with Lacey, phoning Marcy to tell her they were in a study-crunch for nine-week exams. Finally, on day five, she went home, expecting…something. But Jack acted as if nothing whatsoever had happened. Nothing! Yet every time she crossed his path, Rose detected a look of calculated warning, a silent threat. She flatly refused to acknowledge his gaze, refused to speak more than a monosyllable when spoken to, refused to stay home when there was anywhere else she could spend the night. She showered only in the morning.

Evenings, when she sensed she had worn out her welcome with friends, Rose helped the librarians shut down the Summerlin Public

Library at nine. She walked the three blocks home clutching a house key and a bedroom key, letting herself in with one, and, after briefly checking in with Marcy, locking herself up with the other. She positioned a scarred metal softball bat in the bed beside her and put herself to sleep fine-tuning the Plan.

At first, she knew only that she would remain in Summerlin long enough to graduate from high school. Seven more weeks—surely she could avoid Jack for seven weeks. Then she would find a place...an untraceable place...a place at the beach. She'd get a waitressing job—a good one—that would cover living expenses for two. And then, when she had enough money, she would bodily remove her mother from Summerlin. Kidnap her, if she had to. They would spend the summer—where? Maybe in an extended-stay hotel with a kitchenette. Marcy would wake up and understand that she loved her daughter more than she thought she loved Jack. She would agree to evict him. Rose would pay for an attorney. Marcy would go home in late August and Rose would enter the university—the only part of the Plan as yet formally arranged.

The Plan kept Rose focused, gave her purpose. It pushed her to bear down in her AP classes, write her papers, prepare for tests.

But by late April, a few holes remained. How, for example, would Rose actually leave town? Too far from a train station, too young to rent a car, unwilling to steal her mother's, Rose was considering a bus when an opportunity presented itself: an invitation from Lacey's mom to spend a week's vacation in Myrtle Beach. They'd be leaving, she said, the morning after graduation. Rose accepted on the spot, considering the Plan complete. At the end of the beach week, she would simply ask the Brunsons to drop her off at the camp in Windy Hill where she'd worked the summer before. From there, Rose would find a job, a place to live, and a logical way to get Marcy out of Summerlin.

Yes, it had been a workable Plan...until....

A fire truck, its siren screaming, passed the pancake house in a blur. Rose started; it wouldn't help her job chances to sit staring fixedly while the world burned down around her. She turned sideways in the booth and studied the swinging doors that separated the kitchen from the dining room. She studied the way the waitresses carried coffee pots and tried to listen as they took the orders of three families who'd arrived for a late breakfast.

As if her mind had a split-screen and one screen was locked, her thoughts played on. She had come to a place, perhaps not untraceable, but that no longer mattered. She had somewhere to live. Now she was applying for a job. But the point of it all had been lost. Marcy blamed Rose for everything that had happened to Jack. Marcy would certainly refuse to make a home with Rose.

Jack's face imposed itself over a solitary diner sitting in a booth near the door, a fortyish man who kept looking her way. She squeezed her eyes shut, but the leer invaded the space beneath her eyelids. She recited the eight parts of speech, then reviewed participles, gerunds, and infinitives. The proper noun trumped them all: *Jack Bradford.*

Rose could clearly remember the first time he rang the doorbell, still hear him ask Marcy to come outside to watch the sunset. Clever of him to ask so little—it was disarming. In fact, observed objectively, Jack was charming, a consummate networker. He had money, which Rose's mom never seemed to have enough of. He had a small, expensive sports car, a large, expensive boat, and wealthy friends. He had a business of his own—The Suitable, a menswear shop with a reputation for being excessively pricey. He looked wonderful in his Harris Tweed sports coats, but Rose knew the side of him that caused the gross taste to appear in the back of her throat.

One evening—almost a year after moving in with Marcy—Jack had used a key to open the bathroom door while Rose was in the shower. "Get out!" Rose was shrieking, just as Marcy came home early from watercolors, calling out something about the instructor being sick. Jack had backed out calmly, telling Marcy he was giving Rose the bar of soap she'd called for. It was one lie among many but the first of his intrusions on her privacy. Brushing too close to her in the kitchen, lingering in her doorway, touching her fingers as she passed a bowl at the dinner table—all premeditated invasions that culminated on the cold March midnight when Jack had forced himself on her—a girl of seventeen with strawberry-blond curls and her dad's dazzling blue eyes—a slightly stocky girl just slimming down to the point that she was being noticed by the guys her own age.

The restaurant was filling up for lunch. Despite herself, Rose's gaze returned to a twentyish waitress whose uniform fit too snugly around her waist.

Had it really been only ten days since she'd confirmed her greatest fear? Back in April, when her period failed to start, she reminded herself that this was not the first time. Stress always made her late.

"Honestly," she'd heard her mother exclaim, "I've never seen her so moody and rude. I guess it's graduation—she's pushing herself!"

But when six weeks passed without relief, Rose had driven her mother's car to the next town to buy a pregnancy test, bypassing the Summerlin merchants who knew her on sight. She took the test that night. And for a few minutes, the results had turned Rose into her mother: completely helpless in the face of trouble.

By force of will, she'd collected herself. She had to concentrate on the Plan. Staring at the test strip, Rose slipped into the same detached, adult-like persona she assumed whenever she needed to think.

First, she lectured herself sternly, graduation was only one week away. One week! She would need that diploma to get a job…to support herself. The university…At this, Rose drew a quavering breath. She had avidly looked forward to college. Lately, its three-hour distance from Summerlin had seemed a margin of safety, and her scholarship offers would cover all of her tuition and living expenses. But not like this, she told herself emphatically. She refused to factor this development into the Plan. She would *not* enter college expecting a baby.

Above all, she must tell no one she was pregnant. The town of Summerlin, North Carolina, was too small. Her mom's reputation couldn't survive any more talk than she'd already generated for herself. Her pastor? He was a great guy—Rose could picture herself telling him everything—but his wife had once been Marcy's best friend. Somehow, to confide in Tommy Bellamy would betray her mother. Rose couldn't bring herself to show up for youth group, much less for worship.

Even Rose's closest friends, Lacey and Britt, knew nothing past the fact that Rose had been strangely moody since spring break. But since they too were honors-track students, all competing for a GPA that would land them in the top 5 percent of the graduating class, neither had probed too deeply. No, there was no one to turn to. Rose had stared at the May calendar until all she could see was Friday the twenty-ninth, with a tiny cap and gown penciled into the block. On the thirtieth, she would leave with the Brunsons for Myrtle Beach. The Plan was still in place. The Plan was workable.

Until it fell apart. The reality of having her mom discover the matter—that had been too much to handle! Rose had been so careful to wrap up the used test kit. She'd stuffed it—hands shaking—into the outdoor trash can under several heavy plastic bags. The fact that Fondulac, the neighborhood stray, had chosen that same night to tip over the garbage can and string its tell-tale contents across the back steps seemed so supremely coincidental that Rose had interpreted it as punishment from God.

All in all, the discovery added up to a nightmarish Saturday morning: Rose sick in the bathroom, her mom denying the obvious. Marcy kept shrieking, "You haven't even brought home a boyfriend!" And there was Rose, silent but wanting to scream at the top of her lungs, "No, Mom, I didn't have to! You did!"

For once, Jack's face was a strained, contorted mask. Claiming a fitting appointment, he evacuated as Marcy's furious questions flew: "Who is it? He'll have to own up to this! What else is going on behind my back?" Rose just stood there, clutching the bathroom sink, a knot of frustration twisting her stomach. Could her mom really be so naïve? But Rose knew the answer.

She had known it for years. Absolutely. Marcy Kendall's emotional needs were so great and her emotional stability so fragile that she was blind to the obvious. Rose loved her mother with a protectiveness born in the unspoken role-reversal they had acted out for the past fourteen years. Somehow, Rose just couldn't bring herself to inform Marcy that the man she thought she loved had raped her own daughter.

Seizing on a half truth, Rose finally blurted out, "You don't know him, Mom!" and fled through the back door, grateful for the first time in her life that she knew exactly how her mother would cope: with a ripping migraine and three days in bed. That would leave three days to formulate a new Plan.

Rose remembered wanting to pray and feeling incapable. Wherever God was, he seemed tragically absent from her life right now, even though Rose had prayed desperately, begging him to make things right.

Now, as she waited by the window of the Picket Fence, she found herself too paralyzed to pray about something as minor as a waitressing position. *Jack is dead,* she thought over and over. *Mom will never forgive me.* Hearing the carefree giggling from the table of comrades behind her, she wondered if she had ever once lived in their world.

The restaurant manager approached her booth. Rose cleared her head forcefully and produced a smile. The manager extended his hand in introduction. "Miss Kendall?" he said in an overly loud voice as he slid into the seat on the other side. "Congratulations. This is a top-notch application. I can read your writing. You left nothing blank. You can spell! You even signed and dated the application, a very important step that some people"—at this, he looked pointedly at the tableful of girls behind her—"never get around to!"

To Rose he directed a brief series of what he called "semi-personal" questions. She answered him factually, sounding calmer than she felt.

"Miss Kendall," the man concluded, "this is a busy place. I need a detail-oriented waitress I can count on. You can start tomorrow morning at six. Sara here"—he gestured to a smiling, older woman with white hair—"will outfit you with a uniform. I look forward to working with you."

CHAPTER 3

Walking the nine blocks back to Savannah Cole's house, Rose celebrated the good news of her employment for all of five minutes. North Myrtle Beach was so crowded with traffic that she had to sprint across every intersection. But as soon as she left the sidewalks of Highway 17 and turned onto a side street, the mental video resumed right where it had left off. It played without ceasing, getting longer and more detailed, as Rose tried to make sense of the storm that had dragged her from her own home and into Savannah's.

That hideous Saturday morning of the pregnancy test discovery, Marcy had wept uncontrollably. She persisted well into the afternoon. Neither Rose nor Jack knew how to make her stop. Not that Rose didn't try. "Mama, Mama—settle down. Just breathe. I'm okay. Really." But Marcy began shaking when she wasn't lurching from the force of her sobs.

Back from his fitting, Jack prowled the next room, the door open, saying nothing, simply monitoring. "*Why* doesn't he just leave?" Rose asked herself for the thousandth time. But edgy as he seemed, Jack showed no intention of leaving. When the inevitable migraine sent Marcy to her darkened bedroom, Rose had simply collapsed into a chair beside her, accepting her moans as a fitting lament for two shattered lives.

Catching Rose on the front porch that evening, Jack blocked her sidestep and spoke in a low voice that was all business. "We'll take care of this. Have you told anyone?"

Rose paused, absorbing his intentions. *Why should I be surprised?* she thought. Ice in her voice, she responded, "It's already taken care of."

Jack stared at her for a long moment, obviously interpreting her reply to suit himself. "Hmmph!" he retorted. "You're smarter than I gave you credit for." When Rose said no more, he walked briskly back inside.

Whatever he told Marcy the next day was enough to quell her hysteria. She had emerged from her bedroom on the evening of the third day, shaky and holding on to the furniture, unwilling to ask any loaded questions.

Jack's latest charade of tenderness toward her mother raised Rose's suspicions to new heights. There was neither love nor logic to explain it. Why *was* Jack staying there? Marcy was far too unpredictable, too unstable, to be the social ornament Jack had evidently taken her for at first. And what drew him away from the house every evening? Why was he suddenly so busy?

For the next several days, Rose invented reasons to leave their two-story white frame Georgian either a few minutes before or a few minutes after Jack's departure for his so-called evening fittings. Cutting the block, Rose stationed herself in Waterfront Park, crowded with tourists to the picturesque little coastal town. From the World War Memorial, Rose could see every approach to The Suitable.

But Jack wasn't going to his shop. Instead, she saw, every night he was heading for the garage located behind the huge yellow Victorian he had purchased on the aging but elegant side of Summerlin's waterfront battery, a block and a half further north.

The Victorian itself had been enough to blind her mother. Early in the relationship, Jack had promised Marcy that as soon as he finished the daunting job of renovating the 110-year-old monstrosity, they would get married on the front porch, where its circular gazebo overlooked the harbor. The sunset would bathe them in colors as intense as the azaleas they would plant along the curving brick walkways—features that, as yet, existed only in Jack's florid promises. Until then, he had sweet-talked, he needed a place to live—and Marcy had plenty of extra room. Rose had been horrified.

Most incongruous was her mother's abandonment of her long-standing membership in Harborview Community Church. Sure, Marcy might have been irregular in her attendance, but at least she had turned out once or twice a month—until Jack uprooted the fragile balance of their lives. Rose was baffled that Marcy could have been so utterly taken in. How could her mother have allowed any man to move in with them?

Now, Rose thought to herself, *here I am. Stalking the responsible party through downtown Summerlin.* How ironic that Jack never looked back. Even at a distance, she could see the self-assurance in his walk. He spoke confidently to everyone he passed, calling out to the neighbors by name.

For three nights running, Rose watched Jack pull out a key, open the side door to the Victorian's garage, and disappear into the gloom. The third night, just after dusk, a short, robust man with spiked blond hair appeared in the driveway. Jack emerged from the garage to meet him. From behind a huge clump of overgrown azaleas, Rose strained to listen to the conversation in the driveway.

"I've waited long enough," the visitor said forcefully. "Give me half, and we'll call it even."

"I told you, you just have to be patient," Jack said, with a hint of a snarl.

"I'm all outta patience. Half."

Jack sighed audibly. "The buyer says he can be here next week."

"Half."

"You're going to miss the best opportunity you've got."

The voice rose, hard and ugly. "Half. Now. I can find my own buyers."

"Okay," Jack said, with a profanity. "But I can't get to them tonight. Tomorrow night—seven o'clock—at The Suitable. My office is in the back, so come to the back door. Knock once."

"I'll be there at seven," the bulky blond growled, "and you better have 'em. Lemme remind you—I can say a few things to the wrong people for you."

"Watch your own back!" Jack retorted, dressing up his warning with another profanity. "I can name a couple of people who'd gladly see you out of business too."

"Look, man," the blond replied with an explicit epithet, "you just be sure I can find you at seven o'clock."

"Tomorrow," Jack snarled. The visitor turned on his heel and strode angrily down the street.

Rose stayed put for a full minute and a half. Then, tiptoeing into the street to blend in with the foot traffic, she found herself trembling with tension. What was Jack involved in that he would speak to someone so threateningly? Who was the blond man, so different in dress and speech from Jack's usual business associates? This business was clandestine, that much was obvious. Some type of exchange—whether money or drugs or stolen property—was taking place tomorrow night at The Suitable.

Rose was overwhelmed with a wild and elated desire to be there. And so would the police. Oh, she would make sure of it! She would genuinely enjoy seeing Jack caught in something criminal! Her heart pounded strangely; her nerves felt electric. Could she wait until seven o'clock tomorrow night to see the man ruined? She would force herself.

So easy to slip into hatred, she mused, scarcely recognizing her own heart or the way it beat for revenge.

She reasoned through it. She had every right to hate this man. He had stolen her mother, stolen her home, her innocence, her body, her future, even her faith. Rose took a deep breath and tried to relax her neck and shoulders. *In twenty-four hours,* she thought, *maybe this part of the nightmare will be over. And Mom will be safe...Mom will be safe.*

The next morning, Rose woke up at five to the brief, anguished outcry of her mother. The dream again. By the age of nine, Rose had given up rushing to her mother's bedroom to comfort her when the dream occurred. Marcy never remembered enough of it to explain.

Now, Rose tried vainly to go back to sleep, but she was too full of nervous exhilaration. At six, she got dressed as if she were taking a final exam. Marcy was up uncharacteristically early making coffee, oblivious to the fact that Rose had exempted all of her exams and actually had no more classes to attend. Throwing her backpack over her shoulder, Rose headed downtown to scout out the side streets that flanked the rear of Jack's shop.

Never before had she ventured into the alley that backed up to The Suitable. Behind a scuffed green trash compactor, she spotted an unexpected door, jostled the doorknob, and found herself in an unkempt storage room separated from Jack's office by nothing more than a thin wall of paneling. It was far too early for Jack to be up and at the shop—he habitually slept late—so Rose cleared away the thick cobwebs beside a set of metal shelves and prepared a hiding place. Male voices, she reasoned, would carry through this wall sufficiently to hear at least a little of what would take place inside The Suitable at seven o'clock that evening.

In the meantime, she had to find somewhere to spend what promised to be the longest day of her life. She walked to school, pretended to read a novel in the library, then spent the afternoon at graduation practice. That evening, she forced herself to eat dinner at the same table with Marcy and Jack. Her mother was still scarcely speaking to her, and Rose never tasted a morsel she swallowed. Jack left at six, taking his car this time. Rose left at 6:40, knowing it was only a ten-minute walk to Jack's shop. At 6:50, after checking to make sure the car was in the alley, Rose made a whispered phone call to the town's 911 operator. She spoke in a breathless rush. "Something's going to happen tonight—seven o'clock—behind The Suitable. It's important! We need the police." She'd intended to make the call anonymously, not counting on the dispatcher's pressure to identify herself. Aware of the seconds ticking by, she knuckled under: "I'm

Rose Kendall, and something terrible is going to happen if you don't get here by seven!"

Switching off the phone, Rose crept down the alley. The dark, humid storage room smelled of mildew. May had taken all the chill out of the cement block building and left it close feeling. She burrowed into the corner she had cleared that morning and settled in, reviewing a litany of vindictive thoughts.

Did he really think he could use us to lead a double life? Silently, she answered herself. *Of course he did.*

From inside The Suitable, a door opened and shut, but Rose could hear no voices, only the squeak of the floor as someone walked past. She edged a little closer to the paneled wall, wedging herself tightly into the corner, concentrating on silent breathing. Five long minutes went by, five minutes that felt like fifty. Rose nervously entertained herself with mental images of Jack outfitted in prison stripe instead of herringbone. She could imagine him scoffing, "Broad black stripes? How unsuitable!"

And how ironic, she mused, that Jack should give his shop a name that blatantly contradicted his character. Suitable. It meant fitting, appropriate, right for the purpose or occasion. Nothing about Jack was suitable!

Claustrophobic in the dark and aware that her right leg had gone to sleep, Rose was slowly and gingerly shifting her weight when her ankle touched something that felt like a cobweb. She flinched but made no sound. Seconds later, however, a sting pierced her ankle, sharp and hot, and she instinctively jumped, dislodging a dusty book on the adjacent shelf. It teetered, then toppled…and fell to the concrete floor with a *smack*.

Jack's voice rang out, hard and demanding: "Who's there?" Rose could hear him tramp through the office and out the back door. A panic-stricken fifteen seconds went by as Rose willed herself invisible. But Jack moved as if he could see through walls. Throwing open the storage room door, he reached in and yanked Rose into the alleyway, his face slack with surprise. But only for a moment.

"Well!" he smirked, eyebrows raised. "You've come looking for me now?" Rose was far too unnerved to reply. She twisted and wriggled in his grasp, which tightened. "Oh, you struggle!" Jack declared sarcastically, his handsome face distorted in a cold smile. "But you liked it, didn't you? All that fighting and kicking. Quite a show." His French cologne welled sweet in Rose's nostrils.

Rose's throat constricted, and for a moment she thought she would be sick. Instead, she spat out the words: "You think I want you? I *hate* you!"

The words hung in the air for a split second before Jack seemed to process them. "What *are* you doing here?" he demanded. She simply glared at him, and this time he clenched her forearms and dragged her roughly toward The Suitable's back door. She clung to the doorframe in vain. Jack propelled her into the office, artfully dodging her flailing arms and legs. She kicked at him in a parody of helpless dreams, but he laughed. "Think you're stronger than I am? Give it up."

Sirens wailed in the distance, drawing closer by the second, and Jack cocked his head to listen. A flash of defiance leapt from Rose's eyes, and, seeing it, Jack came to a sudden, startled conclusion. In an explosion of profanity, he shook her. "You called the police? *You*?" he burst out, dragging her back toward the door again, curses intensifying. "You'll pay for this little trick, Rosie. Believe me, it *is* payday. Now get out! Get out! You'll see me soon enough!" As the sirens drew closer, Jack kicked open the office door and pushed Rose backwards into the alley, up against the door of his sportscar.

He froze. A look of apprehension seized his classic features. His eyes opened wide, focused not on Rose, but on a point behind and to her left. It was the only time Rose had seen Jack frightened.

Her eyes darted to the face of a stocky man with spiked blond hair. He was standing in the alley, his gloved right hand rising toward them. "Help me!" Jack barked. "Get her out of here."

The blond man looked panicked. He shook his head twice as the scream of the sirens enveloped them. "You ruined it, man. You ruined the whole thing." Rose heard a spurt from the extended gun, watched Jack lurch backwards. Before she could move, he recovered sufficiently to latch onto her shoulders, then fell forward and sideways against her, his weight trapping her between the car and the trash compactor. The blond man flipped the gun over their heads and into the compactor, then raced down the other end of the alley, jamming a camel-colored pouch under his jacket.

Rose was now crushed between a wall of metal and a 190-pound adversary who seemed even heavier. Screaming, she wrestled to free herself from his weight. She could feel his hot blood seeping through her shirt, feel it dripping on her feet. Her screams seemed tamped, muffled by Jack's body.

"Stop it! Get off! Let go of me! Let me go!" But Jack held on.

Finally, he pushed himself up slightly and looked at her, his eyes two accusations. She stared back, mesmerized by the fury in eyes slowly glazing over as Jack lowered himself to the gritty asphalt.

"You'll pay for this," he panted. He slumped forward, one final gurgle escaping from his throat before the ragged breathing stopped.

It seemed like mere seconds before the police swarmed into the alley, two of them yelling, "Freeze!" The order was pointless. Jack couldn't move, and Rose was already frozen.

Now, her own words to the dispatcher came back to haunt her. Something terrible *had* happened here. "A blond man ..." said Rose in a voice that bordered on hysteria. She pointed down the alley.

The officers ignored her, their weapons pointed at her shoulders. "Where's the gun? Hand it over." She shook her head repeatedly, trying vainly to pull her shirt away from her skin, repulsed by the blood that seemed to have fused the fabric to her chest.

"Young lady, this man's been shot and unless I'm mistaken, he's dead. Give me the gun."

"I don't have a gun," Rose responded, her head reeling. "There was a blond-haired man...."

Two of the three policemen finally followed her pointing finger and raced down the alley.

Meanwhile, the questions persisted. "You *are* Rose Kendall. You're the one who called the dispatcher. Now where's the gun?"

Rose's thoughts cleared sufficiently to remember the trash compactor. "It's in there," she said, pointing shakily. "I saw him throw it in there and run."

"Run where?"

"I don't know! Down the alley."

"Did you see a car?"

"No. But I couldn't see the end of the alley. He…he fell on top of me."

In five minutes, the other officers were back, shaking their heads. Nobody else on the block claimed to have seen or heard anything more unusual than a fast-moving car. One officer produced a camera and got to work.

The EMTs arrived, checked in vain for vital signs, and hustled Jack off in the big square ambulance, its siren wailing needlessly.

Meanwhile, a newly arrived detective took one startled look at Rose, pulled out his cell phone, and placed a call, dialing from memory. "Marcy," he said in a low voice, "this is Kirk Landry. Rose is… at a shooting scene. She's okay, but you need to come down to the police station right away."

"Let me transport," he said to the responding officers, and guided Rose, visibly shaking, to an unmarked car, settling her into the back seat. "It's okay, Rosie. It's okay," he murmured. "Just hang on. We're going to get you some clean clothes. Just a few routine procedures, okay? We'll need to ask you some questions, and then you can probably go straight home." He seemed to sigh and shake his head at his own statement.

At the station, a technician swabbed Rose's hands, palms, and arms for a gunshot residue test. A female officer led her to a shower stall, thoroughly swabbed her neck and chest, collected her clothes and bagged them, then turned on the showerhead and adjusted the temperature. The generous stream of warm water, the soap, the shampoo, afforded a few minutes of escape, but the instant Rose turned off the shower, she knew two things: Marcy was in the building, and she was hysterical.

Rose could hear Detective Landry trying to talk her down, but Marcy's voice was rising higher and higher. Rose's shaking resumed, and she scrambled to towel herself dry and slip into the pale blue scrub suit left on a towel rack. The female officer looked at her curiously—not without a flash of sympathy—and led her down the hall toward the "soft room" to calm down.

Two dark green couches faced one another in the carpeted, softly lit room. A leather Bible lay open on the coffee table. Rose sat in motionless dread while her escort went to notify the detectives that she was there, but five minutes went by, ten, twenty, thirty without company. All that reached Rose's room was the sound of the distant rise and fall of her mother's weeping, the words indistinguishable. Finally, the sound stopped, and several minutes later, the detective peered around the doorway. He offered a tight, tired smile, sat down on the opposite couch, waited a second, and said, "We had to call her doctor, Rose. He gave your mom a sedative and took her home."

She nodded in dull acceptance. For the next two hours, Kirk Landry and Sgt. Linwood Bowler asked her all the obvious questions, sometimes two or three times. She answered what she was asked, volunteering little. Finally Kirk said, "Rose, the GSP test showed no evidence that you've fired a gun in the last twenty-four hours. We're emptying the dumpster to make sure that was the only gun in there, but for now, we've only got one murder weapon, and it doesn't seem to be wearing any fingerprints.

"Legally, we don't have any grounds to hold you. But your mom said something that we can only classify as…accusatory. I believe her exact words were, 'I knew she hated him, but I didn't believe she'd go this far.' She thinks you shot him, Rose."

The words sank in.

"Did you have any reason to want Jack Bradford dead?"

Don't tell him! her thoughts commanded. *Keep quiet!*

"Did you?" He asked the question gently but firmly.

"Of course I did," she said. "He stole my mother from me. But I didn't shoot him. And I don't know why the blond man did."

"Why were you really there, Rose?"

"I wanted to catch him doing something illegal and get him out of our lives."

Kirk drew a long, deep breath, thought a minute, then said, "This may be a little unorthodox, but here's what I'm going to propose. I know there's no other family here in town for you to call. And I don't think you need to go home to your mom tonight. Dr. Barber will make sure she's okay. Besides, it's almost midnight. So how would you feel about spending the night right here on this couch? We'll get you some dinner and a pillow and blanket. Under the circumstances—and don't think *I'm* accusing you of anything, Rose—we need to run a blood test, just to rule out drugs and alcohol. We'll let you know as soon as the results come in."

Rose nodded in relief at the burly detective who had been her Sunday school teacher two years before. "That'll be okay," she whispered. "I don't need anything to eat."

Within twenty minutes of the blood test, she fell into fitful sleep, dimly aware that someone was checking on her at intervals during the night. "Why," Sgt. Bowler kept asking in her dreams, "were you at the scene?" Rose simply pursed her lips and shook her head.

The next morning, declining an offer of breakfast and a ride, Rose walked out of the station and, from the viewpoint of the Town of Summerlin, disappeared.

CHAPTER 4

Remorse covered Marcy Kendall like a heavy winter garment despite the fact that it was June. As she stood in the check-out line, wedged between customers in beachwear, she heard a red-haired woman behind her swear at a sturdy little girl who swung on the chain dangling from the next checkout counter.

"Stop that, I said! Just wait 'til I get ahold of you."

The six-year-old looked sad and dropped the "Lane Closed" sign. The remorse that flitted across her face included fear.

Why, Marcy thought, *is this woman making threats in the grocery store? Can't she wait until they get to the car?*

The memory of her own daughter's reproachful looks haunted her. Now Rose was gone.

The irritable redhead broke into Marcy's thoughts again. "I—said—stand—still or Alec's gonna blister you! Do ya hear me?"

"Don't tell Alec," the little girl gasped. "You spank me, Mama, but don't tell Alec!"

"Then stop that whining!" the woman responded impatiently. "You're driving me crazy! Just shut up!"

How many times, Marcy asked herself, had she told Rose, in essence, to shut up? A thousand times Rose had tried to convey her intense discomfort with Jack, but Marcy had been unwilling to listen.

Finally, the man in front of her paid, and the cashier started reaching for Marcy's small handful of items.

"How are you this evening, ma'am?" the cashier asked.

Marcy marveled at her own hypocritical ability to smile and say, "Fine" when she was dying inside, not only from her own stupidity, but from her grief that this other mother was making a grave and familiar mistake. The conversation behind her resumed.

"Mommy, can I have a piece of candy?" the little girl asked, as they edged past a display.

"No!" the woman said between gritted teeth. "For the last time, I said no! You can't have anything. What's wrong with you? Why can't you ever be happy?"

Marcy took her change and moved on, carrying her small bag with one hand and clutching her chest with the other.

Why can't you ever be happy? Why can't you ever be happy? How many times had she asked Rose that question, never realizing the impossibly unhappy situation she had placed her daughter in. And further, what had she ever taught Rose about happiness?

Happiness was a quality that had always eluded Marcy. The quest for happiness had been what drew her to Jack in the first place, and look what it had brought her. His money, his clothes, his looks, his charm had been so magnetic that Marcy had left the comfortable company of her church and her friends for the nearly constant round of parties hosted by the "new people," the ones building the towering resort mansions overlooking the entrance to the Cape Fear River.

For a year and a half, Marcy had ignored Rose when she begged, "Mom, please tell him to leave. He makes me feel weird." Finally, Rose had stopped asking. Toward the end, she had stopped saying almost anything at all.

Reaching her car, Marcy stowed her few groceries, climbed into the driver's seat, lowered her head to the steering wheel, and wept. "My entire life is gone. Oh, God, help me! I can't stand this much pain." The tears fell past the steering wheel and soaked her cotton slacks.

Finally lifting her head, she encountered a sight that hiked the pain level even higher. The little girl and her mother were crossing the asphalt lot toward an obviously irritated man standing only two parking spaces away. "What took you so long?" he barked. "I been out here forever."

"She just wouldn't behave. I couldn't even concentrate on my list."

Through bared teeth, the man snapped, "Get in the car, brat—now!"

A confused, frightened expression covered the child's features. Marcy could see her little mind trying to figure out what she had done, how she could make it better. Couldn't this couple see what they were doing to the child? *How could I not have seen what was happening to my Rose?* Hopelessness swamped her as Marcy started the car to head for the small condo in North Myrtle Beach, where she had spent the last five nights.

She drove mechanically, ignoring the strip of seafood restaurants boasting immense neon crab claws clacking open and shut, open and shut; the tall neon lighthouses casting a searching beam over Highway 17; the beckoning sea captains promising early-bird specials. She likewise ignored the beachwear shops, the outlet malls, the miniature golf courses with their smoking volcanoes. Marcy saw only the highway, and even that with a mechanical awareness, empty of conscious recognition. Mentally, she was still in the attic.

The attic was one of Marcy's least favorite places. But four days after Jack's murder, with Rose missing, the police showing up at least twice a day, the town of Summerlin in an uproar, and its initial gestures of sympathy awkwardly extended and more awkwardly received, Marcy had left her bed in the middle of a sleepless night to climb the narrow attic stairs searching for…what?

Up to her elbows in cardboard boxes, she spotted a small wooden chest that held legal papers, including a deed to the house and the title to the car. Good. She needed those. But Marcy knew that what she really wanted was in the large blue box marked "school papers" that she now spied in a neatly cleared spot under a dormer. In the glare of a single light bulb, she lifted the lid and pulled out the few papers on top. There!

There were the pictures of Rose, the clear-eyed toddler with the irresistible curls. They were neatly filed in order, starting in K-4, with Rose beaming above the straps of the white pique sundress that she had picked out for the first day of school. The K-5 shot depicted an entirely different child—serious-faced, sad around the eyes—a picture made only three weeks after Daniel's funeral. The first-grade photo showed a tentative gap-toothed grin. The second-grade face was turned for a three-quarter profile. There was a mature look in the eyes.

Marcy looked through every picture, conscious that she was intently searching every photo as if for clues. She studied each expression as if, momentarily, the lips would open, the mouth would move, and Rose's voice would call, "Here, Mom! I'm okay." She held up one of Rose's twelfth-grade portraits, one of the proofs taken back in September, and angled her cheek to touch the matte-finished paper cheek. With her finger she smoothed the haunted-looking paper eyes. How could she have possibly misunderstood a look like that? How could she have left even the methodical filing of the school pictures up to her daughter?

Near the bottom of the box was a stack of lined papers, clipped together, and at the sight of them, a bittersweet memory overtook Marcy. Atop the stack was a story Rose had written about her daddy.

Marcy recalled the particular Thursday afternoon when seven-year-old Rose dragged her feet all the way from Summerlin Elementary School's big, wooden front door to the car where Marcy was waiting to drive her to the dentist's office.

Marcy had scheduled the appointment only after Rose complained of a toothache. It was hard to stretch what little money was coming in from Daniel's Social Security check; it didn't allow for regular check-ups. Daniel's parents would give her the money if she asked, but they were already doing so much: letting Marcy and Rose live with them in the rambling white Georgian, covering all the everyday living expenses, buying all the groceries, encouraging her every day to believe that, soon, she would emerge from the dark place that seemed so very much larger than she was, that one day she would genuinely care again.

But she couldn't feel it! Though three years had passed since Daniel's death, Marcy was still basically living in her bedroom. Occasionally she gave in to Mr. and Mrs. Kendall's inducement to go out—to dinner, maybe, or just to walk along the waterfront. But Marcy was in the velvet clutches of depression, and even leaving her room to take her own daughter to the dentist was taking effort. This particular Thursday, as she sat in the car, watching Rose's downcast approach, she thought to herself, *She's walking the way I feel.*

Rose got in the car. Marcy offered her the crackers her grandmother had sent and asked, "How was your day?"

"Okay, I guess." Her daughter spoke with an uncharacteristic sorrow.

"What's wrong?" Marcy asked.

"It's really terrible, Mom."

"What's terrible?" she asked with real concern. *There! That was a feeling, wasn't it?*

"I have to write a story about Daddy. I told Mrs. Harrison I didn't remember much." The little-girl voice had developed the squeak that meant Rose was holding back tears. "She said that maybe it was time to find out a little bit about him. I have pictures of Daddy, but I don't know enough to write about, Mom."

"No, I guess you don't, Rosie, but…I do. After your appointment, we'll go to the park, and I'll tell you. Eat your snack, sweetie."

All these years later, Marcy could still remember that wait in the dentist's office. A struggle had raged inside her. Guilt, because she had not talked about Daniel, hadn't given their child even a loving description to take comfort in. Sorrow that her marriage, the most blissful years of her life, had ended in a near-tidal form of grief that rose and ebbed, sometimes high, sometimes low, but always threatening to pull her under, drown her, and leave her body as dead as her feelings.

She knew she should have returned to the brick cottage she and Daniel had shared before he got too sick to care for without the help of his parents. That might have forced her to cope. But she felt incapable. Besides, Daniel's medical bills were astronomical. The sale of the cottage had covered all but the final forty-five thousand dollars. And so she and Rose had remained in the home of her in-laws, two of the kindest, most generous people she had ever known.

Around the house, they never talked about Daniel. Whenever an outsider brought up his name in conversation, Marcy tended to fall silent, which prompted everyone else to tiptoe around her. That Thursday in the park ended much the same. The conversation turned tearful almost immediately, and Rose promptly asked to go home. Marcy went to bed with a migraine.

For a week afterward, Rose would come to the door of Marcy's bedroom, hang on the doorframe, and say, "Mom, I'm sorry I made you talk about Daddy."

"You didn't make me, Rose."

"But I made you sad."

"I was already sad."

"I made you more sad."

As for the school assignment, Papa helped Rose put a happy face on the biographical facts. Rose's teacher had written the word *Wonderful!* in big red letters at the top of her report. Now, sitting on the attic floor, Marcy read Rose's paper and realized she had utterly failed her daughter. The seven-year-old's account was full of her grandparents' memories and none of her own. It concluded with a two-sentence reference to Marcy: "My mom misses my daddy very much. She cries every day."

Her poor Rose, always picking up the pieces while Marcy incessantly fell apart. Now, sitting in the attic at three in the morning, Marcy was filled with an appalling realization. For the last eighteen months, she had been so busy trying to come back to life again, so busy trying to replace Daniel with Jack, that she had abandoned her precious child in the process. Pulling only the senior portrait out of the blue box, Marcy carefully replaced the lid and returned the box to the exact spot where Rose had left it.

CHAPTER 5

As Marcy unlocked the door, sadness invaded the tiny beach condo even before she did. She set down the grocery bag on the bar that served as both table and kitchen counter, slid the apple juice into the efficiency refrigerator, put the breakfast bars in a basket, and sat down on the end of the bed to continue her self-prosecution.

"I didn't even wake up when you came home, Rose," she whispered to the newly framed senior picture she had placed on the bureau. "I went back to sleep."

It was the sedatives, Marcy rationalized—that and an aversion to hard questions. All things combined had kept Marcy from getting out of bed that morning when she faintly stirred at the sounds of the front door opening and Rose's footsteps moving up the wooden stairs. Couldn't the police have detained her? But no. Rose was eighteen—a legal adult in North Carolina. She didn't have to be released into her mother's custody at all.

Regardless, another twelve hours had passed before Marcy fully awoke, got out of bed, and realized Rose wasn't home. At first she called the police station and learned the facts of Rose's release. She next called Lacey and Brittany, both of whom were full of questions but no answers. Finally, she'd called her cousin Nancy, who lived twenty miles west of Summerlin, and found herself having to tell the whole confusing story from the start.

And Jack—Jack, whom she should have been able to call on for help—was he actually dead? Jack, with his good looks and his money and his contacts and his quick wit, dead? She couldn't believe it. A strange grief overwhelmed her, but not for Jack alone. In a sickening flash of insight, she realized that Jack would have been less than eager to help her find Rose.

Fear and frustration completely overwhelmed Marcy as she considered the absurdity of her daughter's simply leaving without a trace...well, except for the note and the blue scrubs, which had been arranged on top of the bed as if a person were lying there. A small suitcase was gone, and two drawers in the antique mahogany dresser stood empty. The bathroom vanity had been cleared of toiletries and cosmetics. Other than those obvious items, Marcy realized, she didn't know much about what Rose owned, or where she kept them. And how about money? Rose did babysit often. There was no sign of money in this echo chamber of a bedroom.

The police were sympathetic and agreed to issue a missing person bulletin, primarily because their chief witness to a murder appeared to have skipped town. But it might be weeks, they advised Marcy, before anything came to light. Marcy went home in anguish.

For a week she lay in a dark room, struggling up only when the phone or the doorbell rang, alternately crying and trying to pray. Twice, she made the midnight trip to the attic only to return to bed, surrounded by the pictures of Rose, arranged in ascending order by age.

On the eighth day, refusing to acknowledge the gnawing edge of another headache, she forced herself into physical activity. She would clean Rose's room, she decided, dust it, vacuum it. "At least I can put clean sheets on the bed," she told herself when her body began to insist that she stop. The contour sheet was hard to stretch over the thick corner of the mattress, and Marcy found herself lifting up the corner and bracing it with her knee, exposing the box spring below.

And then she saw it. A green journal peeked out from between the mattress and box spring. And in its pages, Marcy learned everything she didn't want to know.

Now, sitting on the bed in a condo fifty miles from home, she opened the journal again, rereading the pages that brought such inexpressible heartbreak.

I'm afraid to tell anyone, she read, her eyes caressing Rose's unmistakable penmanship, with its loopy Es and Fs. *Mom is just blind. She needs his money. He buys her things, and she completely ignores me. Why would you let this happen, God? This is hell.* Rose had underlined the word *hell* eight times.

Does it get worse than this? I have to walk into the house and pretend everything is okay. Mom is accusing me of weird stuff. But he lies and lies, and she believes him.

Two pages later: *He looked at me again across the dinner table. It was like a warning. I've got to get out of here. Please, God! I can only spend so many nights at Lacey's before her parents say that's enough. They're so worried about her perfect 4.0. I almost told Brittany at school today, but I can't. I can't tell anybody. Mom asks me why I don't talk anymore. There's nothing I can say that she'll believe.*

The next entry caused Marcy to bite her lip so hard she tasted blood. *I'm late. Oh please, God, don't let me be pregnant. Graduation is only one week away. I can hang on for one week. Then I'll find Savannah and maybe get a job at the restaurant where she works. Please, God, let me start tonight.*

Marcy couldn't bring herself to reread the diary entry from the day of the pregnancy test. It had taken up three pages so full of agony that Marcy had wept all night.

Two entries later, Rose had written: *Pighead! He thinks I've scheduled an abortion. And I've thought about it. Big temptation. But if I did, I'd be handing him some kind of power over the rest of my life—turn me into whatever he is. Why does he stay here? Any marginally intelligent person would leave! There has to be a reason.*

Maybe I can make him leave. Of course, Mom would blame me. She always believes him. Doesn't she remember me at all?

The final entry was dated Tuesday, May twenty-sixth, three days before Rose would've taken her place in the graduation processional.

The diary read, *Tomorrow night! Finally I have a reason to call the police. I'm sorry, Mom. I have to do something.*

At the bottom of the page Rose had written: *Spiky blond hair. 5'7." 180–190. Maybe thirty. Deep tan. Thin bracelet tattoo on one wrist. White T-shirt reads "Dive." Khaki cargos. Leather flipflops. Southern accent. Metallic blue Camaro, license tag begins with KL.*

Marcy replaced the journal on the condo's counter and tried to collect her agitated thoughts. This person resembled no one she had ever met—man or woman. But the police said this was the description Rose had given of the gunman.

So Jack had been involved in something that had nothing to do with menswear. Far, far worse was the realization that her handsome boyfriend—fiancé, she had always told herself, though he had never presented her with a ring—had raped her daughter. Marcy felt she'd been plunged into ice water. But for the first time in fourteen years, she felt fully awake. Replacing depression with rage and anxiety was hardly a step up, but at least, Marcy told herself, she was thinking and feeling.

Now, Marcy entertained the possibility that she and Rose had been Jack's cover. Quiet, law-abiding mother and daughter living in an old historic neighborhood—who would question them? The realization that Rose had gotten close to a secret spelled danger to Marcy. What if Jack's people had her now?

The journal held numerous references to Rose's plans to leave Summerlin as soon as she graduated. Myrtle Beach intrigued her. Ever since a July retreat there two years before, Rose had corresponded with a girl named Savannah and had worked with her last summer at a church camp in Windy Hill, a few miles north of the main strand. Just before Easter, Rose had even mentioned taking an all-summer waitressing job there after graduation, but Jack had declared it unsuitable.

"I'll be eighteen and out of high school. You won't be telling me what to do!" Rose had declared with uncharacteristic candor.

Marcy remembered telling Rose to sit down and show some respect. Rose had glared at her dinner plate, refusing to make eye contact. From what was written in the green journal, Jack had made her pay dearly for her bold declaration. But why?

Oh, the sickening knowledge that she was responsible! Marcy could no longer abide her own reflection in the mirror. A groundswell of grief drove her to her knees there on the condo's tile floor. The tears came until she couldn't breathe. She wept in a combination of sorrow and fear, crying out between gasping sobs, not caring who might overhear. "I'm sorry! Sorry! So sorry, God, for my selfishness! Please forgive me! Wherever she is, help me find her! *Please!*"

CHAPTER 6

A huge oleander covered in pink blooms hung over the sidewalk at the corner of Fifteenth Avenue North and Ocean Boulevard. Rose rounded the corner and ran straight into a man's chest. Humiliating! As the man stepped back, Rose fought the urge to run. So many times since arriving at the beach, she'd felt a familiar fear, even around men who bore no resemblance to Jack.

Glancing up at the clean-cut, well-dressed, thirty-something man, she blurted, "I'm so sorry! My mind was a million miles away."

"My fault entirely. I wasn't looking. I have an appointment in fifteen minutes, and it takes at least ten to get there." Rod looked at Rose more closely. "You okay?" he asked.

"Fine, sir. I just had a lot on my mind," said Rose. As her strawberry blond hair glimmered in the sun, Rod Butler thought to himself, *Pretty girl.* She looked like she was carrying an emotional load, though. Glancing at the logo on her uniform, he said, "Picket Fence Pancake House! Now I know why you look familiar. I'm a regular. You have the breakfast shift, don't you?"

Rose nodded. "I've just finished my week of training. This morning, I'm on my own. I guess you should watch out if I head your way with a coffee pot."

"I'm forewarned." Rod chuckled. "Can't be there this morning, though. Better run. Have a good day!" he called as he strode away.

"You too, sir," replied Rose.

Sir? he thought to himself. *Am I really so old that teenage girls call me sir?*

Rose walked on to her workplace to pick up her first check. Thanks to Savannah, she was a first-shift waitress at one of the most consistently busy breakfast spots in the bustling beach resort. Most days, she and Savannah worked the same schedule—today was one of the exceptions. The money they made was great in the summer, but from what Rose heard, it dropped precipitously in the winter. That's when her diploma would pay off in competing for a full-time position. Well, winter would have to take care of itself. For now, Rose planned to stay a couple more weeks with Savannah Cole and her family until she'd earned enough money to rent a place of her own.

So far, Rose knew, she had dropped into a sanctuary. Every now and then, the Coles asked a discrete question, but Rose avoided answering in any detail. It was clear that Savannah had begged them to trust her and to refrain from asking too much too soon. How could Rose plausibly explain that she was pregnant, had just been cleared of possible murder charges, and had run away from her mother?

The cold sensation of abandonment crept into her heart every time she pondered why her mother had refused to believe in her. To the very end, Rose knew that Marcy had no clue that the baby she was carrying was Jack's. Well, Rose had made up her mind on that score. She was carrying this baby to term and then putting it up for adoption. What the plans were after that, only God knew—if God was still interested in a screw-up like Rose. *Screw-up,* she thought with disgust. *Slang: substandard English.*

One step at a time, that was all she could take. Today after work she had an appointment with Lifesender, an adoption agency listed in the phone book. From the little she knew of them, they helped pregnant girls who didn't have any money. Savannah had offered to drive her to the appointment, and Rose had accepted.

Then tonight, Rose and Savannah planned to tell her parents the whole story. So far, the Coles had accepted Rose at face value. They had included her in all their family activities, including going to church on Sunday mornings. Rose had nervously agreed to attend, and in that first Sunday morning service, she had tentatively tested the waters of prayer again. Up to this point, the scorching pain of her mom's rejection, her anger toward Jack, and the numbness she'd experienced after his death had left Rose spiritually detached.

Her once open faith had shut down. She had quit talking to God. If he wouldn't help her, she'd decided, she was on her own. But back in the setting of a church again, she sensed, if not peace, the potential for peace at some point in the future. For now, she had to make arrangements for this baby. She knew it was strange, but for the life of her, Rose couldn't bring herself to hate this baby.

Linda Cantrell was nearly hidden behind the neat piles of file folders that covered all but the center of her black metal desk. It had been a busy morning, with no time to file the stack of papers that always accompanied an adoption.

She located her appointment book beneath one towering stack and checked the after-lunch schedule. Next on the appointment list: Rose Kendall. As she always did before an appointment, Linda bowed her head, sat in silence for a moment, and then sent up a petition: *Lord, I pray for your perfect will to be done in this young woman's life. Whatever happens today, guide her to see the truth about you, your plans for her life, and your plans for her baby. Protect this little life, Father. And protect this mother. Give me your words to speak, and your love to share*. Her thoughts returned to a familiar point: *There are so many hurting women, Lord. Send us the ones you want us to help.*

Linda's secretary Joyce stuck her head in the door. "Ready for Rose Kendall?"

"Give me two minutes, Joyce, to move a few of these files. Then send her in."

Outside in the wainscoted waiting room, her face hidden by a gardening magazine, Rose was battling a full-fledged panic attack. All of her worst fears converged on her at once. Today, she knew, she would face the questions she had refused to think about. What if Jack had given her AIDS or some other disease? What if this baby was deformed? Jack's mind had been deformed. Could the ugliness of a father's mind creep into a tiny baby's body?

Savannah, who was actually reading her magazine, sensed Rose's anxiety and patted her arm, just to remind her that she was not alone. Rose's thoughts rolled back to the days before Jack, when she was still attending youth group meetings at church.

During a series of Sunday night discussions, several newlywed couples were invited to discuss the challenges and rewards of reserving sex for marriage. The following week, a physician in the congregation had addressed STDs and teenage pregnancy. The third week, the group discussed abortion—at great length. Some of the kids thought certain circumstances might justify it. But after watching a video on abortion methods—all shockingly violent to the baby—Rose had been uncharacteristically vocal: "I could never do that! Not to myself or to a baby or…to God!" Strong words spoken with passion—but that had been before Jack.

Once or twice, Rose had actually considered an abortion, tempted by a quick solution to her most obvious predicament. She had gone so far as to jot down the phone number of a clinic. But the words she had spoken so bravely to the youth group replayed of their own accord, over and over. For a while, she heard them in her sleep.

These people at Lifesender would have lots of questions. They might think Rose was just making up the story about Jack. Did it matter to them either way? Would they call the police? Contact her mother? Maybe she should simply walk out. Just as the impulse to flee overwhelmed her, Rose heard a receptionist calling her name.

She stood up, and a wave of lightheadedness stopped her where she stood. The stress—it was palpable.

"You okay, honey?" The middle-aged receptionist had a name tag with a cross and *Joyce* written on it. Her accent was decidedly Southern. As Rose made eye contact, she knew her fear was showing. Joyce wrapped a long, angular arm around her shoulders and murmured, "Now, you just take a deep breath, honey, and relax. Come right on in here. We're going to do everything we possibly can."

CHAPTER 7

Linda Cantrell looked up to see an attractive girl, neither slender nor heavy, being escorted into the office. Trying not to stare, Linda took note of the strawberry blond curls cascading past the girl's shoulders. The oversized uniform from the Picket Fence Pancake House fell off her shoulders but betrayed not a wrinkle. The creases in her khaki pants were still sharp even after a full shift of waitressing. Rose briefly shook her hair to the side, and Linda caught a glimpse of a soft and whimsical face. Her features were rounded and delicate, but as Linda looked closer, she saw an aching depth in the wounded blue eyes. "This one is really hurting, Lord," Linda breathed silently. "Give me the words."

Rose sat down in a slightly faded, tapestry-covered armchair.

Linda smiled warmly, and some of the tension lifted. "May I call you Rose?"

"Yes, ma'am," she responded quietly.

Linda offered her most reassuring nod and looked down at the chart before her. "Let's just talk for a few minutes. I'd like to tell you a little bit about Lifesender." From experience, Linda knew that it helped her clients to hear the story of the agency's founding, told with a smile and a sense of awe at all that God had done to establish it. Rose listened carefully. Finally, Linda lobbed her the conversational ball. "Do you think you could give me a little information about your circumstances?" she asked, again with a smile. Rose nodded, and Linda continued, "Have you always lived at the beach?"

"No, only for a couple of weeks. I have a friend here that I met at summer camp two years ago. We'd been e-mailing each other. She told me to come and stay with her family until I knew what to do." That was it. Rose volunteered no more.

From her body language, Linda could see that Rose was afraid. Her breathing was too quick, and she was perched on the front half of her chair, looking as if she would bolt. Linda walked around her desk and placed her hand on Rose's shoulder. "I know this is painful to talk about with a perfect stranger. I'm here to help. Please, just share some things about you," Linda urged gently. "Where you grew up. Favorite subjects in school." She took a seat in a chair beside Rose.

"Okay," Rose responded, taking a deep breath. "I grew up in Summerlin, North Carolina, an only child. My father died when I was four. My mom and I continued to live with my grandparents. But my grandmother passed away when I was thirteen, and then my grandfather when I was almost sixteen. I loved them ..." She trailed off.

"What about school?" Linda prodded gently.

"I love school! English is my best subject. I would've received the senior English award, but...I never actually got to attend my graduation."

Linda watched a shadow fall over her visitor's face.

Rose waited a moment to gauge Linda's reaction. Seeing nothing but a sympathetic nod, she went on. "I don't know if you've read about it in the papers, but I witnessed a murder. My mom's boyfriend. I didn't do it," she hastened to add. "But my mom, she didn't understand. She was...living in her own world. When the police released me, Mom never came to pick me up. I called her several times, but she never answered the phone. She was sound asleep when I got home. So I packed some clothes and caught a bus here to Myrtle Beach. I'm living with my friend Savannah and her family until I can afford a place of my own. I've just started working as a waitress." Rose took a deep breath. It had been a long speech, but she plunged on.

"I know I don't want an abortion. I've thought about it, but I can't do it. I really don't know how to get through a pregnancy, but I hope you have some answers."

"We do," Linda said assuringly. "How old are you, Rose?"

"I turned eighteen on May second."

"What was the date of your last period?"

"March fifth."

"How did you confirm your pregnancy?"

"I bought a home pregnancy test."

"So, how far along do you think you are?"

"Going on three months."

"Any allergies?"

"None that I know of."

"Surgeries?"

"Only one. Oral surgery."

Faced with questions that required straightforward answers, Rose began to relax a little. It felt good to talk. Nobody but Savannah knew it all, and as Rose answered simple questions, she realized she wanted to make some simple plans for the future. Maybe this woman could help.

Then Linda asked the question that caused Rose to quake: "Do you know who the father is?"

"Yes, ma'am," she said softly, "but he is deceased."

Linda disguised the startled reaction she felt to Rose's answer. In ten years, she had never gotten that particular answer to the paternity question. Switching gears to give herself time to think, she said, "Rose, I gather your mom either doesn't know about the pregnancy or didn't approve of your relationship with the young man. Are you in contact with her at all?"

Tears appeared in Rose's eyes, and she made a sudden excuse to get up. "I need to use the restroom," she blurted.

"Two doors down on the left," Linda said.

In the restroom, the anguished reality of her life finally made Rose lose what little she had eaten for breakfast. She stared weakly into the mirror, then washed her face with stinging cold water. She really didn't feel like talking anymore. She would walk down the hallway and out the front door. Savannah would drive her home.

But wouldn't it feel good, she asked her reflection in the mirror, to get the whole thing out in the open? Wouldn't it feel good to know she could forever relax around this one woman who had the potential to help her make decisions—that Linda already knew the worst?

Retracing her steps down the soft gray carpet to the office where Linda waited, Rose braced herself to speak the whole truth. She sat down, clutched her hands together fiercely, and took a deep breath. "Mrs. Cantrell, to answer your question, I was sexually assaulted by my mother's boyfriend on March twentieth. He had been drinking. He threatened my mother's…mental state if I told her. I never told her. Just before graduation, I found out I was pregnant. My mom found the pregnancy test kit the next morning." Rose's voice was trembling, but Linda's obvious concern kept her going.

"So she knows I'm pregnant, but she doesn't know any more than that. The next week, my mom's boyfriend was shot to death in the alley behind his shop. You can read about it in the Wilmington papers from a few weeks ago. A man he was meeting at his business shot and killed him. I had overheard them setting up the meeting, and…it sounded like Jack was involved in something illegal…and I thought I could turn him in and…get him out of our life.

"So I called the police, and I hid near the meeting place. But Jack found me just as the man showed up. I had no idea," she said, her eyes by now brimming, "that anybody was going to kill him." She paused and collected herself.

"The police accused me at first. But it turned out that the gun was traceable. All I know is that it was traced to a blond man who was wanted for forgery and identity theft. The description I gave matched him perfectly. But he's disappeared."

"And your mother?" Linda asked gently.

Rose pushed her chair back and started to stand. "I'm sorry," she said in a trembling voice. "My mother hasn't seen me since the day Jack was killed. She holds me responsible for his death. She doesn't know that he's the father. I just...don't feel like talking about her right now."

Linda recognized that Rose had used up her emotional energy. Nevertheless, Rose had told her what she needed to know. The father of this child could make no claims on the baby, there were no other relatives who might be interested, and Rose was receiving no help from the one close family member she had left.

Linda put on a kind but professional voice intended to be calming. "I want to meet with you at the beginning of next week if that's possible, after you've reviewed the literature I'm going to give you today. At that time, I'll schedule a doctor's appointment for you. After that, we'll make some plans for your future." She smiled. "And Rose, I want you to remember that you do have a future. Joyce has a packet of information for you that will outline some options.

"I can tell," Linda continued, "that you have strong convictions, and I'm really thankful for that. I won't have to describe to you the guilt and grief and loss that follow an abortion. Between now and our next appointment, would you please be praying about the best choice for both you and your baby—a choice you can live with for the rest of your life? I promise you, Rose, I will be praying for you. God understands situations like this. They seem so complicated to us, but he has the answers we don't. May I pray with you before you leave?"

Linda paused to collect her thoughts, then spoke softly and familiarly. "Dear Father, I ask that you take perfect care of Rose. Help her to make the very best decisions, both for herself and for this baby. Let her know that you love her, that you care deeply about the future of this baby, that you are *with* them, no matter how alone they seem. Thank you, Father, for bringing them here to us. Guide my words and actions on her behalf. And Lord, in your perfect time, please help Rose and her mother find the strength to forgive one another. In Jesus's name, amen."

That evening, in the briefest possible terms, Rose told Savannah's parents what she had earlier told Linda, and then went for a walk. As she walked along the beach, the lapping of the waves seemed to drain what remained of the tension from her body. The Coles had accepted the facts quietly, asking very few questions, but clearly recognizing Jack's story from the news accounts on TV. Now Rose was second-guessing herself and offered a whispered prayer into the wind.

"What's happening to me, Lord? This morning, I thought I had everything finalized. But now, I'm feeling major indecision. What if I make decisions that hurt this little one? What if I give the baby to the wrong people? What if the man turned out to be like Jack?"

Rose walked on, past a pavilion where couples danced to a live band playing vintage beach music. Rose stopped to watch, drawn to the sight of a small blond woman in a tropical floral dress. She wore her hair like Marcy's—it was even the same shade. Rose felt a painful throb in her heart. *The mom I used to know would at least be concerned. Where did she go, Lord? I wish she were here.*

From an inner recess of her heart, ten words—words of quiet but absolute authority—filled Rose with the astonishing realization that someone had spoken.

I AM. I will never leave you nor forsake you.

She stood stock-still. "Lord, is that you?" she whispered.

Let not your heart be troubled, neither let it be afraid. Lo, I am with you always. Trust in the Lord with all your heart.

The disconnected—yet oddly unified—verses hurtled through her mind. An amazed excitement jump-started Rose's heart. All those Bible verses from fourth-grade Sunday school! She laughed aloud as she thought of Martha Tyne, the energetic teacher who had given her class special treats for memorizing Bible verses. What would Miss Martha say if she knew that those verses, learned in return for sugar cookies, had come back from the dead?

With pounding heart, Rose ducked behind a sand dune and sank to her knees. The reality of what had taken place astonished her. Right into her mind the words had rolled. She'd had nothing to do with it. A supernatural calm sat placidly at the core of her excitement. God had just declared that he was with her! He said he would never leave her!

"You're here!" she breathed.

Always, the silent voice reiterated. *I am with you always.*

Relief coursed through Rose's heart. For weeks, her thoughts had been invaded by accusations that God was disgusted with the state she was in, that it was her fault, that she had somehow enticed Jack to do those things to her, that it was God's judgment on her that she was pregnant, that God didn't care. But he was *with* her! She felt honored beyond description.

"I believe you," she whispered into the cool night air. "Your words feel…alive. Thank you!" She sat perfectly still, simply treasuring the sense of a supernatural presence. Half an hour later, Rose stood and walked shakily back out to the beach.

She retraced her steps toward the street and stopped to watch a final orange glimmer give way to a stunning indigo sky. The faintest breeze had sprung up, stirring both her hair and her spirit. Never! Never in her life had she felt so awake. She spied an unoccupied bench and took a seat, delighted with every backlit cloud as it slowly deepened to match the sky's ineffable blue.

Fifteen minutes passed. The beach was nearly deserted. She heard a giggle and looked up to see a mother chasing her little girl in a circle of light from a hotel boardwalk, pulling her into her arms. At long, long last, the tears began to flow. "O Lord, I'm so glad you're with me. Mom used to chase me like that. Please, Father… take care of Mom."

CHAPTER 8

In the living room of the condo, Marcy sat sideways on the loveseat, listening to the oddly disembodied voice of her cousin Nancy on the phone.

"You're right." Marcy sighed. "It's almost time to head home. I could stay longer, but I've looked everywhere I know to look. There's sixty miles of beachfront here, and it's full of teenagers! At first glance, Rose has a hundred look-alikes. I see her everywhere I go.

"Realistically, though, I have no idea what she would say if I found her. Probably she never wants to see me again. And . . . in truth, I can't blame her. I don't know what to say to her, either. I have to try, though. You saw the agony I was in, just waiting for her to call."

"I did. That reminds me," Nancy said. "I drove into Summerlin yesterday and checked your messages on the house phone. There were five hang-ups yesterday. It could have been Rose calling. Maybe she just didn't want to leave a message."

"Oh," Marcy exhaled, "I hope she *is* trying to reach me! I just can't forget, though, what she wrote in the note she left on the bed. Rose told me"—at this, fresh tears began to roll down Marcy's face—"she said I had no place in her life if I couldn't believe that she was the victim and not Jack. I'm starting to realize that I never really listened to her. If I had, at least I would have known the last name of her friend here at the beach and some specifics about where she lives. It was a chance I took coming here."

Nancy made a consoling "um-hum" sound and Marcy continued, "I have to be honest. I'm owning up to things, and I don't like what I'm seeing."

This time Nancy was blunt. "I hate to tell you, Marcy, you weren't the same person when Jack was around. He was all you could see. But I could see Rose, watching you, hurt and jealous and confused. Sometimes she was angry and sometimes just plain rude. Now we know why. Of course, I'm not guilt-free, either. Once or twice, I tried to get her to open up, but she just looked right through me and mumbled, 'You wouldn't believe me if I told you.' I thought she was being catty. So I figured, *I don't have to take this* and let it go. I couldn't get past her attitude, but Marcy, she really needed me as a friend."

"Oh, Nancy, she really needed her mother! Today is Saturday," Marcy said. "Where do you think I should go? Abortion clinics won't even talk to me. I'm not the client. But somehow, I just can't see Rose getting an abortion anyway. So what's the alternative? Adoption, right? I called all the adoption agencies in the yellow pages. Most of them are at least willing to listen. I told them my daughter was pregnant and alone and I desperately want to help her. I asked them to let her know that her mother's trying to reach her."

"No luck?" Nancy asked.

Marcy sighed. "No one has called me yet, but they all have this number *and* my home number in case she does turn up. So maybe I'll hear something this week. One agency was closed, so I left a message. Tomorrow, I'm going to the Sunday service at the church that sponsors the summer camp Rose attended. I've parked there and watched for her at least twice a day. The staffers have changed since last summer. They remember hearing about a girl named Savannah, but she isn't working there this summer. Then, on top of it all, the church secretary's on vacation this week. Oh, Nancy, even if Rose won't talk to me, I just need to know that she's safe."

"I know, Marcy. Give me a call when you get back. I'll bring over your mail."

"Thank you, Nancy. Thanks for keeping an eye on things at home." Marcy heard the connection go dead, but she continued to sit with the cell phone to her ear, only dimly awarc that shc was listening to nothing. Home? There was nothing at home without Rose.

Linda Cantrell was pajama-clad and immersed in a novel when the phone rang. This wasn't the first time Joyce had called her at home on a Saturday night. "How was your Friday off?" Linda asked her longtime receptionist.

"Heavenly," Joyce said. "I went to the beach for the first time in six months. But Linda, this afternoon, something kept telling me to check the answering machine at the office. I know you were out of the office Friday afternoon, right?"

"Right," Linda said. "I made two civic club talks—one at lunch and the other at dinner. Then I went home."

"Well, I checked the messages a few minutes ago. Linda, a lady named Marcy Kendall called. She's Rose Kendall's mother."

"What did she say, Joyce?" Linda asked, sitting up with sudden interest.

"She said she believed her daughter was in the area and if she happened to contact us, to please, please let her know her mother was trying to reach her and that she was sorry. Didn't say sorry for what. She left a number for the Sandy Shell Condominiums. That's a small complex in North Myrtle Beach. Just wondered if you brought Rose Kendall's file home with you."

"No, I didn't. She's living at a friend's house, but I don't remember the friend's name. Rose is coming in on Monday, though, to discuss the options and schedule her tests. You know, I want to pray about this, anyway, before breaking the news to Rose that her mother's in town. I could tell there was a lot of tension in the relationship. Joyce, I'm so glad you checked those messages. Were there any others?"

"About twenty," said Joyce. "But nothing that needed immediate attention."

"Great," said Linda. "Let's pray—and pray hard—for Rose and her mom."

Linda settled back into the pillow, fully conscious now. Her pulse rate was up, she realized with a grin. Linda worked for a cause that produced more than the usual number of happy endings, at least for the hopeful couples she worked with. But the clients who moved her most were the birth mothers—these courageous girls, some of them so young, who refused to take the easy way out of a tough situation. They were like children, really, children who still believed in life.

Conscious that Joyce was doing the same, Linda put down her book and started to pray.

One hundred and fifty chattering teenagers in camp shorts and T-shirts filled the right side of Coastland Chapel. Year-round members squeezed into the left side, and a few pulled chairs into the middle aisle. Camp at the Coast was a long-standing project of Coastland's membership, and no one minded the tight quarters that meant summer was here. As three guitarists and a pianist started to play, Marcy slipped into the back row.

Almost two years, she realized, since she'd been inside a church. Jack's romantic attentions and, later, his offer to help with the bills, had come at a vulnerable time. Once Marcy gave in to the physical intimacy, she had allowed him to move in, despite what she knew would be her church friends' disapproval. Sure enough, the friends made it clear that they still loved her, but they didn't approve—and several expressed frank concern for Rose. Marcy had been too infatuated to care. Finally, after ignoring several phone calls and letters, she left an after-hours message on the church answering machine asking that her name be removed from the roll.

But Jack was gone now and so was every friend that Marcy had ever counted on. And Rose! That little girl had been the only reason she had continued to breathe in the dark years after Daniel's death. What in the world had she been thinking, giving in to Jack like that? She had sacrificed Rose for financial security and an exhilarating but short-lived sense of romance. Marcy groaned inwardly.

After several songs and a reading of Scripture, the pastor rose to the lectern, asking first-time visitors to stand. Marcy stood on tiptoe, scanning every row.

As she reluctantly sat back down, the words to a simple old chorus were projected on the wall. Though she didn't sing, she could feel the words tugging at her.

Open the eyes of my heart, Lord. Open the eyes of my heart. I want to see you.[1] As the singing echoed around her, Marcy asked silently, *Would I want to see you, God? I'm afraid to think that you see me. I'm so dirty.*

The song ended, and the pastor stood at the lectern. "Do you *really* want to see Jesus?" he asked the congregation. "Or are you afraid of what he sees inside your heart?"

How did he know? As Marcy looked up with a question in her eyes, the speaker smiled. "It's a challenge to guard our hearts, isn't it?" he asked with a self-inclusive nod. "We live our lives bumping up against each other. Each of us establishes relationships, and, within these relationships, each person stays busy protecting himself, either setting up obstacles or tearing them down. Sometimes the obstacles are set up deliberately. At other times, it's a passive process: we fail to keep in touch, we drift apart, we forget to nurture the relationship. Sometimes a relationship breaks and creates sharp, jagged splinters that skewer our hearts. How many of you, I wonder, have broken relationships that you long to repair, but you just don't know how? Understand that hidden in those broken human relationships are the signs and symptoms of what ails us: issues in our relationship with God."

Marcy's heart sank as she realized that another facet of her guilt had followed her into church. *Oh, God,* she thought, *do I have to face up to this mistake too? I turned my back on you.* Yet from the moment she formed the thought, Marcy experienced a remarkable inner awareness. It was something she had never given herself permission to fully articulate. Jack was not the beginning of her rejection of God. For years, she realized, she had held a grudge against God for taking Daniel so young.

Not until that moment did Marcy realize the impact of such resentment. *This is why I am where I am,* she spoke through her thoughts. *I've been angry with you for years, and all my other relationships have suffered, too.*

As Marcy pulled her attention back to the pastor's words, she felt afraid. *I have been angry with God,* she informed herself in silent amazement. *What will he do to me?*

"Do you know that your God is drawing you to himself at this very moment?" the pastor continued, as if Marcy's conversation had been an audible exchange with him personally. "You can't do it by yourself. The Scriptures say we are dead in our sins, and a dead person can't reach out to anyone. But God is in the business of making dead people alive, and once you've been reconciled to God, he also begins to work in your human relationships. Does someone here have a broken relationship with a parent, a child, or a spouse? Wouldn't you do just about anything to restore that relationship and experience peace between the two of you? Think of God, yearning many times more than you could ever yearn, for that relationship to become what he means for it to be. And picture him having the power to make it happen.

"As we discuss the weapons that God uses to destroy sin barriers, please, open your heart to the Scriptures and allow the Holy Spirit to show you first what stands between you and your God."

Marcy contemplated the pastor's words. How many years now? Fourteen? Her memories were as clear as if Daniel had died that morning...Daniel, husband, lover, best friend, in terrible pain, no way to help, no way to save him. No words to express how difficult it had been. She remembered asking herself almost constantly, *What will I do? I have a small child. I can't do this on my own.* A weed of fear and bitter blame took root in her heart.

In the final days of her husband's life, Marcy had simply grown numb. Still, she could never shake off the memory of the moments preceding Daniel's death. All morning, he had been slipping in and out of consciousness, when suddenly, around two in the afternoon, he gasped, opened his eyes, and locked her in the most joyful gaze she ever remembered seeing on his face. "I see Jesus, Marcy!" he exclaimed in a hoarse whisper. "He'll never leave you!" But Daniel left her, and as he did, Marcy was both mystified and furious. How could he be so alive in the moment of his death? And how could she be both breathing and dead?

Looking back, Marcy remembered days upon days when she couldn't function. Daniel's parents had taken charge of Rose and the probate process. Marcy had been immobilized. When she did go to church, it was with a wall of reserve erected around her heart and mind. Her church became her social services agency, but Marcy stopped believing that God cared.

Now, as tears rolled down her face, she realized that she desperately wanted to believe that God cared. The pastor was winding up his sermon. His next words made her realize that it was time to lay her grudge to rest.

"Have you allowed anything to come between you and your relationship with God? Has that obstacle caused your other relationships to lack depth or honesty or peace? Do you have someone somewhere you want to be reunited with, someone you've hurt and you want to apologize to? Come to the front. Let us pray with you."

As if pulled by a giant chain, Marcy stood and went forward, her only conscious thought that this moment belonged to her. God was calling her back to him. Her knees met the carpet beside the railing; her head dropped as if it were weighted, and she wept for wasted time. *O God, I am sorry for walling you off, for blaming you. I was so angry and so scared. I didn't trust you to take care of us. Forgive me for blaming you when I needed to trust you. Forgive me for Jack—O Father, I knew better. Forgive me for ignoring Rose and concentrating only on me.* Despite her attempts to contain her sobs, they broke free, wrenching in their anguish.

A woman from one of the front rows got up, walked to her side, placed her hand on Marcy's shoulder, and bent her head to Marcy's ear level. "Take the pain, O Lord, and in its place, give peace. Heal these wounds." The woman knelt and continued her prayer in silent companionship until the minister pronounced a final "Amen."

CHAPTER 9

As Marcy finally turned to face the woman kneeling beside her, she encountered a study in brown: brown eyes in a pretty, tanned face, surrounded by short, dark brown hair that curved around her jawline. Even her sleeveless linen dress was chocolate colored. Most notable, however, was the compassion that turned the dark eyes bright. Marcy was disarmed, and she sobbed once again. The woman hugged her.

For someone who'd had no physical contact with another human being for a week of lonely condo nights, the hug was like being wrapped in a down comforter. "Why don't we step into this little room?" the woman whispered, pointing to a door at the side of the sanctuary. Marcy nodded gratefully as a small ensemble led a musical benediction.

Inside and settled on a couch, Marcy wept for a full five minutes—giant sobs that left her chest muscles aching. Finally she drew a breath that seemed to hold a promise of self-control. She felt the need to explain.

Her voice was wavering as she began. "My daughter ran away, and I've been trying to find her. It never occurred to me that I would find God before I found Rose. I've been apart from him for such a long time, but I know that he was speaking to me this morning in that sermon. My life . . . you would never believe. . . ."

The look on the woman's face made Marcy stop short. "What?" The woman was shaking her head, half in denial, half in delight.

"What?" Marcy repeated. "Do…do you know a Rose—Rose Kendall?"

Lisa spoke slowly in a tone of awe. "Yes, I do. She's a friend of my daughter Savannah. I'm Lisa Cole." Lisa stretched her hands toward Marcy's, and her eyes grew huge and filled with tears.

"You've seen her?" Marcy gasped. "You've seen Rose? She's all right?"

Lisa was nodding, even as tears coursed down her tan cheeks. Still, her eyes never left Marcy's. "Rose has been staying with us for the last couple of weeks. Just yesterday, she explained to my husband and me much of what had happened to you both. Before that, Savannah asked us just to trust her. She said that Rose was…hurting too much to talk about things yet."

Marcy leapt to her feet. "My daughter lives with you? Is she all right? Where is she? How can I see her?" Then a dawning realization caused her to ask fearfully, "Do you think she will see me?" Dread blanketed Marcy's face, dread and near panic. Lisa studied this trembling new acquaintance with wide eyes. Marcy looked like a vulnerable schoolgirl—petite, five-foot-two, her charming, classic features marked by stress. Her ash-blond hair fell gracefully around her heart-shaped face, playing up her searching hazel eyes. Lisa had immediately seen in her mannerisms a resemblance to Rose: the way she tilted her head when she talked, the movements of her hands, a tendency to break eye contact.

Lisa smiled at Marcy and hugged her, saying, "God is in control." Stepping to the door, she peered back through the sanctuary, spotted her daughter, and called, "Savannah!" Both women watched the perky brunette stride toward them. She glanced from her mother to Marcy, openly smiling a welcome. Her mother gave her a significant look and said slowly, "Savannah, honey, this is Marcy Kendall."

Marcy saw the protective look spring instantly into Savannah's eyes. But the young woman's training rose to the occasion, and she stepped forward, extended her hand, and said politely, "How do you do, Mrs. Kendall? It's so good to meet you."

"Oh, Savannah!" Marcy exclaimed, bypassing the pleasantries. "I've been looking for you everywhere. I only knew your first name—oh, please, take me to Rose."

Savannah shifted uneasily from one foot to the next, clearly unsettled. A full thirty seconds went by before she spoke. "Please don't misunderstand, Mrs. Kendall. I need to know some things before I can do that. Rose told me what happened. Are you going to blame her for the situation? If you are, then . . . I'm sorry, but Rose isn't ready to see you yet."

There was genuine caring in Savannah's eyes, and Marcy knew that God had placed someone strategic at the point in Rose's life where she herself had gone missing. "No, Savannah," she said. "I am here to take the blame for the entire situation. I know the truth."

The defensiveness in face and posture diminished. "You realize," Savannah spoke more gently, "Rose is being forced to make decisions that will affect her future forever. Mrs. Kendall, I can't understand why you let her leave Summerlin alone. When she was being questioned by the police, you accused her. Do you know what that did to her? And when she got back to the house, you didn't even get up, so she packed up everything she needed and caught the bus to come here to Myrtle Beach."

"Savannah, she took everything that connected her to you. I couldn't find an envelope, an address, a phone number, an e-mail, anything! A few of her other friends remembered your first name, but they couldn't remember your last. I've been here all week searching for you."

"I don't believe that God wanted you to find her without hearing from him first," interjected Lisa.

At that moment, a pleasant-looking man craned his neck around the doorway. "Ready for lunch?" he asked, with an inclusive smile that told Marcy he may have been used to prayer-room strangers going home with his family.

"What do you say, Savannah?" asked Lisa diplomatically. "Let's go home where we can talk in private. Will you join us?" she asked, looking hopefully in Marcy's direction.

Marcy nodded, and Lisa took the opportunity to make introductions. "Scott, this is Rose's mother, Mrs. Kendall."

"Oh, please call me Marcy," she said quickly.

A guarded look flashed over Scott's face as the news hit him. "Is everything okay?" he asked uncertainly, as he looked from his wife to his daughter to Marcy's tear-streaked face.

"Yes, it is, honey. Everything is amazing! Let's have lunch, and then we'll arrange for Marcy to see Rose. Why don't you drive Mrs. Kendall in your car, Savannah," suggested Lisa, glancing at Marcy's red, puffy eyes. "I can fill your dad in on the drive." She reached into her purse for her sunglasses and discreetly slipped them into Marcy's hand.

CHAPTER 10

Savannah got the air-conditioning running in her stifling compact car before asking the big question. "Mrs. Kendall, is it okay with you if I call Rose and let her know you're here?"

"Do you think she'll be upset that I've come looking for her?" asked Marcy.

"Well, that depends on why you're looking for her," replied Savannah, keeping her eyes fixed on the road ahead.

"You're a good friend, Savannah. To be honest, the reason why I came is getting clearer by the minute," said Marcy, automatically scanning the streams of girl campers headed for the dining hall. "I was totally confused when Rose left without a trace. I was in shock, and upset with her for leaving, so undone over . . . the shooting, and . . . everything! Finally, I just had to be near something connected with Rose. I went to her room to clean it. I was pulling the sheets off the bed, and when I did, the mattress shifted and I found this."

Marcy took a green book out of her pocketbook. "It's a journal. She'd been writing about Jack and what he . . . I . . . put her through. After reading it, I understood completely why she ran away." Marcy's blush extended down her neck. "I thought I would self-destruct. Thank you so much, Savannah, for being the kind of friend Rose could run to when she had nowhere else to go." As tears welled again in Marcy's eyes, she looked away, repeating, "Thank you."

Savannah signaled for a left turn and wheeled expertly into the driveway but sat there with the engine running and the cool air blasting from the dashboard vents.

"Mrs. Kendall, my parents are already home. Could you tell them I'll be right in, please? I'll call Rose to let her know we'll meet her at work around two. Maybe both of you can come back here to our house and just sit and talk."

"She's working? Please…tell her I love her," Marcy said in a pleading tone she hoped would be conveyed to Rose. But as Marcy stepped out of the car, she was gripped with doubts that Rose would actually believe it.

A frowning manager called Rose to the phone at the very peak of the lunchtime rush. As rare as it was to get a call at noon, Savannah's announcement was a greater rarity. Rose reacted with a tumultuous rush of emotion. Just when it looked like things were getting simpler, they got complicated again.

Heading to the kitchen to pick up an order, Rose could actually feel the yoke of responsibility settle firmly back onto her shoulders. It was a perfect fit. She had worn it since she was four years old. Fourteen years.

Fourteen years of role-reversal. Fourteen years of learning to always look out for her mother first. Fourteen years of making it look as if Marcy were calling the shots. Fourteen years of reading every facial expression, every vocal inflection, every sigh that escaped Marcy's lips, all in an effort to protect her from the emotional destitution of living life without Daniel.

The mother of her fantasies was responsible, take-charge, attentive, consistent, involved in her daughter's daily life, and Rose longed for her. But that was a Marcy made up of bits and pieces of other mothers, the mothers of her friends. She had watched them covertly—how they treated their husbands, their children, their guests. How long they stood at the kitchen counter without wandering back to the bedroom. How competently or incompetently they dealt with spills, cuts, failed tests, childhood fevers, tax bills, weight gain, job loss, and especially bereavement. Rose had taken notes on them all, applying each newfound skill to her youthful life's work: the unending quest to make Marcy happy again.

Now, within the hour, Marcy would be en route to the Picket Fence, a petite blond question mark. What if Marcy still blamed Rose for taking away the "security" of her life with Jack? What if she were here to blame and accuse and pop a migraine? What if Marcy settled back into her role as the child with Rose as the mother again?

And, Rose pondered, what if she herself couldn't manage all that anymore?

She gulped so hard her dry throat ached. Well, she would know soon enough. Savannah had said she would drive Marcy to the Pancake House as soon as the lunch shift was over. In reality, where could they talk comfortably? Rose hated to take their situation back to the Coles' house. Savannah's parents must think her a lunatic. What if they were no longer willing for Rose and Savannah to be friends? They'd met Marcy, Savannah said. What had she told them? Her hands trembled—*trembled: intransitive verb, past tense,* she heard some distant sector of her brain saying—as she filled the glasses at the corner table. Well, one long hour of nerve-twisting uncertainty and her questions would be answered. Then again, maybe that hour wouldn't last long enough.

"Some dessert?" Lisa asked Marcy as the group finished their lunch of salad and baked potatoes. "I've been experimenting with key lime pie."

"Yes, I think I would," said Marcy. She had enjoyed her lunch with this family of four. Scott Cole was a personable, outgoing real estate agent. Lisa worked part time for an accounting firm. Savannah was preparing to re-enter Coastal Carolina University in the fall as a sophomore marine science major. Her brother Robbie was a rising junior in high school—a decent student but an absolutely outstanding surfer, his parents said. Marcy made note of the fact that all four seemed comfortable discussing the points of the pastor's sermon. Though her heart was too full to join the discussion, her bright eyes and radiant smile made it clear that she had found the sermon a fascination.

When Marcy had helped clear the table, Savannah looked at her with an expectant smile. "Rose's shift ends in fifteen minutes. I'll be praying for you, Mrs. Kendall—that you and Rose will be able to really talk. Let her know how much you love her. She needs that."

The infamous summer beach traffic was bumper to bumper. This time, Lisa Cole had offered to drive Marcy the nine blocks to the Picket Fence.

Lisa maneuvered the Honda Accord past a long motorcycle brigade of middle-age men in ponytails and black leather, gunning their engines at every stoplight. Their girlfriends gripped the passenger seats with their knees and called out to one another as a phalanx of bikes roared away from the intersection. "The tourists are never boring here," Lisa said with a laugh, trying to lighten the moment.

Marcy wasn't picking up the cue. "Tell me how you think Rose is going to react to my being here," she said instead.

"I don't know. Rose has learned really well how to hide her feelings. I imagine she's had a lot of time to sit and think about the two of you. Only she knows the whole truth about what happened to her," Lisa replied, trying to be diplomatic. "Are you ready to hear how she really feels?"

"Lisa, either I face it and overcome it, or we both go on alone. Actually, I need to correct that statement. We go on with God and keep trying. I learned that just this morning. But Rose probably doesn't believe I can talk about anything painful without falling apart. And she doesn't know yet that I've read the journal. That should help...the fact that I already know about...this nightmare with Jack," Marcy responded, hope in her voice.

Lisa, seeing an opportunity to ask for help once again, suggested, "Let's pray as we drive." Despite Marcy's dubious expression, Lisa kept her eyes wide open, fixed on the five-mile-per-hour traffic. "Dear Father," she began, "we're so glad you know every detail of the past. You know that Marcy and Rose didn't break apart in a single day. Please cause them both to remember that their love and trust may not be repaired in a single day either. Lead them step by step and issue by issue until no barriers are left between them—only the beautiful bridge of Christ and his cross. We love you, Lord, and we trust you for the future."

Rose finished clearing the last table in her section, gratefully gathering up a generous tip from the family of eight who had kept her running for drinks. With breakfast and lunch officially over, she tread increasingly uneasy ground. She felt shaky, threatened, angry, defensive. What other feelings would her mother bring out?

Not that she hadn't prayed for a sign that her mother cared. The question was: could Marcy and Rose reconnect with any kind of normalcy? Theirs was not a relationship; it was a minefield.

Over the last several days, Rose had experienced a budding sense of freedom. Despite the feelings of abandonment that ambushed her sporadically, Rose almost felt separated from the past, at least until the baby came to mind. The future had its own plans, its own relentless schedule, she realized. Now the past was about to reclaim her. Just as she was beginning to feel some security, she had to deal with a mother who specialized in the opposite. What would they have to say to one another? How hard would it be to forgive? Could Marcy's love ever be fully trusted?

From the front window, Rose saw Lisa's silver Honda pull into the parking lot and, for a brief moment, beat back the impulse to slip through the stockroom and run. There was still the possibility that Marcy might blame her and leave. Which would be harder, she wondered: bearing that blame or resuming the role of parenting her own mother?

Unconsciously, she crossed her arms over her chest, resting a hand on each shoulder, as if to test how much weight she could carry. Back in Summerlin, she knew what the townspeople said about her. "You're such a responsible girl," they often commented at the bank, at the cleaners, at the grocery store. "You're such a help to your mother." Rose suspected that, behind her back, they were saying, "You *are* the mother." Her friends had talked, she knew—telling their own parents how Rose knew how to cook, wash clothes, pay bills. Her grandparents had been patient teachers. Marcy *had* taught Rose how to drive—a simple task, since Rose had been studying her mother's handling of the car for years—and as soon as she passed the driving test, she had begun driving herself to school. *Responsible Rose,* she thought to herself now. *Always responsible.* Yet how could she possibly go back to being her mother's mother, now that she was pregnant by…No! It was unthinkable.

She felt the insistent tremor of her nerves in the tightness of her crossed arms. *Okay,* she told herself, *I can do this. I'm eighteen now. We are both legal adults. We should treat each other like adults.* She drew a breath so deep it seemed to inflate her entire upper body.

Rose stepped into the parking lot. She didn't want to look too eager. Every instinct told her to hold out until her mom approached her first—and begged forgiveness.

But that resolve crumbled as she saw a small blonde figure step from the car. There was a hesitation in Marcy's movement that Rose recognized as something more than her usual insecurity. It was fear.

Fear. Marcy was as terrified of this meeting as Rose was.

All resolve melted as Rose flew across the steaming asphalt. The two met halfway, Marcy clutching Rose in a vise grip. "Oh, Rose," she sobbed into her daughter's ear, close to sudden hysteria. "Thank God! Thank God! Forgive me, Rose! Oh, God, forgive me! I'm so sorry." Marcy's weeping came in convulsive waves, too violent now for further words.

Rose broke into a sob she hadn't known was coming. Her heart threatened to burst through the surface of her chest. After two interminable years of watching Jack transform her mother into a stranger, Rose soaked up the words that now seemed to gush from a deep fountain. Simple and real, her mother's apology had covered all the main points.

"It's okay, Mom," Rose sobbed in reply. "It's okay—you came." They clung to each other until both knew it was time to let go.

The ride to the Coles' house was made largely in silence, though Rose and Marcy sat together in the back seat, both fighting for composure. At the house, Rose changed into shorts and a T-shirt and wordlessly accepted the two tall, icy glasses of lemon-garnished tea that Lisa handed her. She carried the glasses to a shady corner of the deck brightened by ceramic pots of impatiens, and put the glasses down untasted. Face to face, Rose and her mother sat.

CHAPTER 11

Marcy broke the awkward silence as she and Rose studied one another from their deck chairs. "Rose," she said slowly, still trying to make sense of it all, "it may have been Lisa who drove me over in her car to see you, but it was God who brought me to the Coles this morning. I've been here at the beach for a week. I've looked everywhere for you; I'd almost given up. I felt…I didn't deserve to find you. Finally, this morning, I decided to go to the church where I thought I remembered your summer youth conference being held. It seemed like a last link. I could at least sit in a building where I knew you had been. And Rose, something amazing happened. God showed me that he still loves me, even though I've been so angry with him all these years. Ever since your daddy died."

Rose was listening but not fully understanding. She said soberly, "Mom, it's really good to see you."

"Oh, Rose, you'll never know how terrible I feel. I don't know how you could possibly forgive me."

Rose sat in her sling-back hammock chair, looking out across the Coles' small rose garden, not sure what to say, but feeling pressured. Minutes passed. Both drank the icy tea as if it held the secret to diplomacy. But Rose refused to be dishonest. "I'm overwhelmed at this moment, Mom. I believe I can forgive you, but my feelings are all mixed up."

Why? Rose knew perfectly well the source of the confusion. The Great, Ugly Unspoken sat in the third chair, invisible yet almost tangible. Rose had never named the father of her baby. That fact alone threw her off balance. She was torn between the habit of years, of protecting her mother and the near-desperate need to become a daughter, trusting, dependent, leaning on the person who was supposed to be stronger, wiser, more responsible.

Marcy felt it too. But she was at a loss to explain that she already knew. She made an abrupt excuse: "Let me get you a refill."

She walked to the kitchen, holding up the two empty tea glasses to Lisa with a mute, apologetic appeal. Rose sat still, fervently praying. Life should be getting better, she acknowledged. Her mom was here to help. But the inner struggle was about to consume her. How could such filthy feelings rush to the surface when the happiness of seeing her mom was fresh and strong? Emotions rose up like breakers in hurricane season: resentment that her mom had ignored her, unspeakable hurt that Marcy had accused her, abandonment stemming from the fact that for two years, Rose had felt set aside when she needed help most. In all her dreams of this reunion, it was never with such need to clear the air. She had anticipated feeling angry, but this was so much more! Her breathing felt like seething. *How,* she thought, *am I even going to speak?*

In everything give thanks. There it was, another verse, resurrected from Bible school the year Rose was twelve. She had won an ice cream coupon for memorizing that verse and several that preceded it. Stunned that the Almighty would not only be monitoring this conversation but taking an active part in it, too, Rose took a quick breath and reacted with childlike faith. *Thank you, Lord,* she began in her heart, *for letting Mom find me. What do I do with all these feelings?* She felt a wave of despair. God had to be upset with her for feeling what she was feeling.

Be angry and sin not.

Even as the five words settled into her mind, a calm sense of certainty came over her. It was as if Rose had permission for her angry feelings—permission with limits. Right now she had to express those feelings without stirring up others that were worse. Was it possible?

She heard Marcy's returning footsteps. She would simply have to say it. This was Jack's baby she was carrying. Her mother had to know.

"Mom," she began, but got no further, for Marcy slipped the little green journal into Rose's lap and helplessly shook her head. Once again, Marcy and Rose held each other and cried.

"Rose," said Marcy finally, her voice hoarse, "when I found the journal, I saw the situation I had created. I was ready to die because of what I put you through. Rose, I'm here to help you. I want to carry the burden."

"Mom, I appreciate what you're saying…but…the burden is a baby, remember?"

"I can help you more than you know. After you left, I went through a sort of cleaning frenzy. I found some things in the attic that I didn't know about before. I'm no expert on antiques, but I think they'll bring in a good bit of money."

"Mom, that scares me. It's always been about money, and our lack of it. I'm more concerned about you and me. As long as we have enough to get by on, I'm okay. But I want to know that I can count on you."

"I understand."

"Of course, we're going to have to have something steady—some income we can depend on," replied Rose. "And I can already tell that waitressing is only a short-term way to do it. My tips are great right now—I think I can make enough to cover my expenses until the baby's born. But there's not a lot of future in it—and I don't think I can provide for both of us."

"Rose," Marcy asked, "do you still want to go to college?" As soon as she asked, Marcy knew she had found the key to Rose's heart: the look in her eyes said everything.

"I just want you to know that we're going to find the money for college, if you still want to go. I know the scholarships may be gone, but I'll do all I can. I'm going to get a full-time job," announced

Marcy, to her own amazement. "In the meantime, you and I both need to think through your options."

The word *options* triggered an association that made Rose's temples pulse.

"Mom, if you're telling me I have the option of an abortion, we have to end this conversation right now."

Marcy placed her hand on Rose's and said quietly, "There was no mention of abortion, Rose. I'll admit—yesterday, I might have suggested it."

Rose looked up, clearly hurt by the thought that her mother might have lobbied for something so…unmotherly. Marcy hastened on. "Rose, by options I mean that I'm willing to help if you decide to keep this baby."

Wow! Rose thought. *I didn't see that one coming. Mom is open to the idea of* keeping *the baby?* She shook her strawberry curls slowly.

"Mom, I feel like I need to put the baby up for adoption. I've already made contact with an agency. But to be honest, I'm having a terrible time with my feelings about it. I have these sudden, unreasonable attacks of sadness. I'll never know this child. I watch mothers playing with their children, and"—her voice quivered—"I get really sad."

"Oh, darling, I love that about you. One day, when the time is right, you're going to make a wonderful mother…better than I've ever been. But you're right, we probably need to place this little one with parents who are ready." Picking up the journal, Marcy said, "Maybe we can throw away…no, burn this part of our life, and start a new one."

It sounded too easy to Rose. "Can it ever be closed, Mom? I'll always remember the lies he told you." Again, the sudden flash of anger. "And you believed them. How could you, Mom?"

Tears welled again in Marcy's eyes. "I don't know, Rose. I just know I've been stupid and weak in the past, and I can't promise I'll be really strong in the future. But I want to be. And for the first time in years, I think it's actually possible."

Marcy sat still for a few moments, silently praying. Then she ventured, "Rose, I want to ask you for something very specific. Will you please forgive me for all the years I refused to accept your father's death, and acted like I had died too? Will you forgive me for throwing away our good name in Summerlin? Oh, Rose, will you forgive me for ever letting Jack move in with us and putting you in such danger? And for believing his lies? And for all the times I told you to be respectful to him? And..." She slowed down while her eyes grew wide, "can you bring yourself to believe that something actually happened to me today in church? I feel like a different person," Marcy trailed off, an amazed lilt in her voice.

There were too many loaded questions for Rose to deal with at once. She shook her head sadly. "This whole thing with Jack has changed me, Mom. I'm suspicious, and I can't help it. I shut people out because I don't trust them. Do you know...I cut off my friends back home because I was afraid they would turn on me the way you did? Since I moved here, life has been different. Some things I can never get back, but other things like...hoping and trusting...praying and believing that God is talking back...are actually real to me again."

Rose plunged on. "Mom, I have trouble being around men in general. What's with that? Will I be able to get married and have children? And what kind of man is going to want me?" she blurted bitterly. "Me with all this ugly baggage."

As Rose described the desolation she felt, her mom's silent tears slid past her chin and down her neck. She reached across the table and pulled Rose close, wrapping her in a salty embrace. "I'm so sorry, Rose," she managed. "If I could change it, I would give my life to do it. But Rose, God is at work in me, too. You've got to believe me. For the first time since your father died, I feel hope."

After several minutes of silence, Rose chose to accept that Marcy's plea was sincere. She wondered what to say. How could she issue a convincing statement of trust in the future of a mother-daughter relationship that had been nearly extinguished?

Finally, she slid her hand across the table and angled it upward. Slowly, almost hesitantly, she pressed her right palm against her mother's left in a ritual the two of them had practiced since Rose was tiny. "Look," she said softly, "palm to palm. We match. My fingers are finally as long as yours." Marcy recognized the gesture of daughterhood even as she acknowledged that this daughter had grown up. She sighed with a fragile relief.

They sat for a little while longer, sipping their tea in silence. The sun had turned the sky golden. "Rose," Marcy said, "are you all right to stay here with the Coles just a little bit longer? I have several legal and property issues that have to be cleared up—in fact, I have two appointments back in Summerlin tomorrow. But more than that, what happened this morning at church makes me realize that God is doing some serious sorting out with me. I hope this doesn't sound strange, but I need a few days alone with him.

"I want to make the drive home before it gets too dark, but if you need me to stay here tonight and prove to you—in any way I can—that you're the most important person in my life, then I'll rearrange every detail and every part of my life to be here with you. I will gladly stay! Rose, every move I make now has one goal: to create a future for us." Marcy unconsciously quoted Scripture as she concluded, "A future and a hope."

CHAPTER 12

Had Marcy realized that the two-and-a-half hour trip back to Summerlin would turn into a blitz of buried memories, she might never have climbed behind the wheel of the champagne-colored Buick Regal for the solitary drive home.

She had always been grateful for the car. Daniel's father had bought it shortly before he died, an end-of-the-year special, fully loaded, with leather seats and a built-in satellite locator service. More than once, Marcy had wondered if Mr. Kendall hadn't actually picked out this car expressly for her, knowing his own time was short, wanting her to have something reliable, something that would keep its trade-in value for many years.

Today, however, the car seemed too small. It was suffocating. Talking with Rose had dislodged a carefully fixed seal over the memories of Marcy's early childhood, and now the wild emotions that flooded her heart and mind seemed poised to overwhelm her. Twice she pulled over to the side of the road, rolled down the window, and gulped the hot summer air, finding no relief except in the realization that she *could* escape the car—she was not trapped, not held down, not pinned.

Until she told her daughter the truth about her own parents, she realized, Marcy's ability to serve as Rose's support system was still shaky. There were issues she had never fully resolved. Until she faced up to them, how could she genuinely help Rose?

Ever since the day Marcy had found and read the journal, she had been mentally "seeing things," distorted images of a childhood that never came totally into focus, like slices of scenes from poorly edited films. Sometimes there was sound—broken syllables with echoes. Why had she never told Rose that there were "things" in her own past? Why had she not revealed the fragments of the dream that caused her to cry out in the night? Probably because she could not articulate them yet, could not take hold of the pictures before they slipped from her grasp. They were locked up so tightly inside!

But as Marcy heard Rose utter the words "ugly baggage," her own past surged up and threatened to spill over. Marcy knew about baggage. She carried it everywhere she went.

What was pulling and tugging so hard to get out? Who was? Where? Wha—*Mama, help me!*

The shadow pictures flashed, strobe-like, on the dark screen in her mind.

She remembered...a terrible picture of her father. He was chasing her mom through the yard, screaming obscenities, lunging after her, his size and speed making up for his irregular gait.

In a spliced scene, Marcy's twelve-year-old brother Jesse disappeared through the hedge.

Marcy was under the bed. Heavy footsteps mounting the stairs. Tips of black work boots. Arms...hands coming at her from the side of the bed. Time to scream! Scream! Can't scream!

The smell of alcohol....nausea.

Her own voice: "Nothing! I didn't tell her—"

A blow. A scream.

Pinned! Pinned! Can't breath, can't move!

Blood! All over one side of Mama's face! Sirens! Oh, Mama....

The isolated scenes were shockingly clear after all these years. What connected them was harder to recall in orderly sequence. Where did the story start? And when?

When she was very little. That much she knew.

Her dad had sometimes come into her room. Marcy didn't mind. He shared her pillow and told her stories about growing up in Texas. She was accustomed to his smell—the bourbon was his own distinctive aftershave. She felt special—chosen.

But one night, something changed. Marcy remembered his encouraging her to snuggle closer. He pressed her against the wall, closer and closer. The next time it happened, he called it their "special time." If she told anybody, she would break their secret. If she told, then he just might have to hurt her. Marcy was afraid. She wouldn't tell.

Slowly, slowly she withdrew, afraid that her mother would sense more than Marcy could safely reveal. Looking back, why hadn't she told? Mentally, all she could see was a black boot hovering above her.

On the one evening that Marcy could remember clearly, her father came home walking erratically. Her parents had a noisy argument. Her father left the house in a rage. Marcy's mom came to her room, her hands clutched so tight that Marcy could see the skin stretched white over every knuckle. She sat down on the bed and, after an awkward pause, asked, "Has he hurt you?"

"Who?" Marcy asked, although she knew the answer.

"Your father."

"Not much," Marcy had replied.

"Has he touched you, Marcy?"

Marcy sat quietly, unable to meet her mother's searching gaze, not knowing what to say.

"Has he touched you in a private place?" her mother demanded anxiously. Marcy looked up with fear in her eyes.

They locked gazes for a long moment. Then she lurched out of Marcy's room, Marcy running after her. "Please don't tell him I said anything!" she was crying. "He'll hurt me! He said it was our secret. He said if I told, he would hurt me."

Her mom was so shaken she could only pace up and down, up and down the stairs, wringing her hands. Finally, she made several phone calls. Marcy's brother Jesse came in, and after a hushed conversation, Marcy could hear him arguing, "I'm not going! I'm not leaving my friends!"

"You don't know what we're dealing with, Jesse." Her mother's voice was rising. It was too tight, too loud. "Go pack your clothes. Get your books. Get your glove and your bat. We're leaving!"

Marcy retreated to her room, frightened by the emotional intensity that now seemed to arc like lightning from room to room. Evidently Jesse had been convinced. He started packing, and so did Marcy. They were almost ready to load their hand-me-down suitcases into the car when their dad roared through the back door.

His furious shouts, her mother's shrieks, and the sound of blows tore Marcy to pieces. Mom was shrieking, "Stop it!" The back door slammed shut, but it was no sound barrier for the cursing that fouled the backyard. When Marcy heard her name, she slipped to the door, peering hard into the twilight.

Jesse was positioned in front of their mom, arms stretched wide, deflecting their father's blows. "Take 'em?" her father was screaming, "These kids are mine! So help me, you try to take 'em away from me, I'll put you away for good!"

"They are not yours to ruin! I will not stand for it!"

Dad looked at Jesse and thundered, "Get outta my way!" He picked up a shovel and swung it in Jesse's direction. Marcy saw her brother duck, then take off running toward the neighbors' house.

With attention momentarily focused on Jesse, Marcy's mother took off in the opposite direction. To Marcy, it seemed that it took her father only three or four long strides to catch up. He was swinging the shovel, cursing, screaming. Marcy watched in horror as her father raised his muscular arms in a powerful backswing, stumbling, recovering, and gaining ground with every stride. The sight and sound of the shovel's contact with her mother's skull moved Marcy to flight. In terror, she ran to the safest place she knew. Under the bed...under the bed...and then the boots appeared, and the hands, and the drunken, crushing weight...

A car horn jolted Marcy back to the present. She had crossed the center line, her vision so blurred, her breathing so shallow she was close to fainting. She wheeled onto the shoulder of the steamy asphalt highway, threw open the door, and leapt outside, gulping in air.

So—it had been preserved after all—this documentary of her childhood's defining moments. It was all there—the colors, the sounds, the smells, the fear! Memory had locked it up, waiting for Rose's little green journal to bring it back in detail. Oh, yes, Marcy could remember it all now…the sheriff, the handcuffs, the ambulance, her mother's concussion, the cut on her scalp curved like a shovel blade. The smell of the hospital, her mother's head wrapped in bandages.

"Why does he hurt us, Mama?" Marcy had wept.

"I don't know, honey. But I know this. Before they let him out of jail, you and Jesse and me are leaving this place and never coming back. We can stay with Aunt Debbie in Summerlin. I can get a job. We'll be safe there."

One more memory surfaced, etched in clarity: her mom, standing in her aunt's kitchen, staring at the phone, then firing one- and two-word questions into the mouthpiece: "You're sure? How? When?"

Instinctively Marcy knew. Her daddy was dead. Yes, her mother said, he'd been crushed when his bulldozer turned over on a rocky slope. Marcy understood crushed. The emotional confusion blindsided her. Mixed with a brief sensation of relief was an abject sorrow for the daddy who had singled her out as "special"—even though she hated the way that he had shown it. Sorrow. It made her feel guilty, a traitor to her mother.

Relief. Sorrow. Guilt. They sparred in her memory until they merged into an indistinct perplexity. To survive, Marcy learned to push down the trauma of those months—way, way down—far from conscious recall.

Summerlin, North Carolina, had smiled on the pretty little seven-year-old with blond braids. Her teachers were welcoming, and she had plenty of friends. Marcy's aunt, who had "married well" and lived in a nice house downtown, gave them the guest house located behind her own. For the first time in her life, Marcy became a regular at Sunday school, learning about a loving Father, not an abusive one. In the public schools, she discovered her aptitude for painting. In time, she had come close to forgetting the turmoil of her early life.

Somehow, today, the memories could be held back no longer.

In a moment of insight, it occurred to Marcy that her father's death had been the massive tremor that caused the rest of her immediate family to crack apart, shift like tectonic plates, and push one another away.

Jesse had left them first. Never comfortable in his aunt's social circle, he dropped out of high school, took a job with a local shrimper until he earned his GED, and celebrated his eighteenth birthday by enlisting in the navy.

Soon afterward, Marcy's mother convinced herself that a local seafood buyer would make a stable husband, despite the fact that he traveled year-round and could order drinks in six languages. A year into the marriage, unwilling to admit another case of poor judgment, she opted to travel with him, coming home twice a month until her own drinking became too obvious.

Marcy, though, was happy in Summerlin, happy to move into the pretty house with her now-widowed aunt and her cousin Nancy, happy in school, in art classes, in dance lessons. Yes, she missed Jesse and her mother, but covered up the longing with activity, and only her best friend, Renee, knew about the lonesome spells that periodically put Marcy to bed, even in high school.

Now, standing by the highway, Marcy leaned against the car and drew one shaking breath after another. Why today? Why, when she had just discovered the reality of a personal, communicative God—

why had this serpentine memory slithered out of its hiding place? "Lord," she prayed, "please hide me and protect me! I need to get home." The road ahead seemed endless. Finally, around nine, she pulled into her own driveway, utterly exhausted.

Marcy unlocked the front door and flipped on the light in the foyer. Nancy had already brought the week's mail and stacked it on the library table. The light on the answering machine flashed insistently. Marcy was too tired to care. She climbed the stairs to her bedroom, pulled on a loose cotton gown, made a quick call to Nancy to verify her safe return, and turned out the lights. It seemed impossible that it could still be Sunday, but Marcy wrapped herself around the memory of Rose running toward her across an asphalt parking lot. Of all the thousands of thoughts and emotions this Sunday had generated, this was the one she would focus on. "Thank you, Father," she whispered in the dark.

She drifted off, utterly unaware of the thickset shadow that passed beneath her window around 2:30 that morning and made the rounds of the house, quietly trying doorknobs. A neighbor's dog sounded a raucous alert that Marcy never heard. The shadow moved quietly down the street to a parked car and drove away.

CHAPTER 13

While Marcy was making her torturous drive back home, Rose was facing the fact that she couldn't sit down, couldn't concentrate, couldn't focus. Finally, after a dinner to which she contributed nothing either in preparation or conversation, Lisa suggested, "Why don't you two take a walk?"

"Let's do it!" Savannah said. Rose looked less than thrilled. "Come on," Savannah wheedled, "I need it. You need it."

Rose obligingly disappeared into the bedroom to pull on her walking shoes.

"She needs to get some energy out," Lisa murmured. "We all do."

The roadbed was still steaming underfoot as the girls made their way four blocks down the side street leading to the beach. Neither spoke. Deep in thought, they matched strides without trying. They emerged onto Ocean Boulevard, looked both ways, and crossed, attracting catcalls from a convertible full of college boys. The two looked straight ahead.

Several feet into the dune line, they reached a wooden bench. "Need to rest a minute?" Savannah asked thoughtfully, but Rose shook her head and pushed on past a stream of children coming up the boardwalk off the beach.

At the base of the wooden steps that ended on the packed sand sat a little boy, red-faced, tears streaming. "Mom-m-y," he wailed.

Rose recognized fear in his voice, and, looking in all directions, saw no one who looked like a first-responder.

She glanced apologetically at Savannah and then lowered herself to sit on the bottom step. "Which way did your mommy go?" she asked in a high, light voice.

The little guy continued his wailing but pointed up the ramp.

Savannah turned around and headed back up the boardwalk as Rose cast about for diversion. "What's in your bucket? Are those shells?"

The blond head nodded.

"Can I see some?"

"Only if you gib 'em back. My brudder takes 'em all the time, an' he doesn't gib 'em back."

Rose bent down over the bucket and drew out one of the bigger shells. "Look!" she said. "This is pretty! Do you think a crab lived in here?"

"I saw some cwabs," he offered, his eyebrows arching high over round blue eyes. "They wen' in a hole."

"Oh! Fiddler crabs. Did you catch one?"

"No, they run too fas.'"

By this time, Savannah came in sight, smiling broadly and trailing a mom and three stair-step boys. "Lanny!" the mom said with only a modicum of irritation. "You were supposed to hold Jeremy's hand!"

"But my sannal came off," Lanny said, holding up a chubby leg to offer proof.

Rose, grinning from ear to ear, slipped the sandal onto his foot, reached out to pull the child to a standing position, and gently replaced the shell in the bright red plastic bucket that Lanny still kept under heavy guard.

"He has some pretty shells!" she said lightly. "Bye, Lanny."

"Bye," he replied and reached for his mother's suntanned hand.

Rose and Savannah watched as the caravan trudged back up the ramp. "Okay! Mercy mission accomplished!" laughed Savannah when the group disappeared from view. "Which way would you like to walk?"

"Away from the swash. Let's head north."

"You really handled that smoothly back there," Savannah said with a giggle. "But you should've seen the mom's face when I caught up with her. I thought Jeremy was gonna get it right there."

Rose laughed for the first time that day.

They had walked several hundred yards when Rose asked, "What do you think of my mom?"

Savannah took a step or two to consider. "She seems . . . different from the way I pictured her."

"In what way?"

"She's so petite, I suppose her looks give her a slightly childlike appearance. Actually, she's beautiful."

Rose smiled and said, "She is, isn't she? She was different today. I'm not sure I know her."

"Are you glad she came?"

"Yes," Rose breathed quietly. "Yes. I still don't know what to expect, but yes, I'm glad."

Savannah could sense that Rose was reluctant to go much deeper. Too new, too fresh, the events of the day needed to be processed. She switched the subject slightly.

"I don't get it, Rose. From little things you've told me, it sounds like you took care of your mom more often than she took care of you. And your dad died when you were how old? Four? How did you turn out to be so responsible? And how did you know how to calm down little Lanny back there?"

Rose turned her back to the water and her face to Savannah, her expression lit by the setting sun. "I just wish you could've met my grandparents," she said with a smile.

Rose had remarkably clear memories of the year that followed her daddy's death. Aching, confused, angry, she'd turned defiant, throwing tantrums at the slightest provocation. With Marcy incapacitated, the responsibilities of discipline had fallen to her grandfather. Nothing punitive seemed to help—not lectures, not restrictions, not spankings.

In retrospect, Rose wondered how Papa and Grandmom had stood it. After all, they had just buried their only son—their hearts were raw. How could they have been so patient?

Rose's birthday came. Despite a lavish celebration, Rose pushed every limit a five-year-old could think of. She answered rudely when spoken to. She smashed her drinking glass against a wall. She kicked one of her party guests and refused to say she was sorry. She wasn't.

The following week, she slipped outside with a box of matches and set a brush field on fire, necessitating a visit from the fire department. Banished to her room, she pulled out a set of permanent markers and drew a large rectangle on her bedroom floor. To this day, she had never confessed the reason or the meaning, but in her mind, that rectangle represented Daniel's coffin, and she periodically flung herself down in the middle of it, feet pounding the heart pine planks. That was the week that intensified Grandmom's focus on responsibility. Rose had spent an hour a day for a week scrubbing the floorboards until every corner of her bedroom floor shone.

But Rose was deprived now of both father and mother, since Marcy spent nearly every day in her room, door closed and drapes drawn. When Rose took up sitting on the hall floor just outside the door, her grandmother responded first with cajolery, next with bribery, and finally with spankings. Nothing worked. It was a relief to the adults when kindergarten opened, but after a week, the teacher was sending home notes about defiant behavior.

The final straw, however, was Rose's destruction of a small, china-topped stapler that Rose had lifted from Mrs. Campbell's desk one night when the family was invited over to their neighbor's house for dinner. Marcy had declined the dinner invitation, as she declined everything. But Papa and Grandmom had accepted, taking Rose along for safekeeping. At dinner, Rose ate enough to avoid comment and then slid out of her chair and wandered aimlessly through the house. The stapler was beautiful—hand-painted with butterflies. Rose took it to the back steps and smashed it with a cast-iron doorstop.

Caught red-handed, Rose simply surrendered the remains and refused to apologize in any tone that sounded sincere. Humiliated, her grandmother broke down. "What are we going to do?" she wept. "I love her so much, but I can't get through to her." Her grandfather stood and stared.

"Rosie," Papa had said quietly, "you and I are going for a walk."

The tone in *his* voice told Rose she had crossed a line she had never crossed before. "I don't want to walk," she pouted, but he took her hand so firmly she had no choice. Head down, she struggled to match Papa's steps as he strode through the cool evening air. For the first time in her life, she felt a little frightened of her grandfather.

Fifteen minutes' silent walk brought them to the community ball field. Papa didn't stop until he reached a spot almost halfway between second and third base. "Stand right here," he instructed, pointing to a spot behind the infield baseline. He inhaled and exhaled slowly, his voice growing soft.

"Did your daddy ever tell you how much he loved baseball?" he asked finally. She nodded her head yes. "Mmm, he did love it," Papa said. "This was his spot—shortstop. Your grandmom and I even nicknamed him Shortstop until the year he got taller than both of us."

Papa chuckled a little, even as Rose caught sight of the tears glistening in his eyes.

"You know what, Rosie? The shortstop has the toughest position to play in the whole infield. He has to move fast. He has to think fast. He has to be able to jump high." Papa leaped up into the air, his right arm fully extended and thrust toward the sky. He nabbed an imaginary pop-up and returned to earth. "And he has to be able to throw hard." Papa fired the phantom ball toward home plate, then hooted, "Got him!" He looked at her meaningfully and said, "Your daddy was the best rec league shortstop I ever saw."

Rose was entranced. She had never seen her papa so animated, so lively. She felt excited, proud, privy to a confidence, even though she understood only half of what he was saying.

"But you know what, Rose? Sometimes a batter hit a Texas Leaguer. That means he would hit the ball right over the shortstop's head. Even your daddy couldn't catch it. It wasn't your daddy's fault The ball was just too high." Papa traced the arc of the imaginary ball over Rose's head. "You see?"

Rose nodded.

"And when that happened, there was another man way back here." Papa turned and pointed to the outfield. "He's called a center fielder, and his job is to run forward as fast as he can and yell, 'I got it! I got it!' And then, Rose, he scoops up the ball the shortstop can't catch!

"Rose, when I was a young man, guess what position I played in baseball." Rose watched him, wide-eyed. "I was a center fielder! I had to back up the shortstop. When I saw that the ball was too high and too far for the shortstop to catch, I was the one who had to run and yell, 'I got it!' And when I scooped up the ball, it was very important for me not to drop it. So I learned to hold on tight.

"Now, Rose, I want you to come with me." And Papa escorted her about fifteen yards into the grassy outfield, stopped, and pointed. "Stand right here. Don't move." Alone, he continued his march into the twilight to a spot near the center field wall. He turned. He bent his knees into a slight crouch and placed a hand on each knee, his face turned toward home plate, his body suddenly tense with anticipation. "It's a Texas!" he shouted, and started to run. "I got it! I got it!" Too stunned to get out of the way, Rose watched him rush toward the very spot where she was standing. His arms came forward, his body bent downward, and in a hurtling rush, he scooped her up and kept on running, finally slowing down at home plate. Rose was shrieking, exhilarated! Still, Papa did not put her down, but pressed her to his chest, his heart pounding audibly, his breath coming hard, but his arms strong around her. “I won’t drop you, Rose,” he gasped. “The Good Lord has sent you and your mama to me and to Grandmom, and we’re going to love you and take care of you, and we’re going to remember your daddy together, okay? We’re going to miss him and miss him, every day…together. And we’re going to remember how much fun he was too, and we’re going to laugh. Any time you want to talk about him, we’ll talk, and if you feel like laughing, that’s okay, and if you feel like crying, that’s okay too. It’s okay,” he murmured again, brushing her strawberry curls with his cheek, now damp with tears. “It’s okay.”

CHAPTER 14

Coasting his ten-speed bike, enjoying the freshness of the Monday morning sunrise, Scott Cole made a right turn onto US Highway 17. A quarter of a mile later, a big green SUV intruded on his peripheral vision and almost nudged him off the road. Scott made a quick lurch and ended up in a heap on the side of the road. He stood up with a shake of his head and dusted himself off. No point in getting frustrated this early in the day. "Let it go," he told himself. Summer traffic at the beach was notorious.

Hearing a beep, he turned to see someone waving at him from a navy Toyota. It was Savannah, no doubt on her way to work. Scott gave her a "go girl!" fist pump and watched her merge deftly into the traffic stream. He shook his head in admiration. He and Lisa had learned so much about Savannah this weekend. After watching how she dealt with Rose and Marcy, Scott knew this daughter of his was all about helping people.

When she had first asked if a friend could move in with them, Scott had balked. It wasn't abnormal to have a friend stay over, but this friend couldn't go back home. Red flags had gone up immediately. Scott and Lisa had made eye contact, and the eyes said, "No!"

"Savannah, you know we'd do anything to help you, but we need a little more information here," explained her dad.

"Mom, Dad, can you trust me on this? Rose is my friend. I've known her for three summers. Every time I've ever asked for help before, you've felt comfortable with it because you knew the situation. This time I just need you to trust me. Rose is hurt...nowhere to go. If I close the door to her, she doesn't know where to turn. I can hear the need in her voice—she's desperate.

"What would Jesus do in a situation like this? In my heart, I know I need to help. Can't you please just trust me?" Savannah had pleaded. And the Coles had given in.

Hopping back on his bike, Scott looked both ways and took off again, shaking off the dust. Ever since Rose had arrived, she had proven herself more than worthy of the trust they had placed in a total stranger. What a grateful heart! She thanked them daily. She commented that their home felt safe. She had gone to church with them that first Sunday morning, and every Sunday afterward when she didn't have to work. And having Rose around the house, Lisa had confided, was almost like having a housekeeper. The girl had an enormous sense of responsibility.

Rose had been between a rock and a hard place, Scott realized, now that he knew the whole story. Today, she had hope. How many people, himself included, would've slammed the door on her without ever really getting to know the situation! "Thank you, Father, for teaching us about compassion," Scott murmured into the wind. "Thank you that my own daughter has taught me so much. Please continue to heal the relationship between Rose and her mother. And the baby—who should take care of it, Lord? Only you know. I'm learning to see you at work in all situations, in all people. Show me how I can be part of accomplishing your will. And thank you again for my family—for Savannah, who is being your hands and feet." As he turned the corner onto his own street, he felt thankful through and through. After all, he told himself, he could be dead right now, flattened by an SUV! Instead, he headed into the shower whistling, grateful to God for life, his family, his job, for the opportunity that had been placed in his family's path.

Even the blinds couldn't block the radiance of the morning sun. Rose opened her eyes and rolled over. Only half awake, she reached for the saltines sitting on the night stand. They helped in the mornings; it would be late afternoon, she knew, when the french fry craving materialized. As she munched on a cracker, she heard the garage door close. That would be Mr. Cole, back from his early morning bike ride. Savannah was at the Picket Fence, Robbie would be checking the surf report on the Internet, and Mrs. Cole, already dressed for work, would be scrambling eggs to top a neat row of toasted, whole wheat bagels. This family ran like clockwork.

It was Rose's day off. The appointment at Lifesender was lined up for 3:00 p.m., which should give Savannah just enough time to pick up Rose and drive her to the appointment. Rose had reread the agency's literature last night, and she knew inside what her decision needed to be. It was just a matter of signing the papers.

Still, she wished her mother were here to go through the process with her. So many times she had yearned for her mom's help in making decisions. Yesterday had solidified the desire.

Rose got dressed and stuck her head into the family room as Lisa and Scott were making their way out the door. "Morning, Mr. and Mrs. Cole."

"Morning, Rose! Did you sleep well?" Lisa asked.

"I did. I just want to thank you again for letting my mom come over. It felt so peaceful to wake up this morning and know that she and I are a …a family again."

"You're so very welcome!" replied Lisa, coming forward to wrap Rose in a warm hug. "We were thrilled to realize how God brought her straight to you," replied Lisa. "I'm still amazed!" She gave Rose a second big hug. "You have an important appointment today, don't you?"

"At Lifesender. I have to sign some papers. I've put a lot of thought into it, and I believe I know what I have to do."

The Coles nodded their encouragement without prying and headed out the door.

Rose ate the bagel that Lisa had made for her, noticed the dishes in the sink, and set about stacking them in the dishwasher. She wiped up the crumbs on the breakfast bar and surveyed the orderly kitchen with satisfaction. She made up her bed and wiped down the bathroom sink, then straightened up a few magazines on the coffee table, and finally sat down on the couch to check out the want ads for rentals. The last thing she and Marcy had discussed was the possibility of her mother's moving to Myrtle Beach and looking for a job, perhaps as a secretary. The summertime want ads were plentiful, most of them pleading for hotel and kitchen help. There were only a few ads for professional office positions, but Rose circled them with a purple pen and made a note to pick up a map for her mom.

Back in Summerlin, Marcy rolled over in response to the streaks of morning sunshine peeking past the heavy draperies that covered the wavy glass panes of her window. Normally, she would have pulled a pillow over her head and gone back to sleep—Marcy didn't do mornings. Couldn't. The stress of simply opening her eyes and facing what never went away was too much. This morning, long years of habit caused her to grope for the pillow, but something new beckoned her to life. Rubbing her eyes and stretching, she spied the answering machine light blinking atop the bedside table. Suddenly awake, she thought of Rose. "I wonder if she called before I got home," Marcy said aloud. The thought propelled her feet to the floor and her finger to the replay button. The recording went on and on: hang-up after hang-up. Marcy counted ten. Then, an official sounding voice: "Marcy, this is Kirk Landry. It's Saturday morning, about 8:45. Would you please contact the police department immediately? We need to speak with you as soon as possible." Next: "Hi, Marcy, it's Jason. It's a little after nine on Saturday morning. I need you to call me right away—as soon as you get this message."

By the time she heard the voice of her attorney, Marcy's heart was going a mile a minute. The police had been in and out fairly constantly in the last two weeks, but there had never been the sound of urgency that she had just heard in Kirk's message. And obviously the police were motivated enough to try to reach her through Jason. Several more messages from the police had been left on Sunday.

"What do I do? It's only seven a.m. Do I call the police without talking to Jason first?"

The old Marcy would have stayed in bed, waiting for the phone to ring, debating whether or not to answer. This new Marcy was still shaky, but she felt a measure of unfamiliar strength and something else: a tiny flame of faith that seemed to burn inside her chest. Faith plus strength. Marcy considered checking her face in the mirror to make sure she was still the same person. She had the distinct sensation that before talking with anyone else, she wanted to talk with God. Talk! With God! The idea seemed revolutionary.

She turned on the shower and stepped into the steam, thanking him over and over for making himself so personal the day before, for speaking to her in the sermon. Then she poured out her gratitude for the fact that it was Lisa Cole who chose to comfort her afterwards. That one "coincidence" seemed so miraculous that Marcy felt both euphoric and humbled. And to actually be escorted to Rose! She climbed out of the shower, wrapped herself in a giant towel, and padded to the bedroom to rummage in her nightstand for a Bible that she had only vague memories of ever opening before. It was buried under a pile of papers from The Suitable, and at the sight of them, Marcy flushed with shame. Her fingers located the Bible, however, and she quickly closed the drawer with a mental note to clean it out and burn the contents.

"Where to start?" she asked herself, leaning back against her pillow.

A leather bookmark protruded from the center of the Bible. She had vague memories of helping Rose select it as a Father's Day present for Daniel. "Here," the strip of red leather seemed to say, "start here." She opened the large black volume to the spot where the bookmark had rested undisturbed for fourteen years: Psalm 18. She had barely begun reading when the first verse virtually jumped off the page: "I love you, O Lord, my strength."

Strength. That was precisely what Marcy lacked. Remarkable, she thought, that the first thing she read would command her attention. "I believe you," she whispered. "You know what I need."

Marcy stared at the words for several minutes, only vaguely aware that she was memorizing them. Then, slowly, she read the rest of the psalm. It was long, fifty verses.

The fourth verse, which described being entangled by the cords of death, seemed to address the last fourteen years of Marcy's life. There was a nearly hair-raising description of the power of God followed by a declaration that God had reached down from on high, taken hold of the psalmist, and drawn him out of deep waters.

She felt her face burn with despair at the verse which announced that "the Lord has dealt with me according to my righteousness; according to the cleanness of my hands...." Marcy refused to look down at her hands, afraid she would find them filthy. But then she remembered the pastor's sermon on Sunday. Twice he had repeated that those who entrust themselves to Christ are washed totally clean, made totally righteous in his sight.

Marcy found herself taking special note of the end of verse forty-eight: "from violent men you rescued me."

Violent men. Marcy had had her share. First her father. She had repressed those memories so long that yesterday's recollections still felt new and raw. Then there was Jack. *His* violence had been directed toward her precious child. "You have rescued me from violent men," she whispered. "Thank you."

Closing the Bible gently, Marcy continued her prayer of thanks, letting it grow into a request for help for the day ahead. She felt an unusual sense of peace. She would call her attorney and try to deal calmly with whatever issue now involved the police.

Jason Edwards was a long-time friend of the Kendall family. He had handled Daniel's estate as well as that of Daniel's parents. In the wake of Jack's death and Rose's disappearance, when Marcy found herself alone and short of money, she had called Jason. He had put her in touch with a real estate agent, who was due to arrive this very afternoon. That appointment was the primary reason she had torn herself away from Rose so soon after finding her.

She dialed Jason's number at 8:30, hoping he was at his office early. He answered the phone personally on the second ring. "I'm so glad I got you!" Marcy exclaimed. "What's going on?"

She savored the steady sound of Jason's deep Southern voice. "Morning, Marcy. Good to hear from you. Something's happened down at The Suitable—I don't know what, but there's police tape out front. One of the detectives contacted me Saturday morning, wanting to know where you were. He said they have a thousand questions all leading nowhere."

"Strange," Marcy replied. "I was planning to ask you today to help me get the antiques out of The Suitable. I had hoped to call in an appraiser this afternoon. Those pieces in the shop are likely to bring the best prices of anything I have."

"Ooff," he exhaled. "I don't know how all this is going to affect your antiques. Let me call Kirk Landry. I'll tell him we'll meet him at The Suitable at ten. They'll be glad to hear you're back in town. They've been hounding me all weekend."

"Thanks, Jason. My last session with the detectives made me realize just how little I knew about Jack. Maybe …I can sound more coherent this time."

"I'm sure you will," Jason replied, sounding slightly surprised but courtly as ever. "Park in the square, and we'll walk to The Suitable together."

Marcy hung up the phone. She wanted nothing more to do with Jack's legacy, but she knew that wishing wasn't going to undo a year and a half of reckless living. And she was determined to give back to Rose the opportunity to attend college. To do that, she needed all those pieces at The Suitable: the antique secretary that had been in the Kendall family since the turn of the century, the hat tree, and the Chippendale chair with its wine-colored velvet upholstery. And she wanted the two antique pocket watches—wanted those most of all. Rose had already lost so much of her childhood. Surely these pieces of her inheritance could be turned into college tuition.

CHAPTER 15

Ninety minutes after hanging up the phone, Marcy pulled into the parking space beside Jason Edwards's American-made sedan. He emerged from its air-conditioned comfort wearing an impeccable charcoal gray suit, white shirt, and subdued striped tie. As well-tailored as he was, by now, Marcy knew enough about men's clothing to tell that even Jason had not been one of Jack's regular customers. The Suitable sold clothing lines that very few locals—not even attorneys—could regularly afford.

Marcy joined Jason on the sidewalk. "I'm glad I didn't listen to your message last night. I'd never have gotten any sleep," she said lightly. "What do you think they want?"

"I'm not totally sure myself. They want your reaction to something inside. We want to get inside too, so the way I look at it, this is our opportunity to make sure your furniture is still there and undamaged."

"You're right," she said as they turned the corner and the marina came into view. Across the street from the waterfront, two policemen were waiting in front of The Suitable. They looked excited to see Marcy. She held out her hand to Kirk Landry, the head detective, and Shawn Goodwin, who had recently left the retail lumber business to join Summerlin's small but well-trained police department. It was a congenial, easy-going group. All four of them—Marcy, Jason, Kirk, and Shawn—were within three years of one another in age, Marcy being the youngest. They had all gone through the Summerlin public school system and, as teens, had attended each others' youth group meetings at the Baptist, Methodist, and Presbyterian churches that made up the two-block "church district" on the eastern end of Main Street.

One glance at The Suitable's bay window gave Marcy a clue to the nature of this meeting. The mannequins, normally dressed in Jack's latest and greatest, were strewn naked across the display window floor.

It was a shocking sight. Marcy had always admired the masculine elegance of The Suitable, with its heavy mahogany doors, antique heart pine floors, and its walls of old brick. The shop's artwork alone told the customer that he was doing business in a sumptuous world.

Opening the security lock across the front doorframe, the detectives stepped back. "After you, Marcy."

She crossed the threshhold and gasped.

Before them lay piles of expensive sports coats and suit coats, grossly mistreated. Every lapel had been lifted and slit. Every pocket was exposed and cut open. Every jacket lining was ripped open along the bottom hem. Marcy could pick out the Harris tweeds, the plush cashmeres, the English hacking jackets with their deep side vents and angled pockets, each one slit at the neck, their pockets all exposed, their linings filleted.

She glanced at the wall where her antique mahogany secretary stood. All she could see were ties in a mangled mess. Jack had allowed Marcy to "dress" the desk with an elegant, eye-catching tie hanging out of each small drawer. The other ties—stripes, solids, and clubs in a variety of silks and wools—she had stacked neatly behind the glass doors of the ornate bookcase on top.

Marcy remembered Jack's insistence that she wear cotton gloves to handle the handmade European silk—protection against snagging the fabric with a fingernail. Each tie was made of three layers, he had told her authoritatively; ordinary ties contained only two. Marcy had been stunned by the prices. These ties started at a hundred and fifty dollars each and went up—way up.

Now, Marcy could easily see all three layers exposed in the ties she picked up gloveless. There were at least two hundred, each one slit. Coming out of her thoughts, she saw Jason, Kirk, and Shawn studying her face. Then they looked back down at a rock-like substance Shawn had just discovered beneath a stack of pleated wool trousers.

"We better have this tested," Shawn declared.

"For what?" said Kirk, picking up a small handful and letting it sift to the floor. His chuckle broke the tension in the room. "You think this is about drugs, Shawn? Well, this is not crack. This, boy, is silica. You can see the shoe boxes are all over the place. So are the shoes. Somebody's knifed open all these bags of silica looking for something."

"You sure it's not some weird kind of coke?" Shawn asked, disappointed.

"Test it," Kirk said, "and listen to 'em laughing in the lab."

Marcy looked down at the loafers. All types were thrown together: calf cordovan, brushed deerskin, even crocodile. Jack had boasted about selling the best, and even Marcy had wondered aloud about who bought The Suitable's outrageously priced clothing. "Yachters," Jack had always answered vaguely.

For the next forty minutes, the detectives plied her with questions about Jack's phone calls, appointments, visitors, mail, deliveries, stray comments, any suspicious behavior. They broke the news gently that they would once again have to search her house. In the past, Marcy would have given in to her usual victim-mentality and pleaded a migraine. Today, oddly, she felt strong, even when the detectives asked the long-delayed question that was obviously uppermost on their minds.

"Marcy," Kirk said, "have you found your Rose?"

"I have," she said with a beatific smile. "She's living with a friend in Myrtle Beach."

"That's great! She's okay?" asked the detective. Marcy nodded.

"We're going to need to see her," he continued. "Could you please give us a phone number?"

Marcy nodded. "I have it here in my wallet, Kirk, but would you mind if I…broke the news? She's still pretty shaken up. We just established contact yesterday. She's dealing with a lot."

Jason handed Marcy his cell phone. "Let's call her now, Marcy. That way, the officers will be able to speak with her once you've laid the groundwork."

But there was no answer at the Coles' house except for the answering machine. Marcy left a message asking Rose to call as soon as possible. Kirk took down the number in case he had to make the contact himself.

Jason spoke up in his most persuasive courtroom voice: "Kirk, we really need to get Marcy's personal belongings out of here—that desk, the little hall tree, the velvet chair near the window. Jack talked her into letting him bring these nice things down here to show off all his pricey merchandise. They belong to her and her family, and as we've all just seen, they're not altogether safe here."

Kirk shook his head, equally negative about it. "Sorry, Jason. Every stick of furniture in this building is evidence for a while. This is a real twist. We don't know if this break-in has anything to do with Jack, or whether some druggie was just looking for fast cash. Though I'll admit, I've never seen a druggie pull a stunt like this. All those slit lapels and ties…something different's going on here. It may be six months—longer—before you can get your furniture. But I will do this, Marcy: I'll move it into a climate-controlled storage unit behind the police station and lock it up for you. It's insured there," he added.

Marcy was sorely disappointed, but hardly surprised. Even she could see that The Suitable break-in had just added a bizarre twist to an already baffling homocide. She sighed and said, "Be careful with them, okay? I just want my things back in good condition. You're looking at Rose's college tuition there."

She walked back over to the secretary to retrieve her purse and, on an impulse, pulled out the wide central drawer and ran her fingers behind the tangle of ties, searching for a tiny brass knob on the left rear side of the back panel. She gave the little knob a push.

The panel fell forward as if on a small spring. She reached into the shallow drawer-within-a-drawer and swept her fingers from left to right. In the back right corner, she encountered cool metal, round and smooth, and to her great astonishment, drew out one of her father-in-law's silver pocket watches—one of six in his collection. "I didn't know this was here!" she gasped. Like a small herd of cattle, all three men stampeded to her side and peered into her shaking hand.

"I can't believe it. I gave him permission to use the other two, but not this one—never this one. It was Mr. Kendall's favorite. Jack *took* this out of my house!"

Quickly, she turned back to the desk's newly opened compartment and once more ran searching fingers from side to side. A small velvet bag lay near the spot where the pocket watch had been. "What's this? What's this?" she murmured and bumped heads with three others as they all bent over to peer eagerly at the bag.

Upending it, she shook its only contents into her open palm. It was a dime-sized coin, gold, not silver, clearly American, with oddly worn lettering for a coin that was otherwise so pristine looking. The date 1861 was centered inside a leafy wreath on the back, with a letter D at the bottom.

"Finder's keepers?" she asked playfully. All three men looked at her, and Kirk noted the sparkle he remembered from high school when Marcy had intrigued a number of masculine hearts. He couldn't remember seeing this Marcy in a very long time.

Everything in him wanted to say, "Of course. Take it," but dutiful Kirk finally shook his head and said, "Soon, Marcy. Just as soon as we figure out what the devil this is all about."

"Can I see that, Marcy?" Jason asked, nervous excitement in his voice. He walked into the light at the front window and stared intently at the coin's design, first one side, then the other. He continued to turn the coin over and over, running his fingers over the edges, lightly tracing the raised design and inscription. His inspection continued for three or four minutes until finally he murmured, "Well! Welcome to the new South." Then, turning to the officers, he said, "One favor, gentlemen. Let's find a good copy machine and make a photocopy of this—both sides. You know I'm a Civil War student at heart. There's some history here—I'm virtually certain."

Taking one last look at the mounds of coats, pants, shoes, and ties, they shook their heads and walked back out onto Waterfront Street. No one spoke as the officers carefully locked and double-locked the door. "Well," said Kirk, as the four of them lingered, staring at the disheveled mannequins in the window, "that didn't clear up a thing."

CHAPTER 16

"Linda, Rose Kendall's scheduled to come in today. I've been thinking about her all weekend," said Joyce, studying Linda Cantrell's face. The director looked burdened.

Linda held up a small sheaf of papers. "I went online and looked up some of the news articles about the man responsible for Rose's situation. He led a high profile lifestyle, it appears, but there's very little here about his past. Sounds like the police are at a dead end with their investigation. Let's pray Rose and the baby are safe," replied Linda. "The police have never caught the killer."

"She was so tense. For her sake and the baby's, she needs to relax," replied Joyce.

"I know, I know," Linda murmured as she patted Joyce on the arm. "We'll do our best to help. We'll get her connected with a good doctor and answer as many questions as we can. I wonder how she's going to take the news about her mother."

"Me too," said Joyce. "I've been praying all weekend. Oh, by the way, that application we were looking for is right here. Stephanie said their home study is complete. They're so hopeful. Did you enjoy getting to know them as much as I did?"

"I really did! They seem to have a good time together—until someone mentions the miscarriages. Go ahead and add them to the book, now that the home study's done. Would you call them and let them know? They could hardly wait."

"I'll take care of it right now," Joyce offered.

"Thanks. Are you ready for some coffee?"

Joyce handed a Styrofoam cup to Linda, who set it down absently on her cluttered desktop and resumed her reading of the Internet printouts. Seconds later, Joyce laughed as she heard the director's exclamation of frustration and the familiar sound of the paper towel dispenser.

Marcy had dreaded making the phone call. "What exactly do they need from me, Mom?" Rose asked, a slight tremor in her voice. The first truly tender mother-daughter phone call from her mother had just culminated in the announcement that the police had requested her phone number. "I'm not sure if I can get off to see them," Rose went on. "I'm working the next five days straight. Would they just talk to me over the phone?"

"Maybe. Rose, there's been a break-in at The Suitable. It's pretty obvious that the burglar was looking for something specific." She described the scene in detail. "My guess is that the blond man you saw is looking for something. The police think you might have overheard something that would help them."

"Mom, I don't know…"

"Rose, there are lots of reasons to cooperate. As soon as the crime scene is dismissed as evidence, there are some valuable pieces of furniture in there that we can decide what to do with."

"Is this about money?"

"Partially, honey. It's your college tuition locked up in that store. I don't want the next burglar to take what's left. If you just talk with them—the detective is Kirk Landry, you know him—maybe we can settle this faster. Apparently, you weren't supposed to leave Summerlin without giving the police a forwarding address. Technically, I suppose, they could bring charges. But nobody's going to do that. I think if you help them, all of this will be over sooner. We can move forward instead of always looking back."

"I'll do it, Mom," said Rose, inwardly marveling at the change in her mother and drawing courage from the sound of Marcy's voice. The old Marcy would have been unnerved, unwilling to take on anything with the potential for causing stress. This Marcy sounded—did Rose dare think it?—almost take-charge.

"By the way, Rose," Marcy asked, "did you ever see Jack with one of Papa Kendall's pocket watches? Or some gold coins?"

"Mom, Jack was all over the place. I even saw him come down out of the attic one time! I'm pretty sure he went through all the dresser drawers too. He always seemed to have some reason to work at Papa's old desk, and I'm positive he went through the papers in that. Were there important documents in there?"

"Yes," Marcy said. "The certificates of authenticity for the pocket watches are missing. That's another reason why I hope you can tell the police something. You remember Jason—he's my lawyer—he told me that I need proof of ownership to sell them on a collector's market for collector's prices."

Marcy told Rose about the contents of the hidden drawer in the secretary at The Suitable. "I found one of the missing pocket watches—the most valuable one—and a small gold coin that Jason got really excited about. I'm not sure where the coin came from, but the police want to talk to you, to see if you happened to hear anything in the conversation between Jack and the blond man at the Victorian that night. Anything they can tie together. I'm quoting Kirk: 'There're a thousand loose threads in this strange story, and no two have come together yet.'"

No reply. Marcy continued, "I'm so glad I found that pocket watch. Your grandfather told me several times that the watches were a good investment for your future. I didn't know how good until Jack had them appraised. He took them from our house to The Suitable, supposedly to meet with an appraiser there.

"Anyway, they turned out to be Civil War era. Your grandfather's parents had saved them from their parents. They'll bring in more money than I ever dreamed. I thought it would only be a couple of thousand, but I found Jack's appraisal paperwork, and it said up to twenty-five thousand. But for now..." Marcy struggled to remain upbeat, "the police say everything is evidence. It's just going to take some time to get to the place where we can offer them for sale."

"Wow, Mom. That much money for one watch? And you have six of them?"

"Uh huh. But only three are extremely valuable. And one of them is missing. Every bit of that money is earmarked for your college education, Rose. Do you think it will be enough?" she asked sincerely.

Rose had to laugh. "Enough? Yes, it'll certainly be enough, unless we set our sights on the Ivy League." Again, they were both reminded of their historic role reversal, considering that Rose had calculated the cost of college while Marcy had no clue. Nevertheless, it was Marcy who was now making plans to pay what Rose had calculated. That was a significant switch.

"I'm praying about what to do next, Rose. Everything in me wants to lock up this house and move to Myrtle Beach with you right this minute. But I feel as if I'm supposed to stay put for a few weeks, and...see what happens. So I've set a goal. One month from now, I want to be ready to move. I'm going to put this house on the market today. With an appraiser's help, we're going to sell what we don't need, and find some way to cash in what your grandfather collected for you. Maybe that way, you'll be able to believe that...I really love you. I'm going to do everything I can to give you a solid foundation for the rest of your life. That, my darling one, is not just about money."

Rose chose her words carefully. "Mom, it can be good, but right now, it's hard for me just to hear you speak Jack's name." She softened. "But we need to say what's on our minds. And I'm so glad you're planning to come—the sooner the better. Just this morning, I was wishing for you, wishing you could go with me to my appointment this afternoon." For once, the silence between Rose and Marcy felt comfortable, loving.

Rose steeled herself and said, "Listen, I'll talk to him—Detective Landry. I can't do it today, though. I have an appointment at Lifesender, and I have to get some medical tests done. Why don't you ask him to come here tomorrow, meet me at 2:15? I'll be off work, and I can change clothes and meet him at the beach. That way, the Coles and the restaurant staff won't have to overhear all the gory details."

"Where?"

"Tell him to meet me at the beach access at the end of Thirty-Ninth Avenue North. I'll wait for him there on the bench."

When Marcy called Kirk a few minutes later, he scarcely hesitated. "Take a road trip to Myrtle Beach? Sure! Why not. Wanna come?"

"Can't do it. I'm meeting with a real estate agent today, and I don't know what that will mean for tomorrow."

"Yeah?" said Kirk. "You selling the house?"

"Trying," said Marcy. "Surely somebody will want a creaky old historic house with astronomical electric bills."

"Oh, definitely," Kirk laughed. "Especially the electric bills! Look, I know you have appointments this afternoon, but would you have time for me to drop by the house? I need to check out a few things. Thirty minutes?"

The navy Toyota pulled up in front of the Lifesender office, and Savannah left her foot on the clutch. "I'll be back in half an hour," she said. "I have to get some gas and pick up a book for Mom. Don't worry if you take longer than that. I'll take my notes into the waiting room and study. I have a test tomorrow."

Rose received a personal smile from Joyce, and as she entered Linda's office, the director stood up and walked toward her with her arms outstretched. "I've thought about you so often this past weekend. How are you?" she asked, offering a warm hug.

"Pretty good, actually."

"Wonderful!" Linda pronounced, noting the absence of stress lines on Rose's face. "You're looking good! Has anything special happened, anything new?"

Rose's smile lit up her face. Having seen her so burdened during her last appointment, Linda considered the change wrought by a single smile dramatic.

"Actually, quite a lot has changed since I saw you!" Rose replied. "I can still hardly believe it. My mother was here for a week looking for me. In the most amazing set of circumstances you can imagine, she wound up meeting Savannah's mom in church. I wasn't there—had to work that morning. But Mom and I talked Sunday afternoon for the first time in a month. To tell you the truth, it felt like the first real talk we'd had in fourteen years. She seems different. She knows everything. And she actually wants to help me! I'm really still in shock."

Linda was trying hard to control her excitement. "Oh, Rose, I'm so happy for you! Two people make a family! And I really want you to have a family! You know what? Your mom called here Friday. She left a message on the answering machine, and Joyce got the message Saturday afternoon. So that gave us Saturday night and Sunday to pray for you and your mom. If she hadn't found you Sunday, I would have had the privilege of breaking the news to you today."

"Really?" Rose asked, obviously touched. "That's amazing! I'll have to tell her. And thank you so much for praying."

"So, what are the plans?"

"Well, the situation at home is still confusing. The police discovered some new developments in the case involving the man who…you know." Linda nodded and Rose went on. "It sounds like the police are coming down tomorrow to interview me. I'll tell them everything I know, but I doubt it's enough to help much. I don't want to go back home. I like it here. Mom is already working on selling the house in Summerlin and coming here to the beach to help me…and maybe start over together."

Relief was flowing through every vein and artery in Linda's body. All weekend, the heaviness she had carried for Rose had haunted her. She had prayed for her and committed her to God, but every time she thought of Rose trying to piece together these next seven or eight months alone, it had seemed so hard. This was not a street-wise girl, a tough girl, like many who walked through the doors looking for money. She knew that Rose was staying with a local friend, but friends could come and go. Mothers were less likely to. "Well!" She exhaled, beaming. "It sounds like things really are coming together. Have you checked out the list of physicians I gave you?"

"Yes. Savannah's mom said she knows this Dr. Richardson and likes him."

"He's a good man," Linda agreed. "You'll feel comfortable with him. So, Rose…have you had time to make your decision? Do you know yet what you would like to do when the baby comes?" Linda knew this was a critical moment for both Rose and the baby. Only God knew which decision was best.

"Yes, ma'am. I want to put the baby up for adoption…even though I have a lot of conflicting emotions about it. Sometimes I think I would love to have a baby of my own. But I want her to have a good life. I need to be sure she's in the right hands. I want her to have both a mother and a father who will really love her." Why did Rose feel as if these were the hardest words she had ever spoken?

"What did your mom have to say about it?" Linda asked sympathetically.

"She agreed it was the best thing."

Linda nodded, just waiting, not pressing.

"Anyway, what do we do to start this process?"

"Well," Linda said, "we make sure that your health—and the baby's—are well taken care of. Did you remember the form for financial help?"

"Yes, I have it right here," responded Rose.

Linda scanned the paper. It looked complete. "Okay, let's get Joyce to call Dr. Richardson's office and make you an appointment."

"Will you please ask if he can make it in the afternoon? I work the breakfast shift," said Rose.

Joyce came and went with her characteristic "Will do."

"And—I just thought of this—would it be possible for me to meet with a police detective from Summerlin here in your office? I really don't have a private place to talk. Right now we're lined up to meet on a bench at the beach."

"Of course!" Linda replied. "You can have the conference room."

Linda patted a blue notebook. "We'll look at this a little further along in the process. But I want you to see how many families are desperately hoping for a baby like yours. You play the key role in the placement process here, Rose. Eventually, we'll look through these pictures and profiles, and you'll pick the best set of parents for your baby."

Joyce buzzed Linda to say she had Dr. Richardson's office on the line. If Rose could be there as early as 11:30, there was one appointment open the very next week. Rose nodded. She would simply have to get off work early.

"Rose, you're welcome to come in and talk any time. We have classes on health care that I hope you'll take advantage of. There's a nutrition class and a monthly group session with some other girls going through the same things you are. Should we send mail to the address you listed before—Savannah's house?"

"For now. That may change soon. Mom tentatively set a goal to move in early July."

Rose spent the next fifteen minutes filling out forms, finishing up shortly after Savannah's Toyota buzzed up to the curb.

A peaceful sadness rested on Rose as she left the Lifesender office. Her childhood, her teenage years were gone. The decisions she had made were adult decisions. The feeling of sadness passed, however, replaced by the realization that she was ravenous. She climbed into Savannah's car, grinned, and announced, "French fries, girl! We need french fries!"

CHAPTER 17

As promised, Kirk arrived at Marcy's house at two thirty.

He stepped past the solid oak, raised-panel front door and smiled. "I had forgotten how beautiful this house is!" His admiring gaze took in the thick wood molding around the doors and windows, the hand-cut dentil molding at the ceiling, the six-inch baseboards. French doors with panes of wavy glass closed off the wide central hall from a parlor on the right and a library on the left. The windows in these rooms were unusually tall, with nine-over-nine sashes. By contrast, the stairway's well-worn handrail was at least three inches lower than those found in modern construction—relics of a day when Americans were shorter.

Hanging above many of the antique chests and tables that furnished the downstairs were large, gold-framed paintings—landscapes rendered in bright oils and acrylics. They were Marcy's work, dating as far back as high school. The most recent—a beach scene dotted with umbrellas in primary colors—was dated the year before Daniel died.

"It's good to see the house through fresh eyes, Kirk," Marcy smiled. "Sometimes you can focus too much on the slanting floors and the cost of heating and air. Daniel's parents did a wonderful job of keeping it up, though, didn't they? And they updated the kitchen and bathrooms after Daniel and Rose and I moved in."

"It's a beauty," Kirk said with conviction. "Daniel and I had a hiding place under these stairs when I was little. And when we were old enough to play football, Mr. Kendall set up a goalpost in the backyard. This was like a second home to me. I called the phone number here so often I've never forgotten it. Wish I were here for other reasons so I could really study it, now that I'm old enough to appreciate woodwork." He grinned.

"Any news since this morning?" Marcy asked.

"Nothing. Only more mysteries. About that coin you found at The Suitable—has Jason called you back with any information?"

"Not yet. I can give him a ring. He may not know that Papa Kendall kept a library of books on coins. He was a serious collector. I know—some of those coins paid for the new kitchen and bathrooms."

"Interesting. Okay—I need to take a look at Jack's personal belongings again."

"They're still in the spare room upstairs. I've been trying to figure out what to do with them."

"Lead the way," Kirk directed, noting Marcy's slight, involuntary shudder. For the next hour, they went through every pocket in every jacket, shirt, and pair of pants in Jack's extensive and expensive wardrobe. Kirk collected a small boxful of ticket stubs, receipts, deposit slips, coins, and scraps of stationery bearing notes and phone numbers. Marcy noticed that Kirk was careful to run his fingers along the lapels and the lining of every jacket, pressing the fabric between his fingers.

"What are you looking for when you do that?" Marcy asked.

"Haven't the slightest," said Kirk. "All I can tell you is that I don't think we're going to find any chemical residue in those clothes piled up in The Suitable. I still don't think this is a drug case, but you may know better. Did you ever see Jack under the influence, Marcy?"

"Alcohol." She sighed. "Some nights more than others. Jack loved to party. But no, I never saw anything that suggested drugs."

"Where did he keep his personal papers?"

"Mostly at The Suitable. But he did have the Victorian house over on Fifth Street, you know. And it has a garage."

"I know," Kirk said. "We checked it right after the shooting. But Marcy, I have to tell you something. Somebody broke into that garage last weekend, the same night as the break-in at The Suitable. Ripped open all the cushions on an old sofa and chair. Strung metal parts all over the yard. And you know, we had Jack's sports car seized the night he was killed. We towed it to a lot behind the police department. Well, somebody had the nerve to climb the fence and force down a window in the car—this is all in the same weekend, now!—slit the leather seats, rip up the carpet, rifle through the glove box, the trunk, and everything."

"All this took place last weekend while I was in Myrtle Beach?" Marcy asked with wide eyes.

"Right," said Kirk. "You know, if Rose hadn't followed Jack to his garage and heard him talking with the guy who wound up shooting him, we would have initially treated this whole investigation differently. We would have written up Jack as a victim, pure and simple. But Rose seemed to think Jack was involved in something criminal. Now all these break-ins, all tied to Jack. They certainly make Rose's story more credible, don't they?"

The two sat in silence for a moment.

"Kirk," Marcy began, "there has to be a lot about Jack none of us knew. What did you find in Jack's garage on Fifth Street?"

"Nothing we could make a lot of sense out of. A ship-to-shore radio. Some thin sheets of brass. A disc stamper. Hundreds—no, thousands—of metal button-halves—you know, like blazer buttons where the top with the design fits down over the bottom half. There were a lot of small hand tools. Magnifying glasses. Some high intensity lamps. Polishing cloths, the kind you use for silver. Jewelry dip. A whole box of white cotton gloves. Needles of all sizes. Spools and spools of thread, mostly grays, browns, blacks, and tans. A whole case of disposable hobby knives. Manila envelopes. Except for the metal, I suppose all of it could have been legitimately used by someone in the clothing business—someone whose clients can afford yachts.

But Marcy, there must have been two hundred books in there—half of them on men's clothing and the other half on coins. Some of the coin books belonged to your father-in-law. His nameplate was in about twenty of them."

"Coins," Marcy repeated. "You know, Jack did seem particularly interested in Mr. Kendall's coin collection. Actually, the first time I met him was at an estate auction in Wilmington that had some rare coins for sale."

"What were you doing there?" Kirk asked.

"Papa Kendall asked me to drive him. He'd get tired sometimes behind the wheel, plus I think he liked to have someone to talk to. And I know he thought it was good to get me out of the house. Even then, I was only half there most of the time," she added ruefully. "I've thought back over a thousand things I wish I'd asked him on the drive to Wilmington and back. He died about two weeks after that auction. None of us were expecting it."

"Uhmm," Kirk said sympathetically. "Did Mr. Kendall buy anything that night?"

"Actually, yes. I remember that he and Jack got into a bidding war over a Flying Eagle."

"A what?" Kirk said.

"It was the first one-cent coin designed to be the size of today's penny. Minted around 1856. Before that, American pennies were almost as big as a half-dollar."

"Who won the bidding war?" Kirk asked, amused.

"Jack won that one," Marcy said, "but it was okay, because the next coin they auctioned was what Papa really wanted."

"What was it?"

"An 1864 two-cent piece in mint condition."

"And what was so special about that?"

"Papa said it was the first coin to bear the motto 'In God We Trust.' He had always wanted an 1864. I honestly think he bid against Jack for the Flying Eagle long enough to drive up the price and tie up a large part of Jack's cash. That way, Papa would have less competition for the coin he really wanted."

"Clever man," Kirk observed.

"A good man too," Marcy said soberly. "That motto on the money was Papa's motto too. He really did trust in God…something I'm only beginning to learn how to do."

"Really, Marcy?" Kirk voice was quiet and sincere. "Do you mean that?"

"I do, Kirk. Finding Rose was nothing short of miraculous. God made himself so…real to me. He seemed to be insisting that things be put right between himself and me first. Then he literally escorted me to Rose. One of these days, I'll tell you about it."

"Deal!" Kirk said and smiled. He hated to ask the next question, but he had to. "Marcy, how long was it between Mr. Kendall's death and Jack's first contact with you?"

She blushed. "A little less than a month."

Neither one commented. Kirk scratched down a few more notes and tried to sound matter-of-fact as he said, "That should do it. I better get back to the station and run a few searches through the database."

He was halfway down the sidewalk when Marcy stopped him. "Three questions," she called out.

"What's that?"

"Did you check Jack's boat down at the marina? Had anyone vandalized that?"

"We did check it. No damage. But I've had two people tell me that they've seen lights in the boat cabin during the last week. When my men checked it, they found nothing. I'm posting a lookout, starting tonight. What's the next question?"

"Are you still planning to drive to the beach tomorrow to talk to Rose?"

Kirk nodded.

"Rose called and asked me to tell you that she's made arrangements for the two of you to use a meeting room at a counseling center where you can talk privately. She said she would still meet you at the Thirty-Ninth Avenue beach access and you can drive together to the center." Marcy looked as hopeful as Rose had sounded. "I think she's praying that you'll come in an unmarked car—it would draw less attention."

"I had planned to," Kirk said. "I'll be in plain clothes too. Her plan sounds a lot better than a bench on the beach for a sensitive conversation. What's the third question?"

"Harder to ask," Marcy said. "Sit down a minute."

They sat face to face on a pair of heavy, black, wrought-iron lawn benches. Kirk could tell Marcy was uncomfortable. At length, she cleared her throat, took a deep breath, and said, "Kirk, how much do people know about Rose's ...situation?"

The detective studied her face, wanting to make it easier, but not knowing how.

He deliberately lowered his voice. "You mean about the pregnancy?" He could hear Marcy inhale. "This *is* a small town, Marcy. They ran a blood test on her the night of the shooting. Just ruling out alcohol and drugs. Nobody was expecting a positive on a pregnancy test, but that's what it showed. At least four employees at the lab would've seen the results. When all the publicity came out about the shooting, I suppose those test results were a hot potato—too hot to keep to yourself. So I suppose everybody in town knows."

"But do they know who the father is?" Marcy asked.

"No. Lots of speculation, of course. Most of it centers around that weekend that the state Quiz Bowl Competition was held in Raleigh. Some of the kids remembered seeing Rose with a guy from Chapel Hill. Since she wasn't known to be dating anybody around here, they put two and two together and, right or wrong, came up with a baby."

Marcy nodded. Her hands were trembling. "Thanks, Kirk, I needed to know. Would you wait here a minute?"

She returned carrying a small green journal, opened it almost automatically to a page in the middle, and handed it to Kirk, saying,

"I'm trusting you to keep this to yourself for a little while. I found it just after Rose disappeared. It will probably help you understand Rose's reactions when you meet with her tomorrow."

Kirk read for ten minutes in silence, his big hands clenching and unclenching. He muttered something unintelligible between clenched teeth.

Finally he looked up. "Marcy, in a strange way, this is encouraging to me. You know I taught Rose in Sunday school two years ago. No? Well, I did…and if there was one spiritually awake kid in that class, it was Rose. It was killing me to think she had walked away from her standards…God's standards…like that. I know a lot of kids do, and they realize their mistake." He looked deeply into Marcy's eyes and flushed, realizing that he had just described her own path. "Hopefully, this will all be over soon, Marcy. I'm sorry you've got so much on you at one time. But listen, I think I better check the locks on your doors and windows before I go. Somebody is looking for something connected with Jack, and until we find out what it is, please be careful. Have you noticed anything strange since getting back?"

"Just an unusual number of hang-ups on my answering machine," Marcy said.

"Have you erased them?" Kirk asked.

"No. But the callers' numbers are blocked."

"Are the calls still coming?"

"I don't know. I unplugged the answering machine."

Kirk re-entered the house and jotted down the date and time of each call without a message. He seemed satisfied with the window locks, slightly less so with the door locks, and relieved that there was an electronic sentry system in place.

He was circling the exterior of the house when he called out, "Marcy! Have you had any yardwork done since you got back?"

"No," she replied.

"Any service men, meter readers?"

"No. Why?"

"Because there are footprints under every one of your first floor windows, and they don't look dainty. Don't walk near the windows, will you? I'm going to send a forensics guy over. We got some footprints in the wet ground from the impound lot where Jack's car was parked. I've gotta get some measurements and photos."

CHAPTER 18

Real estate agent Lindsay Fullerton arrived at 3:45, her enthusiasm evident on the doorstep, her energy level much higher than Marcy's. "I've admired this house ever since I moved to Summerlin!" she said, extending her hand in greeting. "Always wanted to see the inside." Lindsay's trim figure in her bright pink summer suit and high-heeled office sandals gave her a look of peppy professionalism. She took quick notes on a legal pad as Marcy led her on a tour, first downstairs and then up—a tour punctuated with sincere-sounding "ooohs." Jason had obviously filled her in on Marcy's recent history; the agent asked no painful questions about her new client's motives for selling.

"I don't have a thing to offer you to drink besides water," Marcy apologized, as she longingly eyed the staircase leading up to her bedroom. "I've been out of town for a week and need to grocery shop."

Insisting that tap water was the only beverage worth drinking, Lindsay proceeded to write up a listing contract as Marcy went to the kitchen for two glasses. At the kitchen window, she took a deep breath and stood for a moment, gazing out over the wide green yard with its old-growth camellias and azaleas clustered beneath a pair of large, spreading oaks. She sighed. She would miss this place, she knew, but right now, she felt only two desires: to sleep and then to get back to Rose. Every surface Jack had touched felt caustic to her; she now thought of the house as poisoned. She shook her head as if to dispel memories and focused instead on Lindsay's Volvo parked in the driveway, a real estate logo on the driver's door. "Thank you, Lord," she whispered, "that we are making such progress."

Back in the living room, Lindsay announced that she had already done her homework. She produced a small sheaf of "comparables"—houses that had come on the market in the past six months that were similar to Marcy's in age, size, condition, and neighborhood. Together, they reviewed the listing prices, the actual sales prices, and the length of time on the market.

"I don't want to be overly optimistic, Marcy," Lindsay said, "but I think you have a fairly quick sale here. This house is old enough to be considered historic. It's in terrific condition. The neighborhood is the most desirable in Summerlin. Price it right, and this house could sell within a month. Now, if you want to speculate"—she grinned—"the house may sit until next spring when the tourists come down for flower season. Of course, you might actually be able to hold out for an extra twenty-five thousand dollars by doing that."

"No," said Marcy. "Price it to sell. I want to sell it fast. It's just that I can't be ready for you to show it for...a week, at the earliest," Marcy calculated, thinking of the deep cleaning that the old house needed from top to bottom. A few minutes later, she signed her name across the contract and put down the pen with a wistful smile. Lindsay headed for the Volvo where she kept a For Sale sign at all times and planted a shiny new one in the front yard, then whipped out her digital camera and took several dozen flattering shots of the front porch, the yard, the dining room, living room, and kitchen. She promised to call Marcy within forty-eight hours to tell her where to look for the listing on the company website and in several publications.

Suddenly, after the longest day in Marcy's recent memory, she found herself alone in the big house. Alone and hungry. For the first time, she realized she had eaten nothing all day. There had been no time. Despite a bone-deep sense of weariness, she knew she had to have something to eat.

She forced herself behind the wheel of the Buick and headed for Summerlin's one buffet restaurant, unwilling to wait long enough to even order from a menu. Taking a left on Steepleton, she passed her former church, Harborview Community. Tonight, the sight jarred her. How many times, she asked herself, had she driven past that church and looked straight ahead? Now, she felt an uncharacteristic desire to pull into the empty parking lot, despite the fact that she was starving at almost seven o'clock on a Monday.

By her calculations, she hadn't physically been inside the church in almost two years—since shortly after her father-in-law's funeral. Once Jack showed up, she had shut down the relationships with the few close friends who had faithfully stuck by her during Daniel's illness and the "missing" years that followed.

And really, it wasn't that Marcy had been altogether incapacitated during those years. About a year after the funeral, she had come out of her grief sufficiently to register with a temp agency that offered short-term clerical assignments. But on the days when she couldn't bring herself to crawl out of bed, she refused the work calls by claiming that she was already "booked." It was her private analogy. Her sheets were the covers, she was the story. Between the sheets, she had passed the hours blocking thought, pushing "pause."

Her friends had been a godsend during the missing years—picking up Rose for sleepovers with their girls, taking her to football games, even planning birthday parties and somehow making it look as if Marcy had done a large part of the work.

Rose had stepped up to the plate as well, soaking up her grandmother's practical lessons in doing laundry, preparing meals, writing checks, and balancing a bank statement. Eventually, Marcy began relying on Rose to go to the bank, shop for the groceries, pay the water bill, the electric bill, the phone bill. Summerlin's business district was so compact that Rose could run most of the errands on foot. She was well known by the town's business people as a sweet, quiet girl who was attentive to the details most teens never looked at. No one objected when she signed her own name to Marcy's checks or took outfits home on approval for Marcy to try on.

In this way, Marcy had lived an insulated life. Always petite, she maintained her figure almost effortlessly—not through exercise, but lack of appetite. Her blond hair had natural body and curl, and her hairdresser understood the art of a near-maintenance-free haircut.

To the town of Summerlin, Marcy seemed both emotionally and physically fragile. The fact that she showed up for church once or twice a month was accepted as a show of health. Even then, only the shell of a person had shown up, a shell who often left early, feeling weak, as if the tiny creature she had become was retracting into the shadowy recesses inside. Tacitly, Summerlin agreed to make few demands of her.

So when Jack Bradford singled out Marcy after the coin auction in Wilmington, no one was prepared for her sudden reentry into active society. About a month after the elderly Mr. Kendall died, the couple was seen in one of Summerlin's good waterfront restaurants. They turned up at a jazz festival on the waterfront, Jack with his small cooler full of drinks.

Marcy had been surprised and pleased to see the mayor, the Downtown Redevelopment director, and the president of the Chamber of Commerce hail her handsome date by name. Jack had made the news twice. Not only had he purchased a huge Victorian house on the National Register, but also a former sporting goods shop on the waterfront, where a contractor was doing a first-class renovation job on what was to open as The Suitable.

In retrospect, Marcy could see that Jack had launched a systematic breakdown of all of her standards. It had been so gradual. At first, she had begun having a glass of wine with him during dinner. Then a drink after dinner. Then a drink before, during, and after dinner. Only three weeks into the relationship, Jack had proposed a weekend getaway at a bed and breakfast in southern Virginia. She declined and he took it like a gentleman, but her fantasy life took on a new dimension. Simply thinking about being with him eroded her reserve. His good night kisses were memorable.

He continued the campaign in tiny steps until she nervously accepted his invitation for an overnight stay in Wilmington to pick out paint and carpeting for the shop. Of course, shopping turned out to be incidental in light of the overwhelming physical relationship Marcy caved into by agreeing to stay the night at Jack's apartment. Eight weeks into the relationship, Jack bemoaned the seventy-five-minute drive from Wilmington to Summerlin, saying that it was eating up too much time. Everything would be so much simpler if he just moved in with Marcy until he got The Suitable up and running and could focus on renovating the Victorian. Telling herself that all engaged couples these days moved in together, Marcy had agreed. Most of Summerlin knew the story within twenty-four hours.

Marcy's hands grew tight around the steering wheel as she remembered how Renee Bellamy, her closest friend, came straight to the point and asked Marcy to tell Jack to move out. Marcy knew that Renee really cared about her, but she couldn't stand the implications of Renee's request and bristled at her suggestion that Marcy had stopped attending church because she was too ashamed. After that, Marcy quit taking Renee's calls and essentially shut down a lifelong friendship.

I'll bet she's saying 'I told you so,' Marcy thought. *But maybe not.*

Somehow, Marcy just couldn't see Renee experiencing any pleasure from the fact that she had been so very right and Marcy so very, very wrong about Jack.

Marcy sighed. She had met Renee in second grade at Summerlin Elementary where, by Christmas, the two were inseparable. Marcy considered it comical that, of the two of them, Renee had wound up marrying a minister. Renee, after all, was the one always looking for fun and getting into trouble.

She thought back to the spring when they were sixteen. Daniel Kendall had invited the two of them to a youth rally advertising a live band, free pizza, and several guest speakers. Renee decided they would go for the music and pizza and then take off for the beach. Marcy had to smile as she remembered how Renee caught the eye of the pastor's son. Like Daniel, Tommy Bellamy was two years older and making plans for college. Neither girl had a clue that they were sharing pizza with their future husbands.

Actually, it was a life-altering rally for Renee, who had responded to the message of Christ that night. It took her only a little longer to respond to Tommy, but within two years, both of them were attending Bible college. They were married the day after graduation and eventually returned to the church in Summerlin when Tommy's father retired. By then, Marcy and Daniel were celebrating their first anniversary.

Renee and Marcy each had a child in the same month. They decorated their houses together. Their families went to the beach together on Saturday afternoons. At church, Marcy headed up the crafts committee for Vacation Bible School. She decorated both the sanctuary and the fellowship hall for the holidays. She shyly but willingly agreed to Renee's suggestion that she teach a painting class at the senior center where Harborview held a monthly outreach program. But no, she never taught a Sunday school class, a Bible study. That was for Daniel to do, for Renee, for people who "understood" the Bible. Marcy had learned the fundamentals of the faith. It had just never become personal to her.

And then Daniel had died, and despite the fact that Renee had hovered at Marcy's elbow throughout his illness, everything changed. Marcy felt cut off. When she and Rose went to church, Marcy could only sit and blame God. Soon she was having panic attacks in the pew, and Rose's grandparents—still grieving—took over the job of taking the four-year-old to church, while, more and more, Marcy stayed at home.

The pattern continued. A full year after the funeral, Marcy realized numbly that she had left early every time she'd attended church.

She declined any request that involved responsibility, but soothed her conscience by sending Rose to Wednesday night suppers, carrying desserts made in the night.

Renee had fervently worked to preserve the friendship, but little by little, Marcy shut her out. Years had gone by without meaningful communication, even though Renee never failed to send a birthday gift, a Christmas card. She never failed to pick up Rose for youth group trips and at least once a year took Rose shopping for an outfit, claiming that since she had never had a daughter, this was her personal indulgence. And Marcy knew it had taken courage for Renee to ask her to stop seeing Jack. *Poor Renee*, Marcy thought, *she isn't laughing. No doubt she's been crying for me all these years. Of all the friends I ever had, this one was real. She cared, no matter what.*

Now, as Marcy carried her tray from the buffet line to the table, she prayed. *Lord, we talked about those broken relationships in the service in Myrtle Beach on Sunday. Let me know what I can do about this one.*

Call her. The directive seemed to blink on and off in Marcy's thoughts, like the tiny light on her answering machine. *Call her.*

I can't do that. Not just yet. I…I wouldn't know what to say.

Call her.

Too embarrassing, Marcy told herself. *I can't do it.* She sat down at a table for two and bowed her head to pray, but the words of thanks seemed drowned out by a message coming from the other direction.

Call her.

Her appetite had disappeared, and she ate only a few mouthfuls of salad before pushing the tray away. She drove home trembling.

By the time she climbed the stairs, Marcy's strength was sapped, and she felt confused, a sensation that only grew stronger when she got home to find her answering machine light blinking. She recognized the perky voice of Lindsay Fullerton immediately, though the Realtor's tone contained just a hint of…what? Nervous excitement? "Hi, Marcy. It's Lindsay…already! Listen, I've just received a call from someone saying he wanted to look at your house. That's the fastest response to a For Sale sign I've ever seen! Only one problem—he's really insistent—wants to see the house immediately—says he's from out of town and has to leave tomorrow. Call me as soon as you can, okay?"

Marcy's negative feelings grew stronger. A small wave of fear washed over her, the first truly helpless emotion she had experienced since Sunday morning in church. The old, fearful Marcy was back, awash in self-doubt, incapable.

Oh, Father, I'm afraid! What should I do? Marcy panicked as she realized that she perceived no peace, only increasing confusion replacing the sense of supernatural intimacy with a new-found Father.

"Don't leave me!" she gasped. "Please, I can't stand it. Please, Father, what should I do?"

Call her. Instantly, Marcy recognized the instruction. Call…not Lindsay, but Renee! Marcy felt herself shrinking back, and her insecurity seemed to grow. *Tomorrow,* she bargained. *First thing tomorrow, I'll call her. Let me think about it for a while first. But what about Lindsay?*

Call her. Marcy felt sick, at the mercy of her confusion. Seconds passed, and the phone at her elbow rang. Marcy jumped, then stared at the phone as if an enemy lay coiled inside the receiver. She could not answer; instead, she counted six rings, waiting for the answering machine to tell her who was calling. "You've reached the Kendall residence," she heard Papa Kendall reciting, as if from the grave. "No one is available to take your call. Please leave your name and number at the tone." Marcy waited for the high-pitched beep and for someone, anyone, to speak, but there was only dead air and then *click.* Another hang-up! The caller ID screen reported that her caller's number was blocked. Fifteen minutes later, the phone rang again, and then a third time after fifteen minutes more. By now, Marcy was pacing her bedroom floor, petrified of the clock, the phone, the gathering darkness outside her window, the cloudy condition of her mind. Finally, as the phone rang for the fourth time, she sped to the bedside table, fumbling for the phone book. She looked up a number, dialed it with trembling fingers and as soon as she heard the deep voice of a teenaged boy, hurried to ask, "Is Renee in?"

"I'm sorry," the well-mannered young man replied, "Mom and Dad left maybe three minutes ago. I don't expect them in until around eleven."

"Do they have a cell number?"

"Yes, ma'am—they usually turn it off during meetings, but you could try. Here's the number."

Marcy dialed, got a recorded message, left her own message, then climbed fully clothed into bed and pulled up the covers. She stared at the bedside phone, which continued to ring at fifteen-minute intervals, until finally, around 11:15, she heard something more than a click on the answering machine. It was the concerned voice of her long-time friend, Renee. Marcy picked up, made the briefest of requests, then hung up. She dialed Lindsay Fullerton's cell phone number, got a recording, and delivered her message: she really wasn't ready to show the house until the following Monday, as originally agreed. But, if the urgent house-hunter didn't mind a half-inch of dust, the client could see the house between 2:00 and 4:00 the next day. Marcy would be out of the house with a friend. She switched off the ringer on the phone, unplugged the answering machine, and turned out the lights. She pulled up the covers, but sleep came only fitfully.

CHAPTER 19

Kirk Landry thoroughly enjoyed the drive down the coast to Myrtle Beach. The day was bright, the water sparkling, the temperature in the low seventies. *A rare Tuesday in June,* he thought, *to be this cool.*

Kirk had topped out at six feet during his senior year in high school. Twenty years later, he still maintained his linebacker weight of 220 pounds through a regular weight-lifting regimen that kept him trim beneath broad shoulders. He had friendly blue eyes, an obviously broken nose, a slight drawl, and a wide, quick grin.

He was one of Summerlin's own, having traded in his football jersey for a police uniform after two years at the local community college. After eight years on the force, he made detective. Three attributes worked in his favor: he was honest, he inspired trust, and he remembered faces. He was also a chronic workaholic, a fact that had fatally interfered with any long-term romantic relationships.

Kirk had watched Rose grow up in Harborview Community Church, but their conversations together had seldom progressed further than the pleasantries that typically pass between adults and children who are unrelated. That is, until the year Tommy Bellamy insisted that he teach the senior high Sunday school class. Kirk had learned that Rose was a serious-minded girl, and willing to tackle the serious questions the class was addressing as they studied the book of Galatians. Rose wasn't a talker, but when she spoke, she was worth listening to.

Today she looked tense, but within sixty seconds of their meeting at the Thirty-Ninth Avenue beach access, Kirk could see that he had put her at ease. He had arrived with two cold chocolate shakes, a recent issue of the *Summerlin Sentinel* in which Rose was listed among the graduating seniors who had earned academic awards, and a slightly creased five-by-seven photograph.

Driving to the Lifesender office, Kirk encouraged her to study the photo while they finished their shakes. "Recognize anybody?" he asked. She shook her head. "Well, the guy on the left is your dad. The good-looking one on the right is me. We were in ninth grade and playing JV football because we knew all the girls would think we were cool."

Rose laughed out loud. But she continued to study her dad's face, and by the time she lifted her eyes to meet Kirk's relaxed smile, he had pulled into the Lifesender parking lot.

"This is great," she said quietly. "Maybe I can make a copy?"

He nodded, and Rose was pleased that Kirk didn't simply offer it as a gift. Obviously, her dad had meant enough to the hulking detective that he wanted to keep the original photo for himself. They moved inside to the small conference room.

"Rose, I'm real sorry about everything that's happened to you. From what little we've found out about Jack, he got what was coming to him. Your mom"—he faltered only slightly—"told me about the journal. Whoever shot Jack…well, he gave Jack a fair trial, as far as I can tell."

His tone was genuine.

"I'm still left, though, with the responsibility of investigating his death. A guy who kills once is likely to do it again, and this time, the victim may not be so deserving. We gotta find this spiky-haired blond guy."

She nodded.

"So let me tell you what we know. As I explained that night at the station, the gun was traced to an Anton W. Johnson, age thirty-six, last known residence, Windlass, North Carolina."

Rose nodded. "He definitely sounded local."

"We finally got a picture of this Johnson guy." He pushed the photo toward Rose, and she nodded immediately in recognition. "His last known occupation was—get this—scuba diving and salvage. He used to work for some reputable outfits, including several that locate undersea wrecks. But he's been arrested twice in the last five years, nothing too big. Small amounts of cocaine, plus a forged check and one iffy case of identity theft. Still, it establishes a pattern.

"But he's disappeared. Hasn't been home since late May, the neighbors say. That fits perfectly. What has me worried is that last week, anything connected with Jack was broken into—the shop, the yellow Victorian, the garage, his sports car. Several people saw lights on Jack's boat. I suspect that Johnson or somebody connected with him is back in Summerlin. Something is of sufficient value to risk coming back to the scene of a murder that's less than one month old. He must think we're really backwater."

"What about my mom's house?" Rose asked. "She hasn't mentioned anything about a break-in there."

"We've tripled the number of patrols through your neighborhood," Kirk replied. "I'm not sure your mom realizes it, but we have that house under near-constant surveillance."

With irony, Kirk realized that he was treating Rose as if she could manage to carry the weight of that unsettling information—information that he didn't trust Marcy herself to handle. There was a sense of age in Rose's eyes, an attitude of responsibility.

"Then I'll do everything I can to help you," she said, adding to the impression.

"Well, I know we asked you a thousand questions back in Summerlin, but I figure you've had time to settle your mind a bit. I need you to think—in the weeks before the murder, did you ever take a phone call from anyone who sounded suspicious?"

Rose thought about it. "Jack used his cell phone most of the time, but reception in that big old house was spotty. He did get occasional calls on the land-line phone—almost always from men," she said, trailing off. She let her mind roam. "He always went into the study and closed the door to talk. One time I didn't realize he was on the phone, and I picked up the upstairs extension. I remember thinking that the man he was talking with must be pressuring him about something. I haven't really thought about it since."

Kirk leaned forward. "Do you remember any part of the conversation?"

"A little. The connection was static-y and we were having a storm, so I thought he might not notice if I kept the phone off the hook for a second or two." She sat still, thinking. "He was talking about a boat. I figured it must have been one of the yachtsmen—maybe one of his customers coming in for a fitting. But they kept referring to some type of tool—a crimper. I remember because I looked up the word later. The man who called said they had found a pneumatic crimper that was precise and wouldn't damage the face."

"Face of what?" Kirk asked.

"I don't know," Rose said. "I hung up during a clap of thunder—didn't want him to know I was eavesdropping."

"Was that the only time you heard the man's voice on the phone?"

"I think so."

"Any other callers?"

"Somebody called on one of the days I followed Jack—just before the shooting. He answered his cell phone at the dinner table, which was unusual. The volume must have been turned way up, because I could hear."

"What did the caller say?"

"He said, 'I'm on the way. Everything ready?'"

"What did Jack say?"

"He said, 'It's ready.' Then he told Mom that one of his customers had ordered an entire wardrobe for a cruise and that he had to go to the shop to make up the bill."

Kirk looked thoughtfully at Rose. "But you didn't see Jack with anybody that night?"

"No, I followed him for the next two afternoons, but it wasn't until the third day that the blond guy showed up in the driveway."

"Which was on the day before the shooting," Kirk prompted.

"Right."

"Rose," Kirk said, "tell me everything you ever overheard Jack say about blazer buttons."

"I'll try," she said quietly. "Why, Kirk? Do you think the guy was after valuable buttons? Gold or silver buttons, maybe?"

"Not likely," Kirk said, "but always possible. Buttons are legal commodities. It's not like you have to smuggle 'em—unless they're stolen. It's just that we found probably two hundred buttons thrown around the workshop. I'll run some computer searches to see if there've been any ultra-valuable, top-of-the-line buttons stolen, but"—he grinned—"I kinda doubt it."

Rose accepted the grin as a friendly invitation to take her time, relax, and think. They sat in silence for several minutes.

"Jack had books about buttons," Rose offered. "He always said that a man could take a cheaper jacket and change the buttons and add about five hundred dollars to the value."

Kirk snorted. "I'll have to recycle a few of my old ones from high school."

"Jack knew all kinds of obscure things about clothes. He showed Mom one time how to hold the lapel of a jacket between her fingers and rub her fingers together to tell whether the interfacing had been sewn in by hand or whether it was heat-fused by the manufacturer."

"What difference would that make?"

"Well, he said that in a quality jacket, the interfacing would've been put in by hand. The lapel would lie flat for years. The heat-fused kind would eventually roll up and pucker the lapel. No self-respecting millionaire wants puckered lapels, apparently."

"No kidding!" roared Kirk, with a combustible laugh that carried down the hall.

"And collars—that was something else. He said the underside of a jacket collar was important in determining the quality of a jacket. Wool—that was what you wanted, not felt."

"Okay," said Kirk. "Jack had champagne tastes. Now, what was he involved in that would make a thirty-six-year-old spiky-haired blond guy shoot him in May, lie low for a few weeks, then come back to town and tear up everything Jack had anything to do with?"

Rose shrugged helplessly.

"My thoughts exactly," Kirk said. "Let me show you some pictures of the garage, since the vandals seemed to have spent more time there than anywhere else." He spread a dozen color photos over the desk, each labeled with an evidence number and bearing the stamp of the Summerlin Police Department.

Rose studied the photos. "He had a lot of books, didn't he?" She held one picture closer. "That's Papa's book! I've seen him spend hours and hours studying that book." She felt anger rising inside her at the thought of Jack coolly appropriating her grandfather's library.

"What book is it?" Kirk asked, craning his thick neck toward the picture.

"*American Numismatist*," answered Rose, pointing to a shot of a large, coffee-table type volume lying on a counter strewn with debris. "Lots of color close-ups of valuable coins. Papa pored over that book. Said he had picked up several nice old coins over the years because of it. He was always studying that book. He said that one day he might run across one of those really rare coins, and he wanted to be able to recognize it when he did."

Rose had little more to add as she looked through the photos and answered Kirk's last few questions. At the end of an hour, the detective stood and offered Rose a ride home. Letting her out in the Coles' driveway, he said, "You know where we are if you need us. We'll come to you anytime you need help." He handed her his business card after jotting down his personal cell phone number on the back.

"Thanks," she said, smiling. "Will you please keep a close eye on my mom?"

"You have my word," Kirk said.

CHAPTER 20

At roughly the same hour that Rose was meeting with Kirk, Renee Bellamy opened the front door to Marcy, pulled her inside, and quickly closed the door. Marcy stood awkwardly, at a loss for words.

Renee reached out to touch her arm. "Marcy, I can't believe you're actually standing here! You've been on my mind so much the past couple of days, and to get a call from you last night meant the world to me!"

"It did?" Marcy asked, conscious of the bags under her eyes—testimony to a near-sleepless night. As embarrassing as it was to have Renee see her looking so awful, Marcy was disarmed by her former friend's statement. "You've…you've been thinking about me?" she asked in a near-whisper.

"Almost constantly. Oh, Marcy, I'm so sorry for all you've been going through."

Marcy felt her cheeks burn. "Go ahead, Renee. Say it: 'You idiot, what in the world were you thinking?' You tried to tell me he would bring me absolutely no good."

Renee protested, "That wasn't what I wanted to say at all. Can I please have a hug?"

Disbelief covered Marcy's features. "Just like that? A hug? How can you let it go? I've hurt you time and again by ignoring you, for no other reasons than anger and…and jealousy! You aren't even going to say, 'I told you so?'"

"Marcy," Renee repeated quietly, "can I please have a hug?"

Marcy stared at her friend's face. There was no malice there, only a softness, a hopefulness, a need. "Oh, Renee," she said, reaching out with both arms. Marcy murmured into her friend's hair, "I'm so sorry. Lately, that's my standard line. I'm just full of regret."

Renee propelled Marcy out of the foyer and into the den, where a pair of wing-back chairs flanked the window overlooking the street.

"Marcy," she said firmly, "I loved you before; I love you now. I couldn't always understand your choices, but I never stopped loving you or praying for you. You can't know how good that hug felt! You have *always* been my best friend. We were together almost from the beginning, remember?"

Renee's comments brought a fresh flow of tears from Marcy. "I do remember. That's all I did for years—remember. I still don't understand why God broke up the foursome," she whispered. The old ache in Marcy's heart was once again real. "You know, the very fact that life was so good seemed to make the hurt go even deeper. I think maybe that was my biggest problem. Daniel and I had such plans. More children, family vacations, even mission trips. Just to enjoy life together. You and Tommy were always part of it. We felt… whole…when we were with you.

"Then, when everything changed, I took the wrong road—several of them, actually. Oh, Renee, I've been angry at God for so long. And I was jealous of you, even when I went to church. Knowing that you still had Tommy and I would never have Daniel again was really hard. We were all supposed to be together." Marcy uttered the last sentence between clenched teeth.

But even as she spoke, she could feel the resentment dying away. It had been good to say those things, but even as the words spilled out, Marcy could feel the death of them. In the place of bitterness, she could hear the words which she had read and reread the night before from the thirtieth verse of Psalm 18: "As for God, His way is perfect."

"Marcy, let's start again," Renee said softly. "I've never been able to find another friend like you. I guess, secretly, I've been comparing my other friendships with ours. Every one of those women is precious to me, but…I just can't find the same chemistry." Renee's words were like strong stitches closing a gaping hole in Marcy's heart.

Amazing! Marcy thought. *Renee still loves me. Every time I've seen her in the last ten years, she seemed surrounded by friends. I thought she was perfectly fine without me.*

Two hours later they emerged from the den, having hit the bottom of the tissue box that Renee had wisely pulled out of her van. Marcy had told Renee everything, including the terrible truth about Jack and Rose. Renee, she realized, had immediately ducked her head and closed her eyes, praying, she later explained, for the ability to forgive a dead man.

But Marcy also went on to describe the incredible morning in the Myrtle Beach chapel, when God had taken her to the very end of herself and then—as Marcy explained it—"offered me himself instead."

Marcy thought she would never forget the look of joy and delight that infused Renee's face.

Marcy described the mental battle she had endured the previous night, aware of an intense inner insistence that she call Renee, but too embarrassed to follow through. "It was the strangest thing," she observed. "The more I fought the suggestion, the less clearly I was able to think. The phone was ringing every fifteen minutes—down to the second—but no one would leave a message on the answering machine, and I was too afraid to answer—oh, Renee, it was eerie. I got really frightened."

"I think I understand," answered Renee softly. "You've just experienced a facet of a God so personal that He's right there inside you—right inside your heart and mind. He really will lead you, Marcy, to do the right thing. And he can take every single event that comes into our lives and use it for something good. But when we resist him, even in a very little thing, confusion sets in, and that great sense of peace goes away. It's really like a warning system. When you're in step with God, you have peace of mind. When you fall out of step, when you disobey him, you usually miss that sense of peace so much that you hurry back to the place of obedience. It's beautiful, when you think about it."

Marcy nodded thoughtfully. "It is. It really is." After accepting a dinner invitation for the following night, she reluctantly opened Renee's front door. They walked out to the car together.

"Renee," Marcy concluded as they stood in the driveway, "the church and the youth group were really important to Rose. All those years, when I had given up, and when Mr. and Mrs. Kendall were gone, you—the church—continued to function as her family. I can't let the church think that Rose is responsible for this pregnancy. I can't let her reputation be ruined when the fault is mine. That's too monstrous a lie."

"What are you suggesting, Marcy?"

Marcy gulped for air as if it had become scarce. "It makes me feel faint to say it," she finally murmured. "But I want to speak to the church."

CHAPTER 21

Lindsay Fullerton arrived ten minutes early for her Tuesday afternoon showing but wasn't surprised to find a small SUV already parked at the curb in front of her newest listing. She waved at a city policeman who cruised slowly down the block, then walked toward the husky, dark-haired man in his early thirties who emerged from behind his car's tinted glass windows. "Vince Miller," he said, without offering to shake hands, and actually preceded Lindsay up the walkway before she could hand him her card.

As Lindsay pulled out the spare key that Marcy had relinquished the day before, she sized up this new client as much by intuition as by the scant replies he had provided on the phone the night before. He seemed wound tightly.

"What was it about this house that caught your eye," she asked lightly, "besides the fact that it's huge and beautiful?"

"Near the water," he grunted.

"Sure is," Lindsay said, opening the deadbolt with the same key. "Only a few blocks. Do you live near the water now?"

"Not far."

Lindsay pushed open the front door and had the impression that sheer willpower held back the man from running her over. "This home was built in 1901," she began, and realized her client was already making a circuit of the downstairs.

Okay, Mr. Vince Miller, she thought. *I guess you're the one who's going to show this house.*

For a man who had insisted on an immediate showing, saying that he was prepared to offer cash, Vince didn't seem to be interested in woodwork, windows, ceilings, or flooring. He was unusually interested in closets—of which there were few—and certain pieces of furniture. He also studied the view of the yard from different windows of each room.

"Furniture come with the house?" he asked brusquely.

"I can ask," Lindsay said. "I know the owner is planning an estate sale soon. But she—they—probably aren't planning to sell everything."

She watched the man's eyebrows rise abruptly over the rim of the sunglasses he had never removed.

He spent no more than five minutes downstairs, most of that in Mr. Kendall's old office, where he inspected the cluttered work surface of the roll-top desk.

Then, without asking, he headed up the stairs, and Lindsay noticed that, as most clients would, he stopped briefly to study the portraits that lined the stairwell. "Who lives here?" he asked, and Lindsay felt a mental flag go up.

"Oh, they're one of the oldest families in Summerlin," she answered truthfully but evasively. At the top of the stairs, the man cast his gaze in a circle.

"This is the master bedroom," Lindsay pointed out and watched her client give it a perfunctory tour, running his hand over the carving above the old brick fireplace. He opened the closet to reveal a rack of dresses, tops, and skirts.

"Second bedroom," the agent said next. Her client made a ten-second inspection of the pale green room with a study desk opposite an antique canopy bed.

"Playroom." Another ten seconds. If this guy was interested, he wasn't showing it, Lindsay thought.

At the end of the hall, beyond the playroom, was a fourth room, nicely furnished in dark woods. When the man had spent an extra twenty seconds giving it the once-over, he suddenly asked, "What about Internet access?"

"Internet..." Lindsay hesitated. "You know, that's something the owner and I haven't discussed yet. I'll be glad to ask."

"You got a laptop?" the man interrupted.

"I do."

"In your car?"

Again, Lindsay nodded.

"Wired or wireless?"

"Both."

"Let's get it, see what kind of signal we get," the man said, then suddenly halted his trip down the stairwell. "I gotta use the restroom. I'll meet you downstairs when you get your machine."

Lindsay felt as if the reins of the showing had shifted entirely to this curt stranger. She started to protest, but he had already closed the bathroom door.

"Well," she said to herself, and walked rapidly down the stairs and out the front door, unlocked her trunk, and picked up the laptop. Back inside she looked up the stairs and noticed immediately that the door at the top was closed. *Must have been a draft when I opened the front door,* she thought. She climbed the stairs and, trying the doorknob, realized it was jammed.

She pushed, pulled, rotated the knob several times. "Mr. Miller?" she called through a crack in the door frame. No answer.

Lindsay waited a second and pushed again. "Sir?"

More emphatically. "Mr. Miller. Where are you, sir?" She repeated herself three or four more times and was just pulling out her cell phone to call her office when she heard footsteps coming from what sounded like the opposite end of the hall.

She heard a scraping sound, then rejoiced to see the door swing open. "Sorry," he said. "I was checking a crack in a windowsill. Heard this door slam almost as soon as you went downstairs."

He brushed past her and led the way back down to Mr. Kendall's office, where he reached for Lindsay's laptop. This time, at least, she was determined to regain control. "I'll turn it on," she said firmly. During the minute or two it took to boot up, Vince opened and closed several drawers of the desk before finally heeding Lindsay's request not to do so.

She was almost relieved to discover that there was no sign of a wireless signal, and that the phone jack was just that—there was no dial-up connection. Vince Miller didn't seem overly concerned.

"I want to make a cash offer," he said, shocking her nearly speechless. "Full price. The furniture too. You'll hear from my banker within a week."

"That's great," Lindsay sputtered. "I'm…delighted! This is a wonderful old house you're getting. What kind of deposit would you like to make? To hold it, I mean."

"My bank'll send you a cashier's check," he said. "Ten thousand?"

She nodded, dazed.

"Two days. Where's your office?"

"Three blocks south. Same street. Here—the address is on my card."

"All right," he said and walked out the door to his car.

"When should we expect you?" Lindsay called after him, but he slid behind the wheel with only a nod.

Marcy was rattled. Lindsay had just warned her that a full-price cash contract was on the way. Would the old house stand up to a home inspection? Within two days, a carpenter, a plumber, and an electrician had come and gone, making small but necessary repairs. Not knowing what she would keep and what she would let go, Marcy packed up nearly the entire kitchen, labeling the boxes in detail and leaving them lined up neatly in the butler's pantry.

It was, she concluded, the worst packing job in the house—so many small items, so many pieces that could break.

From the back of the cupboards, she pulled a delicate collection of green Depression glass that must have been Daniel's great-grandmother's. It was covered in a thin film of dust that clung and smudged and refused to wipe off without a fight. Marcy hadn't even known the glassware was there. A rustic oak pie safe held a collection of cut crystal, ranging from pickle dishes to lemonade pitchers. Marcy could clearly remember her mother-in-law serving cranberry sauce from one particular shallow dish. Now its crystal facets wore their own tenacious layer of dust. It felt almost oily to the touch. And the silverware—it had tarnished from the salty, coastal air, which had penetrated even the sectioned wooden drawers.

Marcy knew she would never "play house" in the genteel Southern style that her mother-in-law had practiced before Summerlin grew too large to entertain everyone in town. She would not keep these lovely things, but some collector would buy them and subsidize Rose's bachelor's degree.

Constantly playing behind her thoughts was the fact that she had asked to speak before the church. At certain points, it was all she could do to keep from calling Renee and backing out.

It was 4:30 on Friday afternoon when the phone rang in the detectives' quarters.

"Kirk," said the edgy voice on the phone, "this is Lindsay Fullerton with Coastal Plus Realty. How are you?"

"Pretty great. Knee-deep, as usual. How 'bout you?"

"Feeling stupid," said Lindsay. "Had. Taken. Used."

"That's not the usual you," the detective laughed. "What happened?"

Lindsay sighed forcibly. "I thought I had the biggest, quickest, weirdest sale of my nearly nine-year career in real estate. The Kendalls' house."

"Oh yeah?" Kirk sat up straight. "Tell me."

"Long version or short?"

"Short. It's Friday."

"Okay. Listen to this. I stick a For Sale sign in their yard on Monday afternoon and two hours later get a phone call from a guy who insists he's absolutely got to see the house the very next day. He barely looks at the house and then asks me to get my laptop out of the car to check Internet access. I'm ninety-five percent certain that, while I was being so obliging, he was jamming the stairwell door closed so I couldn't get back upstairs. Claimed the draft from the front door did it. He finally opened up, went downstairs, got no wireless Internet signal whatsoever, no dial-up, nothing...then tells me he wants to make an offer! Cash! Says within two days I'll get a ten thousand dollar deposit in the form of a cashier's check from his bank. Of course, I camp out at the office, but the check never comes. I haven't heard from the guy since. Naturally he doesn't answer my calls."

"Whoa, Lindsay, you've been cut to the quick!"

"Deeper than that, Kirk! Cut to the heart! And I don't have any real reason to report this, except that it just feels...all wrong."

"Well, it's good you called me. You at the office?"

"Yes."

"Good," said the detective. "I'm coming over for the long version."

CHAPTER 22

It was Sunday morning, and Marcy's clammy hands and erratic heartbeat were indicative of her stress level. Simply driving to the church had taken all of her energy. She actually felt faint.

Renee embraced her at the door and with eyes shining, led her, not to a seat in the back, but straight down to the second row on the right. The walk together was the culmination of five days of forgiveness covering fourteen years. Marcy was deeply comfortable with Renee. The other 120 worshippers unnerved her.

Sensing Marcy's extreme anxiety, Renee handed her a stack of fresh tissue. "You're doing great!" she mouthed. Marcy's look revealed that she was quaking inside.

Despite the anxiety, Marcy also felt a faint undercurrent of excitement as she sat, head bowed, praying once again for the right words. She had given up trying to script her message. Instead, she would trust God to give her the right words to say. A growing sense of joy overflowed toward Renee and her husband, Tommy, who had thrown open his own front door and wrapped her in a joyful hug of welcome on Wednesday night when Marcy arrived for dinner. Tommy had wholeheartedly encouraged her in this decision to speak to the church.

Still, she trembled. Maybe she was going about this all wrong. Maybe it was too soon. This was going to be worse than embarrassing. Just a shake of her head and she knew Tommy would let her off the hook. He had said so.

From the pulpit, Tommy led the congregation through the welcome, the morning announcements, the opening hymn, and a heartfelt prayer. Marcy knew where she fit into the order of the service, and at the very moment of wavering felt Renee squeeze her hand.

Marcy stood up on trembling legs. Tommy made eye contact, and now he announced simply, "There's someone here who wants to speak to us."

Marcy could hear the soft intake of breath over the congregation as she stood. For a moment there was dead silence. Inside, Marcy sent up a quick "Please, God!" And then she stepped to the front and turned around to face the faces.

"Most of you know me." She gave a sad smile. "And the rest of you know about me. My name is Marcy Kendall. I grew up here in Summerlin and I married a member of this church, Daniel Kendall. We were very happy together.

"But about fourteen years ago, Daniel died from a very aggressive form of cancer, and I became angry and bitter inside. I pushed nearly everyone away—and I withdrew from any real involvement with the church. All those years, I've been like a...a broken reed, I think the Bible calls it. I lived as if I were shut up in a box, blaming God. Daniel's parents took care of me and my daughter, Rose. But Mama Kendall died, and then Papa Kendall did too.

"Then, just over a year and a half ago, I met a man named Jack Bradford and thought I had come alive again. I made some choices that were morally wrong. And I let Jack move in with us, even though I knew better.

"Some of you were courageous enough to confront me about my choices. All I can say is that you were right and I was wrong. And I am paying the consequences.

"Worst of all..." Marcy realized she was perspiring. Her voice trembled and broke. "My daughter is also paying the consequences. I'm sure you know the facts: Jack Bradford was shot dead behind his shop. Rose was questioned in his murder but cleared. But while she was being detained, a test came back showing that she was pregnant.

"What I want you to know," said Marcy, struggling vainly for composure, "is that Rose did not turn her back on all your teaching and training and love. I did," she quavered, "but not Rose. Rose is not pregnant because of any moral failing on her part, but because I foolishly, stupidly, willfully put her under the same roof with a man who took the worst kind of advantage of her."

Marcy could hear stifled sobs around the room. She struggled to see through her own pool of tears. "You may be wondering why Rose didn't go to anyone for help. I believe I know the answer: she was protecting me.

"You may also be asking who killed Jack and why. I don't know the answers to those questions. I wish I did. The police are still investigating." Here, she made brief eye contact with Kirk Landry, who was sitting near the door, smiling his encouragement but clenching and unclenching his fists.

"I do know that Rose had learned that Jack was involved in something illegal. She had made up her mind that she could protect me and get him out of our lives by turning him in to the police. She never dreamed the situation would turn deadly. And so, when Rose was being questioned by the police, I accused her of ruining my life, not realizing that all the while, she was trying her best to take care of me.

"I learned the truth only when I found a journal Rose had started for her English class—and later kept for herself.

"I'm here today to beg your forgiveness for all of my rudeness, for the distance that I've put between me and my church family. Let me say this plainly: I sinned, and I am desperately sorry. I've asked for God's forgiveness, and now I'm asking for yours.

"It looks as if I'll soon be moving away to be with Rose. We think we have an offer on the house." There was a murmur around the building. "Rose is doing well, and she's made up her mind to put this baby up for adoption. I'm so proud of her, and I know that much of the credit for her courageous decision goes to you and the teaching you've given her through the years. I know that several of you here taught Rose in Sunday school and in high school, as well"—Marcy caught the nod of her daughter's favorite English teacher—"and I want you to know she hopes to continue her education after the baby is born in January.

"I've wasted so many years." Marcy's voice dropped a moment, and she shook her head as if mystified.

"Please pray for us. I have so much to do to win back Rose's trust, not to mention yours. Anyway, I didn't want to leave Summerlin without making some attempt to tell you that God is faithful. He's made his forgiveness so very, very clear to me. Thank you for loving us and never giving up."

It was an hour and half before Marcy could break away from the surge of both old friends and perfect strangers who surrounded her after the church service. In a state of physical exhaustion but emotional peace, she pulled into the driveway of the house she had lived in for so many years. She fell across the couch, still in her church clothes, and slept until dusk.

CHAPTER 23

Melinda Berry sat in her comfortable "prayer chair" chewing her bottom lip, gazing through the sunroom windows at the pink and orange cloudbank that seemed to rise up out of the lake as the sun made its way over the horizon. Once again this morning, Rose Kendall had landed right in the middle of her thoughts—and stayed there. Melinda's journal lay open to her prayer list, and every time she looked at it, a sense of amazement came over her, an amazed sense of having been used by the Lord of the universe to accomplish what he was best at—reconciliation.

It was Melinda who had given Rose the journal to which Marcy had referred in church the morning before. The veteran teacher clearly remembered finding the little books in the local dollar store, each cover slightly different from the next, looking as if someone had skimmed a sheet of thick wax paper over a pan of floating oil paint. The effect was a textured, paisley-like swirl. Between each journal's covers were stitched sixty-four pages of lined white paper. Struck by the fact that there were exactly sixteen books—no more, no fewer—Melinda had impulsively gathered up every one. There was one for each senior in her Honors English class and one for herself, perfect for their study of *The Courtship of Madame Winthrop*, a collection of excerpts from an eighteenth-century diary. From there, they would consider the daily diary entries of Thomas Jefferson, then the all-too-poignant notations of Anne Frank, and finally the diaries of Colonel William Lamb, the Confederate commander of nearby Fort Fisher.

Like every other English teacher in America, she supposed, Melinda was searching for a way to inspire her students to write often. Twice during the first semester she had asked the seniors to bring their journals to school and read aloud to the class.

Melinda laughed as she remembered several of the boys who had clearly used her gift as an assignment book and then—under the pressure of her own assignment—dutifully recorded how much they'd spent on the previous weekend's date—right down to the price of a pack of disposable razors. Well, she thought, Madame Winthrop's suitor had done much the same.

Several of the girls had used the journals to try their hand at poetry, and some of it, Melinda noted, wasn't half bad. *Some* of it. A couple of students, with the dutiful attitude that made them A-chasers, had created what Melinda dubbed "A Day in the Life of Me" essays: "Alarm clock goes off at 6 a.m. Hit snooze alarm. Alarm goes off at 6:09. Hit snooze again" and on and on. But two of the journals had shown real promise. Those were the ones that combined a recounting of some personally significant moment with an analysis of that moment. And one of those journals belonged to Rose Kendall.

Of course it did. Melinda played no favorites in class, but in private, she had known that Rose would win the Senior English Award hands-down. Rose was the kind of student whose objective tests were graded first and whose analytical essays were graded last—tests first, because an English teacher could quickly use Rose's tests to judge how thoroughly she herself had covered a subject. If Rose didn't know an answer, chances were that no other student knew the answer either, and Melinda would steel herself to throw out that question when she calculated the test grade. Rose's analytical essays were graded last because (Melinda would never admit this out loud) she needed the incentive to keep plowing through the more predictable offerings. Rose's were never predictable. But they were always wonderful, something to look forward to, the best that was saved for last.

Melinda had noticed this gift before in teens who had endured great losses, particularly the loss of a parent. These students seemed to see deeper, feel deeper, write deeper. In a sense, she knew, Rose had lost two parents—her father to death and her mother to grief. Then the elder Kendalls had died within two years of one another. To reflect on such losses in a journal would have been natural, but if Rose chose to do so, she kept it to herself, focusing instead on brief, humorous character sketches—so intricately detailed that Melinda broke her own rule and tried to figure out the true identity of the subjects.

Rose *intrigued* Melinda, she realized. Always had—ever since the ninth-grade autobiographical sketch in which Rose revealed that she mentally amused herself by isolating words and grammatically dissecting them. How many other solid first basemen were tagging out runners while lecturing themselves: *Potential base-hit. Compound noun preceded by an adjective*?

And now, Melinda realized, Rose had continued to use her journal, recording moments of such personal significance—such honest analysis, such uncensored personal reaction, in such vivid vocabulary—that in reading it, Marcy Kendall had awakened from fourteen years of virtual sleepwalking to see that she had subjected her only child to unimaginable neglect. And in the sovereignty of God, that tortured mother set out to find her tortured child—and did find her, along with one much greater. Melinda Berry crossed her arms across her stomach and squeezed, as if to contain the elation that seemed to bubble up within her. Melinda knew a turning point when she saw one.

Yet, despite her elation, she felt perplexed. Why was she unable to tear her thoughts away from Rose? "Lord, what do you want from me?" she prayed. "I feel such a need to *do* something. Is it something in particular, or shall I just keep praying for Rose's protection? I certainly don't understand your ways. I don't know why she's had to suffer to this extent. But I have to trust you. Should I call her?" Melinda sat quietly, asking, until she felt a firm conviction growing. Yes, a phone call. Not to Rose. To someone else.

CHAPTER 24

Cleaning cloths and spray bottles in hand, Marcy looked up at the beautiful antique stairway. Daniel's great-great-grandparents had built the house. Daniel had grown up here. So had Rose. And now, because of Marcy, this beautiful house was about to pass out of the family. *Shameful,* she thought. *Look what I've cost us.* But there was no way around it. Rose had made it clear that she never wanted to spend a night in this house again.

Marcy was avoiding the telephone, which rang at least hourly with another warm message from a member of the church. Tears standing in her eyes, Marcy listened gratefully to every recorded message, but she was emotionally worn out from the day before. She needed to clean. Renee had offered to help, but Marcy had begged off until Tuesday. She needed some time alone.

Marcy could understand Rose's refusal to come home. After the death of her own father, she, her mom, and Jesse had gone back home only once, to pack up their belongings. Reentering their old house had been terrifying. Despite the head-knowledge that her father was dead and buried, Marcy had half dreaded and half longed for his footfall every moment they'd spent inside. Her bedroom, which had once felt like her own little haven, brought back a strange mixture of tender and ugly scenes. Yet some form of closure, some sense of finality, had settled over her during that visit. Rose needed to come home too, Marcy thought, to see the house one last time, now that Jack could never come back. Maybe then they could talk about Marcy's past and be done with it, once and for all.

Behold, I make all things new. Marcy smiled as she recognized that she was not alone.

It was time to call Rose again. Marcy would wait until bedtime.

"What's wrong?" Savannah asked her friend, who had just hung up the phone and was sitting quietly on the bed in the dark. The absent expression on her face was visible in the dim glow from the bathroom nightlight.

"I'm not sure. Nothing physical. Just feeling emotional, I guess. I'm kind of hurting since Mom is gone. But it's good to talk with her on the phone. She's called me every day since she left. It's never more than three or four minutes that we talk. But it's good."

"It's hard to believe how much has changed in a little over a week, Rose," Savannah replied. "It's a good thing that you're missing her."

"I know, Savannah. I feel so good about how we talked, and for the first time in years, I sense that…if I fell, she might catch me. I feel her support, but I keep thinking—what if some other guy spots her as an easy target? Jack had her completely taken in. Nobody could open her eyes."

"God did," Savannah reminded her gently. "God is in control of all things. I don't begin to understand his timing, but I know he's working things out for the best."

But Rose was fighting on the battleground of feelings, and for the moment, she needed to air them out.

"You know, in one way—that I'm kind of embarrassed to admit—it was actually easier knowing that Mom was up in Summerlin, with the past. Now she's part of the future. I'd gotten used to not having to feel responsible for her. She kind of complicates things, Savannah."

"How do you feel about the time you spent with her while she was here?"

"I was amazed. I really liked her. I know I've always loved her, but this time, we enjoyed being together. I felt her support. It hasn't been that way for a long time. It actually felt like...she was the mom, and I was the daughter."

Savannah smiled. "Just think of the range of emotions she's feeling now. She went to church, God spoke to her heart, she found you, and now she has to go home and get ready to put your beautiful old house on the market. Plus deal with a police investigation. I imagine she's really missing you."

"I just don't know if I can really trust her, Savannah. This is all too fast. I mean, one day my mom is so fragile she scarcely leaves the house, the next she has a live-in boyfriend who can do no wrong. She tells me off, refuses to believe that I'm innocent of a heinous crime, and leaves me in police custody. A few weeks later, she says she's made peace with God and wants to move in with me and take care of me."

"Well, I admit, she does sound changeable. But the last part of the story—the making peace with God—can't be just your mom's invention. Remember, God sent my mom straight to her. I still think we've all seen a miracle."

"I want to believe it, Savannah," Rose said. "It's just that... the temptation to hold her at arm's length for a little while is really strong."

"Rose, if you don't give your mom the opportunity to actually be a mom, you may interfere with your own ability to be a good mother someday." Savannah laughed at the expression on Rose's face. "Yes, you, Miss Responsibility. Sounds like a category in the Miss America pageant. But I had to do a sociology paper on family relationships and the patterns they take. You wouldn't believe the number of studies showing that children imitate even the behaviors they dislike in their parents."

"You think I would ever do to my child what my mom did to me?" Rose could hear resentment in her own voice.

"Well, I'm paraphrasing, but I think Scripture says that the people who think they're standing firm need to be careful, because they're the very ones who might fall."

"Oh, Savannah." Rose sighed. "I keep trying to forgive her, but it seems like the hateful feelings come back."

Savannah opened her mouth and then shut it again, lifting her shoulders in a gesture that seemed to say, "Who can explain the heart?" She walked over to the bed and sat down. "Joe, the youth pastor, says forgiveness is an ongoing process. Even after you think you've totally forgiven her, there'll probably be days when you wake up with those old feelings. Maybe when that happens, you can tell God you really want to forgive your mom—that you don't *feel* like it, but because you want to obey him, you've made up your mind to do it. Then ask him to forgive her *through* you."

"You make it sound simple, but it's hard to do."

"God is big, Rose. The more often we hand those feelings over to him, the easier it gets. Wouldn't you like to call your mom back and tell her you love her? My cell phone is right there."

"Thanks. Maybe I will. By the time this is over and I move on, I'll owe you a fortune. How can I thank you?"

"I'll know exactly who to call when the time comes," Savannah said, handing Rose the phone. She looked at her watch and exclaimed, "It's ten o'clock! I'm going to hit the shower and then study some more. Will the light bother you?"

"Never. You know I'm out in no time. I have to get plenty of sleep; that way I'm nicer to the customers. I'll be up at my usual four thirty."

"I'm glad you're here, Rose. I needed a friend too," Savannah replied quietly as she padded barefoot into the bathroom and closed the door.

CHAPTER 25

Kirk Landry was a praying man. All weekend long, he had prayed for insight—for some fresh way to look at the Jack Bradford case, to draw a slipknot around all the hundreds of clues and questions, to see how one was tied to another. Marcy's confession in church on Sunday had done nothing but increase the pressure he felt to dispose of this case, if only for her sake.

After talking with Rose, Kirk was more and more convinced that Jack had been involved in a smuggling or fencing operation—perhaps several. But what were the goods? Nothing whatsoever pointed to drugs or any of the other usual vices.

Kirk kept going back to the vandalism at The Suitable, chewing over the evidence piece by piece. If he could just figure out what the vandals were after, surely it would lead him to the gunman.

His primary goal was to apprehend the man who had shot and killed a prominent businessman in the very heart of the historic district. That, he assumed, would help him close a number of other open files: the break-in at The Suitable, the vandalism of Jack's impounded car, the forced entry into his cabin cruiser. The footprints under Marcy's windows, perhaps.

It galled him to think that a broad-daylight killer could be at large in the familiar streets of Summerlin. At the very least, Kirk thought, he should have some clue about a motive. But what?

On this bright blue Tuesday morning, Kirk longed to stay outside where the air had a salty tang, but he knew where he had to go: the evidence room.

Kirk himself had assisted Evidence Clerk Mary Anne Shealey as she catalogued the items impounded as part of the murder investigation. This morning, Mary Anne was already on her second cup of black coffee when Kirk rounded the corner into her office and held out a cream cheese Danish fresh from the deli-bakery down the block.

"M-m-mm," said Mary Anne, accepting the Danish with a twinkle in her brown eyes. "A research project you're getting me fueled up for?"

"Yeah," said Kirk. "Jack Bradford. I'm stumped." He pulled a second Danish out of his deli bag and settled into the chair facing Mary Anne's desk. "I've followed up on no fewer than twenty-five rabbit trails in this case. Three or four leads seem vaguely promising. But I've got a strong feeling we missed something when we catalogued all the evidence. Can you pull up the manifest for me?"

Within seconds, the clerk summoned a series of files on her flat-screened computer monitor. "Which site are you interested in? The Suitable? Bradford's garage? His house? His boat? The car?"

"Give me all of them," Kirk said with more energy than he felt. When the list was finally printed, the detective rammed a staple through sixteen pages of fine print, then stapled them again for good measure.

"Okay," he said, "I'll try not to illustrate these with coffee stains. Anybody in the chief's conference room?"

"It's all yours," Mary Anne said with a magnanimous sweep of her hand. "Let me know if you need access to the physical evidence."

"Hope I do," said Kirk, settling in for a lengthy read.

Ninety minutes later, the detective was sitting straight up in his leather chair, gently tapping the bridge of his nose with the eraser of a number two pencil—a habit left over from high school. Kirk was trying to trap an elusive thought. Back when Jack Bradford had been classified as a murder victim, the detective had looked at the evidence with one mind-set: the collection of physical evidence that might help him identify the killer. Now that Bradford was posthumously implicated as a conspirator, a perpetrator himself, Kirk had to view the crime scene differently. What had he and the other detectives missed the first time around?

As Kirk saw it, there were four big, unanswered questions in this case. First, why was Bradford meeting with Anton Johnson? Second, what was in the manila-colored pouch that Rose had seen under Johnson's arm as he ran from the murder scene? Third, had Johnson personally committed the most recent spate of break-ins, or had he sent in someone else? And finally, what were the intruders looking for? What?

Kirk had a feeling that answering the fourth question might answer the other three.

He looked back over the sixteen-page manifest. It outlined not only the items impounded from the crime scenes, but also those items left on the premises and checked for fingerprints—an exercise in futility, since Jack's were the only prints that consistently turned up in any two locations. The state forensics unit had sent in an investigator who'd swept the sites for hair, blood and fabric samples, but it might be six months before the state's backlogged lab issued even a preliminary report.

No, this didn't seem like a forensics case—yet. Maybe later. For now, Kirk needed to figure out why Anton Johnson might risk coming back to Summerlin.

For the second time, he scanned the manifest. Rose had said Jack and his unidentified Southern-sounding caller were discussing blazer buttons. In the mish-mash of clothes scattered all over The Suitable, had there been anything unusual about the buttons? He struggled to remember, finally asking Mary Anne to locate the digital photos taken at the scene. Soon he was looking at seventy icon-sized shots of disfigured jackets, suit coats, and overcoats. He enlarged them all on the computer screen and then put them into slide-show mode, specifying a five-second interval. Now *here* was something! The suit coats and overcoats still wore their horn and wooden four-eyed buttons, but the sports coats were buttonless. He ran through the slide show again, this time more slowly, just to make sure. There was not a single metal button in the shots.

He closed the photo file and returned to the sheaf of pages that made up the manifest. Most of the vandalism, he knew, had taken place in two locations: inside The Suitable and in Jack's garage behind the yellow Victorian. The garage had been turned upside down. Every storage bin, box, and drawer had been pulled completely out of place, upended, and its contents splayed across the floor. That meant the vandal was looking for something relatively small—small enough to be stored in the smallest drawer.

Money was always an obvious target, though Jack didn't seem like a cash-on-hand kind of guy. So what about blazer buttons? Some seventy-five photos had been taken of the shop, and Kirk could spy a few metallic buttons amid the images. He isolated those photos on the computer screen and peered at them closely.

"Huh!" he exhaled, recognizing a discrepancy in the seemingly random remains of the vandalism spree. Rather than being strewn across the floor with the others, one group of blazer buttons was in a small plastic storage tub. Actually, he could see, there were two tubs. Side by side. The buttons inside seemed to be unassembled. In one box were the ornamental tops, their intricate crests molded into the metal, but they had no bottoms. The second plastic bin held what appeared to be brass shanks—the bottom halves—but no tops.

Kirk felt himself coming alive. He downed the dregs of his cold coffee, stood up, and stretched.

"Okay," he said loudly. "I'm comin' out with my hands up."

He stepped into the hallway and grinned at Mary Anne. "Aisle six, bin fourteen," he said.

CHAPTER 26

At 11:15 on that Tuesday morning, Rose signed the clipboard at Dr. Richardson's reception desk and looked for a vacant seat. There were two, and she had to make a quick choice. On one side was a hugely pregnant woman taking up almost two seats, leaving only a small space to squeeze into beside the wall. On the other side sat a young mom holding a newborn baby. The mom was cooing to the pink-clad infant in adoring tones.

Rose opted to squeeze. The pregnant lady almost scowled as she slid over as far as she could. Rose sympathized with the woman, but she knew she didn't want to sit so close to the baby girl. "Can I go through with this?" she asked herself. Every little murmur from the mother made her heart jump. "What will I feel every time I see a baby? On the other hand, why would I even consider holding a baby that was Jack's?" Rose commanded herself to think about the new patient form in front of her.

But within seconds, a nurse came to the door, calling, "Mrs. Randall?" The uncomfortable lady beside her stood and waddled through the doorway. Reality set in. As long as Rose didn't show, her situation could go unnoticed, but as soon as she got big, people were going to ask questions. How could she field those questions honestly? And would the questions always dredge up these desires? A glance in the direction of the newborn brought a yearning to hold her, yet the fact that she could be facing Jack in any form made Rose feel physically sick. "Lord," she prayed, "I'm having a hard time. I wish Mom were here, or Savannah."

Savannah slipped in the door just as Rose was called by the nurse. She stepped up beside Rose and asked the nurse if she could go in to wait with her friend.

The nurse looked disapproving but said, "That'll be okay. Wait outside while she gets her exam gown on."

Savannah nodded and told Rose she'd be in the hallway.

"Ready," called Rose after a few minutes, and Savannah followed the nurse into the room.

"I have a few questions, and then you can wait for Dr. Richardson to come in. The chart says this is a prenatal exam. Have you had a pregnancy test?"

"Yes, ma'am, two—both positive."

"The father…you don't have him listed?" the nurse asked cautiously.

"He's deceased," replied Rose with trepidation in her voice. Now the questions would start, bound to take her to the deepest levels of embarrassment.

"Oh, how awful!" The nurse looked up, compassion in her tone. She was ready to go on, but Savannah's expression stopped her in her tracks. "The doctor will be with you in a moment," she said, slipping out and closing the door behind her.

Rose exhaled so audibly that she was certain she could be heard in the next room. "Thank you, Savannah, for showing up just when I need you. How'd you know?"

"It just popped into my mind."

"Do you think the doctor will let you stay while we talk?"

"We'll see."

"I really hope so." A few moments of silence elapsed, and then Rose erupted. "It was terrible sitting out there in the waiting room. Sometimes I can almost push away the reason why I'm here. But today, I can't. Everything about this appointment is wrong. I shouldn't have to be here. I've been raped. I feel filthy. And now

I have to tell another perfect stranger about it." Savannah saw the panic rising in Rose's eyes.

"God is in control, Rose," she said soothingly. Just as tears started to trickle, the doctor tapped on the door and stepped in.

"Don't tell me you don't like me already!" he said with big eyes.

Rose had to smile as she wiped her face with the back of her hand. Dr. Richardson was disarming: boyish-looking even in his sixties, a warm smile lighting up his face.

"Allen Richardson," he said, extending his hand first to Rose and then to Savannah. "You are," he said to Savannah, "the friend I've heard about?"

"I suppose," she replied with a smile. "I'm Savannah Cole."

"It was good of you to come," he said simply. Both girls relaxed a little.

"So, my dear," he said to Rose, "let's talk a few minutes. Have you been examined since you found out you were pregnant?"

"No. I just took a couple of pregnancy tests." She choked.

"I know," the doctor interjected before she could say more. "Linda Cantrell filled me in—she told me about the man and the murder. Took me an hour to level out my blood pressure. So, Braveheart, how did you withstand what must've been a lot of pressure to end this pregnancy?"

Rose relaxed so visibly that both Savannah and the doctor smiled. "Well, I confess, there were days when it seemed like a sensible choice. But I have a picture in my mind of standing before God and being asked why I killed a baby. I begin offering God all the arguments. And he just looks at me and…that's enough. I've seen videos of abortions, Dr. Richardson."

The doctor sat quietly for a moment, then said, "So he's that real to you, Rose?"

She just nodded.

With a tone of respect, Dr. Richardson declared, "You know where you stand! Okay. How about your eating habits? Tell me how you're taking care of yourself."

"I try to stay balanced, but I know I wasn't at the beginning."

He ran down a clipboard full of questions on diet, exercise, and medical history, then looked at Rose keenly and said, "Remind me sometime to share with you just how I know God is in control. Let's get you up on the table, and we'll see how you and the little one are doing. Savannah," he said, "when you open the door, the nurse will come in. You can wait right outside."

"Thanks, Savannah," Rose said, following her friend with her eyes.

As the nurse entered, Rose shrank. This was repellent, repulsive, even more humiliating than she had foreseen, but the doctor continued in his easy tone, "Rose, let's talk while I do your exam."

"Okay," she said gratefully, her eyes glued to the ceiling.

"Did you get to graduate from high school?"

"I finished all my requirements. It was the last week of school when all the chaos took place. So I didn't attend graduation."

"What are your plans?" he asked again.

"Really, I don't have any yet…just to get through this and find the right people to adopt the baby. I had plans to major in literature in college, but I don't know now."

"Well, I'll help you all I can medically, and there's more help available, if you're willing to apply for it."

"I've been doing that."

"Good. I'll give you vitamins, and if we have other samples that you might need down the road, you can have those too." Rose winced as the doctor prodded.

"Are you working, Rose?" he asked, and she filled him in on her morning routine, glad for the distraction as Dr. Richardson pushed and prodded some more.

"Okay," he said at last, "Let's get you up and moving. Your due date is around December twentieth. On your next visit, which should be about two weeks from now, we'll take an ultrasound to verify. We'll also see if we can hear the baby's heartbeat. You know, some fortunate couple is going to have their prayers answered through you."

"I hope so. I really want the baby to have a happy life."

"I'll be praying about that," Dr. Richardson said, with a sincere look. "You'll have to have some blood drawn before you leave, and here's some literature to look over. If you have any questions, just write them down, and we'll take time to answer them."

The door opened, revealing Savannah sitting in full view. The nurse, more sympathetic than the first, beckoned to Savannah as she wrapped an elastic band around Rose's arm and prepared the needle.

"Where would you like to go for a snack?" Savannah asked in a blatant attempt to distract her. "Maybe we can run past a few consignment shops when we finish. There's a great one on the boulevard."

The nurse was removing the needle as the decision was made. "All done," she said.

"How many more of these do I have to get?" Rose asked.

"Sweetheart, you'll have to have several more tests during your pregnancy. The delivery—well, that all depends on what's needed at the time. You might even get used to needles," she stated with a half smile.

"I'm not counting on it," Rose said.

CHAPTER 27

The evidence room was a grim, sterile-looking, twenty-by-forty-foot box without windows. Its acoustical ceiling tiles were intended to dampen the echoes that bounced between the white tile floor and the black concrete-block walls. Heavy steel shelving units divided the room into aisles.

Filling the shelves from ceiling to floor was a hodge-podge of bulging cardboard boxes, brimming with the flotsam of interrupted lives. Orange biohazard stickers indicated boxes containing human body fluids stored in sealed plastic bags. Otherwise, a yard sale assortment of items stuck out of the boxtops: electric drills, basketballs, a waffle maker, golf shoes, a dollhouse, a grass edger, CDs, a booster seat. Boxes and boxes of electronics—from computer keyboards to big black amplifiers—loaded the bottom shelves. A golf cart sat forlornly in a dark corner, while two full-sized surfboards, listed in the computer records as "recovered stolen property," looked equally out of place in this sunless, breezeless, wave-less world. On the other hand, a large garbage can full of confiscated weapons looked right at home.

Kirk was searching for a box marked Bin Fourteen on aisle six, barcode number 0389563. He found it, carefully lifted it from an upper shelf, and carried it to a small desk beside the door. Near the bottom of the box, he found what he was looking for, the two small plastic tubs of button parts. Selecting the tub containing ornamented tops, Kirk pulled out one button, then another and another.

Other than their weight and the intricacy of the embossed crest, there was nothing extraordinary about these forty buttons—except for the little gold lip designed to be crimped over the shank half. Each lip was pried outward in one spot along the perimeter. Kirk figured the prybar to have been a small flathead screwdriver.

Next, he checked the tub of button-backs. They were quality, he had to admit it—no dull grey stainless steel designed to be hidden where the eye didn't see. No, these were solid brass-shanked button backs. Kirk counted. There were forty, each one dented, wearing the impress of a flathead screwdriver. Unless he missed his guess, the forty tops had once covered the forty shank-backs—and someone had pried them all open. Why?

For the first time, Kirk seriously considered the possibility that this was actually a drug case. After all, at least 75 percent of the evidence in this room came from cases involving drugs, either directly or indirectly. But there was nothing to indicate drugs—no weeds, no pills, no powder, nothing granular. In fact, the only reason the two tubs had been taken in as evidence was that there were smudges on the outer edges of the rims. The detectives had tested to see if the smudges were human blood. They weren't.

So what would you smuggle in a button? Crack? It seemed a cumbersome, impractical means of delivery. Some really high potency hallucinogen—a dot's worth, perhaps? Again, there were far simpler ways to hide it effectively. Still, in the absence of other evidence, Kirk could no longer rule out drugs.

He looked through the tubs one more time, hoping to spot something he'd missed the first time. It wasn't there.

"Good enough," he said to Mary Anne. "Let's get these to the lab in Raleigh this afternoon. Tell them we need to know if there's any chemical or material residue whatsoever—powder, crystal, leaf, liquid, fiber, anything. Tell them it's urgent. Tell them we have a broad-daylight killer who's wreaking havoc in Summerlin looking for his stash."

Lindsay Fullerton had shown the Kendalls' house four times in ten days, and Marcy had grown accustomed to forty-five minute walks through Summerlin's shady streets while the potential buyers poked into cupboards and closets. Now, coming in from the grocery store where she had scavenged more boxes, Marcy's eyes caught the blinking light on the answering machine. She automatically pressed the button.

"Hello, Marcy. This is your hardworking real estate agent. We have ..." Lindsay paused for effect. "A full-price, cash offer on your house! It's real this time. I have a deposit check in my hands." The next words threw Marcy's mind into a whirlwind. "The buyers need to close immediately. Like in the next two weeks! Call me back as soon as possible. These are anxious people, and there's another house in the historic district that they may settle for if they can't move in quickly. It's already empty. But they like yours better. Call my cell phone if you don't get me at the office."

Marcy stood there in shock. Then an immense gratitude filled her heart. *Full price! Cash! Thank you, Father! This is happening so fast!*

"I'm a little overwhelmed right now, Lindsay," Marcy said when she returned the call.

"I imagine you are," said Lindsay. "What can we do to get this moving good and fast? These people have cash on the table, and they need to have a residence set up no later than two weeks from now."

"Well, Lindsay, it'll be a miracle if I can do it in two weeks, but I've seen a lot of miracles lately. What do you need me to do?"

"Stay where you are and let me bring you this contract to sign. I'll also bring you the phone number of the auctioneer I told you about. His name is Mitt Radcliff. He's a character, but he does a good job."

"I'll be right here," Marcy laughed.

"I also need some paperwork from you showing your electric bills, water bills, and taxes. They're just curious about the daily costs so they can plan ahead. Because they're asking you to be out so fast, I suggested they throw in your closing costs. They've agreed! Can you believe it?"

"I can! Lindsay, do you mind giving me Mr. Radcliff's number now? If I have two weeks to get ready, I'd better get moving."

Lindsay read off the number, and Marcy dialed it as soon as her voice stopped shaking.

"Mitt Radcliff, please," she requested, and waited a full two minutes for a deep, down-home voice that caused her to hold the receiver slightly away from her ear.

"Ma'am," he said in an elongated drawl once she made her request, "it is virtually impossible to have an estate sale this quick. First of all, it is ab-so-lute-ly essential to have the sale listed in the Saturday and Sunday papers—at the very least for one weekend. And second, I am completely booked up."

Marcy started to say thanks and hang up but surprised herself by saying, "I really need to do this right away. Could you please double-check your book?"

The man came back a minute or two later, sounding surprised. "My shinin' light of a secretary has just informed me of a cancellation on Saturday, July fourth. I can't believe it. I have just enough time to yank their ad and put yours in. Whaddaya say, little lady?"

"You mean do it on the Fourth of July? Will anybody come?"

"That's one of the best days to do it in a town like yours. Tourists all over, especially in the historic district. They're gonna buy a souvenir somewhere!"

"I say let's do it," Marcy said, feeling electrified.

Her very next call was to Renee: "Help!"

Renee dropped everything, arriving ninety minutes later with her van stuffed with boxes from the merchants at the local mall. In the meantime, the auction firm dispatched the "shinin' light," who arrived with a sheaf of instructions on how to get ready for the sale. She took photos, wrote up an ad for the Internet and the newspapers, and had Marcy sign a legal agreement. Clearly the woman was impressed with the quality of the furnishings that Marcy wanted to sell—but intimidated by the amount of work it would take to clear out such a large house.

"You've only got ten days. You sure you can do this, honey?" she had asked.

"I've got help," Marcy said. "Human and superhuman."

"You'll need it," the woman had declared.

CHAPTER 28

Rose picked up a gigantic pair of baggy pants from the consignment table, held them up to her waistline, and called out to Savannah, "What do you think?"

Savannah laughed and said, "I think you're crazy!" She searched quickly through the stack of clothes in front of her. "Now this is more like it, Rose." She picked up a glitzy red dress covered in sequins. *Vintage* was too kind a word.

"I'm sure I'd look great in that!"

"Your stomach's hardly noticeable."

"Believe me, I can feel it in my clothes," Rose said, distracted. "Come on. The lady at the cash register said anything on this table is a dollar a bag."

"Really?" asked Savannah.

"Yeah! Let's get to work. Where's the bag?" The hunt continued until the bag was full of interesting items, including two pairs of nearly-new looking jeans with a stretchy waistband. Savannah found three knit tops for school, one of which still had its store tags dangling from the sleeve.

The french fry craving surfaced as they headed for home. "You're going to turn into a fry," Savannah said teasingly. "And you told Dr. Richardson you were trying to be balanced! Good thing Mom makes up for it with all her salads." Both girls laughed. Lisa was famous for tossing together a host of unconventional ingredients and calling them a salad.

"I only eat fries twice a week," said Rose, defending herself. "I *am* trying to be balanced."

"I guess it's time you made up for all those weeks you were wasting away," Savannah said, half seriously, as she pulled into the line of cars at the drive-through window of the Triple Deck.

"Here's the money, Savannah."

"Fries are on me today. You've been through a lot."

"Not really. It's been a good day. I now have some comfortable clothes, thanks to my loyal friend and taxi driver's willingness to go digging with me. I have a doctor who is very kind. And the low point of the day—the exam—I survived because of you. I think I owe you fries."

"Oh, no, Rose, you owe me much more than fries! For sitting in the same room with a needle, for digging through old slinky dresses, for being your taxi driver through thick and thin, I need… chocolate!"

"Coming up," Rose said. She leaned over Savannah to shout into the microphone on the big, colored kiosk, "One small fry, please, and the biggest chocolate shake you've got!"

At the pickup window, Savannah was surprised to see the laughing face of Ricky Belden, a friend from church and a fellow Coastal student. "Hey!" he said, "Is this the car that nearly knocked my earphones off?" Both girls laughed with him.

"Didn't expect to see you here," Savannah replied.

"Where've you been, girl? I'm the assistant manager," Ricky replied, craning his neck a little to see into the passenger seat. "Who's your friend?"

"Rose Kendall," said Savannah, accepting the small bag that was giving out the tantalizing smell of hot, freshly salted french fries. "She's working with me this summer at the Picket Fence Pancake House. Come in one morning and yell for some syrup. One of us is bound to come running." She laughed, accepted the chocolate shake, and waved good-bye.

Savannah's cell phone rang just as she pulled out onto the highway, and Rose was surprised to hear her say, "Well, hi, Mrs. Kendall! Just fine! How are you? That's good! Sure, she's right here."

"Mom?" said Rose, accepting the phone with a tinge of concern. She was unaccustomed to hearing from Marcy in the middle of the day. "Are you okay?"

"I'm fine. How was your doctor visit?"

Rose was touched. Clearly, Marcy had remembered the day and time of the appointment and had timed her call.

They briefly discussed the appointment, with Rose exclaiming, "He's the nicest person. He's someone I would feel comfortable with even…afterwards, you know? And you too. You would like him."

Rose could sense her mother's brief moment of tension, but Marcy dispelled it with a gentle statement: "That's wonderful. I prayed all morning for you. I knew you were dreading the appointment."

"You prayed for me—all morning?" Rose felt tiny tears of pleasure prick the inner corners of her eyes.

"I did. It was a privilege." The two said nothing for a second. "Rose, I've waited a little while to tell you, but we have a solid offer on the house. It's full price—cash! The only catch is that we have to be out really quickly. I'm in the middle of organizing the house for an estate sale. It's set for July Fourth. I know that's quick, and a strange day to do it, but that's when the auctioneer had an opening. I'm trying to decide what to keep and what should go. I really need to know which pieces are special to you. And Rose, I still have all your dad's things here. They've been stored away in boxes for fourteen years. We never threw away a thing!

"I know I've got to let most of this go. We need to start over. But you deserve to go through these things and decide what brings back happy memories. Do you think there's any way you could come home—even if it's just one day—and tell me what to hang onto for you?"

Rose felt her stomach lurch. "Oh." She exhaled. "I don't know if I can get there. There's my job, and I don't have a way to get to Summerlin." Another second, though, and Rose was wavering. She realized she was mentally walking through the old family home, stopping in doorways, looking inside the wallpapered parlor, the pale blue dining room, the library, the sunny den. She could clearly see the kitchen with its small, round breakfast table, her grandmother setting the table with blue china, and in the summer, adding a vase of happy-faced zinnias.

Reluctantly, Rose realized, she was leaving the kitchen and walking up the stairs, running her hand over the polished banister. Upstairs, she stood in the middle of the wide central hall, then stopped in the doorway of her grandparents' bedroom and lingered. The posts of their old mahogany bed were topped with hand-carved pineapples, which Grandmom had said were a sign that Rose was welcome there anytime. Next was her mother's bedroom; the sadness that seeped from its walls was virtually tangible. Rose closed that mental door.

On the opposite end of the central hall, she carefully avoided the small suite that had once been furnished as an upstairs parlor. Jack had taken it over as his own. It was filled with his clothes, his papers, his books, his desk, and an antique bed. Rose hadn't been in that room for two years. She wasn't going in now.

In her mind's eye, Rose could see her old playroom next. Here she actually stepped through the mental door, went inside, touched the shelves of toys and books, ran her hand over the smooth, strawberry-colored hair of her doll Lucinda. She saw herself select a book and walk to the goose-neck rocker that had been her dad's favorite chair. She curled up in the seat and looked dreamily out the window.

She remembered the attic door, accessible only through the playroom. No one ever locked it, and Rose had climbed its sturdy, rough-hewn stairs on countless rainy afternoons. Her box of school pictures—it was there in the attic. Mentally, Rose lifted the box top. Everything was in order. She descended the stairs.

Only one room remained—her own bedroom, and as Rose watched herself walk toward the door, she stopped short. Except for three softball trophies and a mitt, there was absolutely nothing she wanted from that room. Nothing whatsoever.

"Mom," she said at last, "are you asking me what furniture I might want?" Marcy replied that she was. "Well," said Rose, "I'd like to have my dad's chair, Papa and Grandmama's bedroom furniture, and the old breakfast table and chairs.

"Of course."

"And the bookshelf in the playroom, and my music box, and Lucinda. My softball trophies, my mitt, and the box of pictures in the attic. I think that's it."

Marcy hesitated, not wanting to push Rose, but not wanting her hasty decision to lead to regret later on. "You're welcome to anything in the house—upstairs or down. Think about it, Rose. You don't have to decide immediately. If you're willing to come here just for the day, I'll drive to the beach and pick you up."

Rose promised to think about it, and the two hung up. She looked down at the french fries and thought, *French. Previously a proper noun. Now a common noun and no longer capitalized.* The fries were cold, she realized, and she didn't really care.

CHAPTER 29

Anton Johnson ran his thick fingers through his spiked hair in frustration. He wasn't much closer to finding his property than he had been a month ago—and no closer to his dream of the twin-engine jet boat that would make his fortune. For an hour now, he had been sitting on the end of his overturned surfboard, staring out over the waves, casting about for a fresh idea, a new plan for getting back into that woman's house without bringing out the whole screaming, small-town police force.

For the millionth time he cursed Jack Bradford, extending his curses all the way to the day he had first laid eyes on him. Weird how he could still see Jack at the age of nine, wearing a navy blazer, perfectly creased khaki pants, white shirt, red tie, and kid-sized loafers, his dark hair combed to one side. A photographer was positioning him beside his father, dressed identically, for a newspaper ad for the Father and Son Clothiers. Even then, Jack had a glitter in his eyes that took in everything and everybody.

Anton had hung back in the mall's interior, watching the stylishly outfitted father put his hand proudly on Jack's shoulder. What would it feel like to look up and see pride in your father's eyes, he wondered. Before the thought fully surfaced, he felt his own father's rough tug against the collar of his corduroy jacket. He turned without a word and followed him back into the maintenance room.

Other boys looked forward to Saturdays; Anton dreaded them. None of the other boys he knew had to go to work with their dads, emptying trash bins, dumping cigarette butts, mopping bathroom floors. Not that he had always spent Saturdays this way. He used to stay home alone. But ever since the Social Services woman had come to the door, Anton had spent every Saturday at the mall, incurring his father's irritation to a deepening degree with every hour that passed. Little boys who didn't have a mother didn't have enough sense to stay home by themselves, his father ranted, and since it was probably Anton's fault that his mother had left the town of Windlass, North Carolina, and never come back, he was going to have to pay for it—at least until he was old enough to take care of his own worthless hide. His father customarily ended that speech with another drag on the bottle in his jacket.

It was impossible to grow up in Windlass and not follow the progress of a golden boy like Jack Bradford. Anton watched him from afar until the year he scratched out a GPA just high enough to earn a spot on the basketball team and stay there. Basketball was Jack's sport too, and on the court they developed, if not a friendship, a working relationship forged in the dynamics of teamwork.

No one, it seemed, was as good at getting the ball down court as Anton, who quickly learned the drill: to pass off as soon as Jack had planted himself in the "sweet spot." Jack could shoot predictably from that one spot only, but he was good for three points every time. When the final buzzer sounded, though, Jack and Anton went in separate directions, Jack with a new girlfriend every other month. In a small town like Windlass, Jack quickly racked up a reputation for being cavalier.

Jack graduated without academic honors, but with great family fanfare. Anton graduated with neither. Jack went to a state university, where he lasted one year. Anton, who had spent his summers crewing on a shrimp boat, opted for a job at a dive shop on the coast. It was far enough away from his old man, who—by now—was intent on embalming himself. Anton found his own substances to abuse, twice landing in the county jail for possession of small quantities of cocaine. He had since learned to be much more discrete in his buying and selling. He had earned big money only once—but it hadn't taken long to develop a taste for it.

Twelve years after their high school graduation, Anton spotted Jack leaning against a piling on the docks, surveying the waterfront. He was genuinely surprised when Jack suggested walking down to a waterfront bar for a drink, but the reason came clear soon enough.

"Don't you do some diving?" Jack asked. "I've got a site the state doesn't know about."

"Yeah? How old?"

"Civil War."

"What kind of cargo?"

"All kinds," Jack had answered vaguely. "I've got a buyer for some of it."

They talked for two hours before Anton was convinced that Jack was probably more than the average treasure hunter. He ran into those all the time—men with excitement in their eyes, but never enough money to conduct a quality salvage job. Jack, however, had a backer—that much was clear. He had equipment, and he had an offer that would more than pay Anton's bills for the next six months.

Anton briefly entertained the thought that this could be a set-up. Had Jack gotten into some kind of legal trouble? Was he looking for somebody to shift some blame onto, somebody to leave tracks all over some cop's investigation?

Over the next few days, Anton made inquiries. Jack had inherited the Father and Son, and within two years, had taken it under, leaving him a half million in debt. People said he had tried to take the shop's inventory up a notch—or ten—by putting in a line of exclusive menswear and pricing it twice as high as the locals were accustomed to. The regular customers couldn't afford the prices, though for a while there had been a number of new clients, many of them foreign.

So, what would a clothier know about diving, about salvaging wrecks? And what had Jack found that allowed him to support himself in the manner that his car, boat, and wardrobe all seemed to suggest? At their next meeting, Jack opened up a well-known history magazine and pointed to an article entitled "Sinking Under the Weight of Gold: An Escape That Failed."

The story he told Anton involved a prominent Washington socialite in the 1860s. Rose O'Neal Greenhow was a Confederate spy, so daring in her espionage that some people called the widow "Wild Rose." At least once she was imprisoned by the Union army, but eventually gained her freedom and sailed to England, where she published a book claiming foul treatment at the hands of the Northern forces.

The book sold well, and Greenhow collected her royalties. On the night of October 1, 1864, she was aboard a British steamer trying to slip past the Union blockade into the port of Wilmington. They were near the mouth of the Cape Fear River when a violent storm blew up, and the ill-fated steamer, *The Condor*, ran aground on a sandbar near Fort Fisher.

Afraid of being recaptured, Rose secured a leather money bag to her body and demanded to be taken ashore in a smaller boat. Apparently the lifeboat swamped, and Greenhow drowned in the surf, weighted down by official British dispatches and the two thousand dollars in gold sovereigns in the leather bag.

Her body washed ashore and was found by a soldier who took the money but returned it when her identity was disclosed. According to some accounts, as the Confederate ladies of Wilmington reverently prepared Greenhow's body for burial, they found even more money sewn into her dress.

"All this to say what?" Anton had asked. "Sounds like her money was recovered, right?"

But Jack claimed that Greenhow's money was a pittance among all the gold that got wet on the sandbars off Cape Fear that night. He claimed to know about a second stash that had upended in the bucking boat, strewing coins underwater in a swath that stretched half a mile. A few of the gold dollars and half-dollars had been recovered—Jack produced one to tantalize Anton further. And Jack claimed to know the coordinates of the discovery.

The trouble, of course, would come, first, in locating individual coins buried under years of silt; and, second, in keeping them, if word of a major haul got out. Inside the territorial limit, even the discovery of a sunken gunboat usually erupted into a brawl among federal, state, and private entities.

Anything they found, Jack stressed, would have to be kept secret—a doubly difficult job since the dive site was visible from heavily trafficked Fort Fisher and its state-run aquarium.

"So," Anton had asked, "how're you gonna make money off these coins if you can't tell people you found 'em?"

"Private collectors," Jack had answered. After a pause, he added, "Foreign."

Anton's raised eyebrows eloquently expressed his skepticism even before he asked: "And how're you getting these coins out of the country?"

"I'll show you that later," Jack had said, smiling and walking away, reinforcing Anton's impression that Jack looked "up market" even in seersucker shorts, a polo shirt, and deck shoes. Turn his clothes inside out, Anton figured, and you'd probably find coins sewn into his inseams too.

CHAPTER 30

Anton Johnson didn't know much about nineteenth century coins, but he did know that a good pulse induction metal detector could lock onto a coin buried a foot deep in silt and mud. He knew that a compressed air blower could blast holes in the ocean bottom and stir up items buried several feet deep. He also knew that a dredge pump could suck up and strain out silt to leave behind whatever relics had come up in the vacuum.

Nevertheless, he had been fairly stunned when Jack showed up for their first offshore run in a fast, shallow-draft cigarette boat carrying a top-of-the-line underwater metal detector, a hand-held blower, and a halogen light mounted on a diving cap. The GPS he consulted during the ride offshore was a more sophisticated unit than Anton had ever seen up close.

It was approaching low tide when Jack cut the engine, dropped anchor, and handed Anton a smaller GPS unit to strap on his wrist. "Figured it out?" he asked brusquely, pointing to the metal detector that Anton had been examining throughout the ride, flicking through its digital menu. Anton nodded. "Okay, then. The GPS is pre-programmed. It'll take you straight to the coordinates two hundred yards away. I'll stay here with the boat, doing a little fishing, in case anybody's watching us. Anything you find goes in this." He handed Anton a mesh bag of black rubber with a belt clip. "You've got two and a half hours. Make it count."

Anton slipped over the side of the cigarette boat and entered the murk of the Cape Fear Inlet. No dazzling, clear blue water here—the chop of the waves and the shape of the shoreline kept these waters constantly stirred up. Atlantic hurricanes had disturbed the ocean bottom so regularly that it was highly unlikely any sunken cargo remained in its original resting spot for long.

Still, you had to start somewhere in the Graveyard of the Atlantic. Anton knew that Jack was counting on the likelihood that last year's hurricane had vacuumed some long-buried coins back up to the surface. Perhaps they were just lying there—the silver coins looking tarnished and gray, but the gold pieces still glinting in any light that penetrated their cloudy bathwater.

The GPS unit's lighted face pointed even further offshore, and Anton calculated that Jack had positioned the boat almost directly between Fort Fisher and the dive site to deflect the gaze of any curious onlookers should Anton suddenly pop to the surface. Somehow, he thought, he needed to get his own fix on the sandbar, just in case Jack got greedy and forgot to share.

When the helpful unit strapped to his wrist indicated that Anton was over his target, he switched on the headlamp strapped to his forehead and blinked behind his goggles to find himself approaching a large school of silvery fish. He let them pass, then drove a two-foot stake into the sandbar and attached a fluorescent yellow flag to the end, watching the current pull it straight out like a streamer. He swam to a spot about twenty feet away and hammered in another stake, attaching an orange flag this time. Twice more he staked the sandbar, creating a square. This would give him a visual field in which to start his search, and keep him from drifting past an area he hadn't yet covered.

All of the preliminaries had taken nearly thirty minutes. Anton started near the red flag and headed toward the green one, watching with satisfaction as the GPS on his wrist faithfully tracked his course. Satisfied, he turned his attention to the sandbar, sweeping it with light as he turned his head slowly from side to side.

It was an oddly pleasant world here, where the bubbling of his oxygen played musically in his ears. At the point of low tide, Anton saw that there was no more than twenty-five feet of water above him, and a shaft of bright sunlight gave him better visibility than usual. Still, neither he nor the metal detector noticed anything unusual until, about an hour and a half into the dive, he drew near the orange flag and spotted a slight dimpling in the sand. He swept his hand over the spot and immediately felt substance there. It was round, about the size of a quarter, and yes!—it was a coin. He held it close enough to read. This quarter had been minted in 1992—a relic, no doubt, of a fishing boat slapped by a strong wave. It was worth exactly twenty-five cents.

Methodically, Anton moved on. He was laying out his third quadrant—aware that he had only five minutes left before he was due to surface—when a quick pass with the metal detector produced a strong pulse. He pushed into the silt with his gloved hand and closed his fingers around what felt like another quarter. A yard away, he found another. Out of time, he dropped the last two finds into the mesh bag, marked his position with the GPS, and swam upward toward the light.

Anton found Jack hard to read, but he was fairly certain that Jack was more excited over the last two coins he'd found than over the two sea bass flipping in the fish cage that hung from a rope off the side of the boat. The coins were gold, dated 1859. Jack flipped them over several times, asked a slew of questions about their location, and reminded Anton three times to make sure he had the GPS coordinates.

Now it was Anton's turn to ask questions. Did Jack recognize the coins? Did he know if they were common or rare? What did he think they were worth? Who did he know who might buy them?

Jack insisted he had to look them up in a reference book before he could tell anything about the coins' value. But he was clearly pleased. Fired with enthusiasm, they agreed that Anton would switch air tanks and head back down. This time, before staking out squares, Anton let the GPS take him back to the site where the last coins had been found, then turned east for fifty feet. He picked up one more coin that way, then, assuming that whatever had scattered the gold pieces had done so in a band perhaps ten feet wide, retraced his route, scanning five feet to the right and left of the original line. Not a single pulse shone from the metal detector.

So, he thought, maybe the strewing had taken place in the opposite direction. Again, Anton used the GPS to establish a line linking the three discoveries. This time he headed west. His heart rate picked up as he detected more objects buried beneath the silt and sand, but these turned out to be buttons. Still, he stashed them in the mesh bag. Plenty of collectors paid for period buttons.

He worked the site north and south, always saving his route on the GPS. When his time was up, he surfaced—one coin and five buttons richer.

Those first few coins went to a local collector—quietly. Jack said that he had gotten between six and seven hundred dollars each, and gave Anton a third of the sale price—in cash. Another third went to the backer who owned the boat and search equipment. Jack held onto a third for himself.

A month of sunny weather kept Anton diving at least every weekend. Knowing that the sandbar was a viable site prompted Jack to suggest using the blower—the first Anton had ever handled. Coins were spread here and there all over the sandbar, and by blasting shallow craters in its surface, Anton was often able to bring up seven or eight per dive, bypassing chunks of rusting metal that told the story of tackle boxes and small boats lost in sudden squalls.

At first, Anton had been satisfied with making an extra five to seven hundred dollars a Saturday, but after four months, he was bringing up fewer and fewer coins. Clearly bored with salt-water fishing, Jack had begun bringing along coin books, studying them under the shade of the boat's bimini top. Apparently, his local buyer was up to his spending limit, temporarily sated with the Flying Eagles Jack delivered.

Anton had taken note of the way Jack cared for the coins—simply soaking them in soapy water, avoiding anything but the softest brush against the face of the gold. Likewise, Anton had noted the name of the book Jack consulted, and one rainy weekend, he had gone in search of the book at the public library. "Your timing's good!" the librarian told him. "This book is put out annually. We just got the latest edition. There's also a supplement that lists market prices."

Not much of a reader, Anton nevertheless soaked up the fact that Jack's buyer was giving them only half the market value—a stat he lost no time in pointing out to Jack. "He's not keeping the coins," Jack had answered gruffly. "He's got expenses getting them out on the international market."

"So what's keeping us from selling direct?"

"I'm working on it," Jack replied, but Anton could tell from his tone that Jack wasn't pleased with his new interest in business.

Kirk felt both relieved and pressured to get a call from Lindsay Fullerton announcing that the Kendalls' house was under contract—this time to a buyer who'd stuck around long enough to sign papers and hand over a cashier's check for a sizeable down payment. That was good for Marcy, Kirk thought, but a potential complication for the case. Kirk was not a beat cop, and he had too many other investigations in process to simply stake out Marcy's house night and day. But one thing was obvious: someone had tried to get inside the Kendalls' house—and every other piece of property that Jack Bradford owned or held interest in. And now, if this guy saw a Sold sign go up, he'd be facing a deadline.

The estate sale made Kirk nervous. Too big a house. Too many people to keep an eye on. Too trusting a seller. Recognizing that he—and the rest of the world—had to stop coddling Marcy, Kirk decided to explain the situation plainly. He needed free rein to come and go throughout the sale. And he'd need reinforcements.

But who? Lindsay was an obvious choice, and when Kirk dropped by her office to present the idea, she took a few minutes to digest. "That weird guy? You mean…I may've shown the Kendalls' house to the man who shot Jack Bradford?" Her hazel eyes grew big. "That would explain a few things—like the sunglasses indoors and the monosyllables and the rudeness! My internal alarm was going off every ten seconds, but I didn't know what it meant. So, do you really think he'll come to the estate sale, knowing I might be around?"

"Yeah, my gut reaction is that he'll be there, but I suspect he'll look a little altered. Think you'd recognize him just from his build and facial features?"

"Maybe."

"Did he look like this?" Kirk produced a new photo downloaded from a national crime database. It was two years old, taken after Anton's arrest on drug charges.

Lindsay studied the photo with a scowl. "Pretty close," she said. "His hair wasn't blond or spiked like that. The sunglasses covered most of his face. But the shape of his head—his jawline—it was very similar. How tall is this Anton Johnson?"

"Five nine. Hundred and eighty pounds."

"Yeah, that's about right."

"What was he wearing the day you met?"

Lindsay scarcely had to think about it. "Dark gray suit. Off-white shirt. Shoes that were a little too…outdoorsy for the suit," she said, working to explain herself. "I remember thinking his coat sleeves were too long—almost down to his knuckles. He looked like he'd borrowed the outfit from three different people."

"Any jewelry?"

"Not that I remember."

"Distinguishing marks—tattoos, scars, birthmarks?"

"No—sorry. I do remember noticing how tan his hands and face were."

With a knot in his stomach, Kirk placed a call to Marcy. She drove over to the realty office and pulled up a chair in front of Lindsay's desk. Kirk closed the door.

CHAPTER 31

Ruminating over his dealings with Jack, Anton knew there were three days he would never forget.

First was the Saturday, five months into the search, when they found the largest bed of coins. For several weeks, Anton had been bringing up just enough to indicate they were following a trail: a dozen, then fifteen, then twenty-five. Jack was nervous to the point of switching boats. To divert attention, he was anchoring farther and farther from the center of the search—forcing Anton to swim nearly half a mile to reach the last GPS plot of the day before. The longer swim, of course, cut down on search time. But one slightly overcast morning, when the sea was unusually clear, Anton was coming within sight of the latest grid when he was drawn to a large, dimpled section of sandbar just a few degrees west. Three passes of the metal detector and he knew. The machine was recording hits as fast as he could move it.

He marked the spot on the wrist recorder, surfaced with a hammering heart, and summoned Jack with a two-fingered wolf whistle and a wave of the distress flag he carried in his belt.

Jack responded quickly, heeled the boat around to close the distance, and for once, followed orders instead of giving them. He unlocked the vacuum hose, unreeled about twenty feet of it on the port side away from Fort Fisher, waited for Anton's signaling tug on the message line, and flipped on the power. Within seconds, he was seining water from the sand, sand from shell fragments, and shell from gold and silver that caught and threw back the feeble rays of sunshine poking through the cloud cover.

They ended the diving day with a haul of 474 coins of all sizes and ages. Anton would never forget their jubilation. For once, Jack acted like a buddy. The two went out to eat, ordered drinks, left the dockside hooting.

Over the next five dives, they brought up nearly a thousand coins.

But in the days that followed, as the numbers dropped, it was hard to stomach Jack's calculated inspection, his look of subtle suspicion, each time Anton surfaced and emptied his bag. When it appeared that the site was exhausted, Jack announced they would take some time off. He had to find buyers, he said, and pay bills. Within a week, he fairly dazzled Anton with a payoff of forty-seven thousand in cash. Add the nearly eight thousand that had already trickled in over the five-month search, and the prospect of future collaboration left Anton feeling reasonably secure about his future. For a weekend job, this was paying off way beyond his expectations.

The second most memorable day was when Anton surprised Jack by turning up at The Suitable two weeks after it opened in Summerlin. It was a warm October morning, and there were no customers in the shop when Anton arrived in khaki pants, a black tee shirt, and an unlined linen jacket that looked like it belonged in Miami. "Man!" he said to Jack, as he scanned the shop's handsome furnishings. "You can make fifty-five thousand go a long way!" Jack looked defensive.

There was a short and awkward pause. "Isn't it about time we go fishing again?" Anton asked, laying a gold coin about the size of a dime heads-up on the sales counter. He never took his eyes off Jack, who quickly flipped over the piece to study the back.

"Where'd you find this?"

"Old Fort Fisher."

"Our spot?"

"Not too far from."

Jack had to clear his throat to query, "How many did you find?"

"Let's say several," Anton answered.

"Just like this?"

"Just like it."

A deep-throated bell rang to signal the arrival of a customer. Jack looked up with tension in his face, replaced it with a forced smile, spoke to the arrival, and turned back to Anton. "Come back at noon," he told Anton under his breath. "These fittings take a while. We can get lunch."

Anton raised his eyebrows, consulted the diving watch on his wrist. "I'm meeting somebody," he said, determined to maintain control of this day's negotiations. "Make it one."

"One," Jack said. Anton held out his palm for the dime-sized coin, which Jack surrendered with obvious reluctance, and Anton snapped it into a small flat box which he buttoned into the breast pocket of the linen jacket.

On his way out, Anton couldn't help but notice that Jack's customer showed little interest in the shop's winter line of wool sports coats and tartan ties. At the huge mahogany door, he turned to see the man disappearing into the inner office and closing the door.

At 1:08, when Anton casually turned the corner to approach The Suitable, he noted with satisfaction that Jack was waiting outside with a salesman. "I'll be back in a hour or so," murmured Jack and fell in step before Anton could slow to a stop. "There's a sandwich shop two blocks down," he said, and Anton nodded.

"I know the one."

Anton entered first and headed for the most isolated table. Once they gave the waitress their orders, he lost no time but leaned forward and addressed his partner. "You know, Jack," he said gravely, "I played it straight with you. I gave you every cent I found on that sandbar—kept nothing back. And as far as I can tell, you played it straight with me. But I admit I was curious about the book you were always reading. Pricy. Bought my own copy. That's where I found a picture of this." He held up the coin that had riveted Jack in the shop. "Found it down inside the cuff of my diving glove after you dropped me off on the dock that last day. You pulled at least one other like this out of the dredge from the vacuum—I remember it. I decided to keep this one as a souvenir, figured it wasn't worth much. Looked like one side had been mashed in the minting machine, see? The U in United States is almost gone. Based on the date, though, I thought, *Hey, maybe it's in the book.* And it was. Was it ever."

Jack bobbed his head ever so slightly, offering nothing.

"Y'know, Jack, I never got to see everything the vacuum brought up. You find any more of these in the wash?"

"Only the one," Jack replied and waited.

"You're sure about that? I've been checking an online website. Three of these sold last month through an auction house in Britain. An 1861-D doesn't turn up often, far as I can tell."

"Had to be somebody else's."

"So…" Anton paused deliberately, "how much did you get for the one I found?" He gave a slight emphasis to the word *I.*

Anton watched the wheels turning behind Jack's eyes, tried to imagine his thought processes. Clearly it would be profitable for Jack to handle the future sale of any more coins like this one. And he would need to sell them for the highest price possible to keep Anton from trying to find another middleman. But that would also mean giving Anton between six and fifteen thousand dollars on the spot for the one already sold. And Anton was certain Jack wasn't in the mood to admit owing him a thing.

"You did get your split from that first coin," Jack began predictably. "It was in poor condition. It only brought five thousand."

"Then you must have slammed the cabin door on it," Anton replied. "It wasn't bent. It wasn't badly scratched. It wa right in the place it was supposed to be."

"Five thousand," Jack repeated without flinc get—I've never marketed a coin of that rarity. T probably sold twice again before it got past the collector."

"Jack, Jack," Anton crooned softly. "You sold one of the rarest gold dollars in US history for five thousand? A coin that brought in nearly $150,000 in 2008? You expect me to believe that?"

"My mistake," Jack conceded. "But it worked out in your favor. Word got out, and I met somebody who buys direct. He knows my shop. He comes into the country three or four times a year. He… let's say…has good taste in menswear."

"Well," said Anton, and his voice grew hard and flat, "I need to know how much per coin my take is going to be before we do any more business. This time, I'm both the boat owner and the salver. And I'm taking bids for the best price."

"You got a boat?" asked Jack, mildly surprised.

Anton nodded coolly, not revealing that the small runabout was twenty years old and that the engine had to be coaxed into starting every time he took it out. "GPS. Metal detector. Vacuum. You'd be surprised what you can get on the used market. Not so shiny as yours. But they work."

"Well," Jack said, and stopped. He started again: "I'll do research. But the first thing my contacts are going to ask is exactly how many '61-Ds you've got. Keep in mind," Anton could see the wheels continuing to turn, "if you dump a bunch of them all at once, the purchase price'll go down."

"You and I both know there never was a bunch of them. But I've got enough to keep things lively for a while. Tell 'em I've got one piece. See how much you can get. Later, tell 'em you've heard a rumor somebody's found, say, forty-five. See what they do.

"Besides," Anton continued, displaying the breadth of his newfound interest in library research, "I don't believe the purchase price will drop too far on these. Somebody's going to be willing to pay for the whole collection."

Now, a year later, Anton sat on the beach cursing Jack Bradford d reliving the circumstances that created the third most memo- day.

All that Anton knew about Jack's buyer was that he was a native Egyptian and a pain to work with. Jack had been right about one thing: the buyer was demanding to know the exact number of Dahlonega dollars Anton was holding—in fact, demanded digital photos taken under strictly specified lighting conditions, coins laid out in rows, fronts and backs. According to Jack, the man was prepared to buy all forty-five of the 1861-Ds, but wanted them five at a time at three-month intervals. On top of it all, the buyer was insisting that Jack find a way to conceal the coins for the trip back to Port Said against an all-too-likely search by a customs crew, whether in an airport or on a coast guard cutter. Apparently the Egyptian buyer was a businessman who made quarterly trips to Charlotte and rather liked to take home some choice souvenirs, sometimes by air and often by yacht. As he told Jack, his least favorite part of the sea trip was within territorial waters. After that, he felt free to enjoy himself.

Jack's solution, initially, had been to sell his client some exceptionally fine winter sports coats. Along with some flat, monogrammed gold buttons that Jack custom ordered for the buyer, the client left with the coins stitched behind the jacket's thick wool lapels.

In the next shipment, they used the coins as weights in the vent plackets, ostensibly to make them lie flat. Yet another shipment went out in flawlessly sewn shop labels stitched into the backs of neckties, forming the flat strap through which the narrow end of the tie could be held in place. But each method had its drawbacks—and would immediately raise the suspicion of any coast guard inspector with a metal detector.

Anton had insisted on being kept apprised of Jack's shipping methods, but the two men didn't work well together off the ocean. The day arrived, however, when Jack was convinced he had hit on a method that would work for all twenty-five coins that remained to be shipped over the next eighteen months. A pneumatic crimper—that's what he had asked Anton to scout for, and Anton had finally found one that would do the job perfectly.

And then, the buyer backed out.

For months Jack had searched for other buyers but claimed that the market was skittish. At one point, Anton had shown up at the shop, demanding to see the coins. He was horrified to realize that Jack was keeping them in a tiny lockbox behind the cash register drawer. "Any thug on the street could break in here and clean us out!" he ranted. "It's the first place they'd look!"

Finally, Anton's mistrust of his partner got the better of him. He demanded that Jack give back the coins, and when Jack began making threats that hit too close to home, Anton backed down a little. Half. That was what he demanded. In the end, Jack had agreed.

And then—as he replayed the scene, Anton let his profanities become audible—that idiot had turned his shop into a love nest on the very day Anton was due to pick up the coins and the proceeds from the last sale—money Anton had already committed to the fastest boat he had ever seen, one that would take him down the Intracoastal Waterway to the Keys. A little side business of his own was getting increasingly profitable now that he had some working capital.

He had never intended to kill Jack. Scare him if he had to—yes. Jack had let him down, had fallen behind on his payments, twice making promises he had failed to keep. That put Anton behind, too. He really hadn't intended to use the gun, only wave it around if Jack didn't immediately pay up. But it was the timing—to have Jack burst out the back door into the alley at the same time the sirens started—to see Jack wrestling with a high school girl—all that reddish blond hair! What was he *thinking*? She was looking right at Anton—recognized him, apparently. And then Jack was ordering him to "Get her out of here"? Right! The girl had to be pinning something on Jack, and Jack was planning to push her off on an innocent party—probably hoping she'd get hurt. And when she did, it would look like Anton's fault.

Anton had pulled the gun almost out of reflex, had fired without really thinking, had gaped at the blood that instantly covered the couple in their struggle, and had then sought to distance himself in the stupidest way possible by throwing the gun away. In the dumpster! With the girl probably watching! How could he have been such an amateur?

All his years of self-protection crowded in on him. He knew he probably had half a day to disappear. The handgun was easily traceable—he spat curses on his stupidity. He had owned it only a week; the paper trail was nice and fresh.

Anton's trip to the Keys was not the pleasure trip he'd planned. He had driven all night and all the next day, stopping finally in a rundown motel on the outskirts of Ft. Lauderdale and leaving its plumbing full of hair dye the next morning. He found the most disreputable-looking used car lot on the boulevard, produced one of two fake IDs, traded his car for way less than it was worth, and kept on driving. He traded again in Homestead, paying cash for a ten-year-old sedan with a huge patch of Bondo and a bad paint job on the passenger side. He made a point of asking both employees in the dank-looking office several questions about stops along the Everglades Parkway. Then he headed, not into the Everglades, but due south, down through the Keys, where he spent two miserable weeks in a mosquito-ridden backwater cabin making plans.

Sick as he was at having killed a man—and Anton was sick to the point of sleeplessness—he knew he was probably the only person still alive who knew that a fortune was hidden somewhere among Jack's belongings. Second, he was fairly certain the strawberry blond had been on the run too. According to a news article he pulled up online in the library on Duck Key, her name was Rose Kendall, a resident of Summerlin. The girl—good night! She was only eighteen—had been cleared in the shooting but never went home and was being sought by the Summerlin Police Department.

Right now, the police weren't necessarily the biggest of Anton's worries. He had creditors of a mean sort—the kind who wouldn't take the time to read him his Miranda rights. Fortunately, they shouldn't have any reason yet to tie him to the small town of Summerlin. He could hide there almost as safely as in the Keys. He weighed the options and decided it was worth the risk to go back.

Anton chose a new moon to revisit Summerlin, figuring that after two weeks, the cops were unlikely to still be staking out Jack's stomping grounds. On that first dark night, he searched Jack's boat at the marina but found nothing of interest. He tore apart The Suitable, leaving chaos. He moved on to the Victorian, which he found almost completely empty, and spent three hours in the garage out back. Nothing. There were no coins to be found anywhere. Desperate, he even climbed under the loose portion of the wire fence surrounding the impound lot where he'd spotted Jack's classic sports car. Celebrating the fact that the Triumph was too old to have a built-in security system, he forced down a side window. Other than the usual loose change lodged behind the driver's seat, he came up empty again.

So, if the yellow Victorian was empty, not even cordoned off with police tape, where had Jack been laying his head every night to sleep? The next morning, Anton searched out the *Summerlin Weekly Times*, asked if he could buy copies of the last two weeks' issues, and found a wealth of detail that the larger, statewide papers hadn't gotten the first time. Most important was the news that Jack had never actually lived in the Victorian but with a woman named Marcy Kendall. The paper had run a photo of Jack with a pretty little blond at a Chamber of Commerce fundraiser.

And while it was clear that the police were being close-mouthed about it, the following week's story stated that the detectives were still searching for the eighteen-year-old daughter of Marcy Kendall.

But surely Jack wasn't using two women at the same time—mother *and* daughter? Anton hated to go to such a public place, but he changed his shirt and sunglasses, stuffed a different cap over his ears, and asked the librarian at the front desk of the town library for the most recent issue of the Summerlin High School yearbook. Two minutes of research was all it took. The girl who had locked terrified eyes with his was definitely Rose Kendall.

A phone book. The K section. Another two minutes and Anton had the street address of the only Kendall residence in town. It didn't really surprise him that the house turned out to be on the oldest, most well-preserved street in town. Jack had always had good taste.

Now, all Anton could do was wait and watch—without being watched himself. No car loitered in the Kendalls' driveway, and the door to the ancient detached garage had six inches of lush grass growing up in front of it. Still—you never knew who might be lying low inside the house. He dialed the home phone number repeatedly, always hoping that a live voice would answer. If so, he would find a way to get his foot in the door. But the only voice he ever heard was that of an old man, saying, "You've reached the Kendall residence...."

He timed his patrols at two-hour intervals—sometimes by car, occasionally on foot, but always taking pains to change shirt and hat. By the end of his second day in Summerlin, he was confident that no one was at home. Once he watched a heavy-set brunette woman collect a handful of mail from the box by the front door, only to return to her car and drive away. That night he ventured out after midnight, entering the side yard and ducking under the huge oak trees that afforded cover almost up to the house itself. The place was really dark—not even equipped with automatic timers to give the appearance of being occupied. Anton tried every window and door and found them locked up tight and wearing security system stickers. Were they for real? He honestly didn't want to find out the hard way.

The motel in the next town was so run-down that Anton figured it was checked regularly by the local cops. He drove another seventeen miles inland to a manufacturing community that had seen better days, explained that he had a short-term tool and die job and might need a room for as long as a week. He paid cash up front for two nights and arranged to pay day-to-day after that.

On his fifth night's prowl of Summerlin, Anton was elated to see a Buick in the Kendalls' driveway and a dim light shining in an upstairs bathroom window. Clouds gave him enough cover to quietly test the doors again, but they were locked, and a neighbor's dog was threatening to give him away. The next morning, he traded cars again, settling on an older, beige, late-model sedan that, at a distance, looked remarkably like Marcy Kendall's.

He absolutely had to get inside the woman's house when the security system was off. Anton knew his limitations well enough to reject any thought of finessing his way inside by posing as a repairman. No, it would take some strong-arming—a prospect he dreaded only slightly less than losing the sum total of his investment.

So when the For Sale sign showed up almost immediately in the front yard, Anton considered himself the most fortunate of men. The following morning at a Goodwill store, he located a charcoal suit that, to his untrained eyes, looked faintly like one of Jack's. Lindsay Fullerton, the enthusiastic little agent who used an actual key to let him in the house he'd been casing for a week, would have easily succumbed to the strong-arm, but Anton was determined to avoid any possibility involving the police. Since his dark-of-the-moon vandalism spree in downtown Summerlin, the cops were already patrolling too regularly. By now, he knew them and their cars at twenty yards.

His real estate tour of the Kendalls' house told him exactly what he wanted to know: that an armoire upstairs was stuffed with expensive looking men's clothes. At least that identified Jack's bedroom. And the office downstairs held plenty of potential too. He knew he had wowed Lindsay Fullerton with his declaration of intent and figured he could talk her into letting him back in again, once he figured out a ruse for going upstairs alone.

But again, fortune seemed to smile. A new sign went up in the Kendalls' yard announcing an estate sale only two weeks away. Now no subterfuge was needed, only patience. Anton had once worked for a salvage company that cleared out old houses after estate sales.

It was hot, dirty work, and many of the employees were day laborers who sweated for a few weeks and then found something better—Anton among them. But he knew enough to contact Mitt Radcliff and talk his way into a job. For a week and a half, Anton toiled in a series of hundred-degree attics and garages and overstuffed closets, hauling out everything from heat-damaged furniture to faded plastic funeral flowers—and losing ten pounds in the process. He worked steadily and quietly, building up the talkative old man's trust by listening to his stories and laughing when he had to. By the day of Marcy Kendall's estate sale, Anton, trimmed down and sporting a full beard, was crew chief of the day laborers.

CHAPTER 32

The crime lab in Raleigh had responded with unusual speed: Kirk had gotten his report within forty-eight hours. There was no sign of any known drug residue in the two tubs of buttons. Square one.

Feeling only slight satisfaction that his instincts had been correct, Kirk's irritation quotient ("My IQ," he liked to tell colleagues) was steadily mounting. It wouldn't do to get irritable. On the afternoon before the auction, the big detective decided to drive over to a favorite spot along the Cape Fear River.

Marsh Point was a quiet neighborhood of old-growth oak, maple, and hickory trees overhanging seventies-style ranch houses. The streets had been thoughtfully laid out to preserve the biggest trees, and where the avenue swung wide to avoid asphalting over the root systems, the developers had left small pockets of green space along the riverfront. Kirk's favorite "pocket" was furnished with a lone concrete bench scenically sited beneath a live oak. It faced a broad, shallow stretch of the Cape Fear, which today gave the impression of flowing over millions of two-carat diamonds.

Kirk settled onto the bench and waited. The spot almost always had the same effect: it quieted his restlessness and somehow sorted his thoughts—helped him decide what to keep or discard, what to file and what to analyze. Best of all, it leeched away his anger at the people who hurt *his* people. And at this juncture, Kirk felt angry.

But it was pointless to harbor anger against a perpetrator. It got in the way of clear thinking.

Looking up into the oak limbs shaggy with moss, Kirk found himself talking out loud, reviewing the Kendall case in sequence, starting with everything he knew about Jack Bradford.

Thirty minutes of mental review mixed with prayer, and he was right back to the buttons. They were the key to something important—he was sure of it. Kirk closed his eyes against the nearly irresistible sparkle of the river, sitting motionless, listening. There was a faint breeze coming off the water, cool, refreshing.

A familiar scrabbling sound broke his reverie, and Kirk opened his eyes to see a gray squirrel running barber poles up the trunk of the tree, heading toward a choice, mossy branch with an exceptional water view. The squirrel's mouth stretched wide to accommodate a hickory nut, a big one half the size of the squirrel's head. Kirk shook his own head, imagining how much power there must be in squirrel jaws to bear down on a nut of that size. Suddenly, Kirk pictured Jack—not prying open but clamping down on a blazer button, crimping its ornamented top over its shanked bottom. Yes, he had seen the crimper that Rose had mentioned, had even examined the strike plate to make sure there was no button still inside. But this was a pneumatic crimper. It was fed by two tubes connected to hoppers that could be loaded and reloaded with tops and bottoms. Kirk had personally checked the hoppers, and they were empty. But had anyone thought to check the tubes?

Another squirrel approached the bench, spotted Kirk, and froze, its long tail snapping forward over its back. "Have at it," Kirk said, gesturing toward the bench. "Your buddy's already picked up dinner."

He leapt off the bench and strode to the cruiser. "Dispatch?" he said into the radio on his dashboard. "Kirk Landry. I need you to locate Ronald. Tell him to meet me in the evidence room."

Ronald Dupree, Summerlin's city electrician, had been only too glad to leave the heat of the municipal recreation complex, where he was monitoring the installation of a scoreboard at the softball field. The evidence room was the coolest spot in the city's administrative complex, and Ronald was hoping fervently that the HVAC unit was turned on high. He spotted Kirk beside Mary Anne's desk and grinned. The two men maintained a running rivalry during baseball season.

"Whassup?" Ronald called out. "Hope you catchin' crooks better'n the Braves are catchin' flyballs."

Kirk responded with a matching grin. "Hope you're lighting up that scoreboard better'n the Phillies in St. Louis last week."

Pleasantries out of the way, Kirk said, "Lemme show you something," and led the way to the evidence room, where he had already placed the crimper from Jack Bradford's garage on a table near an electrical outlet.

"Whatcha got? Looks like my great-grandma's old orange juicer. I could use me a glass right now!"

"Crimper," Kirk said. "Pneumatic. I'm hoping mighty hard something's jammed in the feeder tubes. But if it is, we need to get it out without bending or breaking it—or electrocuting anybody. That's why I called you."

"Can't promise a thing," Ronald said crisply, already plugging in the cord, pressing buttons, listening to the whine of the motor. "You run anything through it yet?"

"No, I was waiting for the expert. I'm pretty sure these are what's been in it, though." Kirk held out his hand to reveal both the top and the shank of an unassembled button.

Ronald turned over the parts in his own hand and nodded. "So this crimper just clamps the top down over the bottom? Leaves it hollow in the middle?"

Kirk nodded. "Apparently."

"Good," he said with efficiency. "Let's see how this fella's put together."

Ronald opened up the crimper's top, which resembled the top of the office coffeemaker. He reached into each round hopper in turn and stuck his index finger as far as he could up into the feeder tube. "Can't feel a thing," he mused. "Let's try it from the other direction." He unscrewed the protective caps at the top of each feeder tube and inserted a finger, but touched nothing from that side either. "Hmmm," he said musingly, "this main tube's about eight inches long. There's a section in the middle I can't get to. But I got something that can."

He reached into his canvas bag and pulled out a tool that resembled a long bottle brush with a thin wire hook on the upper end. "Let's be safe," he said, and unplugged the crimper from the electrical outlet. He inserted the brush end into the left feeder tube and gently ran it all the way down to the hopper at the bottom. "Nothing in that one," he said.

Kirk tried not to sigh.

Ronald repeated the process on the right tube and met resistance about halfway down. His eyes lit up. "Congrat-u-la-tions, Kirk. You got yourself an arterial blockage here! Want me to do one of those fancy angioplasties like the surgeon in Wilmington did for me last summer? It'll only cost you twenty-seven thousand dollars after insurance."

"I don't have time to do that much paperwork," Kirk said, his pulse quickening. "Let's take a traumatic approach. Just don't bend it."

"You need to keep this machine?"

"It *is* evidence," Kirk said. "But I need what's inside worse."

"Good. I'm gonna perform radical surgery. We gonna take this entire a-orta right out. But first"—he grabbed the hopper above the feeder tube—"this here kidney's gotta go."

"Ronald," Kirk said, "there are surgeons and there are butchers. I admire your style."

"Right," said Ronald, his eyes fixed on the spot where the bottom of the tube emptied onto the mechanism that positioned objects in the tubes to meet on the strike plate beneath. "I do believe we can disconnect this ri-i-ight here." With a pair of pliers, he clamped down on the bottom of the tube and pulled. It didn't budge.

"Oh! Quality workmanship," Ronald grunted, and picked up the entire crimper, inverting it in his lap to examine the bottom. He removed six screws, flipped the crimper right side up, and tapped on the strike plate to push it downward, away from the twin tubes. This time, both men could see some separation. "Come on-n-n, big fella," Ronald coached, pushing harder, until finally the right tube came off with a satisfying *pop*.

He held up the length of translucent plastic piping to the fluorescent light and peered through it. "There's something white in there, right smack in the middle," he said, meeting Kirk's eyes and realizing that the big detective was using all his self-control not to jerk the tube out of his hands.

"Just stick a pencil in it," Kirk said.

"Patience, big guy. You said you didn't want it damaged. But you didn't say nothing about damaging this tube. Lemme show you my complete medical arsenal."

Out of the canvas bag came a small rotary tool to which Ronald affixed a tiny circular saw blade. "I offered my cardiologist this thing, but he declined."

With the flick of a small button, the tiny blade began whirring round and round. Ronald bent down over the tube and sliced off two inches. He lifted it to his eye again. "White cotton," he said. Kirk felt dull-headed.

Ronald inserted his finger and this time touched the obstruction. "It's wedged," he said. "Like a penny caught sideways in a penny roll." Inverting the tube, he sliced off two inches from the opposite end, peered inside, and announced, "Something gold."

As if he'd had shock treatment, Kirk's heart restarted, and his breathing quickened.

"I can see a little clear space." The electrician inserted his bottle brush again, hook-end first. He worked the tool gently back and forth, made certain that the hook was touching cotton, and eased it toward him. The obstruction tilted, shifted, and gave way, allowing Ronald to draw it out into the open, where Kirk's hand—now gloved—hovered just underneath.

"Got it," Kirk said, more calmly than he felt. With one fingertip, he brushed aside a badly wadded piece of cotton and turned over the crested gold button top, revealing beautiful embossing and an inscription that looked Arabic. "Any tweezers in that bag?" he asked.

Ronald produced a heavy-duty chrome pair. Kirk reached into the button's hollow interior and used the tweezers to grasp another layer of cotton. He lifted it away. Underneath, wedged tightly in the button top, was something small and round, disk-like, wrapped in a final layer of thinnest cotton batting. Kirk rotated the disk out of the button top, placed it on the table, and used his index fingers to gently separate the batting. Glinting in the light lay a gold coin about the size of a dime, wearing the noble profile of Lady Liberty and the date 1861. Kirk took a deep breath and strode to a filing cabinet of small metal drawers, opened one, and lifted out a tiny plastic bag labeled "Break-in at The Suitable." Inside was a dime-sized coin, identical to the one sitting on the table in front of him.

CHAPTER 33

Rose and Savannah arrived in Summerlin two days before the estate sale and pitched in, sorting, packing, labeling, cleaning, and discarding. Marcy was grateful to see that Savannah seldom let Rose out of her sight. *She reminds me of Renee!* Marcy thought as she watched Savannah anticipate the next need and take steps to fill it.

And she loved their banter. Midafternoon on Thursday, Rose's stomach grumbled audibly, and Savannah called out, "Fry alarm!"

Rose swatted her on the arm, exclaiming, "Some friend you are!"

"You can't blame me! That was Ricky."

"Don't you blame Ricky. That was *your* idea. You know it was!"

At Marcy's quizzically raised eyebrows, Rose finally explained, "You won't believe what she did to me before we left. We stopped to get a drink—all I wanted was water, Mom, really—and Savannah pulls up at the Triple Deck because she insists she has to have *a triple chocolate* milkshake!" Rose paused and glared pointedly at her friend, whose innocent look was a mite *too* wide-eyed. "There *had* to have been some kind of code, because when we reached the window, there was Ricky Belden—a conspirator, obviously—holding out a gigantic tray containing one cup of water, one milkshake, and a *mountain* of french fries spilling all over the place. I was so embarrassed."

Savannah smiled sweetly at Marcy and said, "I'm pulling french fries out of every corner of my car."

At dusk, Rose, Marcy and Savannah retreated to the Bellamys' house for hot showers, a good dinner, and the luxury of clean guest rooms. Renee, who was bagging up homemade blueberry muffins for Friday morning, announced that both she and Tommy had cleared their calendars for the final day of packing.

On Friday evening, Savannah hugged everyone good-bye and left to get ready for work the next morning. Rose was noticeably lonely without her.

Now, back at the Kendall house early on the Saturday morning of the estate sale, Marcy sat down with her to-go cup of coffee and opened the Bible once more to Psalm 18. It was her morning habit to reread short sections of that psalm before turning to the book of Matthew, which she was reading straight through. On this, her last morning in the house, she wanted to remember it peacefully.

At 7:15 the doorbell rang. Marcy closed Matthew and got up to greet the team of workers waiting on the doorstep. The leader of the pack stuck out his hand and boomed, "Mitt Ratcliff. Call me Mitt." He looked out over the yard and asked, "Okay to set up over there under the oak tree? From the calls we're getting, this is gonna draw a crowd."

"You'll be setting up outside?" Marcy asked with an unsure voice.

"Yes, ma'am," he grinned. "We'd never fit all those people in the house. I need t' be able to see people when they're biddin.' We've had noses punched 'cause I didn't have a clear sightline."

Mitt proceeded to escort Marcy down her own front steps, walking her regally through the front yard. "Here's where to set up the chairs." Motioning to the four men standing over by the truck, he called out, "Over here—a hundred to start with. Put 'em in straight lines of ten. Need more, we got more."

Next they inspected the registration table, where three women waited patiently for instruction. Mitt explained that not everyone who attended the auction had to register—only those who intended to bid. Each bidder would receive a numbered paddle from Rachel, who was responsible for recording the winning bids on the inventory sheet that Marcy had filled out Thursday afternoon—now color-coded and glowing on a laptop plugged into a small portable generator.

"Lynette here"—he indicated a woman of about fifty in a hot pink jumpsuit direct from the seventies—"is gonna be stationed inside the house, downstairs. Charlene"—a younger version of Lynette—"is gonna do the honors in the garage. They accept payment during the preview for the small items we're gonna sell outright. After the preview, we bring the auction items outside, one roomful at a time. Miss Marcy, would you mind showin' us all around the house?"

Surprise flitted across the man's face as he walked into the living room—a picture of order and organization.

"You're hired!" he said admiringly. "You've isolated everythin' you plan to keep?"

"Right," Marcy said. "They're in two rooms—one upstairs and one down. The downstairs room locks. Unfortunately, I can't find the key to the room upstairs. But I've closed it off with Do Not Enter signs."

"Perfect," Mitt said. "Now, let's take the tour."

Even as she led the small caravan through the house, Marcy herself could scarcely believe what she, Renee, Tommy, Rose, and Savannah had accomplished in such a short time. Very little of the formal furniture would go with them. Instead, they had chosen the most comfortable pieces to furnish a den and a breakfast room, two bedrooms, and an office "for Rose to study in," Marcy insisted. Daniel's chair. Rose's grandparents' bedroom furniture. Marcy's bed and dresser. Not one item from the handsome suite that Jack had claimed when he moved in.

Marcy's skin crawled as she led Mitt to that end of the second floor. Against her will, she could still hear Jack's refined drawl, his announcement that he would give Marcy the privacy of her own bedroom. "You can visit me," he had murmured. "It will be more exciting that way." And, he explained, when the town snoops asked, Marcy could truthfully say Jack had his own separate quarters.

Indeed, the quarters were somewhat separate—the result of a quirky renovation in the sixties that had enabled the Kendalls to install a central heating and cooling unit upstairs. Jack's suite, once an upstairs parlor, had been enlarged by taking in two smaller rooms, one of which was a bath and the other a dressing area.

It had been a beautiful suite. A fireplace at one end faced a comfortable couch and a coffee table. At the other end was a bed and a bureau. Jack had supplemented the tiny closet with a tall walnut clothespress pulled in from another room.

Now, from the small *en suite* bathroom, the scent of Jack's distinctive cologne greeted Marcy as soon as she and Mitt opened the door. The day after Jack's murder, in utter despair and confusion, Marcy had actually spritzed herself with the cologne before hurling the bottle to the floor. The smell had never completely disappeared.

Now, all of Jack's elegant clothes were crammed into the closet. The clothespress, the bureau, and the bed had been moved to the center of the room. A quartet of muscular men would eventually carry those pieces down the stairs.

"That's it," Marcy said, turning to Mitt.

"That's plenty," replied the auctioneer.

Five minutes later, Marcy heard the microphone being tested. The noise rang through the house—she was certain the sound would carry all the way to the waterfront. "Ladies and gentlemen," Mitt was booming, "welcome to the sale of the season!" As the yard began to fill, no one noticed that the stocky foreman of the moving crew was slipping upstairs at regular intervals and locking himself into the suite that was Jack's.

Six hours later, Rose and Lindsay Fullerton stood inside the entryway of the nearly empty house. "I think it was a success, don't you?" asked Lindsay.

"It seemed to be. Mom got really excited when some of those huge items sold. I even saw Kirk take a hop in the air when they sold the highboy for so much."

"He did seem to be paying attention to everything," Lindsay agreed. "I don't know if you know it or not, but Kirk asked me to be here—to keep an eye out for the guy who shot Jack."

"Really?" Rose asked with a nervous lurch in her stomach. "You've seen him?"

"Well, we think so." Lindsay gave Rose a brief version of "The Showing to End All Showings." Rose's face grew tense.

"Have you seen him today?"

"No, you would've known about it if I had. Kirk's been ready to close in on him all day."

Two of Mitt Radcliff's burly crew members, wearing their bright yellow T-shirts imprinted with the auction house logo, pushed through the front door, mumbled something that passed for "Excuse me," and walked between Rose and Lindsay to mount the stairs to the second floor.

"We need to look upstairs," one told the other. "Mitt said to double-check an' make sure we got all our equipment."

"So how is Myrtle Beach?" asked Lindsay.

Rose wasn't quite sure what Lindsay actually knew, so she chose to expound on her job, her friend Savannah, and her favorite spot at the beach. Finishing up, she smiled at Lindsay and said, "I really like it."

The two made way for a crewman coming down the stairs hoisting a furniture dolly in one hand and a plastic bag full of duct tape and furniture coasters in the other. "Good day," he mumbled.

Rose and Lindsay next made room in the foyer for Marcy, who looked tired but elated. "I'm not very good at mental calculations," Marcy said, "but my rough addition tells me we did extremely well out there. Two of those bidders apparently recognized the living room lamp—you know, Rose, the stained glass one—as a genuine

Tiffany—I had no idea! And they fought it out for nearly half an hour. The final bid was over fifteen thousand dollars!"

"Are you sorry we didn't keep it, Mom?"

"No, honey! We have a new life. That money is earmarked already," she said, with a meaningful look.

Mitt walked toward the front door and signaled to Marcy, who accompanied him into the yard.

Lindsay looked around one more time and said, "Well, I'm glad I wasn't really needed here today."

"Me too," said Rose. "And I'm glad I didn't know that you might have been."

"Well, time for me to call my clients and tell them we're actually ready to close day after tomorrow. There were a few pieces of furniture that they were interested in keeping with the house. They left a sealed bid, and I need to go see which pieces turned out to be theirs. Mitt should know by now. Take care, Rose. I wish you and your mom all the best at that beautiful beach of yours."

"You too, Lindsay. Thanks for all you've done."

Rose watched as Mitt's men loaded the last of the folding chairs into the truck bed, folded up the blankets used as padding, shut down their laptops, stored away the folding tables and the auctioneer's podium, rolled up their extension cords, and roamed across the front yard, tearing down the Auction Today signs and picking up discarded paper cups and bidding paddles. The big truck pulled away. The women who had recorded bids left shortly afterward in a minivan. Mitt remained on the front porch with Marcy, his pencil flying over a print-out of the items that had sold. Kirk was at the curb, leaning against an unmarked car.

Rose ducked into the powder room. Something was wrong, but she couldn't decide what. She felt unsettled, uneasy, almost… forewarned. She ran cool water into the ancient pedestal sink and splashed it over her face. Drying her hands on a paper towel, she heard a soft thump over her head. That wasn't a sound this creaky old house normally made, even when the wind blew. Another car door, she decided—but it had sounded so close.

She exited the powder room and looked around her. Her grandparents' house, stripped of its drapery and furniture, looked stark and sad. She wandered into each room in turn, remembering. Certain corners harbored distinct emotions. She stood at the big bay window of the dining room, overlooking the side yard with its magnolias, remembering the hours she spent perched in their limbs. She smiled wistfully, recalling how the backs of her khaki pants had turned green behind the knees when she hung upside down on the thin-skinned magnolia branches. But the unsettled feeling remained. It was hard to say good-bye to the past.

A step. The sound of something closing. A sticking drawer. Suddenly Rose envisioned two men walking upstairs and only one man coming down. Was Mitt Radcliff's crew member still working upstairs? Which one, she asked herself? The shorter one. Husky. A dark beard. Sunglasses.

She walked to the bottom of the steps and listened. Yes, there was movement upstairs. "Hello?" she called upward. The movement stopped. The stairwell itself seemed to listen. Rose waited. She was on the verge of stepping to the front door when a bright yellow T-shirt appeared at the top of the stairs. The owner's face was obscured by the stairwell's low ceiling. "Miss?" called a tense voice. "Can you come up here a minute? I have a problem with the inventory list for this room."

"I…I don't know anything about that," she said. "My mom's the one who pulled all that together."

"Oh." The man waited. "It's just…I can't read this handwriting. I thought you might recognize it."

Rose glanced out the front door and saw that Marcy had walked to Mitt's truck and was conferring with Kirk and three other men whom she recognized as active bidders. They were starting to load furniture into their small, enclosed trailers. Marcy was pointing to certain pieces and shaking her head. Rose assumed these were the pieces that would stay with the house.

Her mom was already tired. Why not try to lift one little task from her shoulders?

"Okay," she called, and started up the stairs. The man backed down the hall, turned to the far end, and entered…Jack's room. *No,* she thought. *We don't have to deal with anything in there. Anything left is being picked up by Helping Hand.*

"Here it is," the odd man called.

Her heart thudded strangely at the thought of even entering this room. She walked tentatively to the doorway and halted. "What is it?"

"It's over here."

As she crossed the threshold, a meaty hand closed over her forearm and pulled her forcefully into the room, even as the door slammed behind her. In a split second, she recognized a scene all too like what Marcy had described at The Suitable—coats and ties strung from one end of the room to the other, linings gaping, lapels knifed open. With her free left hand, she struck out at the man's face and clipped the edge of his sunglasses. As they fell, she recognized a pair of brilliant blue eyes that she had seen twice before, though never at such close range. Jack's driveway. The Suitable's back alley. The eyes looked stressed, over the edge.

"What do you want?" she asked.

"Where are they, Rose?"

He knows my name?

"I've looked in every drawer of every piece of furniture that came out of this house. I've looked in every corner, every closet, every piece of clothes your high-style boyfriend"—his tone was snarling—"ever wore."

"What are you talking about? What do you want?" Her eyes were flying around the room, looking for a gun, finding nothing. A knife then. He'd been opening boxes. Almost certainly he had a knife.

In response, he pushed her up against the wall and held her there, his thick forearm stretching from shoulder to shoulder and pressing down on her collar bone. Her eyes, wide with fear, teared up—and even as they did, she recalled Miss Martha leading the nine-year-olds through their memory verses. *Whenever I am afraid, I will trust in you,* she could hear her classmates reciting in unison.

Lord! She flung the silent prayer to the heavens and waited, breathing raggedly.

"All right," the man snarled, "I'll spell it out. Where are the coins?"

"Coins?" She looked at him helplessly. "I haven't seen any coins."

"Don't tell me that." He pressed harder. "Jack Bradford kept coins here."

"I don't lie," she said gasping for air. "I don't know…anything… about where Jack kept coins."

He pressed harder, now against her throat, and Rose felt the panic start to rise. She flattened her back against the wall, trying to breathe. *Whenever I am afraid…* She forced herself to think. *Help me, Lord!* Her vision was starting to blur, her ears were ringing, his voice sounded farther away, and a black cloud enveloped her. Her chin fell forward against his arm.

From far away, she could feel the stocky man shaking her. "Wake up!" He slapped her across the face, and she collapsed on the floor, striking her head against the doorframe. For a moment, she lost consciousness. As she came to, she realized that she was being hoisted over someone's shoulder, and that, together, they were clumping down the hallway toward the playroom.

CHAPTER 34

Anton dumped Rose without ceremony in the middle of the playroom floor. "Don't move," he growled. "I'll be right back, and you're gonna tell me what I want to know." He stepped out into the hallway and locked the door—undoubtedly with the key Marcy always left above the door casing—leaving Rose to make a desperately quick survey. Just where Marcy had stacked them, the mattresses were still upended over the playroom's low closet door, forming what a child would see as a half tent. The fact that the mattresses were undisturbed told Rose that Anton hadn't found the attic yet, since it was accessed only through that room.

Without hesitation, she slipped between the mattresses and the wall, opened the door to the closet, and squeezed inside. A second, identical door in the closet's back wall opened to her familiar touch, and Rose raced up the stairs on tiptoe.

Very few of the attic's childhood delights remained now: the furniture and vintage memorabilia had been borne downstairs a week earlier and organized into categories for the auction. Rose dashed rapidly to the lone window and looked out over the backyard. No one there. The window was painted shut. *O God, help me!* She reached for her jeans pocket, felt the outline of her mom's cell phone, and pulled it out just as she heard a door slam downstairs. Thumbs and fingers flying, she typed out a frantic, unpunctuated text message and hit the button to "send all." She could only pray that somebody out there on her mother's short call list would hear the signal, check the message, and figure out what in the world it could mean.

"Rose!" came an angry roar from downstairs. How *did* he know her name? She heard the scrape of the mattresses being shoved aside and glanced around frantically. He had found the little closet door… now the stairwell door. Maybe, just maybe.…She wedged her body up under the eaves beside a built-in cedar chest that had once stored quilts and winter blankets. An old chenille blanket, pale blue, was lying across the top, and she pulled it down over her body and made herself small, leaving just a sliver of visibility. At the last minute, as she heard a rapid tramping up the attic stairs, she grabbed an old black umbrella hanging from a nail in a rafter, and returned to her trembling crouch. She would stab the man if she had to. *Stab,* she thought. *Vivid transitive verb followed by its object: man. Stab the man. Stab the man.*

Heart pounding furiously, she sat there gripped with fury at… of all people…a dead man! Would he never be gone? The old hatred pumped through her, and she tightened her grip on the umbrella and realized she couldn't pray! What did this mean? *Lord*…she started and got no further.

As we forgive our debtors, rang a silent voice in her ears.

"What? I'll deal with that later, Lord. This is urgent."

The steps drew closer.

As we forgive…

Lord, please!

Closer.

Forgive…

Rose sat there, eyes squeezed shut, resisting, monitoring the approach of the footsteps on the stairs. The eighth tread from the top always creaked. There it was. The footsteps had reached the wide, unvarnished pine planks of the attic floor.

Insistently, the voice confronted her. *Forgive us our debts, as we forgive those.…*

More was at stake, Rose suddenly realized, than her immediate physical danger. The hatred she felt was a spiritual danger of equally deadly proportions. Could she accept unconditional forgiveness without extending it too? But did she really have to deal with this now? Was God helping her clear her slate? Was she going to die?

Lord! she appealed. *I'm being stalked by a murderer!*

And instantly she realized that God's son had been stalked too—stalked, captured, tried, and tortured. And still he prayed, "Father, forgive them...." Could Rose love her forgiving God and simultaneously hate her enemy?

Oh Lord, she prayed silently, even as the footsteps approached her. *I know I can't live without forgiveness, but I don't feel like forgiving Jack or this man Anton. I don't even know how to forgive them. Help me, Father.* At that moment, the chenille blanket was ripped away.

Lindsay Fullerton was saying her good-byes to both Marcy and the auctioneer when Kirk Landry bounded up. Before he could say a word, two cell phones beeped simultaneously. Amused, Kirk and Lindsay each said, "You calling me?' and burst out laughing. Looking like mirror images, they flipped open the phones and brought up their text messages. Marcy watched as nearly identical furrows creased Kirk's and Lindsay's foreheads, and their eyes locked in confusion. Both screens read: "Help in the attic hurry rose."

There was a nanosecond of interpretation before Kirk broke into a run, screaming, "Marcy, how do I get to the attic?" The mini-stampede halted at the front door. It was tightly locked from the inside. No one on the porch had a key.

Rose dropped the umbrella and held out her hands in the "wait a minute" gesture. "Mr. Johnson," she began, and watched the shock register in Anton's distinctive blue eyes. She knew *his* name?

"Please," she said shakily. "Will you tell me exactly what you're looking for? Maybe I can help if I know what you want."

"You know perfectly well, girlfriend," Anton said, gripping her arm and jerking her to her feet, snagging her shirttail on one of the rafters and drawing the shirt tight. His eyes widened as he saw her stomach, hard and round. "So—I guessed right! There *was* a little love tryst. The newspapers didn't mention this. No wonder your mom was so undone. What'd he give you, Rose?" He shook her hard. "All that money he took from me?"

Rose choked back her revulsion. "Is that what you're looking for? Money?"

"I just want my coins—the coins I found."

"Okay!" Rose said, as frightened by the continued silence of the old house as by Anton's intensity. Had everyone left with the auction crew? Remembering the voice, however, she summoned her courage and...was that a small sense of pity she felt? Rose steadied her own voice and tried to make it gentle. "Tell me what your coins look like. How many are there? I'll help you look."

Anton hesitated. Then, despite himself, he held up a beefy thumb and forefinger to form a circle about the size of a dime. "That big. Gold," he spat out. "Got a woman's profile on the front. She's got a crown-like thing on her head. Dated 1861."

Rose worked hard to keep her voice low. The man's nerves were about to snap. He would hit her again, she knew, if sufficiently provoked. He might hurt the baby.

"How many coins? What size container?"

"Twenty-five," he blurted. "I don't know what size container. I just handled the diving; your boyfriend handled the shipping."

"Not...my...boyfriend," Rose said, so quietly but firmly that Anton didn't contradict. Her ears had picked up the sound of feet on the front porch. Surely she would hear voices any minute.

Kirk had bolted off the front porch and raced around to the back door, but it too was locked. His only option was to break a window, but he dreaded giving away any element of surprise. Marcy, who—for the first time in weeks—looked like she was coming unglued, suddenly shrieked "Mrs. Campbell!" and fled across the street, reappearing moments later with the spare key that her neighbor had guarded for years.

The little group—Marcy, Lindsay, the auctioneer, and now an audibly panting Mrs. Campbell—huddled under the back porch awning and listened to Kirk's low, rapid-fire instructions. Only he and Mitt Ratcliff would enter the house. Mr. Radcliff would check the downstairs and then station himself at the bottom of the stairs. Lindsay would please take off those tom-fool high heels and be prepared to use one against anybody who ran out the front door. Marcy and Mrs. Campbell would stretch this rope—Kirk lifted a length of yellow nylon ski rope used to cordon off the back door during the auction—across the back porch. They had his permission to clothesline anybody who tried to escape. "Ladies," he blurted, "police backup will be here any second but with no sirens. When they get here, move out of the way and keep praying. Mr. Ratcliff, follow me."

As Kirk made his way toward the staircase, he took his own directive: "Father," he prayed with an urgency he never remembered feeling before, "I have failed to protect Rose from a dangerous man. Please, Lord, do what I can't do. And calm Marcy. Now, give me wisdom. And help me see the man before he sees me."

"I suppose," Rose said to Anton, "you've looked all over the second floor."

"And the first. Inside every piece of furniture. Under and behind every drawer and cabinet. Inside every piece of clothing. I found nothin.' So that tells me you and your mama have my coins." Anton's grip was so tight that Rose could feel the blood thumping in her shoulder.

She shook her head. "Do you honestly think Jack would have left valuable coins someplace where we could've just picked them up?" She strained to hear movement downstairs. There was none.

"So where else would they be?" Anton growled, pushing Rose's head back against the wall with his free hand.

"I don't know!" she answered with a suppressed cry. "But this is a really good place to look. There are all kinds of hiding places up here."

"Well, suppose you just show me." Anton said nothing more; instead, he opened the palm of his right hand to reveal a small knife handle; its blade flicked out at the touch of a button.

Rose came close to fainting. But she remembered how close and clear the voice had sounded. The only thing Anton Johnson had in his hand was a knife—all the man knew of power. Rose herself was in the hand of God. She took a deep, trembling breath.

"Look, Mr. Johnson, Jack took advantage of me—and my mother. It sounds like he was all set to take advantage of you too. But I don't know anything about these particular coins. Look over here." Rose deliberately led Anton to the built-in chest of rough-hewn drawers that always produced a loud screech when a drawer was pulled out. "Nobody's gone through these yet."

"Stand right there where I can see you," Anton ordered, jabbing the knife blade into the top of the chest and hauling drawers out onto the floor. In less than thirty seconds, he had dumped out every one, producing a flurry of faded photographs. He upended the drawers to check the undersides, the backs, the sides. Finally, he shoved the drawers carelessly up against the old brick chimney. "Next?" he said through clenched teeth.

Halfway up the stairwell, Kirk looked behind him. For such a big guy, Mitt was proving exceptionally light on his feet. The auctioneer moved silently into place at the base of the stairs and simply nodded when Kirk double-checked his position. The detective realized that the burly auctioneer probably had no idea why he'd just been sucked into a stake-out, but Kirk was glad to have him on hand.

Now, from over his head came the muffled sound of voices and a sudden screech that sounded like unprimed wood on wood.

"Middle room on the left…with the mattresses!" Marcy had told Kirk frantically. "The little door!" Kirk gently tested the doorknob to the playroom, drew his revolver, and pushed his way inside. Mattresses were lying at odd angles all over the floor, but the little door was fully exposed. Silently, Kirk tested that knob, opened the door and immediately encountered another on the back wall of the closet. A loud thud sounded above him! A second screech, a second thud! Kirk timed his opening of the stairwell door to coincide with what he hoped would be a third screech-and-thud.

Thinking fast, Rose pointed to the chimney. "I think there…there's a hollow brick," she stammered.

"Show me."

Anton pushed her toward the chimney with obviously growing impatience. Rose deliberately dragged a drawer out of the way; Anton grabbed two more and simply threw them over his shoulder.

Oh, Lord, Rose prayed, *let somebody pay attention to all this noise!*

She grabbed an old metal screwdriver and began rapping the handle sharply against the bricks, listening for the sound of a hollow brick. Detecting an echo, she pointed. "There!"

Anton reached up, pried out a dry wedge of mortar, and wiggled the brick loose. A long rectangle of jewelry box cotton was nestled inside, covering…folded squares of paper bearing a scrawl Rose recognized as her own. Childhood poetry! She had forgotten ever hiding it there. As Anton cursed furiously, Rose felt despair. Then she heard a familiar creak, and a wave of hope swept through her.

"Sorry!" she said. "I thought my mother might have told Jack about that brick. Try the floorboards in this back corner. One of the boards lifts up."

Anton glared at Rose as if to determine if she were playing him for a fool. He growled audibly, but dropped to his knees in the corner and began running his fingers over the joints in the floor.

Through the echo chamber of the attic stairwell, Kirk could hear Rose speaking in a tone that simultaneously knotted his insides and flooded him with gratitude. The girl was doing what she did best—taking responsibility. Still, he could hear the tension in her voice.

And he could hear a man—terse and tense—moving like a bull from one spot to another. Now, a steady tap-tap-tapping was pulling Kirk upward, orienting him to his quarry. He crept upward. Only eight feet away from the square opening into the main attic floor, a tread beneath him creaked, and Kirk froze, listening. Had he given himself away? Nothing upstairs indicated that he had. Instead, he heard what sounded like crumpling paper and a furious curse.

But listen to the girl! She was magnificent. "Sorry!" she was saying. "Try the floorboards in this back corner. One of the boards lifts up. There's a prybar hanging on a nail right beside you."

As he approached the opening to the attic, Kirk was counting heavily on Anton Johnson facing away from the stairwell as he examined the floorboards. Was he? *Keep him occupied, Lord. Don't let him see my head.*

Rose had heard the creak! She would recognize that eighth stair tread anywhere. A wave of hope swept through her. "Can you feel it?" she asked Anton with an urgency she tried to disguise. "One end of the floorboard sticks up a little more than the others. You have to press on it hard to make the latch give way."

Kirk took a deep breath, grasped the handrail at its highest point, and eased up until he could see where Johnson squatted, his back to the stairwell, a knife at his right elbow and Rose right beside him. Out of the corner of her eye, she spied Kirk's head emerge from the square opening in the attic floor. Her eyes widened, but she made no sound. Silently, Kirk signaled her to move away. Then, just as Johnson, in a storm of dust, ripped a floorboard completely out of the floor, Rose leapt to her left, ducking behind the brick chimney as Kirk catapulted himself onto the attic floor. Their sudden and simultaneous movements jolted Johnson off balance. He stumbled as he jumped up and struck his head hard on a low rafter. "Freeze!" Kirk shouted, but like a bull, Anton ignored the order and charged straight for the attic's lone window, striking out with the pry bar and sending shards of glass raining down into the back yard. "Stop or I'll shoot!" Kirk bellowed, but Anton was already diving through the window as Kirk fired.

The bullet passed all the way through Johnson's right calf and lodged in the windowsill. Amid the clatter of falling glass, Johnson landed on the tin porch roof and slid, falling the final eight feet to the ground. He jumped to his feet and managed to run about ten yards before a Summerlin policeman executed a tackle that knocked him to the ground. The last thing he remembered before blacking out was the sight of two women hurtling toward him with a yellow ski rope.

CHAPTER 35

Fireflies were lighting up the woods behind Tommy and Renee Bellamy's house when Marcy finally walked out on the back porch and met her friends' questioning eyes.

"She's asleep," Marcy said simply, and the couple nodded. Renee slid over and patted the cushion beside her on the wicker settee.

Marcy sat.

As if he knew conversation would be too taxing, Tommy picked up his well-worn acoustic guitar, drew his fingers lightly across the strings, and half-picked, half-strummed a ballad that Marcy remembered studying in high school. Without a word, Renee got up and padded barefoot to the kitchen, coming back with a tray of green grapes, late strawberries, crackers, and brie. They sampled in silence, appreciating the frog chorus that took up where Tommy left off.

Crickets joined the frogs as a light breeze blew in off the marsh, and still no one spoke. Tommy began to pick-strum a medley of pop tunes. Eventually, as they always did, his fingers began to express the emotions of his heart, and now, as the fireflies continued to rise, so did Tommy's need to express the gratitude they all felt. Simple worship choruses sprang from the strings, and finally, Tommy began to sing softly to a plaintive old hymn that he had recently rediscovered. He especially loved the final stanza, which began,

My name from the palms of His hands
Eternity will not erase.

Impressed on His heart it remains,

In marks of indelible grace.[2]

"Is that true, Tommy?" Marcy blurted. Realizing that she had interrupted, she felt herself coloring in the dark.

"What's that, Marcy?"

"That our names are on Jesus's hands?"

"By implication," Tommy said thoughtfully.

"Meaning?"

"Well, the verse is actually from the Old Testament," Tommy said slowly, mentally dredging up the context. "Isaiah. God is promising that he will never forget his people even when it looks like he *has* forgotten them. You want to hear it?"

"Please."

Tommy reached for his "porch Bible" and flicked on the tiny lamp he kept clipped to the book's cover.

"You often read in the dark?"

"Now and then. Just looking up things that come to mind." There was a quiet rustling of thin pages turning. "Here it is—Isaiah 49, starting at verse fifteen. It's kind of unusual to hear God comparing himself to a mother, but he asks, 'Can a woman forget her nursing child, and not have compassion on the son of her womb?'

"Of course, we might think the answer would be no. But God says it *can* happen. He says, 'Surely they'—meaning anyone, even a nursing mother whose body would ache for her child—'may forget, yet I will not forget you. See, I have inscribed you on the palms of my hands....'"

Marcy sat perfectly still, transfixed by the thought. Her mind seemed to race through her life, through the last two years, the last month, the last two weeks, and especially through this particular Saturday. A bizarre mixture of emotions dammed up her chest, and she nearly gasped for breath. "Tommy...Renee...I had forgotten you, forgotten Rose..." She choked. "I had forgotten God. But...he *never* forgot his children, never forgot us." The dam broke, and she doubled over, forehead touching her knees. Renee stretched herself over Marcy, encircling her, dampening Marcy's back with her own thankful tears.

Tommy—stunned by yet another disclosure of how God speaks—closed the Bible and looked far into the woods, past the fireflies, filled with wonder.

Anton Johnson was calling for his lawyer even before the emergency room doctors could begin tending to his leg, his dislocated shoulder, and several dozen cuts and bruises. But Kirk had seen enough to know that his stocky prisoner not only fit the physical profile of Jack Bradford's murderer but also of Lindsay Fullerton's mystery man. "Measure his feet for me, will you?" he barked to a deputy, remembering the footprints beneath Marcy's window and those in the impound lot.

After conferring with the hospital's security director, Kirk pulled aside the ER physician to suggest that, if he had to keep Anton overnight, he should keep a guard posted at the door. "And I need to see his shoes, his wallet, his car keys—anything in his pockets."

Mitt Ratcliff had come puffing into the waiting room on the heels of the EMTs, agitated that one of his own employees was implicated in a crime. Kirk offered him a cup of coffee and a chair in a small conference room. A community affairs officer was waiting for him, ready to take the first statement.

It was dark outside when Jason Edwards arrived and snagged Kirk's elbow as the detective stepped outside the conference room. "Kirk, you got a minute?"

"For you, yeah." Kirk smiled.

"The whole town's stirred up about a shooting at Marcy Kendall's house. Is she ..."

"Marcy's fine. So's Rose—by the grace of God. Unless I'm mighty wrong, Jack's shooter came after her and was holding her hostage while he searched the attic."

The ever dignified Jason sounded as if the breath had been knocked out of him. "Did he hurt her?"

"Roughed her up some. She has bruises on her arms and neck. But that's one cool-headed little girl—she held him off with brainpower."

Jason shook his head in admiration, waited only a second, and then said, "Kirk, you remember the coin Marcy found in the hidden drawer at The Suitable? I made photocopies of it in Jack's office that day, remember? I want you to see the fax that came in just as I was leaving the office."

Kirk leaned against the wall and devoured the brief message from the curator at the National Numismatic Collection at the Smithsonian. The note read simply, "Mr. Edwards, we would be extremely interested in examining the original coin. Your photocopies are consistent with all identifying marks of an 1861-D. Feel free to contact me directly."

"So what's the story on this coin?" Kirk asked.

"Do you have time for this?" Jason asked. "It may take a little while."

"Your timing's exceptional. Hold on, let me check my patient first. I'll be right back." He was gone less than three minutes. "Looks like the surgeon'll be working a while. How about some coffee?"

"Not for me," demurred Jason. "You won't have one normal nerve left after drinking hospital coffee."

"What're you saying?" Kirk grinned. "This is how I maintain my lightning-quick reflexes." The two men settled in at the conference table, and Kirk inhaled deeply across the top of his steaming Styrofoam cup.

"Kirk, that little gold coin that Marcy found was an 1861-D…a Dahlonega dollar. Does that ring a bell?"

The detective shook his head.

"It's considered the second rarest US gold dollar out there. Some collectors will buy them regardless of condition. Back in 2000, a low price for a '61-D in average condition was around seventeen thousand dollars. Those in great shape go for a lot more. In 2008, a top quality piece went for $149,500."

It was Kirk's turn to shake his head. "For a one-dollar gold piece? Why?"

"A sense of romance," Jason smiled. "And being a Southerner, you'll understand it. Here's the short course. You remember studying the Cherokee Indian culture—how a deer hunter on Cherokee land supposedly stubbed his toe on a rock that turned out to be gold? There was a decent-sized vein of it there. Remember how the government eventually rounded up the Cherokee and all the other Southern tribes and marched them out west on the Trail of Tears?"

Kirk nodded.

"Well, that particular gold strike was near Dahlonega, Georgia, and the gold was especially pure. Once word got out, it was too dangerous for the miners to take their gold all the way to the US mint in Philadelphia, so the government set up a branch mint in Dahlonega. Ever been there? It's a pretty little mining town in the mountains—scenic. The Appalachian Trail runs right by it. There's a gorgeous old brick courthouse turned into a gold museum.

"Back in 1837, this little branch mint could turn out a gold dollar every second. They also made a quarter eagle coin worth two fifty, and a three-dollar coin, and a half-eagle worth five dollars.

"Trouble was, after a while, there wasn't enough gold coming in to cover the overhead. That's why all the gold coins minted in Dahlonega are considered rare today, because relatively few of them—about 1.3 million—were made. Apparently, that's not many for a twenty-eight-year operation.

"But you haven't heard the interesting part—at least from a collector's standpoint. In 1861, when the war broke out, Georgia seceded from the Union, and Mr. Kellogg, the director of the Dahlonega mint, submitted his resignation to Abraham Lincoln. That was supposed to end Georgia's coin production. But it didn't. Some people say that Confederate soldiers seized the Dahlonega mint by order of the governor and used what little gold bullion remained to make these coins. But others say the mint employees simply 'transferred their allegiance' to the Confederate States of America, and that they're the ones who made the 1861-Ds.

"Either way, the handful of coins that were made after the mint came under Confederate control were weak strikes—almost as if the men handling the equipment didn't fully understand how to set it up. Or maybe they were in a hurry, and the planchets—the little gold disks to be stamped—were sloppily prepared. See? Look at this picture."

Jason produced a sheet obviously printed from an Internet site. He pointed. "This is the heads side, the obverse. See how the letter U in United States of America is really weak? Now, look at the decorative edge—the reeding around the edge of the coin. Underneath Lady Liberty's profile, see, the reeding looks worn away. But the problem isn't wear. It's a weak strike." Kirk simply nodded, and Jason went on, pointing to the second picture.

"Here's the tails side—the reverse. This is supposed to be a wreath of corn and grain circling the inscription." Kirk studied the photograph. There was a large numeral 1 centered over the word *dollar* on the second line and the date *1861* on the third. The mintmark D for Dahlonega sat below the ribbon at the base of the wreath. Instead of being crisply outlined, the wreath looked slightly overlapped. A section of reeding along the bottom edge was missing.

"One thing's for sure," Jason went on. "The 1861-D was unique. Two new dies for a new reverse had arrived in Dahlonega in January 1861. They'd never been used. So in April, somebody put a new tail on an old head, and produced a coin that has no counterpart.

"So," Jason summarized, "you see how these little dime-sized dollars capture people's imaginations. There's so much that's unique and historical and emotional attached to their story."

"How many were there?" Kirk asked.

"Some experts say between a thousand and fifteen hundred, but others say up to thirty-five hundred. Nobody really knows. Coin collectors can account for maybe a hundred. And as I said, the value just keeps going up and up. So"—Jason paused for effect—"if Jack and his business partner stumbled onto even a few of these, maybe some that were unknown to collectors, they had the potential to make big money—no minting machine necessary."

By now, Kirk was feeling a pleasant sense of weariness. He leaned back in his chair, unbuttoned his breast pocket, and pulled out a small plastic bag containing two gold coins. "Jason," he said, "Have you ever met a pneumatic crimper?"

CHAPTER 36

At Tommy's and Renee's insistence, Marcy and Rose remained at the Bellamys' house for several days. When the local TV news crew arrived, Tommy gave a stand-up interview in the front yard. His account covered the basics: A man entered the Kendalls' house during an estate auction, apparently looking for valuables. Rose encountered him upstairs and was taken hostage and locked in a room. She managed to reach the attic, sent an urgent text message on her mother's cell phone, and thus alerted the police, who surprised the intruder in the attic. Diving through the attic window, the intruder was shot in the leg and then brought down by members of the Summerlin Police Department.

Most of this, of course, the reporters already knew from the official police report, but Kirk had provided Tommy with several additional details, each carefully chosen—the wording of the text message, a physical description of the playroom door to the attic, the location of the attic window—to help flesh out the story. The reporters were appeased, if not satisfied. In his quiet, trust-inspiring way, Tommy deflected questions about any connection to the murder of Jack Bradford by saying, "Y'know, the police are looking into that." Rose, he said, was shook up. She had bruises on her arms and neck. But, he added, she had shown tremendous faith and courage, and he was proud of her, proud of Marcy. To persistent personal questions, Tommy replied that he couldn't jeopardize his pastor/parishioner relationship but fervently hoped that the reporters' questions could all be answered soon.

A day later, when Anton Johnson was officially charged with murder, taking a hostage, possession of a lethal weapon, attempted robbery, assault and battery, and resisting arrest, the news crews shifted focus to Anton's hometown, which gave Marcy and Renee the opportunity to slip out of the house early the next morning to oversee the loading of a moving truck parked in the Kendalls' backyard. At the last minute, Rose surprised them by asking to come along. "I don't want to be alone," she said simply.

To the women's surprise, a dozen teenagers were waiting quietly on the Kendalls' back porch. Hair uncombed, sleep still in their eyes, they grinned sheepishly when their spokesman explained that Tommy had called the church youth group and asked for their help. "We've never had a youth group meeting this early in our lives," one said. Tommy pulled up as the boy was speaking, carrying three dozen ham biscuits and two gallons of orange juice.

"Figured we could take care of this in an hour with some extra hands," said Tommy to the pair of muscular men leaning up against the moving truck, drinking coffee. They looked pleased to be offered a hot ham biscuit. The teenagers gathered round and claimed their breakfast.

It was an awkward moment for Rose, who stood behind Marcy and Renee, fervently wishing she had stayed behind. Then two of the girls, Kara and Crista, spotted her and separated themselves from the rumpled group on the steps. "Girl, we've missed you so much!" said Crista, who hooked her elbow through Rose's and hustled her off as normally as if they were leaving the locker room after a victory on the softball field. "We brought you your yearbook. Look—page sixty-three. There's the whole team at state!"

Squeezing onto a bench beneath a big oak, the three girls bent their heads over the team photos. In spite of herself, Rose was soon giggling over the action shots that made several girls look airborne as they stretched to catch a hard hit ball.

"Rose," said Kara after a few seconds of silence, "I hope you don't mind, but we got some people to sign your yearbook for you, since you weren't there for the signing party." She gently flipped open the book to the inside front cover. Not an inch was left unsigned, not just names but messages, short and long. Silently, Rose turned the pages, front and back. Every available spot on the signature pages was covered in handwriting. Many of the photos were too. The faculty page was fully covered. Rose couldn't help but recognize Melinda Berry's familiar red pen. The message said, "Please call me—very important," and concluded with her phone number and the initials MB.

"We told people not to write on the softball pages," Kara said. "We didn't want you to miss these shots." Rose shook her head, unable to speak. She held the book to her chest and watched as, one by one, the other members of the youth group stowed away a dresser, a chair, a box in the moving truck, and then walked over to the bench. Self-conscious, a little awkward, their brief embraces said even more than the messages of encouragement that covered Rose's yearbook.

Two hours later, Marcy and Rose followed the moving truck to Highway 17 and turned south toward the state line separating the Carolinas. "It's a really cute little cottage, Mom, about three blocks from the beach. The owners are an older couple, friends of the Coles. Their last name is Morrison. They own quite a bit of beach property, I hear."

"I can't wait to see it," Marcy assured her, and the two lapsed into a thoughtful silence.

"What a miracle!" Rose suddenly blurted about ten minutes later.

"What?" asked Marcy.

"The kids...I thought they would judge me. But they didn't. You took it all when you explained to the church."

"Oh, Rose," said Marcy, who was equally moved, "I only wish I *could* have taken all of it."

About a mile past the city limits sign in North Myrtle Beach, the moving truck pulled in beside Savannah's little Toyota, and Rose and Marcy spotted a group of strangers, both teens and adults, gathered under the trees. Marcy looked at Rose, who was definitely feeling the effects of the trip, and asked, "Is it normal for that many kids to be here? I'm not sure either of us is up to meeting a lot of new people right now."

But Savannah jumped out of her car, calling, "Surprise, guys! The youth group from church told me yesterday to let them know when you were due in. They're here to help you unload."

"Are you kidding me?" asked Marcy. "Total strangers?"

A man and woman walked toward her, and the man held out his hand.

"I'm Joe," he said with a genuine smile. "I'm the youth pastor at Coastland, and this is my wife, Jessica. Welcome to North Myrtle Beach! It looks like you already have a moving crew, but we figured you'd be too busy to worry about meals, so the ladies at church made lunch and dinner! How can we help?"

"This is wonderful!" Marcy said. "You know, I haven't even seen the inside of the house yet. Let us take a look, and we'll be right back out." She motioned to the moving men, who were standing by the cab of the truck, stretching and waiting for their directions. "We'll be with you in a minute."

"Rose!" Marcy whispered. "I didn't know people did these things! Twice in one day?" They walked up the four steps onto the porch of the white frame bungalow. Savannah came up behind them, gave Rose a welcome-back hug, and produced the key.

A 1940s charm was evident throughout the cottage despite a number of renovations. Instead of sheetrock, the white walls were covered with three-and-a-half-inch horizontal boards. The ceiling was beadboard, lower in some rooms than in others. Beautiful old heart pine floors were aged to a mellow honey color. "Oh, that reminds me of home!" Marcy said lightly.

The two bedrooms shared the one bathroom, with its ancient clawfoot tub and its pedestal sink, all scrubbed and clean. Best of all, a deep porch lined the front of the house. "I can see where I'll spend my free time," said Marcy. "Look." She pointed to two hefty hooks in the porch ceiling. "It's already set up for your grandmother's porch swing."

Suddenly, Marcy went to the door and signaled to Joe and Jessica. "Could you come in for just a minute, please?"

The couple came in, and Marcy said, "Joe, everything in that truck is a part of the past. This house is a new start for Rose and me. Would you pray for us before we move our things inside?"

"I'd love to," said Joe. The four formed a small circle on the front porch, in full view of the crew waiting outside. After the "amen," the moving men followed Marcy's beckoning hand and began lifting the couch from the back of the van. Despite the hired help, the teenagers were in no mood to stand idly by.

"Okay," Joe called out. "You've all done this before. Light stuff for the girls, heavy stuff for the guys."

It wasn't hard to figure out what would go where. The unloading and set-up took no more than forty-five minutes. The bed frames were put in place, awaiting the delivery of new mattresses. The kitchen was stacked with boxes that the youth group insisted on bringing in themselves. Rose didn't recognize all the teens, but she did spot Ricky from the Triple Deck, grinning widely. The second time he passed her he asked, "Had any good fries lately?"

Rose was humiliated. "Savannah Cole," she hissed. "Why did you ask Ricky to come? He's forever going to think of me as a big, fat, french fry!"

Savannah blinked, not sure how to reply. "How do you want him to think of you, Rose?" she asked.

"It's not that, Savannah. It's just that I'm gaining weight as it is, and he probably thinks I shouldn't be eating fries at all!" At that, Rose realized how tired she was and how petty she sounded.

Savannah simply hugged her and turned to touch Marcy on the arm. "The Morrisons were in town this week, Mrs. Kendall, staying at their summer house—the big one you can see right out that window. They told me they were putting some snacks in the fridge. They also sent someone over to clean so moving right in wouldn't be a problem."

"Oh, my," Marcy said when she opened the refrigerator. It was stocked full! "Complete strangers, Savannah!" There were essentials like milk, eggs, and bread, and nonessentials too: a watermelon, some ice cream bars, and a gallon of tea. "This is overwhelming." She pulled out a kitchen chair and sat down. It was almost too much to take in at once.

"Mrs. Kendall," came a male voice. "We have people here who want to know where you want furniture to go."

"Okay, okay, let me see some more of God's blessings," Marcy said with a joyful laugh.

"Sometimes they seem to come in a big rush," said Savannah, who was stacking boxes of kitchenware on the floor.

"That's true!" said a notably brighter Rose. She was looking at her mom, who had tears in her eyes. The movers were bringing in Daniel's chair.

"Right here," she said. "Thank you! Thank you so much."

The Coastland youth group pulled away, having devoured the cold watermelon at Marcy's insistence. Ricky Belden stared out the van window on the drive back to the church parking lot, thinking of how hard the whole morning must have been for Rose. She couldn't possibly be happy about what was happening to her. It showed in her face—self-conscious, uncomfortable. Wouldn't meet his eyes. He didn't know all the details, but Savannah had explained enough. Ricky couldn't shake off his concern. But he didn't know how to feel.

Climbing into his old Trailblazer, Ricky decided he was not going to feel sorry for Rose. He was going to be her friend, instead. And given the opportunity, he thought with a sad smile, he'd give her lots of fries.

The month of July passed quickly. Marcy received a sizable check from the proceeds of the auction and within the week took Rose shopping for a car. Rose was clearly touched—at first protesting, but finally giving in when her mom insisted that they needed two cars. "A Volkswagen," Rose had surprised her by requesting. It was light blue, with an off-white, retractable fabric top. With only thirty-four thousand miles on the odometer, it was in great shape, and Rose was thrilled. "This is our fun car, Mom," she said. "I'll share it whenever you want it."

Marcy was euphoric to land a job as a receptionist for the water department in North Myrtle Beach. The city, she quickly discovered, was an unusual mix. It had a large base of permanent residents and, on any given day, an even larger group of vacationers, snowbirds, and conventioneers. With hospitality as the basis for so much of the local economy, the city insisted that its staffers show a friendly face to everyone who walked in the door. Marcy's smile these days was genuine, and her coworkers quickly grew fond of their soft-spoken front-woman.

Every evening after dinner, Marcy and Rose walked on the beach, amazed that their life contained this element of being on perpetual vacation. Surrounded by vacationers who had left their to-do lists at home, they found laughter contagious and relaxation communicable.

Still, the reality of her circumstances never fully left Rose's mind. She was now four and a half months pregnant. She had seen Dr. Richardson for the third time. Everything looked normal, he said. The baby's heartbeat was strong, its movements vigorous.

She could no longer avoid the nagging question: was the baby a boy or a girl? For so long, she had regarded it as a girl—ever since that night on the beach when she'd heard a little girl call for her mommy…when she herself, feeling helpless and small like a very young girl, had cried out for her heavenly Father, and he had filled her mind with his words. She just couldn't bring herself to ask the baby's sex, though, for fear she'd begin picturing its features.

Partially out of a growing appreciation for nutritional health and partially out of fear of running into Ricky Belden, Rose had shut down her fast-food addiction and contented herself with cooking at home with Marcy. Working together in the kitchen gave them plenty of time to talk.

"I don't feel like me," Rose confessed one night. "What else is going to happen to my body? I'm afraid." It was the first time she had actually voiced her fear. Marcy felt a wall go up.

"Oh, honey…you'll be fine," Marcy answered, suddenly uncomfortable. *Why?* she asked herself. *Why am I uncomfortable? And why am I so spineless that I can't let my daughter talk about how she feels?* Out of some dark mental corner came an image, dreamlike, threatening. The memory of her father pressing too close, touching her. *My body!* She felt a cry start deep in her throat but choked it back.

"Mom? What's wrong?"

Marcy looked at Rose as if she'd forgotten who she was. "That dream…" she began, but couldn't go on.

"What dream? The one that makes you call out in the night? Can you tell me?"

Marcy opened her mouth to speak, but nothing came out. She shook her head finally and said, "I can't." She looked at Rose imploringly. "I want to, but I just can't."

CHAPTER 37

A month after the move, Marcy shyly approached Scott Cole for some advice on financial planning. Scott and Lisa agreed to come to dinner one night, and Marcy laid out the picture of her assets: the house sale, the auction proceeds, two cars, her new salary from the city. Several valuable antiques were due to be released by the Summerlin Police Department, according to a call that afternoon from Kirk Landry.

Then Marcy laid out her wish list. At the top was a good college for Rose. After that, Marcy desired little more than a safe investment plan that would provide her with enough income to live. "I think," she said, looking around her, "I could stay here for the rest of my life. But, once Rose is gone, I don't know how I'll feel. So I don't want to tie myself down."

"That's a really smart way of thinking," Scott assured her. "There've been so many sudden changes in your life. I'd hate to see you make any big decisions too fast. Do you have a budget?"

Marcy laughed. "I've never had to make one by myself. But I can tell I need to now."

With the discussion turning to numbers, Rose and Savannah wandered out onto the porch to sit in the wicker swing in the twilight. Lisa interrupted the financial session with a nod in the direction of the porch and a softly worded question: "How's she really doing?"

"She keeps going. But people are starting to ask her the questions expectant mothers usually enjoy answering. She's embarrassed. I see her withdrawing when we go out in public. She doesn't want to meet people, doesn't want to talk. I certainly understand. But it's not the Rose I know.

"She could stop work anytime, but she says she wants to finish out the summer—says she told the restaurant owner she'd be there through the busy season. She's responsible. She refuses to leave him in the lurch." Lisa and Scott nodded solemnly and turned back to the columns of numbers in front of them.

"You know," Scott finally said, "you brought in a very good price from the sale of your house and furniture. By investing some and spending carefully, I believe you can live on the proceeds for at least fifteen years. Longer than that, since you're working."

"What about college for Rose?" Marcy said. "That's my top priority."

"Well, it depends on where she goes. If she follows Savannah's lead and lives at home, you're still talking about a minimum of fourteen thousand a year for tuition, books, gas, and incidentals. Add another eight to twelve thousand if she lives in a dorm and buys a meal plan."

Marcy bent her head over the page full of figures, absorbed and serious. "Show me my options, Scott. What kind of investments?"

It was almost a month before Rose woke up one morning wondering how long the honeymoon with her mother would last. The day before, she had been forced to buy a new looser uniform for work. No one who saw her in profile could now miss the fact that Rose was pregnant. She felt clumsy and had actually dropped a full tray of drinks in the restaurant kitchen, causing a clatter that was heard in the farthest booths in the back.

Irritable, she came home, and for the first time looked around the beach house and compared it to her childhood home. It looked plain. Cozy suddenly became cramped. The furniture seemed an odd collection of mismatched pieces chosen without a plan. It was not home, and for the first time, Rose realized she could never go home.

An overwhelmingly empty feeling rolled through her, muddied by guilt. She had what she'd desired most. Reunion. Safety for her mother. How could she be so ungrateful?

But did she and Marcy really communicate? Were they transparent with one another? Could they speak freely without one of them drawing back? No, Rose admitted. Even though they were talking more than ever, there were still barriers, places you didn't go.

Could she accept a life like that? Were they going to create a new version of their old lives, climbing back into only partly modified roles, Marcy functioning on the surface but allowing Rose to come only so close emotionally? Would Rose spend the rest of her life silently crying out for her mother?

What did she want from Marcy, anyway? She hardly knew. But Rose recognized that she was going backward, back to the spot outside her mother's bedroom door, where she had often posted herself for hours, just waiting. Waiting for some indication that she mattered. That she was loved for being Rose, not just appreciated for being responsible. Responsibility! Rose felt a surge of fury. Jack had caused Marcy to forget even that hallmark of motherhood.

By the time Marcy came home from work, Rose had worked herself into a state. She struggled heroically to stifle it, hold it in. She pasted a smile on her face and helped Marcy put away the two bags of fresh vegetables she'd picked up from the open air vendor at the corner. She pled weariness after dinner and went to bed, where she tossed and turned, unable to get comfortable. No matter what, she warned herself, she would not undo the fragile sense of peace that covered this house like a mosquito net. *Simile,* she told herself without pleasure. *A direct comparison of two unlike things. This one inadequate. Peace is more than a mosquito net.*

It was mid-August. Rose was painfully aware that Savannah and her friends were heading back to class on the same day that she was scheduled for her next appointment at Lifesender. That afternoon, through a heat-and-humidity wave that turned her hair into damp corkscrews under a surface halo of frizz, she drove over to the agency and dragged herself into the air-conditioned office, turning clammy all over as the moisture condensed on her skin.

It would have been easy to growl at Joyce, but when Rose looked at her face and saw sympathy, when she felt her embrace tighten—not draw back—from Rose's sticky arms, she relaxed a little. "Hey, sweetheart!" Joyce purred. "We've been missing you."

Linda drew Rose into her office with an equally warm hug and exclaimed, "You look wonderful—your complexion is so clear and pink!"

Linda's file confirmed that Dr. Richardson was pleased with her progress at the five-month mark. He noted that she had gained only two pounds this month. "If I've gained only two pounds," she queried, "why do I feel so fat?"

"It's something nobody can explain," the doctor had offered. "Every woman reacts differently. Some women actually feel more beautiful when they're pregnant."

Rose had grunted in disbelief, and Dr. Richardson had simply laughed and patted her on the shoulder.

Now, in Linda's office, Rose felt the pressure of making some final plans. "I've been reading the book you gave me on adoption," she said, "and I've thought about it a lot over the past few weeks. I'd like to leave my contact information with you in case the child ever needs me. But I want to lock the door from the other direction. I don't want permission to contact the child. I need that door shut, because I think I would be tempted, and it wouldn't be fair to the new parents to leave them wondering if I'm going to suddenly show up and create conflict."

Rose paused, aware that Linda was staring at her as if she had two heads. "What's wrong?"

"Nothing! I'm just impressed with how well you've thought all this through—and put yourself in other people's shoes. You've made some generous choices. I'm proud of you."

The words were said quietly, but they resonated in Rose's heart.

"So you don't see any issues I haven't thought of?"

"Not really. Of course, you're the one who'll live your life wondering if the phone will ever ring. And you can decide if you want progress reports on the child as he grows up."

"I…right now I do. I'm still praying about that. And I'm praying about the adoptive parents too."

"Good," said Linda. "So are we. In fact, there may be hundreds of people praying about this baby's future. Now, I have some things for you, Rose." She pulled out a bagful of lotions and other personal products, tied with a beautiful organza bow. "We have generous volunteers. They come into the office once a month and make these gift bags for our clients. And I know that they pray for the recipients the entire time. And there are many, many other kind people praying for you and your child. That's powerful!"

Rose was on her way out to the waiting room when she heard the front door open and another effusion of delight from Joyce.

"We promised we'd be back to see you!" came a second woman's voice.

Rose turned the corner to see a woman carrying a diaper bag. She was followed by a dark-haired man carrying a car seat with a baby nestled inside. It had to be a little boy—he was decked out in blue—and he had to be very young, judging by his size. His eyes, only half open, were brown, his nose straight, his lips deeply bowed over a double chin. He had no more than a suggestion of brown hair. There was a tiny red birthmark on his neck. He was beautiful.

As Rose looked from the child to the mother to the father, she knew two things: she wanted a baby, and she wanted a father for the baby. She wanted a father who would look at her baby like this one was looking at his, as if he could see into his future.

As Joyce and Linda bent over the carrier, Rose edged toward the door, but not before she was caught in an eye-lock with the mother. What did it mean, Rose wondered with an inward cringe, that the woman's eyes filled with tears?

"There's a nutrition class next week if you're off on Thursday afternoon," Linda called.

"Thank you," Rose responded mechanically. She felt as if she'd taken a blow to her stomach. Would her baby look like that? Could she possibly give him up? Yet with every thought of keeping the child came a mental picture of Jack. There was no way, she thought, that she could look at Jack every day and live. It would be best if she never saw her baby. That way, the memory of his face would not hurt her. His face? Her face? She hated to admit it, but a little boy would be easier to give up. He would seem more like Jack's, a little girl more like hers. In utter confliction, Rose decided she would ask to be put to sleep.

But deep in her soul, she asked the question she was afraid to voice: "O God, will I have another child? Is this the only child you're going to give me, or will there be another? I didn't expect to feel so connected to this one."

CHAPTER 38

The call from Kirk Landry wasn't totally unexpected. From time to time he had e-mailed Marcy at work, keeping her up to date on the case against Anton Johnson. The grand jury hearing had been an open-and-shut process, he reported, and the solicitor's office was gathering evidence. They had decided to try Johnson on the murder charge first. But he had admitted nothing concerning Jack's murder or the break-in at The Suitable. Kirk speculated that Anton was weighing whether to make a deal or take a chance on an acquittal.

For now, Kirk said, Rose was needed to give depositions. Of course, he added, she would be called to testify when the case went to court.

Marcy's protective response emerged immediately. "Kirk, is it really necessary for Rose to testify in person? Can't she give a statement?"

"She was the only eyewitness to both of the major crimes he's charged with, Marcy," said Kirk. "No way we can make a good case without her."

"Can you delay the trial itself? At least until after the baby comes?"

"Well, the DA's in control of that, but I imagine Johnson's attorney feels honor-bound to drag his feet. So I'd say there's a real good chance that this won't go to trial until late January, early February. Remind me—when's the baby due?"

"Late December."

"I believe it'll work out. And remember, since this is a capital case, it won't be tried in Summerlin. This will go to Wilmington."

It was slim comfort for Marcy, who dreaded breaking the news to Rose that the solicitor was asking to speak to her.

Maybe at dinner tonight she could broach the subject. She hoped Rose would take it calmly, but lately, Marcy could tell, Rose was keyed up. Savannah would be meeting them for dinner. Then they were planning to shop for one or two maternity items. Marcy knew that Rose hated the shopping trips, hated being around other women who would question her about due dates and baby names. But the few times Marcy had tried to shop for her, the clothes hadn't fit. With Savannah in tow, Marcy figured, they could deflect most of the seemingly innocent questions.

She felt a tugging in her heart, a desire to hear from someone who understood it all. It was time for lunch. She took her devotional book with her to the break room and sought out a quiet corner, praying that the Lord would give her wisdom. She turned the page to August 28. At the top of the page was the verse "Bear ye one another's burdens and so fulfill the law of Christ."

Obviously, the day's selection had been written by a man.

> Do you notice when others are carrying a heavy load? Just yesterday, a friend came over to help with one of mine: laying sod in the backyard. My friend was not his usual upbeat self. He seemed preoccupied. I tried several times to get him to open up. First, I asked him if he was okay. He said, "Yeah, I'm fine." Half an hour later, I asked him again, and he said, "Yeah, man, I'm going to be okay." Knowing my friend like I do, I knew all was not fine. We stopped laying sod, took a break, and got a drink. We sat face to face. He still had a hard time getting the words out.
>
> While we waited, I was thinking about how Christ commanded us to bear one another's burdens to fulfill the law of Christ. What is the law of Christ? I believe it is to "Love the

> Lord your God with all your heart, soul, mind, and strength, and to love your neighbor as yourself."
>
> In other words: care deeply. Christ does. Finally, after a few more minutes, my friend opened up. A battle was going on in his mind. He was feeling guilt over a situation he had no control over.
>
> He told me later that simply talking through the thoughts ended the battle.
>
> I've seen this before. Satan loves for us to feel closed off to others, but when we open up and expose him, he can often be stopped in his tracks. Two are better than one when fighting an onslaught. We are in Christ, and Christ is in us. Sometimes it helps to have someone remind us of that. Observe your friends. Care when they are hurting. Love the way Christ did.

Marcy sat quietly, thinking, praying. "I haven't wanted to talk with Rose like that, Lord, to go to the hard places. But Rose is sending me signals that she needs more than I'm giving her. Why can't I open up to her? And why can't I invite her to open up to me? Will you show me what to say?"

The trio met for dinner at 6:30 at a beach restaurant that featured a big bin of roasted peanuts near the door. Diners were free to scoop up a bucketful and take it to the table, throwing their empty shells on the wooden floor. Marcy snagged a front porch table that provided a great taste of beach ambience. By the time the ordering decisions were made, the drinks had come, and Marcy prepared herself to sit back and listen as Rose and Savannah caught up. But both girls sat there with somber faces, munching peanuts and absently dropping shells.

"Okay, girls, this is supposed to be a celebration. I've just had my first job review, and it looks like they're going to keep me. What's up with you?"

"Oh, just the start of classes," Savannah said vaguely.

Rose just shrugged. Everyone studied the salad greens.

Marcy tried again. "Do you have a heavy course load, Savannah?"

She nodded but didn't elaborate.

The conversation was slow-going, and Marcy wasn't used to leading. Might as well practice on Savannah, she figured, as the salads arrived. They all dug in, and Marcy took two or three bites before laying down her fork and saying, "Is something wrong, Savannah?"

Apparently it was the fork that convinced Savannah that Marcy wasn't going to let it go. "Oh, it's decision-making time for me. I'm signed up for a lot of classes I'm really not interested in anymore. I'm trying to decide whether or not to switch majors, but I don't want to start over completely—I already have thirty-two hours toward graduation."

Empathy for her dilemma took up the next ten minutes of conversation. Marcy was able to eat and nod sympathetically while Savannah weighed the benefits of majoring in psychology versus marine science, and Rose asked an occasional question.

The salad plates were replaced with a platter of mini-burgers—and, of course, a small plate of fries—before Marcy found the courage to look questioningly at Rose. "Honey, you've been looking sad. What's wrong?"

Rose looked pleasantly surprised but quickly opted for the usual ploy of keeping anything upsetting out of Marcy's airspace. "Nothing really, Mom. I've just been thinking a lot the past few days."

But the words didn't ring true. There was a quaver in Rose's voice that told a different story. Both Marcy and Savannah were startled to see tears well up.

"Actually," Rose murmured, "I am so scared."

There. The words sat on the table like granite boulders. There was no way to ignore the statement or change the subject.

Marcy sat, praying for wisdom, waiting outside Rose's imaginary door, just as Rose had sat outside Marcy's. Yes, she admitted to herself at that moment, she had known.

When no one else spoke, Rose lifted her eyes, found a stronger voice in her throat, and said, still quavering, "I'm scared about having a baby. About what's going to happen to my body. Of…dying, maybe? And I'm scared of making the wrong choice of parents. And of never being able to have a baby of my own." That did it: the tears spilled.

"One minute I'm so angry that I have to carry this baby, and then, I see a total stranger's baby, and all of a sudden I want to *hold* my child—*my* child—I want that so much I can almost touch her." Rose screwed her eyes closed in a futile attempt to stop the tears; her voice cracked. "And then I'm scared that I won't ever have a baby I can keep."

The others sat tongue-tied. It had always been hard for Rose to get out what she wanted to say, but they had no doubt that she had just revealed her deepest thoughts and feelings.

"Well," started Savannah, clearing her throat and turning in her chair to give Rose her complete attention. "What stable feelings are you having in the middle?"

Marcy was struck by the wisdom of Savannah's unusual question. It would never have occurred to her to ask it. She was especially intrigued after Rose took a moment to think about it and then answered more calmly, "I'm swinging like a pendulum. I guess the middle would be to carry the child and love it until I give it to someone better equipped to raise it."

Rose wiped the back of her hand across her eyes. "I saw a family today at Lifesender. They had a tiny baby. A boy. They all looked so happy. I guess I wonder if I give away this baby, can I be sure I'll have a chance to have another and be happy like they are?"

Again, Marcy and Savannah just sat there. It was a hard question. Neither answered before Rose jumped back in. "I know I can't logically keep this baby. Even if I could provide for it. Because I couldn't look at him—or her—without thinking about Jack and the havoc he played in my life and yours." She looked at her mother, who closed her eyes and nodded.

Grateful that her chair back was turned to the rest of the diners on the porch, Rose shook herself and took a deep breath.

Marcy finally spoke: "I guess we need to go. We still have some shopping to do." Looking unnerved, Marcy stood up, gathered her cardigan and pocketbook, and walked to the ladies' room.

"Oh, Father," she managed under her breath, "I wasn't expecting such a reaction. And I shut Rose down, didn't I? I wasn't expecting her to be *that* open. Did I carry even a little of her burden?" Walking to the car, she slipped her arm around Rose's disappearing waistline and kept it there, pulling her close. "I love you," she murmured, and kissed her daughter's warm, damp forehead.

That night, Marcy went to bed replaying Rose's transparent confession. Knowing Rose's fears created a fearful lump in Marcy's stomach. She thrashed from side to side, unable to get comfortable, unable to think of anything but the anguished voice of her daughter. Finally, sometime after 1:00, she drifted off to sleep.

From a great distance she heard thumping. *Hide!* she told herself. *Hide! Under the bed!* She slid under quickly, trembling all over. The chattering of her teeth would surely give her away. The thumping was coming closer and she heard her name: "Marcy." The voice didn't sound quite right.

Would he find her? Should she answer? Part of her wanted to keep quiet, while the other part nearly called out, "Daddy! I'm sorry I told!" She was both scared and remorseful. Boots! The floor shook as they entered the room. She heard a voice that didn't sound exactly like her father's. "Come out from under there!" he ordered.

How had he seen her? The bed lifted away from her crouching form, exposing her entire body. She pressed her face tightly against the baseboard. A hand closed around her upper arm, jerking her up sideways. She clinched her eyes shut, didn't want to look, didn't want to see how angry he was. "Look at me!" came the voice, and as she opened her eyes, she cried out in fear. The face that hovered over hers was not her father's. She saw Jack! Her cry turned into a scream. "No, no! Leave me alone! Leave us alone!"

Just as Jack lowered his hand to cover her nose and mouth, Rose broke through her terror. "Mom! Mom!" she shouted. "What's wrong? I've never heard you scream like that!"

It was an hour before Marcy stopped shaking, an hour of walking the living room floor while holding a cup of tea between two hands, thinking she had conquered the sobbing and then finding out otherwise. Rose sat on the couch, her knees pulled up as high as her protruding abdomen would allow, her worried eyes following Marcy's path.

"Mom, you have to go to work tomorrow. Maybe you should try to get some sleep."

"I can't sleep. I have to finish this tonight."

"Finish what?"

"I should have told you a long time ago."

Sensing that this was important, Rose sat silently. Marcy covered the length of the cottage twice before speaking again. "I'm cold. Can we both fit in your bed?"

"Sure."

Rose pulled the coverlet from Marcy's bed and added it to her own. They left the lights on, climbed under the covers, and waited.

Finally Marcy collected herself, took a deep breath, and said, "Rose, I heard you tonight when you said you were scared. My fears have paralyzed my whole life. Until tonight, I couldn't grasp how wide a wall we've built between ourselves. You and I don't really talk, do we? You learned to tiptoe around me. And I learned to ignore your need to talk to me as your mother. I'm sorry! We've missed so much over the years. I'm determined to do better. I want to know you. I want you to know me.

"You've asked me a hundred times about the dream. It wasn't until this past June—the day I went to church and met the Coles and they took me to you—that I could remember what really happened. Up to that point, I could see only bits and pieces. You know how dreams are—people and places seem to change in mid-dream. But this one always went back to the same scenario. There was something…wrong with my relationship with my dad.

"I was driving back to Summerlin that wonderful Sunday afternoon and suddenly the whole story came clear to me. I was so unnerved I had to stop the car and just stand there beside the road. You remember how hot it was."

Rose nodded, and Marcy took a deep breath, just remembering.

"My father was a heavy equipment operator—I think I told you that. He ran bulldozers. He went to work every day in a hard hat, a pair of overalls, and big black boots. When he was sober, he was so much fun. He played dodge ball with me and my brother Jesse. He used to take us roller skating. We went to the beach, and Dad made a sand castle exactly my height.

"Dad lost his job the summer I was five, and that's when he started drinking. He finally got a new job about two months later, but by then, he had established a pattern. Mom had taken a waitressing job that kept her out late. She and Dad were fighting a lot. I remember walking into the kitchen one morning and hearing my mom say, 'You're supposed to be taking care of them but look—this bottle's empty!'

"My dad began coming upstairs every night around bedtime. No doubt it was innocent at first…he was probably lonely for mom. He'd climb in my bed and tell me the most wonderful stories. But after a while, even as young as I was, I knew something wasn't right. That wasn't the way a daddy was supposed to hold his little girl.

"And I wasn't supposed to tell my mom about our 'special times,' as he called them. One day, though, he must've gotten pretty drunk and said something that tipped her off. That's when she came and asked me, and she got really upset and told Jesse and me to pack up. My dad came back late in the afternoon, and this time he was really out of control. They got into a screaming battle, and, Rose, I was so scared! I watched him chasing my mom through the yard with a shovel, swinging and missing and swinging and missing. Finally, he hit her in the head. I heard it! I saw it! And I ran. I ran upstairs and hid under my bed and in a little while I heard him coming. He was stumbling, falling against the wall of the stairwell, and calling my name. He grabbed me, Rose"—Marcy's eyes were wide as she stared into the distance—"and he fell on top of me and I thought I was being crushed to death. And then, the police came. They took him away that night and I never saw him again. We moved to Summerlin, and about a month later, my dad turned over his bulldozer and it killed him."

Marcy was trembling violently, her eyes closed tightly now. "My whole family just came apart, Rose. And somehow, in my mind, it was all my fault. My fault for telling my mom. My fault that she got hurt and had to go to the hospital. My fault that my dad got arrested. And that we packed up and moved away. My fault that he died.

"Mom and Jesse and I moved in with my aunt, remember? My aunt was really good to me, Rose, but I had to learn to live in her world. They had more money and more education than my parents did. They had a social life that was more…polished, more respectable. I learned to be who she wanted me to be.

"And when I met your daddy, he already fit that world. He seemed perfect." The tears began rolling down Marcy's cheeks. "I still miss him so much. When he died, I sort of lost myself. Who was I? Who was I supposed to be? I knew I was still your mother, but, Rose—your dad was the one who'd kept me on course. And all those memories of my own father started coming back, and I felt like I was the one at fault again. God must be mad at me, I figured. I hadn't deserved Daniel.

"Shortly after the funeral, the dream started. It changes from time to time. Sometime Dad is chasing Mom. Sometimes he's hitting her with the shovel. Sometimes he's coming for me. And you know what's the worst part? I can almost work up the courage to come out from under the bed. Almost. But I can't, I can't move.

"Tonight, the dream was different, Rose." Marcy was crying audibly now. "I opened my eyes thinking I was going to see my father…and it was Jack. I don't even know what that means. And I'm not asking you to understand, or interpret it or fix it or anything. I just want to be honest with you. My decisions hurt you in a horrible way. You are free to talk about it whenever you need to. I'm not going to run away anymore. If I try to run, bring me back. Remind me of this conversation."

Rose pulled Marcy into a hug. "O Mom," she whispered.

September arrived, and so did the first small wave of snowbirds, taking the place of the family vacationers who vacated the beach after Labor Day. The Picket Fence Pancake House was brimming with white-haired couples with Northern accents. It seemed strange, but these diners were harder for Rose to contend with than the excited groups of beach-goers during the summer months. They had more leisure time—and more personal questions.

Six weeks earlier, Scott Cole had run interference for Rose with the restaurant manager, explaining why she was pregnant. Mr. Williamson had been indignant—infuriated—that anyone would do such a thing to "a sweet girl like that. I tell you," he said to Scott, "I've employed hundreds, maybe thousands, of teenage girls in my thirty-seven years here, but that one—she just shines. She's patient, she's accurate, nothing is ever too much trouble. She works extra hours when some of the other girls call in late or sick." He shook his head. "It ain't right…ain't right."

That was considered a statement of extreme sensitivity for a man as blunt as Mr. Williamson. When the golfers began pouring in in October, he kept an eye on Rose's tables. Too many customers showed up hung over, likely to make suggestive comments. One morning, his wife, who could be equally hardnosed, called Rose into the office and handed her a plain silver band. "Try this on your left hand, honey. This can be part of your uniform—not that it makes much difference anymore. That kind"—she jerked her head toward a particularly rowdy table—"they don't stop at much."

Ricky Belden began stopping in for breakfast at least once a week on his way to class. Rose noted that, after the first week, he always figured out which section was hers and sat there, generally ordering blueberry pancakes with a side order of hash browns. Determined to keep things comfortable, Rose tried to joke with him a little. "I can get you an order of fries with that," she offered one morning and noted that Ricky's grin seemed to cover his entire face. Ricky kept the conversation light and friendly until the morning a couple of golfers at a nearby table went too far.

"Whaddaya say, sweetheart? Looks like you been playing a round or two y'self, huh? Wanna go out with us tonight?"

Almost instantly, Rose was aware of someone standing behind her. Ricky had drawn himself up to his full five feet eleven inches. Loudly enough for the whole restaurant to hear, he announced, "Time for me to go, babe. You grilling tonight, or am I?"

The golfers turned red and studied their bill as Ricky put an arm around Rose's shoulder and led her to the coffee station. "Have a good one, Rose," he said simply and walked to the check-out desk. A week later, when Ricky showed up for his usual breakfast, Rose paid for a triple order of hash browns and delivered them to his table without a word.

After another week of watching Rose field crass invitations, Mrs. Williamson cornered her husband and announced, "I need help in the office. Send her upstairs to me, please."

For the next month and a half, Rose was delighted to fill the role of an office assistant. Mrs. Williamson quickly discovered that she'd gotten more than she'd asked for. Rose rewrote the menus, added graphics, and updated prices. She cleaned the office, organized half a year's worth of receipts in anticipation of tax season and hung up civic club appreciation plaques that had cluttered dusty shelves for years. She counted money, made out deposit slips, and soon was trusted to take daily deposits to the bank.

By the middle of November, business was so slow that the pancake house curtailed its hours, and all but a skeleton crew of seasoned veterans were laid off. "Will you be back next year?" Mr. Williamson asked, but Rose surprised him by answering with a gentle hug. "I don't know what next year holds, but I'll be in touch," she said. "Thank you both for everything."

The layoff was perfect timing. Rose was withdrawing from virtually everyone as the days went by—everyone but the growing baby whose knees and elbows she could sometimes make out as it turned somersaults inside her.

CHAPTER 39

From the living room window of the beach house, Rose could see the sun topping the horizon, sending up bands of pink and purple. Accustomed to getting up early for work, she found it hard to break the habit. Marcy was still asleep—it was Saturday, and Rose figured she had another hour before her mom would wake up. She flipped on a lamp, adjusted the pillows on the couch, stretched out sideways, and propped her Bible on her stomach. She loved the quiet. For half an hour, she read from the Gospel of Luke, wrote her response in a little notebook, and prayed.

This morning, her prayer was especially heartfelt; she was now exactly one month away from her due date of December 28. She could no longer put it off—she had to select the adoptive parents for the baby. Suppose she went into labor early without making her choice? The task seemed overwhelming, but she'd scheduled an appointment at Lifesender for first thing Monday morning. It had to be done—and now. More than anything, Rose wanted her baby to have a complete family. At last, she thought, she knew exactly what one looked like.

Two days earlier, Rose and Marcy had celebrated Thanksgiving with the Coles. Lisa and Marcy spent hours in the kitchen together. Rose and Savannah had set the table and decorated it with the first-blooming camellias. "Shouldn't these be orange instead of pink?" Savannah asked rhetorically. They washed a seemingly endless procession of mixing bowls and baking pans and filled cups with ice and stored them in the freezer. Finally, the two begged off long enough to take a before-dinner walk on the beach and returned just in time to see Robbie and Ricky pulling into the driveway. Self-conscious, Rose slipped an apron over her head and let its ties hang loosely down her back.

Rose was relieved to see that Ricky kept the conversation lively. He was obviously interested in surfing, parasailing, off-shore fishing—the usual pre-occupations of guys who live at the beach. He was also an amateur filmmaker, though no one would have accused him of artistic talent. Tonight, he had brought his movie camera and was shooting the laden table, insisting that no one could eat until he had documented the feast in its "before" state. Rose kept pushing her chair further and further from the table, out of lens range. "Get back over here, Rose!" Ricky ordered, his eyes glued to the camera screen.

"And wind up on YouTube? No thanks!" she responded. It touched her, though, that Ricky didn't prove himself the usual immature jerk. He swung the camera over to Lisa and said in his best broadcast voice, "How does it feel, Mrs. Cole, to have prepared roughly sixty-five pounds of food per person?"

Lisa rolled her eyes and asked, "Can we just pray, please?"

"Signing off," Ricky intoned.

Scott's prayer was wide ranging, beginning with praise to his heavenly Father, thanks for the meal, and a mention of every person at the table. He asked for safe travel for Ricky's parents, who were visiting relatives too far away for Ricky to make the trip and still get to class the following Monday. He ended his prayer "in the name of Christ the Savior, who equips us to approach our God in confidence."

Rose smiled, remembering the lighthearted mood that Ricky seemed to create once the serving and sampling began in earnest. He'd surveyed the table one more time and inquired, "No fries for Rose?"

"No hash browns for Ricky?" she felt confident enough to bounce back at him.

"No, darlings, you'll both have to settle for 'smashed' potatoes," Lisa responded. "That's what Savannah used to call them when she was two." With the conversation neatly diverted, the dinner had been a pleasure, and Rose had relaxed a little. But there was something about Ricky that still unnerved her. Even when he wasn't looking at her, she could tell he was listening to her, conscious of her movements, almost as if he were trying to read her thoughts. Sometimes his comments were bumbling but never deliberately hurtful. "Why?" she wondered. "Why does he notice me at all?"

Now, sitting on the couch as the sun rose, Rose remembered Scott's sincere compliments to Lisa and Marcy for the delicious meal and how he had rounded up Robbie and Ricky for kitchen duty. The racket from the kitchen was deafening—pots, pans, glassware, china, and laughter. It sounded genuinely happy.

Yes, the Coles were a complete family—with Christ at the head. That was what Rose wanted for her baby. That was what made her morning prayer so fervent.

Marcy was still asleep. Rose flipped through the magazines on the rustic coffee table and found nothing of interest. Just that week, Marcy had brought home a small bookcase and had unpacked several boxes of books. It was there that Rose rediscovered her yearbook. She hadn't looked at it since the day the Summerlin youth group had come to say good-bye.

She marveled again at the pages and pages of signatures. Turning to the faculty page, the red ink stood out again across Melinda Berry's photograph. "Please call me—very important," the inscription said, along with a phone number. Rose programmed it into her own cell phone and pressed save. It was now 8:30. Was it too early to call? Maybe she should wait until 9:00.

At 9:00, Rose walked to the front porch and dialed and almost instantly got a recording. She left her name and number and walked back inside to start breakfast. It was Saturday—she would make yogurt and walnut sundaes, and Marcy would make French toast.

Still Marcy slept. With a deep sigh, Rose retrieved a little canvas briefcase from her bedroom and pulled out the form. She'd put it off long enough. The Lifesender questionnaire asked about her interests and talents, her education and skills, as well as those of her parents and grandparents. There was a section to fill out about the baby's father too. What would she possibly write there?

- *Education:* menswear magazines
- *Interests:* coin-collecting
- *Talents*: acting
- *Skills:* tying neckties

Rose realized she was thinking cynically, but it was hard to shake. It took a major act of will to write serious answers to her own side of the form. She tried to remember how it felt to have an interest in life outside her own body:

- *Interests:* softball, literature, travel
- *Talents:* writing, chorus
- *Education:* high school
- *Skills:* waitressing, organization

Rose gave up. None of the answers seemed like her any more. She hadn't read or written anything for pleasure in months. Softball belonged to another life. There was no music in her soul. High school had no closure. Travel was a fantasy.

A knot of tension built up in her shoulders. Without direction, she paced the living room and finally sat down in her dad's favorite chair. She ran her hand over the tapestry arms and imagined *his* arms wrapped all the way around her. For a moment, she was flooded with warmth and relaxed in the imagined embrace. She had very few memories of her daddy, healthy and whole, enveloping her in his sweeping hugs. But certain memories were buried just under the surface. At times, she thought she could still sniff his aftershave. What was the game they used to play in this chair? Her dad would criss-cross his arms across her stomach and....

Rose sat straight up. Not even her dad would be able to cross his arms across her stomach now. Not even Jack. No! Her mind tried to press delete as soon as Jack's face appeared, but the X wouldn't work. There he was.

In disgust, she hauled herself out of the chair with a scowl just as her mom came down the hall, tying the belt of her robe.

"What's wrong, Rose?" she asked in genuine concern. "Are you...in pain?"

"Just the emotional kind," Rose snapped. "The kind that doesn't go away." Count to ten! she told herself. Don't say anything. Stuff it. Stuff it! But the rage she felt toward Jack—the fact that he had infiltrated even the precious thoughts of her father—overcame her usual self-control. The reservoir burst.

"*Why* did you have to let that man into our life?" she burst out. "He ruined us! He even seeps into what few memories I have of my own dad! I *hate* what he did to us! In fact, I hate *him*. I'm tired of tip-toeing around, pretending Jack wasn't too bad, that maybe he hurt us just a little. No! He *destroyed* me! He destroyed us and the plans I had for us! I was going to go to college and take care of you, Mom. Couldn't you have just waited for me? But you had to humiliate us both—can you imagine what it's going to be like for both of us to testify in court in front of the whole town of Summerlin?"

Marcy stood there, ambushed, dumbfounded. She'd never seen Rose lose control. Marcy felt poised to run to her room, climb back in bed with her old partner Despair, pull up the covers, and disappear. But seeing Rose doubled over and sobbing, she couldn't run.

From violent men you rescued me.

That was Psalm 18, she realized with a jolt, the very first psalm she had turned to on that memorable morning when she began reading the Bible, just after locating Rose in North Myrtle Beach.

"Lord," she said out loud in a trembling but genuine voice, "You have delivered us from a violent man. I thank you. I praise your mercy…and forgiveness. I was far from you, and you came to my rescue." Marcy's voice grew fervent. "O Lord, rescue Rose. Deliver her from the memory…and the consequences of my exposing her to this violent man. It was my sin, Lord, not hers. Show me how to be her mother.

"Lord," she continued, certain now of what she needed to pray, "we plead with you to guide Rose as she chooses a family for this baby. Provide a mother and father who know how to love and trust and discipline and train. Grant salvation to this child from a very early age. And please, guide every second of this delivery—keep Rose safe; keep the baby safe.

"Finally, Father, I pray for Rose's future. I pray that, in your perfect time, you will send her a good man she can love and respect…a man like Daniel. And I pray that they will have beautiful, healthy children to love. Let them always remember how Jesus loved little children, and let Rose find forgiveness in her heart for everyone, living and dead, who has wronged her." She was about to end the prayer when a fragment from the middle of Psalm 18 seemed to insert itself. She paraphrased it slightly: "You have drawn me out of many deep waters.…You have brought me out into a spacious place. Please, Lord, help Rose out of this terrible, narrow place in her heart. Bring her out into the spacious place, too."

Marcy recognized the breath of peace that wafted into her. "Thank you, Lord," she whispered. Then, gently, she called, "Rose, come here, please."

Rose didn't move. She had never heard her mother pray more than childhood bedtime prayers and a formulaic blessing at meals. Who was this woman?

Marcy walked toward her daughter and pulled her into a tight embrace. "This has all been too much, hasn't it?" she whispered. "Dealing with the police, coming here, finding a job, making a life with all that you're facing. Having to figure out how to stop being a mother to your own mother. Please, can I just hold you?"

She pulled her daughter down beside her on the couch, both feeling faint and tipsy about the truth, neither willing to tackle two-way conversation. For some time they sat in silence, gently rocking in place, Rose soaking up her mom's strange if tender strength, Marcy praying for guidance out of the wilderness in which she had lost them. She was struck again by the peace that came from holding her child.

Rose finally stopped crying and looked at her mother through drying pools. "Mom," she attempted with a quavering voice, "do you remember the time I took Papa to his limit? I stole that pretty little china stapler of Mrs. Campbell's and smashed it." She took a long breath, hiccupped, and steadied herself. "It was right after we lost Daddy." The sad, faraway look in Rose's eyes revealed the pain that a small child had stored away and never allowed to dissipate.

"I can't remember it all," she continued. "I must have been terrible, throwing tantrums all the time. But Papa just kept putting up with me until that night. He looked so serious I thought I was really going to get it, but in reality, the only thing I got was more understanding.

"He made me walk with him to the baseball field, the one where Daddy played ball when he was young. He let me see that he missed Dad too and it was okay for me to feel so bad. He was asking me to trust him that it was going to be okay. Just knowing that…helped me change and pull myself together a little. You just brought back that memory. Papa hugged me for a long time that night. It was a turning point for me. Maybe this is it for us. I need you, Mom." Her voice grew muffled. "And I need every one of those things you prayed for."

CHAPTER 40

Whenever Rose looked back on the Monday that followed her mother's prayer, she pictured a giant window in heaven, a window that opened and let down a matrix. Into it, all the strands of her life were being woven into a whole. It was a glimpse of a great Plan.

She awoke that Monday feeling lighter in spirit. Her body was growing, but it was as if Marcy had shouldered the extra weight. And Rose needed that support, particularly today. She was due to meet with Linda and Joyce at 9:00 for a final trip through the Lifesender notebook. She didn't look forward to it.

Every time she looked over the notebook's pages and pages of tenderly written letters, most of them starting with the words "Dear Birth Mother," she sensed the deep need behind the careful phrasing and imagined the aching desire these women and men must have felt as they struggled to choose the right words.

The photos, she had to admit, counted tremendously. The lighting was exceptionally important. A photo taken in a dark room seldom drew her like a picture taken in the sunshine. Green grass and bright flowers were a plus—she wanted her baby to see beauty. But most important were the eyes of the prospective fathers and the smile of the prospective mothers. Were they happy people, even without a child? Rose caught herself virtually measuring the distance between the couples' heads. A husband who stood too far away lost points. Perhaps he was in this only for his wife. But one who leaned too close sent up red flags too. Rose felt sorry for all the couples, certain that they had simply picked what they considered the most flattering pictures, having no clue that they were being judged on her peculiar, subjective criteria.

The letters...well, they were too much alike, too long, too painful sometimes. But why wouldn't they be, she asked herself, as she settled down in the Lifesender conference room and reached one last time for the notebook, aware that she was sitting in one of the most powerful seats of her life.

Linda Cantrell stuck her head in the door. "I've been looking over the forms you filled out—that must've taken a while."

Rose nodded.

"One question," Linda continued, stepping fully into the room and locking gazes. "Rose, do you want to meet the parents after you pick them out?"

She hesitated for a full fifteen seconds.

"Not necessarily," Rose said slowly. "Part of me would like to, but would it serve any purpose for them to know me?"

"Rose, you're a beautiful person, with a good head on your shoulders. You have a lot to give anyone who gets to know you. But it's totally up to you."

"I think I'd like to write them a letter. And write one to the baby too."

Out in the waiting room, a familiar voice was greeting Joyce. "Is that Savannah?" Rose asked with delight and jumped up to greet her friend. "What are you doing here?"

"My professor's plane was delayed on his way back from his Thanksgiving reunion, and he didn't make class. I remembered you had this appointment, so I just thought I'd stop by. I'll take you to lunch when you're finished."

"That's great! It'll keep me moving. Savannah, I need you to pray. This is so much harder than I thought. I would invite you into the conference room, but the book is confidential."

"I'm fine. These chairs are really comfortable. Take your time. I'll be praying."

Rose returned to her lonely seat. Linda wandered in and out of the conference room between phone calls and appointments. The phone seemed to be ringing constantly.

"Line two," Joyce would call, or, "I need your signature." To Rose, she asked "Ginger ale or limeade?"

"Oh! Limeade, thanks," Rose replied and discovered that it came with a plateful of sugar cookies. She broke off a corner of one to be polite, and shoved the plate as far to the other end of the table as she could.

Linda had just joined Rose for the third time when Joyce popped her head around the corner to report, "Rod and Stephanie Butler are going to be a little early."

"That's fine. I'm going to sit here with Rose for a little while. Let me know when they arrive."

Twenty minutes later, Rose was still only two-thirds of the way through the notebook when Linda received an urgent call from a family court judge. "I have to take this in my office," she said. Rose continued plowing through, but after ten minutes, she needed to stand up and stretch. *Bathroom break,* she thought.

Out in the waiting room, Savannah realized she had been drifting off to sleep when the sound of a door opening roused her. Some prayer warrior she'd turned out to be! A couple in their early thirties walked through the door and smiled. Savannah thought the man looked familiar, but after serving breakfast to half of North Myrtle Beach for the last two years, most men did. The woman greeted Joyce warmly.

"Linda's expecting you," Joyce said. "But she just got an important call. She should be free in a minute."

"That's just fine," the woman said, and joined her husband on a small couch. "I'm so glad you came with me this time," she said to him, gently tapping his knee.

"I hated to miss the last time," he said. His voice dropped to a murmer, but Savannah was close enough to hear. "Steph, I just want what God wants. You believe me, don't you?"

"I do. You helped me see that we have to get on with life. It's hard, though, you know. I guess it's like putting a project on hold until you can find a different way to finish it."

"Exactly." Comprehension seemed to dawn in Rod's face.

Savannah was observing as covertly as possible, but the office was small. She couldn't miss the fact that the man was twirling a strand of his wife's strawberry-blond hair with one finger.

Their summons to Linda's office came just as Rose was exiting the bathroom to return to the conference room. Rose looked up to see the back of the woman's head but met the eyes of the husband as he stepped aside to let her pass. He smiled. A look of recognition passed between them, but neither spoke.

I've seen that man before, Rose thought, and suddenly remembered his friendly wave across the Picket Fence Pancake House, repeated once or twice a week ever since the morning she'd run headlong into his chest on her way to work from Savannah's house. She stepped into the lobby to check on Savannah. "I'm down to the Cs."

"The Cs! We could be here all night!"

"No. I went through the book backward. Savannah, you know I'm strange."

"Go ahead. My stomach's growling, but I'll live. We'll eat either when you're finished or famished."

"I can leave now, Savannah. I have several possibilities marked."

"No, go ahead and finish. I'm only teasing you. We'll eat when you're through." Rose nodded and returned to the lonely job of turning pages, scanning letters and studying pictures.

She had come to the Bs when suddenly she found herself looking down into the same set of eyes she'd just encountered in the hall. Her heart accelerated. The photo showed a couple sitting on a sailboat, blue water sparkling in the background. On the shore bloomed a huge bush of brilliantly colored bougainvillea. The man and woman were laughing, shoulders touching. Rose immediately looked down at the letter. It was a single page, handwritten, not typed, half of it in a neat feminine hand and the rest in a bold scrawl.

"Precious One," the first half began.

> Some unforeseen situation has probably brought you to this decision, but God knew it all before time began. He knit you together in your mother's womb just as he is doing now for the baby you are carrying. I can't imagine the pain that has brought you to this point, but I want to thank you for giving of yourself and giving up this child, whether to me or another grateful mother. God knows your heart—and ours.
>
> Praying for you,
>
> Stephanie Butler

"Courageous One," began the second letter.

> I write this note today asking you to consider my wife and me as parents for your unborn child. We love God, and we love each other. I believe these are the true building blocks of a strong family. I have a deep desire to provide a safe and supportive home for a child. The Lord has given me the resources to do so. He has plans for your child, and if we are the ones chosen to help carry out those plans, we will do our very best. I pray that you will be "filled with the knowledge of His will in all spiritual wisdom and understanding."
>
> Waiting on God,
>
> Rod Butler

Rose liked the letters. They sounded straightforward, articulate, and sincere—but not desperate. With a sense of mounting excitement, Rose turned to the couple's personal worksheet. She scanned it quickly. Both had finished college. He owned a sign- and trophy-making franchise; she handled the accounting for the business. They taught a Sunday school class in their church and had gone on three mission trips to the Ukraine. Rod was a former football player who still loved sports. Stephanie was an avid reader, a "middling" pianist, and an occasional poet. They both loved to sail and one day hoped to travel "to all the mountainous places in Europe." Was it wholly coincidental that their garden contained more than forty varieties of roses?

At the bottom of the form, the Butlers had stapled a photo, apparently taken at a church picnic. A vivacious-looking white-haired couple smiled above an inscription: "Your baby will have the most wonderful grandparents!" It was at this point that Rose caught her breath.

The older gentleman was smiling right into her eyes. In his hand was a well-worn softball.

"Oh, Lord," she prayed, "You know all things. You've drawn my heart to this man and woman. If they would make good parents for my baby, give me peace of mind. If not, Lord, please close and lock the door."

With trembling fingers, she wrote a brief note, popped open the metal clasps of the notebook, withdrew the Butlers' page, and slid the note inside its plastic cover. She placed the page on top of the notebook and carefully glanced down the hall to make sure Linda's door was still closed. Joyce was not at her desk. She placed her finger against her lips as she collected Savannah and steered her out the front door. Noting that Rose's smile lit up her eyes, Savannah knew that something good was happening.

CHAPTER 41

At the Beachside Deli, Rose had just ordered a turkey on wheat when her cell phone rang. She didn't immediately recognize the number, but she did recognize the area code and the first three digits that identified Summerlin's most long-standing telephone customers.

"Savannah, I have to get this," she said, and quickly caught the voice of her English teacher.

"Mrs. Berry! How are you?"

"I'm fine! Just got back from a weekend trip. It's so good to hear your voice, Rose! The English Department isn't the same without you." It was a personal joke. Melinda Berry was a one-woman department in Summerlin's small high school.

Rose laughed. "I'm not the same without the English Department. I miss writing all those essays."

"I believe you're the only one who misses them, my dear."

"Mrs. Berry, I'm sorry I waited so long to contact you, but it was just two days ago that I really looked through the yearbook. You'd written a note there to call."

"Yes, I did. And if you hadn't called me by New Year's, I'd have sent Kirk Landry after you."

Rose laughed. "He definitely knows where I am."

"You sound good, Rose."

She hesitated only a moment. "God has taken care of me, Mrs. Berry…and my mom."

There was a deep intake of breath on the other end of the connection. "I believe it too, Rose. He's put you on my heart so often I feel I'm supposed to relay a message."

"A message?"

"An offer too. Rose, maybe you know that I used to work as a grader for the Advanced Placement essays. Every summer for nine years, a roomful of high school teachers and college professors went to Raleigh and spent a week passing essays around a long table, assigning scores. The chairman of our group is now the department chair for the English faculty at the Wilmington campus of UNC. Anyway, shortly after your mother spoke to the church, I felt…compelled…to call Dr. Cuthbert. I told him a little about your circumstances and made the case that he'd never regret giving you some help going to school. Most colleges give their best scholarships to freshman entering directly from high school. Dr. Cuthbert said he'd be willing to make an exception."

"An exception?" Rose squeaked.

"A fairly notably exception," laughed Mrs. Berry. He's offered you a full scholarship. You can have your choice: enter in January or wait until September. The money is yours. All you have to do is fill out the application, and I'll place the call to tell him it's on the way. I believe in you, Rose."

Savannah was so elated over the news that she insisted on ordering a slice of key lime pie with two forks. Rose was too breathless to taste it. It was three o'clock that afternoon before Rose pulled up to the beach house to find Kirk Landry's car parked out front, a small trailer attached to the hitch. Marcy and Kirk were sitting in wicker chairs on the front porch, drinking a pulpy concoction of orange, pineapple, and strawberry juice.

"Have one," Marcy offered, as Rose pulled a rocker from the living room to the porch. "It's supposed to be a smoothie."

Rose obediently took a sip. "Delicious!" she declared. "A little… chewy…but delicious." What was going on? Every person she sat down with was insisting that she eat something, drink something.

For the moment, the conversation was focused on Marcy's job. Rose resigned herself to the fact that it probably wouldn't stay there. She really didn't want to think about Jack Bradford today, or Anton Johnson, or any other detail of an epoch she was trying hard to forget. Today had been too wonderful. Parents for the baby, a full scholarship offer. She couldn't find a break in the conversation to share her amazing news with Marcy.

But to her surprise, Kirk said nothing about the investigation. He'd just spent a week's vacation on the coast of Maine, and kept Rose and Marcy in hysterics describing "a southern boy's attempts to communicate with Mainelanders." He'd had to learn to "pahk mah wicked cah in the wicked dahk," he insisted.

Switching to an exaggerated North Carolina drawl, Kirk announced, "Ladies, Ah've had a cravin'—a cravin' for fried…not steamed, not baked, not broiled, not casseroled, but *fried*…seafood, ever since I got back from the fah, fah nawth. Allow me, please, to take you two to dinnah in Calabash." To Rose's surprise, Marcy didn't even hesitate.

"You go ahead," Rose considered suggesting. "I've just eaten." But here was something she didn't want to miss—the sound of her mother's laughter mingling with that of a good man. Determined to order nothing more than a salad, Rose climbed into the back seat of his car while Kirk unhitched the trailer.

"What's back there?" she asked Marcy.

"Several pieces of antique furniture," her mother answered. "Kirk promised he'd deliver them as soon as they were no longer considered evidence."

"Which pieces?"

"A secretary, a hall tree, and a wine-colored velvet chair. Plus a pocket watch. Interested?"

Rose smiled politely and shook her head. "Me either," Marcy said. "But they're valuable, and I thought I'd try to find a buyer. Put the money in savings." She actually giggled. "Of course, I might want to buy a smoothie-maker first." Rose raised her eyebrows, unseen, in the dark.

The trip to Calabash took only fifteen minutes; the line at the cinderblock restaurant took forty-five. But the smell of fresh-cooked shrimp and flounder was irresistible, and Rose gave in twice to Marcy's offer to sample from her plate. Best of all was seeing the joy spring up in her mother's eyes when Rose finally told her about Melinda Berry's call. Kirk's enthusiastic fist-pump threatened to overturn the table. In celebration, he ordered three slices of chocolate cake.

It was 8:30 when Kirk unloaded the furniture and, at Marcy's request, simply lined up the pieces against the living room wall. She wanted to give them "a good vacuuming," she explained, and call in an antiques dealer she'd met at city hall. Kirk nearly flattened Rose's shoulders in a last congratulatory hug before heading for the car and back to Summerlin.

She was just putting her feet up when a knock came at the door. Marcy popped up, thinking Kirk had forgotten something, but instead, she opened the door to admit the entire Cole family, with Ricky in tow.

Lisa Cole was hoisting a bottle of sparkling grape juice in each hand. "Rose!" she cried. "Congratulations! Savannah just gave us the news!"

Hugs all around. Voices raised in excitement. The grape juice fizzing in clear plastic cups. Rose looked from face to face. All she saw was love. Her heart beat in time with the laughter. And still, she realized, Marcy didn't know the biggest news of all—that there was a potential father and mother for her baby. A man and a woman she didn't really know, but had seen enough of to believe that they were positive, hopeful, caring people. People whose letters revealed that they belonged to Christ. Rose cherished the secret, anticipating the pleasure of sharing it when she and Marcy were finally alone.

At 9:30, the Coles said their good-byes. Marcy and Rose walked them to the car. Ricky—who had driven his parents' sedan—lingered in the yard.

"Are your parents back from their trip?" Marcy asked him.

"Almost. I'm picking them up at the airport around midnight. It should be a good night for flying. The moon's really bright," he noted, looking up at the sky. "Would you two like to take a walk on the beach?"

"Oh, no, not me," Marcy said. "I have to go to work in the morning."

"I'd better not," Rose said, shaking her head.

"Come on, Rose. You don't want me hanging around the video arcade on the front beach, ruining my reputation."

She laughed. "So that's how it happens," she said.

"Yeah. Come on. I'll drive you right up to the access path. A little sand will do you good."

"Go on, honey, if you feel like it. I've got to go to bed." Marcy yawned.

Rose was torn. She was wide awake, but the prospect of a one-on-one with Ricky Belden wasn't comfortable. Still, a walk was exactly what she needed. She was brimming with energy.

"Okay," she conceded. "A short walk. You don't need to drive. But I do need a sweater."

Rose pulled on a heavy knit cardigan with a hood while Ricky extracted a denim jacket from the trunk of the car. They walked the three blocks to the beach, threading their way through the overhanging myrtle bushes that crowded the sides of the access path. As soon as they reached the strand, Rose was thrilled to see a giant full moon casting a silver path straight up the beach. "Oh, it's gorgeous!" she breathed, and Ricky smiled and nodded.

The late November breeze was changeable, coming first from the north and then from the south. "Not many people left," Ricky said, nodding toward the row of dark-windowed condos that lined the beachfront. They walked another block in silence. Once or twice, Rose made an attempt at conversation, but Ricky didn't respond. Then, staring straight ahead, he cleared his throat.

"Rose, I've been thinking a lot since Thanksgiving. I need to talk for a while." She looked at him sharply, but Ricky's eyes were turned to the horizon. "I know you're not going to understand this, but I've had a hard time looking at you—because of me. You don't really know me or my past, but there's something I need to explain."

Rose settled the hood of her cardigan around her neck, making it serve as a scarf. It was a nervous reaction, giving her a moment to prepare for what might follow.

Ricky continued, "I'm nineteen next month, and I'm grateful to be in college, but if I'd gotten what I deserved, I'd be in jail right now. A year and a half ago—my senior year in high school—I got interested in this really hot girl. She had long blond hair, blue eyes, and…she was just gorgeous. By the time my parents knew I was dating her, we were cutting class and sneaking out to her friend's car in the middle of the day. Smoking cigarettes at first. Then smoking pot. Did I mention that she came with a whole set of friends who were into shoplifting? I'm embarrassed to tell you this.

"Anyway, she'd call and I'd jump. She'd say higher, and I'd jump higher. I was crazy about her. I thought she cared about me too. When I look back, it's sickening. My friends at church kept telling me, 'She's big trouble.' If you can believe it, I thought they were jealous." His voice grew caustic.

"One night, six of us stole a car. I was so scared I thought I was going to throw up, so I made the guy who was driving stop and let me out. I actually dragged my girlfriend out of the back seat. About half an hour later, the police arrested everybody else in the car.

"Anyway, to make a long story short, Keri found out the next week she was pregnant. Rose, she was totally nonchalant when she told me, like it was nothing. And then…." Ricky paused and shook his head. "She asked me to pay for the abortion. I must have looked really shocked because she laughed at me. Then she said, 'What did you think? That it couldn't happen?'

"I felt like I'd been hit by a truck! I said, 'Keri, you told me you were on birth control.' She said, 'So I missed a few. I'm only six weeks. It's no big deal. I've had one before.'

"I said, 'This *is* a big deal. You can't have an abortion.' And she said, 'Oh, yes, I can. I'm going to college next year. I'm not going to mess that up.'

"I told her I thought we were together, and you know what she said? 'We've had fun, Ricky. But that's it.'

"'Keri,' I said, 'I have some say in this. It's my baby too.'

"But she said, 'This is not a baby. It's just a blob. And I'm getting rid of it. Too many complications. If you're not going to help me, I'll take care of it myself.'

"Rose, I was so upset and so mad and just…so mixed up. Finally Keri ran off and left me. I was a mess. I didn't know where to turn. By now, all my real friends had just about deserted me. I wandered around in a fog for two or three days. I went to see my youth pastor, but he was out of town, and I didn't want to talk about it on the phone. Maybe something could be done legally, I figured. I just couldn't stand the thought of God watching me walk away from this baby. I'd known all along that what I was doing was wrong, but when Keri told me she was pregnant, it woke me up.

"And then Keri called and asked me to meet her the following night. She said we needed to talk. I had already tried to call her a dozen times, but she didn't answer. Anyway, she met me that Friday night with a bottle of wine and two glasses. 'Time to celebrate,' she said. 'I did it. I talked to my mom, and she took me yesterday. That's why I wasn't at school. Don't you feel better?'

"I just sat there, stunned. 'Better?' I said. 'I feel sick, Keri. This was not just your decision to make. That baby was mine too.'

"All she'd say was, 'It was not a baby, Ricky. It was a blob of blood.'

"'Well, where do you think babies come from?' I asked her. 'Where do you think you and I came from?'

"You know what she said, Rose? 'I guess I'll go find somebody else to share my bottle of wine with.'" Ricky's voice was so choked that he had to stop and swallow, his eyes looking past the night sky to something darker.

"Rose, you can't imagine how I felt. I was eaten up with guilt. Over the next month, God made himself real to me. I'd heard about forgiveness all my life. But it wasn't just that. I finally understood what Jesus was all about. He actually paid, with his life, for my guilt. In my place. I finally understood.

"When my dad got transferred from Greenville here to the beach, it seemed like a gift. It was a chance to start over. My folks offered to let me stay in Greenville and graduate with my class, but I said no. I went looking for a different set of friends, somebody to hold me accountable. I know I'm a little old for the youth group, but I need them. And I look at Scott and Lisa Cole and see how Savannah and Robbie care for each other, and I can hardly stay away. That's what I want, Rose. A chance for a real family.

"Then you moved to the beach. I didn't know why. When things got…obvious, I asked Robbie why his sister was hanging around with a pregnant girl. I was blown away when he told me. If anybody ever had a semi-legitimate excuse for an abortion, it was you."

Ricky's next words were like water to a dry land, and Rose felt the sting of tears rolling down her face.

"You've been so brave, Rose. Going through hell for what you believe. I figured the best thing I could do was treat you like a normal person. Make you feel like part of things. I didn't realize my kidding around hurt your feelings.

"Anyway, it all got to me this weekend. My baby, that somebody could have adopted, was aborted a year ago yesterday. Keri just took it out of my hands. I've never really told anybody else."

The wind was picking up, growing steadily colder. Up to that point, it hadn't registered with Rose that they'd been walking against the wind. But now, they'd reached the wide swash at the end of aptly named Windy Hill and were forced to turn around. As usual, Rose was struck by the fact that when she turned, the walk became noticeably easier. The wind was actually pushing her gently forward.

Ricky apparently noticed the same thing. "When I was walking against God, it seemed like every step was a battle against a force I couldn't see. But when I turned, everything changed. I could sense him in me. Helping me. You know what my biggest battle has been? Forgiving Keri. And the people who did the abortion. Forgiving myself for not fighting harder. But I'm doing what the Bible says, Rose. I literally cry out to God sometimes. And I know—I'm absolutely certain—he's forgiven me. And I'm working on forgiving Keri every time she comes to mind.

"Can you understand why I was watching you, listening to you? I think you're amazing, Rose. I think you're beautiful, inside and out. Your life will go on, and this will have been the hardest season of your life, probably, but you'll have no regrets about this decision. You'll know in your heart that you did the right thing. You'll walk on, with the wind at your back, not in your face, knowing that you did all you could do."

Rose stopped in her tracks and looked at the young man whose story had thoroughly surprised her. "You can't imagine what I've been thinking. I felt like you had me under a microscope, watching me and wondering how I could've let such a stupid thing happen to me. Sometimes I felt like such an outsider. I know I've been supersensitive, but it seems like whenever you'd tease me, I already felt as big as a blimp. You think I'm doing well, but I'm really struggling…I'm scared…and I still have a month to go! Sometimes I'm not sure I can make it. But…you've just helped me so much."

Far down the beach, two children shrieked as they played chase between the dunes in the moonlight. Rose and Ricky turned in unison toward the sound.

"That's why I had to talk to you, Rose," Ricky said gently. "I'm not the enemy. I want to help. What can I do, Rose? What would take away the biggest load?"

"I don't know," she said wonderingly. "A lot has happened today, Ricky—all of it good."

"Would you tell me? I still have almost an hour before I have to leave for the airport."

Rose studied his face in the street light as they prepared to cross the street. Maybe he would listen to her recital of this crazy, wonderful, life-changing day—celebrate with her. Every part of it had lifted a weight from her heart.

"I will," she said, as they headed up the street to the cottage, "But Ricky, so far today I've turned down sugar cookies, key lime pie, a seafood dinner, and most of a piece of chocolate cake. And now I'm hungry. Would you follow me over to the late-night drive-through to get some fries?"

He looked down into her face and laughed.

"You want a large?" he asked.

"Only if I have to share," she answered.

CHAPTER 42

Marcy awoke the next morning to the sound of Rose at work in the kitchen. She had cut up a bowlful of fresh fruit—the remnants of smoothie-making—and was slicing strips of cheddar to make cheese toast. Marcy's coffee was already brewing.

"For a dream, it sure smells real," murmured Marcy, running a brush through her hair.

"Morning!" said Rose, with a lilt in her voice. "Can you be dressed in ten minutes?"

"If I have to. Why ten?"

"I have some news. I need at least forty-five minutes to tell you about it. Hurry, Mom!"

Marcy hurried.

"Eight minutes," she announced. "Have I missed any buttons or zippers? Shoes match? Makeup okay?"

"Picture of perfection. Pray for us, Mom."

Marcy asked the blessing and served the plate Rose had set at her usual place, noting the camellia floating in the bowl in the center of the table. Savannah had brought it to Rose the night before. "Please," she said, "tell me."

Rose studied Marcy's face. "Mom, when I…had my meltdown on Saturday, you covered a lot of ground when you prayed for me. Yesterday was a day like no other. As wonderful as it was to get the call from Mrs. Berry, I wouldn't have been prepared to get it if I hadn't gone to Lifesender first."

"What happened?" asked Marcy, her eyes glued to Rose's.

"Eat your toast while it's hot, Mom. I've already eaten"—she laughed—"so I can talk nonstop. Anyway, I was feeling so much pressure to choose the parents for the baby. That notebook system has its pros and cons. There's only so much you can learn from words and pictures. I had to know inside my heart."

She described the small things that, to others, might have seemed like coincidence, but which to her mounted up to one strong impression. "I need you to pray with me about this, pray that I'm hearing God clearly. But I have to tell you, Mom—from the minute I walked out of that office, I've felt nothing but peace."

"What are they like?" Marcy asked, her face glowing.

"Well, Savannah was sitting right across from them. She said the husband seemed really thoughtful toward his wife. Instead of reading magazines, he actually looked into her face and talked. They weren't in a hurry. It was like he wanted to be there. And she *had* to be there. They seemed...transparent with each other, Savannah said, comfortable. He was playing with her hair."

"What do they look like?"

"Well, first of all, she's got my hair! Same color. Otherwise, she's kind of nondescript looking, but Savannah said that when she smiles, she's transformed. Average height, average weight—nothing I can really describe well. But the smile in her photo seemed real. She wears bright, happy colors.

"He's pretty handsome. Dark hair, dark eyes. About five feet ten. Dresses neatly. What I like most, Mom, is the fact that I kind of know him."

"You do?"

Rose told the story of the grand collision and Rod's connection with Scott Cole's breakfast group at the pancake house. "I've had a chance to watch him for months, not really knowing why, and I like him. I think he'd make a good father.

"It struck me as more than a coincidence that we had made appointments at Lifesender for the same time. And that I saw them in the office just before I got to their page in the notebook. And that everything on their pages sounded healthy and happy." She told her mom about the photo of the grandfather holding a softball.

"And then, Mom, Savannah took me to lunch, and Mrs. Berry called. I came home to tell you, but Kirk was here. At first, I got tense that he was going to question me and destroy the whole day. But he never brought up anything at all. That seemed like a miracle. And it was good to see the two of you together, laughing, just having fun, and then we came home, and I was going to tell you everything, and the Coles showed up, and that was so much fun. I loved it. But I wasn't too excited about a walk with Ricky."

In brief terms, Rose explained only that Ricky had tried to clarify their relationship. He had surprised her by asking to be of help—to be her friend.

"Is there something deeper there, Rose?"

"No, there really isn't. Just friends. Just what I need it to be."

"Well," said Marcy, "I'm going to have to really concentrate on keying in those account numbers today. I wish I didn't have to go to work—I could just sit here all day and ask questions and look at your eyes. Breakfast was great. I love you, Rose."

Marcy pulled out of the driveway, leaving her daughter to survey the beach house with a satisfied sigh. She rinsed up the breakfast dishes, made up Marcy's bed, freshened the bathroom, put a load of clothes in the washer, and then turned her attention to the three pieces of furniture Kirk had delivered the previous afternoon.

They blocked the window and made the living room feel crowded. Marcy had said she wanted to clean them thoroughly before calling in the appraiser. Rose gave her mom a quick call to ask what cleansers to use. Marcy recommended little more than a thorough dusting and vacuuming. "They're not badly scratched," she pointed out. "We could use a little lemon oil on the wood."

Rose checked the laundry room for lemon oil, found it, and grabbed the vacuum and the dust cloths.

She suctioned the dust out of the exposed springs under the seat of the velvet wing chair and set the seat cushion on the front steps to air. The vacuum attachment lifted the nap on the arms as it drew out layers of dust, making the wine-colored velvet look instantly richer. Rose wiped down the chair legs with lemon oil and—satisfied—slid the chair into a corner. Moving slowly, conscious of the contrast her own round bulk created beside the slender hall tree, she rubbed down the century-old wood, enjoying both its scent and its sheen, remembering Papa's hat and coat resting on designated hooks.

The antique secretary, with its many angles and crevices, she had saved till last. The spiders had had a field day with this piece; they were everywhere. Puffing a little, Rose eased herself down on the floor to vacuum underneath its slender carved legs. The bottom of the drawer, she noted, was solid wood, not thin veneer. Back on her feet, she opened up the secretary's glass top and wiped down its one wooden shelf, brightening the door panes with glass cleaner.

She had saved the most time-consuming task for last. It took a key, extracted from the bottom drawer, to open the drop-leaf that folded out into a hinged writing surface. Before her lay a myriad of letter slots, drawers, and cubbies. Randomly pulling out a drawer, Rose was disgusted to find a nest of nimble spiders. "Uckk," she shuddered. "I'm going to have to pull out everything that isn't nailed down."

Soon the floor was littered with thin wooden dividers and dovetailed drawers wearing tiny brass knobs and a century's worth of ink stains. Rose leaned deep into the desk's interior, suctioning and swabbing out the corners, then tackled each little drawer and divider in turn. A rub-down with lemon oil, and the mahogany regained its youth. No longer dry and dull, it looked regal in the beach house amid shafts of morning sun.

Rose was reinserting the components when she realized that the wide center drawer looked too short and shallow for the amount of weight she was hefting in her hand. In its left rear corner, she spied a tiny brass lever. Remembering Marcy's description of a secret drawer—the one in which she had found a coin after the ransacking of The Suitable—she gave the little lever a push. A panel fell forward, revealing a shallow drawer within a drawer. It was empty except for cobwebs. Rose stuck the vacuum attachment up inside, not wanting to touch the interior with her fingers.

Withdrawing the nozzle, she was dismayed to see a thin panel of wood clinging to the nozzle. A half-inch loop of narrow faded ribbon was tacked to the top.

Oh, no! she thought. *I've dismantled the part that makes this desk really valuable!* Convinced by now that spiders could infiltrate anything, she got up and walked out to the enclosed front porch, tilting the drawer to the sun.

She was looking, she realized, into yet another chamber behind the first one. She could easily see to the back of it. It was about three inches deep, an inch and a half tall, she gauged, but as wide as the main drawer, which was at least fourteen inches across.

In the back right corner, something dark was wadded. Sure enough, it appeared covered in a fine lace of spiderweb. Afraid to trust the force of the vacuum, Rose's courage failed and, lacking gloves, she ran for kitchen tongs and a pair of red oven mitts. She was pulling on the mitts just as Marcy stepped up into the porch.

"I came to fix you lunch, but it looks like…I may be too late," said her mother, peering quizzically at Rose, who looked outfitted for a barbecue.

"Don't laugh," ordered Rose. "You know I can't stand spiders." Handing Marcy the drawer, she said, "This is your secret drawer, right?"

"It is," Marcy said, "but all I had to do was push a little lever."

"Well, I did that—and the door opened just fine. But when I stuck the vacuum nozzle up inside, this came out." She held up the thin wooden panel by its bedraggled half-inch of ribbon. "So I brought the whole drawer out here on the porch so I could see up inside. Look, there's something stuffed up in the space behind the inner drawer—but it's pretty messy."

"Well, Dr. Rose . . . Chef Rose . . . let's pull it out."

Rose stuck the tongs far into the back, closed them around something soft and heavy, and drew it out. "A dirty sock?" Three or four spiders exited its folds, and one raced up the tongs toward Rose's hand.

"Drop it, Rose!" Marcy ordered, and the tongs fell with a clatter into the largest drawer. "We'll take this outside." Shaking her arm, Rose ran out the door.

Marcy carried the entire central drawer, tongs, sock, and all, to the front steps. Intending to toss the sock into the garbage can, Rose picked it up in her mitt-clad hand and watched the toe sag heavily.

"There's something heavy in there," she said, and both she and Marcy felt a tingle of anticipation. Momentarily forgetting her arachnophobia, Rose grabbed the gray, subtly patterned sock. Its product label was still attached, identifying it as a ninety percent cashmere, ten percent nylon dress sock that retailed for $150 a pair. Unceremoniously, Rose turned it upside down, and with her fingers worked a clump of material toward the neck. It was a fist-sized wad of cotton.

"What in the world?" Marcy exclaimed. Rose felt all the way down the sock, turned it inside out to be sure it was empty, then gave her attention to the large wad of cotton, now lying in the larger drawer. Marcy peeled back the outer layers, which appeared to have once been used to line the boxes for designer neckties. Inside was a familiar pocket watch plus a handful of what appeared to be cotton disks secured with tape.

"Open one, Mom!" cried Rose.

Marcy pulled off a piece of tape. Into her palm dropped a gold coin the size of a dime. A woman's profile stood out cleanly from the front face. The inscription read "nited States of America." Marcy flipped the coin over and ran her finger over the flattened reed marks on the reverse.

"I have to call Kirk right away," she whispered. Marcy pulled her cell phone out of her purse and pressed a speed dial button as Rose counted the cotton disks. There were twenty-three. Rose did the math. Twenty-three plus one in the drawer plus one in the crimper.

"Mom," she said breathlessly, "ask Kirk to stay for dinner."

"But I don't have time to fix dinner," objected Marcy. "I won't get off work until five."

"Well, let's just order a pizza, Mom. I'll make a salad. And a dessert."

"Oh, really?" asked Marcy appraisingly.

"What? Why are you looking at me like that?"

"Nothing. You're sure you want to do all that?"

"I'm sure."

"Detective Landry here," came a deep voice.

"Kirk, this is Marcy. How are you?"

"Doing great! I was just thinking about you two. Is everything okay?"

"It is, thanks. Listen, Rose just discovered something we knew you'd want to see. It was in the antique desk you delivered. Rose found a hidden drawer even I didn't know about. There was a sock stuffed in the hidden compartment, and inside the sock, there were twenty-three little gold coins, all just alike. They're dated 1861."

Both Rose and Marcy jumped at the sound of Kirk's whoop!

"From what you've told us, we don't feel entirely safe sleeping in the same house with these little treasures," Marcy said, laughing. "I don't suppose you have an armored car, do you?"

"No, but I can come heavily armed."

"How soon can you be here?"

"Well, unless one of my deputies pulls me for making this U-turn or for grossly exceeding the speed limit, I should be there in two hours. When do you get home?"

"Not until just after five. Rose is in charge of dinner."

"Rose can cook?"

"I heard that, Kirk," Rose called out. "Just come and see."

"You're on. I'm going to need to photograph the desk and the coins and take a statement. But we should be finished by the time you get home, Marcy. Know what? I think you've just turned the tide of this whole case."

"In a good way?" asked Marcy.

"I do believe so," said the detective. "See you shortly."

Rose felt her energy flagging half-way through the salad preparations. It was entirely gone by the time she finished the chocolate peanut butter pie. She felt heavy, and when she looked down at her feet, they were swollen. Kirk's arrival and his exuberant examination of the coins, however, revived her long enough to give him a statement. By the time Marcy got home, Rose had lost all interest in dinner and pled weariness. She lay down on the couch and tried her best to take part in the lighthearted conversation at the dinner table.

Kirk was clearly elated by the discovery of the coins. "They're called Dahlonega dollars," he said, as if Marcy and Rose might not remember. Over and over, he pulled out a coin and pointed out some distinctive feature or recounted the uncertain details of the Confederate seizure of the little mint in the Georgia mountains.

"So the soldiers actually produced the coins?" Rose asked from the couch.

"Some people think so. Others say the mint employees might have done it under orders from the Rebel soldiers. Either way, they must have been working under pressure. It just wasn't a professional job. And that's actually a large part of what makes these coins so valuable—that and the fact that there are so few of them."

Rose was stunned by how valuable the little gold pieces had turned out to be.

"Forty thousand, fifty thousand each, according to a website on collectible coins," Kirk said. Somebody sold a really fine one for $149,500 back in 2008. Multiply even the smallest number by twenty-five and you can see why somebody with criminal leanings might take a big risk."

Rose wasn't sure what time Kirk left. She had fallen asleep on the couch. She awoke at eight-thirty with pain in her back and a tightening of her stomach muscles. "I'm feeling funny," she told Marcy. "It's not the first time."

Ten minutes later, Marcy watched Rose get up to go to the bathroom. As soon as she heard the gasp, she reached for her car keys.

CHAPTER 43

Over the hospital noises, Rose heard the cry as she held tightly to Marcy's hand. Groggily she asked, "A girl…or a boy?"

"A girl, honey! With light-colored hair. Not a lot, but enough to brush. Oh, Rose, she's beautiful!"

"Seven pounds even," they heard a nurse call. "Nineteen inches long."

"Thanks…for being here, Mom."

"I wouldn't be anywhere else," Marcy whispered, choking.

Rose faded in and out.

"Ms. Kendall," the nurse said, "would you like to see her?"

Rose opened her eyes to see a nurse standing beside her, and when she nodded, the nurse unwrapped a remarkably small bundle. She lowered the bundle to Rose's eye level, and for a long minute, Rose looked into a pair of navy eyes blinking in an attempt to focus. A hand, three inches long, peeked out over the edge of the blanket that swaddled the rest of her. Rose reached over and smoothed the tiny knuckles.

Something leapt, unpremeditated, to her mind.

"I need to tell her something," she said blurrily. "Can you bend down a little more?"

The nurse moved the baby closer.

"Can you remember this?" Rose whispered into the seashell-shaped ear. "It's a question. Who…can separate us…from the love of Christ?"

Rose tucked the little hand inside the blanket and took one last look at the eyes that had momentarily stopped blinking and seemed to be fixed on hers. She whispered the answer, waited, and added the benediction: "I'll be praying for your life."

Rose closed her eyes, and when she opened them again, the baby was gone, and a different nurse was saying, "Ms. Kendall, we're moving you to your room now. I'm going to slide you over onto the gurney."

Rose was exhausted. Never, though, had she felt more loved and cared for by her mother. As the gurney turned the corner, Rose opened her heavy eyes and looked into four expectant faces: there were Savannah and Mrs. Cole, a beaming Linda and Joyce. The nurse patiently watched as they patted Rose's arm and gave her half hugs. "You did it, Rose! We're so proud of you," someone said, but Rose was too woozy to pick out the voice.

Trying to focus on Linda's face, Rose asked, "You'll take care of everything, right?"

"Yes, honey, you've done all the hard work. We notified the parents, and they're almost too excited to breathe. They're on their way."

"Did you see her yet?" asked Rose, her eyes closed.

"Oh, yes, honey. She's so healthy and beautiful, just like you. We'll be by this afternoon to see you. We just wanted you to know we were here, praying for you."

"Thank you," Rose whispered, and nodded off.

Marcy, Savannah, and Lisa stood in the hallway, waiting for the nurses to get Rose settled in her bed. Then, by pre-arrangement, Savannah announced that she was going to "take the first shift while you two get some lunch." Marcy acquiesced without a fight—it had been a long labor, and she had been stretched in her new role as the supporter rather than the supported.

The chill December beach wind bustled them into Lisa's car. "What could you enjoy eating, my dear friend?" asked Lisa. Marcy shook her head helplessly.

A five-minute drive took them to an oceanfront restaurant, its entry swallowed up in garlands and sparkling Christmas lights. Lisa requested a table by the window, and they sat down delighted with their unobstructed view of the strand.

"What are your plans for the holidays?" Lisa asked, once the waitress had taken their orders for the lunch-sized portion of the establishment's famous crabmeat au gratin casserole.

"Actually, I'm only now at the point that I can make any plans," Marcy said. "I've been going into the office an hour early every day to build up a little leave time. I'm off today and Monday, so that gives me four days with Rose. I'm glad Christmas Day will be on a Friday. That will give us another long weekend coming up."

"Well, Scott and I are hoping you and Rose will join us for dinner on Christmas Day. We'd love to have you."

Marcy looked into Lisa's eyes and saw the sincerity there. "Assuming that Rose is feeling fine, I'll say yes," she smiled. "What can I bring?"

"Well, how about a couple of pitchers of your good iced tea and a dessert?"

"Sure! I'll also bake a pan of yeast rolls."

"Perfect. My family was hoping you'd say so." Lisa grinned, and for a moment, Marcy was reminded of Renee. Christmas, she knew, was a busy time for the Bellamys, with their full schedule of church programs and visits with the congregation. Nevertheless, she would call Renee later that afternoon.

On the night of the twenty-third, Rose answered the door to find a balsam pine, already mounted in a tree stand, obscuring all but Ricky Belden's face. "My dad's selling these for the Optimist Club," he said, walking in and setting the tree on a low table near the front window. "We're almost sold out."

Marcy came out of the kitchen and exclaimed, "Ricky, how did you know?"

"Know what, Mrs. Kendall?"

"That we hadn't had time to go out for a tree."

"Well, I rode by a couple of times. Didn't see any sign of Christmas here. I hope you like this kind."

"Oh, it's beautiful! Just right!"

"Do you have ornaments? I didn't even think about that."

"Where'd we put our box of Christmas things, Rose?"

"The hall closet, I think."

"Want me to get it for you?" Ricky asked.

"Please!"

Rose laughed for the first time in days as she and Marcy made identical moves from opposite sides of the tree—leaning forward and breathing in the scent of Christmas. Ricky emerged from the hall with a box marked "tree." Not since the delivery had Marcy seen a spark of life in her daughter's eyes. Rose had always loved a live tree; every Christmas she spent at least one night sleeping beneath the tree on a pallet on the floor, lights ablaze. Until the last few years.

"Thank you, God, for Ricky," Marcy whispered.

"I told Dad I'd be back by nine. But I have time to put the lights on for you, if you'd like me to."

Rose was quiet, but Marcy didn't hesitate. "Wonderful," she said. "I'm stuck in the kitchen right now, but I'd really appreciate your help. I'll put on some Christmas music."

The division of labor was quickly established. Rose sat on the couch, untangling the tiny white lights, while Ricky fed them around the tree and down the branches. When all the bulbs had been strung, he flicked off the overhead fixture. The accumulation of several hundred tiny lights illuminated the living room so well that no other lamps were needed.

"The Coles have invited my family for dessert on Christmas Day," he said. "You'll be there?"

Rose smiled and nodded.

"Good. Call me if you need anything—will you?"

Another smile and a nod.

To a chorus of thank yous, Ricky made his exit, and a second later, had both Rose and Marcy shaking at his roaring rendition of "White Christmas" delivered from the front steps.

"We now have a tree!" said Marcy. "What else do you want to put on it?"

"Nothing for now," said Rose. "It's beautiful the way it is."

It was uncharacteristic of Rose to stop at the lights and refuse the ornaments, to stay out of the kitchen, to lie on the couch and stare off into space. But Marcy knew that she and Rose were erasing memories this year.

A picture flashed through her mind of the Christmas before this one—Rose holed up in her room while Marcy and Jack attempted to conjure up the impression of a family as they decorated a tree. Marcy also knew that Rose, still tired, was grappling with turbulent, mixed emotions—both freedom and loss, relief and sorrow. She prayed there was no anger in the mix, but suspected there was. That would explain why her daughter had so little to say.

The timer on the stove went off, pulling Marcy back to the kitchen, where a dinner of challenging proportions was underway: one, she hoped, that would graft new memories in the place of those she was working to erase. The dinner had multiple purposes in Marcy's mind. She wanted to celebrate the changes in her spiritual life, to honor the Christ-child and the deliverance he had brought them. She wanted to see Kirk again, and feed him, and hear his laughter, and watch Rose relax in his presence. God had used a human agent in sending Kirk into Marcy's life, and she wanted to tell him so. She wanted to hear him ask the blessing. Small things, yet big too. Things that had been lacking in her life for so long. Now she had eyes to see.

Fortunately, the city had given its employees both Thursday and Friday—Christmas Eve and Christmas Day—as holidays. Marcy thought she could pull together the ambitious meal by herself, given a night and a whole day to cook. Tonight, she was icing a five-layer chocolate cake and decorating it with candy canes. On the stove, a dozen white potatoes were boiling in anticipation of a thick cheese sauce. Earlier, she had stirred up a marinade for the flank steak they would grill on the little hibachi on the porch.

The dining room table was already set. With artistic flair, Marcy had turned it into a holiday tableaux, centering a round mirror on a white damask tablecloth and circling it with greenery. In the center she placed a small china church housing a music box, and against its side, fanned a short spray of red pyracantha berries. She had no holiday plates—only her plain white china with the platinum band—but had bought a set of red goblets and holly-sprigged fabric napkins. Marcy placed a votive candle in a clear cup at each of the three place settings, lit them to judge the effect, and declared it satisfactory.

"I like it, Mom," came a voice from behind her, and Marcy felt the incredible comfort of a pair of arms slide around her waist. Tears welled behind her eyelids, but Marcy commanded them to stay where they were. Mother and daughter stood linked together, staring out across the flickering candles on the table and on to the shimmering tree light, and once again inhaled simultaneously.

CHAPTER 44

The next day, the temperature never rose above the low forties. Driving a Jeep Cherokee with a twenty-inch cedar wreath wired across the front grill, Kirk arrived in the late afternoon and wrestled a giant red poinsettia—clearly a florist's—out of the Jeep and up the front steps. Rose took note of her mother's expression as she welcomed him at the door. Joy and trust played across her face.

"For you both!" Kirk announced.

"It's beautiful!" Marcy declared. "Poinsettias always make me feel...rich! One big poinsettia, and the decorating's nearly done."

Kirk pulled off his windbreaker to reveal a bright green cable-knit sweater over a white shirt. "I'm the rest of the decoration," he pointed out. Marcy took his coat, complimented the sweater, and allowed him to follow his nose to the stove, where a pot of apple cider was simmering, casting up fragments of orange pulp, cloves, and cinnamon.

Kirk admired the tree, admired the table setting, and clearly admired Marcy's hair, which had grown out enough to sweep up in a ponytail.

He insisted on manning the hibachi, where the charcoal had just reached the right temperature for grilling. Soon, he was carving thin, diagonal slices of steak to add to the colorful buffet of scalloped potatoes, green beans cooked with cranberries, a bowl of shrimp salad, and a basket overflowing with yeast rolls. The candy-cane-decked chocolate cake tantalized them from its spot on the coffee table.

"I have something for Rose," Kirk announced, when he had polished off his second serving of everything and produced a flat, wrapped package tied with red curling ribbon. Opening it, Rose drew out an old eight-by-ten photo mounted in a new redwood frame, and looked up wonderingly.

"State champs. Baseball. Summerlin High School, 1985," Kirk explained. "The baseball caps make us all look alike, but that's your dad in the back row, fourth from the right. The ummm…bulky guy beside him is me. That's Tommy Bellamy kneeling down in the front row."

In delight, Rose looked into Daniel's youthful eyes; they seemed to look right into hers. She studied the teenaged version of Kirk's nose—the picture had obviously been taken before football action broke it for the last time. Tommy Bellamy had a faraway look on his face, caught thinking about…what? A date with Renee?

Staring at the photo, she realized that the three teammates were within a year or two of her own age. A sudden sensation of youth startled her. *I'm only eighteen,* she thought. *I've been so much older.*

Rose realized that Kirk was studying her face. "Good-looking guy, wasn't I?" He grinned. "Can you believe your mom picked your dad over me?"

They both looked up at Marcy, who instantly turned pink. "You do know your dad moved in on me the same year I took your mom to homecoming."

Rose simply smiled and shook her head silently. "This will go on my bedside table," she said, with a look of gratitude that Kirk couldn't miss. "Thank you so much."

"Glad you like it," Kirk said with a manly blush. "You seemed to like the flag football picture I showed you earlier. This is a better shot."

For Marcy, Kirk produced a similar sized box, much heavier and also wrapped in white with red ribbon. Inside was a leather-bound study Bible with wide margins for taking notes. Her first name was stamped in gold on the cover. Over cake, they bent their heads over the Bible, leafing through its maps and charts, index, and concordance. Rose looked at them for a long, long moment. "*Suitable*," she thought to herself. *Right for the purpose or occasion.*

Marcy had tied one box atop another to wrap her gift to Kirk—a CD and a boxful of homemade cinnamon rolls. "Oh, you know me well!" he declared, sampling a sugary corner and rolling his eyes with pleasure. "What a shame we've eaten up all this good food. I could come back again tomorrow night!"

In the kitchen, the three of them made noise commensurate with the clean-up of a large meal. "Rose," Kirk said when all the dishes were put away and the counter wiped clean, "I have one more thing for you."

Out of an envelope, Rose pulled a news story clipped from the Wilmington Star-News. Its headline read, "Diver Charged in Summerlin Murder Enters Plea."

Marcy got up nervously and stood behind her as both began to read.

> The man charged in the May shooting death of prominent Summerlin businessman Jack Bradford has confessed to the killing and submitted a plea in district court.
>
> Anton Johnson, 36, of Windlass, NC, appeared before the court on Monday, where he reportedly provided evidence to federal authorities that implicates several native and foreign-born shippers in a smuggling ring.
>
> Judge Haynes Greenbaum is expected to rule on the plea within the week.
>
> If the plea is denied and he goes to trial, Johnson faces a possible death sentence. Other charges pending include piracy within the three-mile salvage limits, breaking and entering, unlawful entry, kidnapping, and resisting arrest.
>
> Johnson is a licensed scuba diver who previously spent several months in jail for forgery and drug possession.

Bradford, the murder victim, was owner of The Suitable, an exclusive menswear shop. He died May 28 after being shot in the chest in the alley behind his shop. In documents submitted to Greenbaum, Johnson claimed that he and Bradford were partners in an underwater salvage operation off Fort Fisher, within the three-mile territorial limits.

Johnson claims that he fired at Bradford in an attempt to protect an eighteen-year-old Summerlin student, Rose Kendall, whom Bradford shoved into the alley, pinioning her arms behind her and apparently using her as a shield.

Johnson says he shot to wound Bradford, not kill him, and has provided police with details of a coin-smuggling operation in which he and Bradford were supplying salvaged coins to foreign collectors. Johnson's role was to locate the coins underwater, while Bradford's was to deliver the coins for sale.

Some of the coins Johnson found are believed to be 1861-Ds, otherwise known as Dahlonega dollars, which are among the rarest and most collectible of US coins. The 1861-D is the only coin ever struck by a US mint under Confederate control—an event that took place shortly after the firing on Fort Sumter, which inaugurated the War Between the States.

No one knows for certain how many coins were struck—there are estimates of up to 1,500—but fewer than 120 have been accounted for. The unusual history of the dime-sized coin made it sought after by collectors, who have paid between $45,000 and $75,000 per coin in recent months, depending on condition.

On the evening of the Bradford shooting, Johnson says he went to his partner's shop with the intention of collecting his portion of proceeds from the sale of several of the coins. Bradford, he said, was having difficulty finding a buyer for about twenty-five more, and Johnson intended to demand that half the coins be returned to him.

Startled by Bradford pushing the girl toward him and by the sound of police sirens, Johnson said he assumed he was being

> set up. Because the girl was resisting Bradford vigorously, Johnson said he fired, threw the gun into a dumpster, and ran.
>
> Several weeks later, he returned to Summerlin and broke into Bradford's garage, his shop, his car, and his boat, searching for the unsold coins. Failing to find them, he determined to search the Kendalls' house, where Bradford had been living. Realizing that the house was for sale, he secured a job with a company hired to conduct an estate auction there on July 4.
>
> Given the job of moving furniture on the day of the estate sale, Johnson took the opportunity to search the house and its furnishings but failed to find the coins. Spotting Rose Kendall in the house, Johnson forced her to help him search.
>
> When a Summerlin detective surprised him in the attic, Johnson dove through a window in an attempt to escape, sustaining a gunshot wound to the leg as well as multiple cuts and bruises. He was detained by Summerlin police in the yard and placed under arrest.
>
> Police say the coins were recently discovered in a hidden compartment of a desk that Johnson had searched unsuccessfully in Bradford's shop. The coins are currently being held by the North Carolina Attorney General's office, awaiting a decision on rightful ownership.

Rose finished reading and looked up, searching Kirk's face. "This means . . . ?"

"You don't have to testify. Judge Greenbaum accepted the plea this morning. Gave him thirty years for involuntary manslaughter and dismissed the other charges. The state can decide how to handle the piracy issue."

Rose continued to study Kirk's face.

"You know what I think happened?" he continued. "After you found those coins and I went to the jail and showed them to him, told him where they'd been hidden, it just broke his spirit. I think he'd been willing to risk a trial for the chance of getting out to look for his stash. Now he had to decide just how close he was willing to come to lethal injection."

Marcy and Rose sat quietly for a few minutes. "No trial?" Rose asked, wanting to hear it one more time.

"No trial," Kirk said, gently shaking his head.

CHAPTER 45

Bundling up against the wind, Kirk, Marcy, and Rose climbed into the Jeep for the five-minute drive to the church, where a candlelight service was scheduled for 8:00. Rose stared out the window, trying to decide what feelings were being added to the already volatile mix. Until this evening, she hadn't realized just how much she'd dreaded appearing in court to face the questions and insinuations of a desperate defense attorney.

Was Anton Johnson's sentence fair? Rose had no idea. What was fair in a situation like this?

Rose stopped trying to insulate herself, stopped trying to avoid thoughts of the baby. It was impossible at Christmas. She almost welcomed the pain that flayed her. *This is how a very big loss should feel,* she told herself. To seek an emotional anesthetic would be to deny what had passed between her and the baby in the delivery room. The child would not remember, but Rose would never forget those eyes, with their gentle look of trust.

It was normal to be weepy, but on this particular night, Rose was one blink away from a tear-fest. Settling into her chair near the back of the darkened church, she closed her eyes and bowed her head, hoping fervently that the Prince of Peace was hard at work in her.

She looked up to see the elementary choir filing in, beaming at parents, parents beaming back. They took their places behind a row of brass handbells, and at their director's nod, adopted an expression of solemn, intense concentration. At another nod, they lifted their bells to peal out the notes to "Infant Holy, Infant Lowly." A short pause and a third nod from the director introduced "Silent Night."

Rose mentally supplied the words. "Sleep in heavenly peace, sleep in heavenly peace."

Peace. It was welling up within her, bigger and bigger. She had done the right thing! She had stayed the course. After all the months of hurt and confusion and fear, she had done a hard thing and finished it. And suddenly, Rose knew that this was a gift she would lay at the base of the manger, if she could. Obedience. The baby she was picturing in the manger had grown up to be a man, a God-man who said, "If anyone loves me, he will obey my teaching." All she could give him was her decision to protect a little child at great personal expense.

Yet the Christ in her heart was requiring one gift more. "What is it?" Rose whispered.

The answer was clear: *Forgive as I have forgiven you.*

Forgive Jack. Forgive Anton. Forgive Marcy. Hold nothing against anyone. Make the decision every day, if need be.

She drew in a deep breath and held it. Where to start? *Forgive me first for hating,* Rose exhaled silently. *Help me now to hold nothing against anyone. Scrub my heart clean.*

On his twelve-string, the guitarist was beginning a complex arrangement of "What Child Is This?" when Rose felt someone slide into the chair on her right. It was Savannah, cheeks and nose pink from the cold, eyes seeking Rose's as if to judge the health of her heart and mind. Beside her slid in Ricky and Robbie, both looking excited to be there.

Rose glanced to her left, saw Marcy regarding them all with a tender look, heard the pastor issue the call to worship.

Worship, Rose thought. *An act of giving, not taking.* The music leader announced the next song, and Rose was the first on her feet.

ENDNOTES

1 "Open the Eyes of My Heart" by Paul Baloche
2 "A Debtor to Mercy Alone" by Augustus M. Toplady